Distress Call

Sentinel Corps
Log One

By
Rod Galindo

v2.0

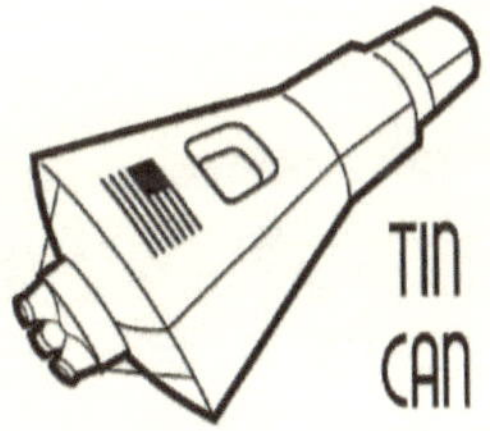

an imprint of Wordwraith Books

ISBN-13: 978-1-946921-35-2

Wordwraith Books, LLC
705-B SE Melody Lane #147
Lee's Summit, MO 64063
www.wordwraiths.com
@Wordwraiths

Cover art by Levi Hoffmeier
https://www.levihoffmeier.com/

Rod Galindo's website *www.rodgalindo.com*
Rod Galindo's Twitter *@RodAGalindo*

Content Warning

This book contains subject matter and situations that may trigger certain emotions and anxiety in some readers. Subjects include quarantine, dead and decaying bodies, corpse-related gore, grief, discussions and descriptions of parental death and child death, and an extremely brief mention of sexual predation and murder.

Dedication

This book is dedicated to the incomparable Jeff Buker and the ever-wise Jim Shoemate, whom, over several years, finally pounded it into my skull that the real Navy is NOTHING like Star Trek. Thank you for your patience with me. Not only on this, but countless work assignments and wargame exercises, too!

Honorable mention goes out to about a dozen beta readers and those who simply helped me talk stuff out. You guys and gals made this book what it is.

And I can't leave out my Wordwraiths, past and present. This was the first real novel I started, which somehow took me ten full years to fully realize and get out the door. Without you, this book, nor any of my other writing projects, would surely never have made it past its initial draft.

Rank structure and a brief history of the North American Sentinel Corps (updated 11 November 2532)

The North American Sentinel Corps (NA SENTCORPS) follows a similar rank structure as the Republic of North America Naval Forces (RNA Navy).

Records are incomplete due to a chaotic time, but an ancient file cabinet containing water-damaged but legible paper documents, dated nearly 500 years ago, were discovered at a construction site in Sentinel City, Freeman Province (formerly Seattle, Washington). These documents hint that the Corps was established sometime in the 2050s, only a few years after Civil War II and the fall of the United States of America. To this day, SENTCORPS proudly retains its headquarters in Sentinel City.

By contrast, the RNA Navy was founded at the same time as the RNA itself, on 4 July 2142. Therefore, the Corps predates the Navy by almost a full century, and retains a proud history of the primary naval force that stood between the invading Eastern armadas and the West Coast. Much of North America found itself unofficially governed at the time, and were it not for the SENTCORPS and a hodge-podge of land and air forces still being manned by former US soldiers, airmen, and marines, the land belonging to the USA would have been divvied up by whichever military got there first.

Both the NA Sentinel Corps and the RNA Navy retained most customs, traditions, rank structure, sea-going warships, bases, and of course, slang originally belonging to the US Navy, the seafaring force of the long-dissolved United States.

The following chart illustrates the rank structure in the time period in which the top secret events of Distress Call occur.

Officer Ranks of North America SENTCORPS

Grade	Officer Rank	Abbr	Desc	Insignia
O-11	Fleet Admiral	FADM	All silver design 1 3-cm stripe 4 1-cm stripes	
O-10	Admiral	ADM	All silver design 1 3-cm stripe 3 1-cm stripes	
O-9	Vice Admiral	VADM	All silver design 1 3-cm stripe 2 1-cm stripes	
O-8	Rear Admiral (Upper Half)	RADM	All silver design 1 3-cm stripe 1 1-cm stripe	
O-7	Rear Admiral (Lower Half)	RDML	All silver design 1 3-cm stripe	
O-6	Captain	CAPT	All gold design 4 2-cm stripes	
O-5	Commander	CDR	All silver design 3 2-cm stripes	
O-4	Lieutenant Commander	LCDR	All silver design 2 4-cm stripes 1 2-cm stripe	
O-3	Lieutenant	LT	All silver design 2 2-cm stripes	
O-2	Lieutenant Junior Grade	LTJG	All silver design 1 4-cm stripe 1 2-cm stripe	
O-1	Ensign	ENS	All silver design 1 2-cm stripe	

Enlisted Ranks of North America SENTCORPS

Grade	Enlisted Rank	Abbr	Desc	Insignia
E-9	Fleet Master Chief	FLTCM	3 Chevrons + Rocker 2 Silver Stars Star in lieu of Rating	
E-9	Command Master Chief	CMC	3 Chevrons + Rocker 2 Gold Stars Star in lieu of Rating	
E-9	Master Chief Petty Officer	MCPO	3 Chevrons + Rocker 2 Silver Stars Gold w/12 years svc	
E-8	Senior Chief Petty Officer	SCPO	3 Chevrons + Rocker 1 Silver Star Gold w/12 years svc	
E-7	Chief Petty Officer	CPO	3 Chevrons + Rocker Gold w/12 years svc	
E-6	Petty Officer First Class	PO1	3 Chevrons Gold w/12 years svc	
E-5	Petty Officer Second Class	PO2	2 Chevrons Gold w/12 years svc	
E-4	Petty Officer Third Class	PO3	1 Chevron Violet only	
E-3	Starman	STN	3 Violet Stripes	
E-2	Starman Apprentice	STA	2 Violet Stripes	
E-1	Starman Recruit	STR	1 Violet Stripe	

Muster Roll

Ship (GSCS)	Registry	Type	Function	Date
Nightingale	AHR-47	SSS	Hospital /Rescue	1 February 2541

	Name	Rating	Rank/ Rate	Billet Title	Admin	Nat
1	Elwick, Moses		CAPT	Captain (CO)		RNA
2	Osterland, Quinton		CDR	Executive (XO)	TAD: Navigator	RNA
3	Kitner, Lance		LT	Pilot/Navigation		RNA
4	Connelly, Guy	MC1	PO1	Communications		RNA
5	Burgess, Maximus	(NR)	STA	Pilot/Nav Apprentice	Striking for ST	RNA
6	Galloway, Gwendolyn		CDR	Surgeon		AUS
7	Jorgens, Alyssa		LT	Head Nurse		RNA
8	Stevens, Frederick	HM1	PO1	Corpsman		RUS
9	Bailey, Gennifer	HM1	PO2	Corpsman		RNA
10	Lawrence, George	HM2	PO2	Corpsman		GBR
11	*(Vacant)*		LCDR	Chief Engineer	(vice: Dent)	
12	*(Vacant)*		CPO	Chief Mate	(vice: Robinsen)	
13	Crawford, Kelly	BM1	PO1	Boatswain's Mate	Exo Colony recruit	ERP
14	Pruitt, Kurt	QL1	PO1	Second Engineer		RNA
15	Girard, Cody	EM1	PO2	Third Engineer		RNA
16	Cabón, Carlos	MM2	PO3	Machinist Mate		PR
17	Masterson, Dale	OS	CIV	SAR Chief	SAR Team	RNA
18	Bruno, Antonio	MM	CIV	SAR XO	SAR Team	RNA
19	Gilbin, Daniel	FC	CIV	SAR Firefighter	SAR Team	AUS
20	Vereau, Rose	DC	CIV	SAR Biohazard	SAR Team	CAN
21	Ebersbacher, Jan	MT	CIV	SAR IT	SAR Team	GER
22	Abiodun, Hamidi	ND	CIV	SAR SCUBA	SAR Team	NIR
23	Laskey, Barbara	NC	CIV	SAR Counselor	SAR Team	UK

NASC FORM SC-242-1, MAR 36 PREVIOUS EDITION IS OBSOLETE **PAGE 1 OF 1**

1

Interstellar Civilian Transport Vessel *Emerald Pearl*

A jolt of electricity yanked Rae out of hibernation. She gulped the icy air as if she had just burst to the surface of a deep, dark ocean. *Where am I?*

Her arms flailed. She searched for something, anything, to make sense of her world. On all sides, cold metal and glass met her fingers. It was several inches from her face so it was not suffocating. Not yet. Confusion assaulted her mind. If only she could see! *Am I dead?*

She breathed deep. Cool, crisp air filled her lungs. She smelled ethyl alcohol. A tanginess offended her tongue. *Calm down, Rae, calm down. Remember what Mom said. Think before you act. Deep breaths. Breathe in, breathe out, breathe in...* She was breathing, feeling, smelling, tasting. *Okay, not dead, it seems!* Two senses remained. Sight. Hearing. She opened her eyes, but saw nothing. But there were noises. Muted, muffled, but present. She recognized none of them except the thump, thump, thump of her own heart.

Something pulled at her skin when she moved. It made her cease her frantic movements. Rae carefully ran a hand up the length of her left arm. She found a small tube and a string. No, a wire. Then another. She discovered several more tubes and wires jutting from her body. A chill ran down her spine.

Her breathing quickened. *Pull them out or leave them in?* She didn't know the answer. *Maybe they are keeping me alive?*

A yellow flash filtered through her eyelids. *What was that?* Rae held her breath. A pulsing in her neck matched the now pounding sound in her ears. She opened her eyes again. Or had she? *Do my eyes not work, or is it just too dark in here?*

Where is here!?

She counted her racing heartbeats to calm herself. *One, two, three—* Another flash. *There it is again!* Her arm dropped to her side, and the familiar texture of clothing brushed against her palm. Her hand instinctively returned and pinched it twixt her fingers. *Is that my blouse? The violet one? My favorite?* She remembered picking out her favorite top for… for what? First day of seventh grade at her new school? No. Not yet. A trip? Yes, the long trip from Earth—

A sound louder than her own heavy breathing crept into her consciousness. It was an alarm. No. A klaxon, like on a sea-going vessel. *That's right. I'm on a ship.* But not at sea, not this time. The yellow flashing every three seconds now made sense. The flashing, combined with the alarm, meant one thing.

Danger.

I want my daddy. Rae's chest tightened. *Where is Da—*

"Emergency. Emergency," said a muffled, feminine voice. It was oddly calm. *"Hull breach detected. Life Support and Environmental Systems at risk of failure. Immediate evacuation recommended. Emergency. Emergency…"*

2
Galactic Sentinel Corps Ship *Nightingale*

Captain Moses Elwick hunched over his beat-up, Navy-issue desk. He choked down the last of his jet-black coffee that had long-since grown cold. A lone tear fell upon the treasured document before him, and he dabbed it with his sleeve.

Petty Officer First Class Kelly Crawford slouched across from him in a chair too small for her towering form, elbows on the desk. Fingers that would be too long for a human being born on Earth partially covered an embroidered black patch on her upper left tricep. It sported three violet chevrons, a large silver eagle, and two crossed-anchors between the stripes and the bird. The anchors represented her job, or "rating," of Boatswain's Mate, the senior Non-Commissioned Officer on board. This made Kelly responsible for the well-being of all the other Petty Officers and lower enlisted Starmen on the *Nightingale*. She ran a finger over her handiwork from months ago: her own initials she had absent-mindedly carved into Elwick's ratty old desk. He had never had the heart to buff the "KC" out.

Moses went back to leafing through the thick, haphazard sketchbook before him. It was chock full of colorful drawings and short poems. Hasty scribbles filled the margins. "For Mom" was scrawled next to some, "For Dad" next to others. Some notes better explained what the illustration or poem was meant to be about. Turning the pages, Moses paused on a colorful butterfly. It sparked a memory of a peaceful afternoon at home seven years ago, the last stress-free day he'd spent with his daughter before shipping off to war. On that day he would have been wearing his shiny new lieutenant bars on his collar, recently promoted from Lieutenant "JG," or junior grade. Still bright-eyed and bushy-tailed. What he would give to return to those days. But would he want to relive the intervening years?

If it meant even just a few more days with his daughter, then yes. Absolutely.

The moisture in his eyes blurred everything. A tear fell onto his sleeve, making a dark spot on his navy-blue tunic.

"I brought ya a little somethin'," Kelly said, breaking the silence. Out of a small box she pulled a chocolate cupcake with pink icing and holo-candle jammed into the center. She set it between them on the desk. The little cake looked completely out of place in the cold, gray, military environment.

"Oh, Kelly." The sweet smell of sugary icing and chocolate made Moses' stomach growl in anticipation.

"It was Zoey's idea," she whispered.

At the mention of Zoey's name, Moses' chest tightened, and his jaw set. A subconscious reflex.

But when the candle flickered to life at Kelly's touch, the tension released. He stared at the faux flame and drew a long breath, which he held for a moment. "Happy birthday, sweetheart." Moses looked up into the intimidating red-head's hazel eyes. Of course, they had already welled up with tears. Kelly's soft, round, girlish face—a hard contrast to her thin but masculine physique—glowed warmly in the candlelight, which "burned" in an uncannily natural way. Almost like the real thing, Moses mused.

Kelly reached two long arms across the desk, her violet tunic's sleeves taut against her sinewy form. She covered Moses' hands with those unusually long fingers. "Make a wish for 'er," she suggested. Her touch was gentle, despite the potential strength those grease-smudged digits possessed.

Moses thought for a moment, and tried to come up with something his baby girl might want. Nothing material of course; Alena was above such things even in life. He nodded to himself when he landed on the perfect wish. Something his little girl would surely wish upon if she could see him now: that he would forgive her mother, reunite, and regain the happiness he once had. *Happiness!* he thought. *Where would such a thing come from?* He pictured her eyeing him from her Heavenly perch, disappointed in him for more than one reason. But he simply could not help how he was feeling. He wasn't ready to forgive her for her negligence that day.

As if Kelly could read his mind, she burst like a Valkyrie through his self-pity party. "Zoey still loves you, ya know. No matter how ya might feel 'bout her."

"Kelly, don't even start. Today's not the day," he added, wiping his face with his hands and then rubbing his temples. "I want to enjoy my baby's tenth birthday, not spend it arguing."

She puckered her lips and stared him down. "I just don't get you. Ya know, keepin' up this charade is probably why you've been havin' trouble with yer tummy lately."

"Charade?" He instantly flashed to anger. "You think I'm *pretending* to be furious!?"

"Who are ya furious at?"

"Are you kidding me?"

"Not my big sis? Why in all the worlds would you be furious with—"

"She killed my baby girl!" he shouted, launching himself out of his chair.

"She did not!" Kelly screamed, also jumping to her feet. Now she was an entire head and shoulders taller than Moses. "Don't you *ever* say that again, Moses Elwick!"

"Captain? Ozzie here," a disembodied voice interrupted.

"So, I guess ya believe I had a hand in killin' her, too?" The imposing figure before him seemed to ignore the XO's call, and continued to bore a hole through Elwick's skull with her powerful hazel eyes.

He glanced down to see the screen embedded into the dingy, gray desk had illuminated itself. Text poured down the small, holographic display at a high rate of speed. "Well, that's odd." He touched a virtual button labeled "21MC" on a smaller, adjacent display, activating the 21 Main Circuit, which would connect his cabin directly and discretely to the bridge.

"We'll continue this later," Kelly whispered through clenched teeth.

Moses took a deep breath. God, he didn't want to continue this conversation. "Elwick here," he finally said, still staring into the hard, accusing eyes of his sister-in-law.

The voice of the *Nightingale's* Executive Officer, Commander Quinton Osterland, resonated in Moses' cabin once again. "Captain, a couple of minutes ago we began receiving a QE-qué from what appears to be a location on the other side of the galactic bulge. It's constant, and seems to be a distress signal."

"Understood, XO. Let's hear it."

"It's not audio; text only, and a whole lot of it. Connelly was able to pull out location coordinates, a ship registration number, time of—"

"Is that's what's flying across my screen now?"

"Aye, sir," the XO replied.

Kelly moved around to Moses' side of the desk, eyes squinting as she studied the numbers herself. She blinked and let out a breath. "Don't know 'bout you, Cap'n, but I ain't never seen no text-only emergency message."

Moses couldn't recall the last time he'd seen one, either. Back in his training days, maybe, when he had first donned an RNA Navy starman jumper. The Quantum Entanglement communications Device, or "QED," usually displayed recorded three-dimensional holograms, two-dimensional video, or an audio recording at the very least. Never just text. "I can't make hide nor hair of this. Just go with the Delta-Lima-Tango."

"Petty Officer Connelly will relay."

Another voice cut in, that of the *Nightingale's* comms officer. "Evening, sir, Connelly here. Delta-Limo-Tango follows. Distance: twenty-eight thousand, four-hundred-seventy-two point three light years. Approximate Time-to-Intercept with standard, emergency-authorized 7,500 light year jumps…" His voice trailed off.

Kelly looked up.

Elwick gently shook his head. "Computer is probably still working that out. They like to call me earlier than—"

"Sorry, sir," said Connelly, "the nav computer is still calculating."

Kelly smiled. But then seemed to remember she was mad at him, and scowled.

"Alright, sir, the XO tells me Nav has calculated the time to intercept at just over three hours."

Moses had been reaching for his flight jacket when he froze. "Say again TTI, Connelly?"

"I say again, three hours."

"What would cause us to take more than an hour and half, two at most, to travel a mere twenty-eight thousand light years? And you forgot the location."

"Well, sir," the XO broke in, "there's a complication."

Moses' gaze locked with Kelly's as he removed his jacket from the back of the chair and pulled his arms through the sleeves. Frustration crept into his voice. "Ozzie, where exactly is this ship?"

"Oh, nowhere of any import," Osterland replied. "Just deep inside the Hades Quadrangle is all."

Moses closed his eyes and acknowledged the unfortunate sarcasm of the XO's words.

"Shit," Kelly whispered.

"You know, Ozzie, I've prided himself on having successfully avoided such regions of space my entire military *and* civilian career."

"First time for everything," he answered.

Kelly lowered her voice. "I've read 'bout that particular region o' space. About three outta every ten ships don't never come outta there."

He smirked. "Better odds than you'll get on the tables at Mylar's."

"True." She moved gracefully back to the appropriate side of the desk.

Moses spoke again to the circuit. "Officer of the Deck?"

"Lieutenant Kitner here, sir."

"Lieutenant, am I to understand there's no other SARCOM or SENTCORPS ship in this sector who can take this call?"

"Actually," Kitner replied, "there is another Triple S nearby, The *Mary Seacole.* And she's already in the Empyrean Straights, about six thousand light years closer than we are."

"Ah, Captain Shoemate's boat. What say we pass the coordinates on to him and ask—"

"I've already done that, sir."

Moses paused. "Oh, good. Well, I'm sure his boys and girls will do just as good as job as we would—"

"Sir, they have orders not to deviate from their present course under any circumstances."

Elwick lowered his head. "Of course they do."

Osterland spoke up again. "Captain, they're en route to deliver a boat-load of inoculations and respiratory equipment to the colony in the Altair system. The one with the respiratory epidemic, remember?"

"Oh, right."

"Epidemic?" Kelly asked. "I must have missed that on the news feeds."

"Apparently the virus has jumped to all thirteen outposts in the colony," Moses explained. "It's a full-blown outbreak, and they're 100% quarantined. Only emergency vessels are allowed in; and no one jumps out. The *Seacole's* crew will probably be stuck there a month or two, if not more, even if they take precautions and no one on board gets sick. Those are orders that came down straight from the Septagon in Liberty Province."

"Wow," Kelly replied.

"Yeah." Moses cringed. "I believe I'll take the Hades Quadrangle over that." He closed his daughter's sketchbook, then bent over the desk and blew out the candle. The holographic flame went out exactly as it was designed to do, using the magic of tiny, invisible sensors built into the wick. *Time to get to work.* "Ozzie, start analysis on the best jump route."

"Already started, Captain," replied the XO, who was also officially serving as navigator.

Elwick glanced at the timepiece strapped to his wrist. Orange digits read "18:46." He had put off evening chow in lieu of a depressing and angry walk down memory lane. His stomach would have to wait a little longer. "Connelly, alert SARCOM of the situation and forward that distress call. I'm on my way." He closed the circuit before his comms officer could acknowledge.

"Time fer me ta git below decks. Make sure Pruitt's gettin' the boiler ready," Kelly said. "Oh, and I'll be back later with this week's duty roster fer yer approval. And to finish our… conversation."

He nodded. He had not the time nor energy to fight her right now.

In only three of her long strides, she was at the door to Elwick's cabin.

"Kelly?"

She glanced over her shoulder, crouched in anticipation of passing through the standard-sized, round-edged, airtight door, which was only about four-fifths her height.

"Thank you."

"For what?"

"For your uncanny ability to switch from personal to professional in the blink of an eye. It's impressive."

Her features softened in an instant. Three more long strides back, and Kelly Crawford was crushing him with a tight hug.

"Oomph!" he winced.

"Sorry," she said, breaking the embrace. She patted him hard on the shoulder, then disappeared through the door, leaving it open.

Before leaving his cabin, Moses looked up. On a panel above the door through which Kelly had just exited was a silver, metal plate engraved with five Latin words. He stared at them for a moment in quiet reflection.

UT DEUM GUBERNARE NAVEM VERO

"May He steer the *Nightingale* true, as he always has," Moses whispered. He then departed for the bridge with a purpose.

3

Emerald Pearl

"Emergency. Emergency. Atmospheric System failing. Environmental System failing. Immediate evacu—"

A different muffled sound now accosted Rae's ears. It sounded like a voice. But not like the one she had just heard.

"Addy!" it called.

Addy? The voice seemed louder than the lady making announcements. That voice had been mechanical, like a computer talking. This one was not. *This* voice sounded human.

"Mommy! Daddy!" came another muffled call.

Her mind found focus, and her eyelids shot open for the first time. "Tabby!" she croaked. Light now filled her vision; she had only thought she had been surrounded by darkness, when in reality her eyelids had been shut tight this whole time. Rae saw a familiar room before her, but a scratched window stood between her and it. She lunged forward and pushed with all her might, and the lid to her hibernation pod began to rise, albeit reluctantly. The motion pulled hard on the tubes and wires inserted under her skin. It was an uncomfortable, nauseating feeling. Finally, the transparent wall had risen high enough for her to tumble from her coffin-like prison onto the cold floor. On hands and knees, she tried to move forward, but couldn't. With clenched teeth, she yanked herself free, tumbling to the ice-cold tile. She turned 'round to see the many plastic "strings" now dangling behind her. No puddles of red or clear fluid pooled on the gray floor; built-in breakaway joints on the tubes had allowed her to escape without making a bloody mess of herself. She thanked the Great Mother Nature for what her own mother called small favors. The yellow light flashed again, brightly now, every three seconds. She ignored it.

Rae breathed. She found it hard to do so. She couldn't feel her hands, though they were right in front of her. She lowered her head and saw her knees, both wrapped in black leggings. She couldn't feel those, either. She lifted her head and looked around the darkened room. "Tabby?" She had no idea whether her voice worked or not.

She tried to climb to her feet. Rae's legs wobbled like a foal just learning to walk, and she fell back onto her knees hard. *Oww! Why won't my legs work? How long have I been asleep?* She tried again, this time turning in a slow circle back toward the cryo pod from which she had recently tumbled, and used its vertical surfaces for support.

"Ayyyy!" came a muffled voice.

She looked to her left. *Tabby!*

"Rae, get me out!" Her younger sister stood in the illuminated stasis pod next to her own, banging away at the curved glass.

Rae dove to her sister's chamber, arms and legs screaming as a million invisible needles pricked at every muscle. "It's okay, Tabby! I'm here!" Rae dug her fingers into the seam of the door. It didn't budge.

"Get me out of here!"

"I'm trying!" Rae noticed a lit screen to her right. It flashed words she didn't care to read. She pounded on the display, first with her palm, then with her fist. It flashed green, and the glass door hissed. It took *forever* to rise. When it finally had, Rae flung her arms around little Tabitha. The ten-year-old fell onto her, sending both girls to the floor in a heap. The fall made quick work of the tubes and wires that had been plugged into Tabby.

Her sister looked around. "What happened? Where's Mommy?"

"I don't know," Rae replied. She had a full view of the cryogenic stasis chamber now, as she lay on her back and turned her head from side to side in a futile attempt to avoid Tabby's long pigtails from tickling her nose. Visual and audible chaos assaulted her from all sides. And every three seconds it became bright as day as the emergency beacon flashed again and again.

"Daddy!"

Rae looked "up" from her perspective to where Tabby pointed, and waited for the recurring yellow flash.

There!

Their father stood in the pod across from Rae's. "Daddy, thank the gods!" But something seemed wrong. It was as dark as the others, but—

"Mommy!"

Rae followed Tabby's gaze to the pod next to her own. In another three seconds she saw their mother's face and upper torso in full display behind the glass of the "coffin." "Looks like she's not awake yet," Rae said.

"Neither is Jamie."

Next to Mother, Rae saw their brother Jamie in a fourth pod. Four more pods lay beyond a wide door that opened to a small alcove.

"Attention. Attention," said the ever-calm lady, who Rae decided must be nothing but the ship's computer. The voice echoed in the metal room. *"Hull breach detected. Life Support and Environmental Systems failing. Immediate evacuation recommended."*

Tabitha pulled herself off Rae, and now sat up. She looked over her shoulder toward her father's cryo pod, and saw three others beside his, then four more on that same side in the alcove. Sixteen pods in all, two empty now. The small data screens jutting out to the right of each pod were dark. When Rae looked back at her mother's screen, it had several blue, jagged lines plodding across it. Words labeled each line, "Cardiac," "Respiratory," "Neurological," among others. Jamie's read the same, as did the other four next to his. Her father's screen showed none of these things, nor did any of the other seven along that same wall. *What does it mean? That they're simply turned off, or broken? Surely all eight can't be broken! There are people inside!*

Rae dragged herself to her mother's pod, made her way to her feet, and touched the small screen. At her touch, soft white lights snapped on in the interior of the pod, illuminating her mom's body. The light glinted in multiple hues off the precious, holy stones adorning the woman's neck, ears, and nose. The center lilac-colored amethyst mineral embedded in the pewter Triple Goddess pendant that hung between Mother's collarbones shone with a brilliance Rae had never before seen. Tiny shards of amethyst embedded in the crescent, metal moons on either side of the center circle seemed to sparkle with a life of their own. The Wiccan symbol of maiden, mother, and crone. It made Rae smile. Her eyes fell downward upon the sleeveless, forest-green dress her mother wore for the trip. It had gracefully caressed the floor when she walked, but now the metal casing of the pod concealed everything below the waist. Their mother's flowing, brown hair returned golden hues in the new light, and had been pulled to one side as if in a hurry. She did that often, out of habit. It had probably been the last thing she did before settling in for the long sleep. *She looks like an angel,* Rae thought. *So peaceful. I almost hate to wake her up. But I have to!*

She turned to check on Tabby. Sis rubbed her legs in vigorous fashion, as if to restore the circulation. Rae's own legs still tingled as well, but she didn't have time for such things. The small screen began displaying additional information, and she navigated through a simple menu. It appeared possible to interrupt the hibernation process, but each friendly blue virtual button she touched turned an unfriendly red, and a nasty notice appeared on the screen. *"No authorization to perform this function."* She tried various approaches and received similar messages. Mother did not wake up. She didn't even seem to be breathing as far as Rae could tell. But all indicators said she was alive.

Rae limped over to her father's pod. Her legs ached with each step, but at least the needles had begun to subside. She touched the small dark screen on his pod several times. Nothing happened; the pod didn't light up like Mother's had. Rae could see her father's face through the glass that separated them each time the yellow light flashed. He didn't look peaceful like Mother. His face looked all twisted up, like he was in pain. *Or had been in pain...* Tears filled her eyes, and her heart seemed ready to burst from her chest. "Daddy!" she shouted. But no reply came. Her lower lip quivered. *No…*

4

GSCS *Nightingale*

"Captain on the bridge!" Petty Officer Guy Connelly announced. He was usually the first to see anyone arrive to the nerve center of the search and rescue ship *Nightingale*, as his communications station stood along the port wall and faced the center of the semi-circular room.

Lieutenant Lance Kitner, the current, and perpetual Officer of the Deck due to manning shortages, spun on his heel and saluted. After Moses returned the large, quiet man's appropriate gesture, Kitner stood "at ease" and went back to hovering over the pilot and navigation stations, known collectively as the helm.

The ship's current pilot-in-training, Starman Apprentice Max Burgess, looked a bit uncomfortable with the lieutenant, a man the size of a football lineman, standing over him. The young sailor had acknowledged Elwick when Connelly had first announced his arrival, and now his attention was back to the myriad controls and displays that allowed the *Nightingale* to maneuver and traverse the lightyears.

Moses reached one of the two tall but narrow Command Pillars, located in the central area of the bridge directly behind the helm. Designed to be operated while standing, one pillar was reserved for the Captain, the other by the ship's Executive Officer. But the XO, Commander "Ozzie" Osterland, rarely left the navigation station, pulling double duty. Something the man didn't seem to mind.

As if on cue, Ozzie glanced over his shoulder and nodded to Elwick, acknowledging his presence, then turned his attention back to the holographic navigational displays.

"Where are we with the calculations, XO? Are all jump waypoints assigned yet?"

"The computer's still fine-tuning the calcs for what looks like seven jumps," replied Ozzie. "I'd give her five more minutes."

"Aye. Starman Burgess, have you battened down the hatches in prep for our first jump?"

"Pre-jump checks are complete, sir, half-way through operational checks; plasma injectors primed, Zee Dee initialization ready."

"Excellent, good job, Pilot." Always good to encourage the young sailors even when they're merely doing their jobs, but especially during their apprenticeship.

Ozzie added, "Captain, you should know that Dale is still securing the submariner rover. His team was in the middle of training on when the distress signal came through."

"Aye. Officer of the Deck, please let me know when the good Master Sergeant reports back that everything is tied down and we're ready to fly."

"Aye aye, sir," replied Lieutenant Kitner.

Moses took the next few minutes perusing the data pertaining to the recently-received distress signal. He frowned and touched a virtual button on his command pillar labeled "2MC," opening the intercom to Engineering. "Petty Officer Pruitt?"

A short silence followed before an unusually dainty female voice filled the bridge. "Crawford here, Cap'n. What can I do fer ya, sir?"

"Just checking on Zee Dee drive status, Kelly. Are we about there?"

"Core is green! Quark soup is comin' to a boil in, let's see… a little less than two mikes now."

Elwick checked his watch, but before he could say anything else, he heard what sounded like a yelp of pain. Ozzie did a slow spin in his chair towards the bridge center with one eyebrow raised.

"Is everything alright down there, BM1?" Elwick asked.

"All good, sir!"

He and Ozzie shared a stare as he spoke to the disembodied voice of his sister-in-law. "Where's Petty Officer Pruitt?"

"He's um… Well, he's 'otherwise detained,' ya might say."

Moses clinched his eyelids and sighed. *Oh, Kurt. Not again.* "Not that I'm defending him, Kelly, but I'll remind you that he's in charge of my engines and that giant motor we're fixing to fire up. I need all his digits and limbs in less than two pieces."

"Don't worry, Cap'n. He's still got one good hand ta push buttons and turns wrenches with."

Moses heard snickering around the bridge, then over the comm, a male voice. "Crawford! Come on, you need to relax!"

Her tone turned guttural, intimidating. "Oh, way wrong thing to say!"

Moses gritted his teeth when he heard a disgusting snap, followed by another, louder yelp. He sighed, certain the other voice belonged to the person he had tried to reach to begin with. "Was that Kurt Pruitt?"

"Aye, sir," Kelly said, returning to her sweet tone. "He can't come ta the phone right now, he's busy learnin' some gentlemanly manners."

"Alright, alright!" Pruitt's yell distorted the small speaker on Elwick's pillar. "I'm sorry! I get it!"

"I don't think ya *do,* or we wouldn't be havin' this conversation." Kelly spat through what sounded like clenched teeth. But then her tone turned dainty once again. "Anythang else, Cap'n?"

"Um, yeah, when you're finished pulling Pruitt out of the Bosun's Locker, tell him and his team to expect seven standard jumps. Oh, and tell him to get those maintenance notes completed and submitted on time this week."

"Will do, Cap'n!" There followed a thumping and a clang that echoed even over the intercom.

"You're insane, you know that, Crawford?" Moses heard Pruitt shout, somewhat more distant than before. "I can't believe—"

The 2MC circuit switched off on the other end.

Ozzie shook his head and turned back to the nav station. "Kelly, Kelly, Kelly. Never a dull moment."

Moses sighed. "That Amazon will be the death of me," he muttered.

"More like the death of Pruitt," Connelly muttered from the far side of the bridge.

Moses inwardly agreed, and pushed the "1MC" this time, connecting him to all decks of the *Nightingale* at once. He waited for the automated Bosun's pipe to sound attention before speaking, which came across as a long whistle followed by an upward tick. "Now hear this. The *Nightingale* has received a distress call that we will investigate immediately. It's pretty far out; the first of seven standard, 7,500-light-year jumps will take place in approximately five mikes. The Officer of the Deck will call out each jump, as usual." He nodded to Lieutenant Kitner, who returned a nod of acknowledgement. "Heads of Medical, Engineering, Navigation, as well as the entire SAR team will report to the Bridge Conference Room at 1930 for the initial mission brief. That is all." He switched off the circuit and directed his attention to the helm.

Max nodded, and activated the Zhédié Shikōng core. In Chinese: 折叠 时空. In layman's English: "Folded-space motor." In sailor's tongue: the "Zee Dee drive."

It didn't annoy Moses that, although the Chinese word "Zhédié Shikōng" was actually pronounced "Juh-dee-dah Skee-kong," everyone used the slang term "Zee Dee," because, well, that's what it looked like when written in English. Not only easier to say, but considering all the trouble China had given the Republic of North America all of Moses' life, he had to all but force himself to maintain any respect for the country or their various, often out-of-control government factions. Not to mention one faction in particular, led by a notoriously sadistic general named Wu Heng Guang. Wu had, in Elwick's Navy days, destroyed a quarter of the Republic fleet, and forced Moses' commanding officer to sacrifice herself to save his sorry ass in a sneaky maneuver out at Jupiter. The Battle of Europa did end up creating a life-long friend out of the man who was now his civilian SAR team's leader, but that seemed to be the only good thing that came of it.

"Aye," Lieutenant Kitner said into a comms panel at the helm. "Captain, Engineering reports quark-gluon plasma at optimal parameters and ready for core insertion."

"Aye, Lieutenant, let's get this show on the road."

"Aye aye! Helm, activate Zee Dee drive."

"Activate Zee Dee, aye!" Starman Burgess repeated, and outstretched both arms in order to push two amber-colored virtual buttons simultaneously. The buttons had been installed a meter and a half apart to avoid unintentional operation.

Now Elwick's bridge crew had a solid three minutes to sit and wait for the gargantuan magnetrons in the aft section of the *Nightingale* to spin up, plus a couple more minutes after that for the Zhédié ante-chamber to compress the plasma—what the Engine Rates referred to as "quark soup"—to a critical pressure. At that point, Elwick's small rescue ship would be ready to break every law of the standard physics model dating back hundreds of years. "Ozzie, in the four or five minutes we have before my stomach turns inside out, what type of ship are we looking at? What's her compliment?"

"Civilian passenger vessel. Small crew. Took me a while to find the schematics. Had to do a general search on the Exonet."

"Really?" Moses' jaw dropped. "It wasn't on the SARCOM registry?"

"It seems to be an extremely old ship, Captain. Not in service anymore, far as I can tell. I just pushed the data to your pillar."

"Sir," said the comms officer Connelly, "Just received an ACK from SARCOM that they received and are reviewing the distress transmission, and they've already approved the first waypoint on our proposed flight plan provided by Mr. Osterland. We have an authorized go for our initial jump."

Elwick smiled. "Timed that out just about perfectly. Connelly, make sure they're fully aware of the issues with the target's location and the reason for our long TTI. I agree with the computer's prediction that it may take us a full hour after reaching our Zee Dee exit point to navigate the Hades Quadrangle and rendezvous with the target."

"Aye aye, sir."

"Ozzie, show me your flight map. I want to see the route I trusted you with that Petty Officer Connelly just sent to SARCOM."

The XO brought up a digital rendition of the galaxy in which the human race called home. It entirely filled the far-right of seven bay windows made of transparent graphene that wrapped around half the bridge. The map rotated so the viewer flew above the "north pole" of the barred spiral that was the Milky Way.

"As usual, the orange circles represent our jump in/jump out locations," Osterland explained. "The red square is our target, and the bright blue square is us." The points indicated a curved line from the bulk of the humans' colonized systems near Earth's Sun, followed along the right side of the bright, central bulge of the galaxy, and then led away to a point the far side of the galactic disk.

Light blue lines broke the galaxy up into sectors, with text labels for each one. The bright blue square that represented the *Nightingale* glowed inside the Inner Orion Spur, while the red square took residence inside an area labeled "Ryker's Hope." Additional text labeled various other points of interest.

"Seven jumps programmed," Osterland announced, "but I can probably shave that down to three or four if allowed to kick it in the—."

"Seven will be fine."

Osterland glanced over his shoulder. "Will it?"

"Yes, XO."

"Aye aye," Ozzie said, a bit dejected.

Elwick took note that a star named Scheau Blao VW-2 C27-77 was near their final jump destination. "What do we know about that star near our final exit point?"

Osterland shook his head. "Just a random K-type yellow-orange star, approximately 33,800 light years from Earth. Nothing unusual about it." He added under his breath, "'cept it's on the far side of the galaxy where no one ever goes…" Then louder, "No one's mapped that system yet, so no data on number and type of planets. Why do you ask, sir?"

Kitner broke in. "Magnetrons will reach full charge in one minute, Captain."

"Noted, Lieutenant."

Kitner touched a virtual button on the XO's command pillar that sounded the proper Bosun's whistle once again across the ship to alert them to attention. "All hands, this is the Officer of the Deck. Prepare for space folding. We will initiate the first of seven standard jumps in one minute. Distance per jump: seventy-five hundred." Then he added, "Prepare accordingly. Standby."

Moses sighed, knowing what lay ahead within the next sixty seconds, but there was no getting around it. Jumping 7,500 light years was standard jump procedure on a rescue ship when lives were on the line. They could drop down to a pitiful 2,500 when in the recovery/resupply phase if they wished, or even a thousand; his insides didn't reel as much when they dropped that low. He only now realized he was still staring at the map, and his XO had asked him a question. "No real reason. Just... what a desolate place to be stranded. On the other side of the galactic bulge, thousands of light years from any hint of civilization."

"The closest human presence is a plasma station in the Norma Arm," Ozzie said. "Speaking of which, we might want to stop and top off the tanks before heading all the way out to the quadrangle."

"Lieutenant, verify the current status of our plasma."

Starman Burgess, anticipating Kitner's next order, flipped to the correct virtual readout, then leaned back so the Lieutenant could better see the display.

"Quark-Gluon Plasma level at ninety-seven percent on tank one, one hundred percent on tanks two, three, and four," Kitner said.

"Aye."

"Magnetons charged," Kitner announced to the bridge. "All systems indicate green. Ready to jump."

"Aye, Lieutenant," Elwick said, then grabbed his command pillar with both hands. He took a deep breath and swallowed before ordering, "Initiate jump."

"Initiate jump, aye!" Kitner replied, and once again sounded the proper Bosun's whistle from the XO's pillar. "All hands, this is the Officer of the Deck. Space folding commencing in five... four... three... two... one..." At "one" he nodded to Starman Burgess.

Max Burgess nodded in reply and yelled a little too excitedly, "Initiating jump!" The Starman touched the same two virtual buttons on his console that he had before, only now they had turned from amber to green. Moses heard the expected thunder rising to a crescendo from astern. He thought about risking a look to see if anyone noticed his knuckles whitening, but he soon couldn't, not with his eyes squeezed so tightly shut.

The giant magnetrons that labored at a respectable level twenty-four hours a day to produce the *Nightingale's* protective magnetic field—which stretched several kilometers from the ship in every direction and protected its organic cargo from deadly cosmic radiation—had been instructed to spin at ungodly speeds. The magnetrons charged the system that fed the four-million-degree quark-gluon plasma from the *Nightingale's* massive, electromagnetic storage tanks into the car-sized Zhédié core, where the engine would alter the structure of spacetime within a pre-designated radius not much larger than the ship. The engine then initiated a quantum pulse that lasted anywhere from nanoseconds to several seconds of relative ship time inside the bubble, but to an observer, the event appeared to complete itself before it began. This is also exactly when Elwick's insides twisted up into a knot, as happened to most people when traveling in such a manner over such great distances, until they got used to it. Moses thought he had gotten used to it long, long ago.

He had no good way to describe the sensation of being inside a fold in the fabric of spacetime to his friends and family who stubbornly remained planet-bound. So, when they asked, he enjoyed quoting from an ancient science fiction novel written three and a half centuries earlier. It talked about "jumping to hyperspace" rather than "folding space" like a piece of paper and sticking a pen through it, but it was still the best description he had ever found. It went something like this: during a jump, your eyeballs turn inside out, your feet leak out the top of your head, and you're left sliding into your own navel. The truly remarkable thing being that this author—a Twentieth Century Englishman who worked in comedy rather than physics—could not have had the slightest clue what such a thing was actually like. Nevertheless, he nailed it perfectly.

"Jumping" was the only way the human race had yet found to cover cosmic distances without either taking several generations to complete the journey, or forcing equally undesirable relativistic effects upon travelers; the speed of light was simply too slow. But even if advances in structural materials allowed humankind to travel at or very close to the speed of light, no one wanted to end their trip only to find everyone they knew dead and buried in the decades or centuries that passed across the rest of the universe, while they enjoyed a cocktail and competitive game of cucumber ball. Moses thought it was bad enough humans had built engines that pushed a spacecraft to one-quarter of lightspeed, which still garnered relativistic effects to some degree, though it usually meant only a few minutes were lost due to the short distances involved (the Earth-Europa run, for instance). However, he had to admit that losing those few minutes was preferable to the nausea and disorientation of being turned two-dimensional and back again.

After what seemed like ten minutes, but in reality lasted only a handful of seconds, the ordeal ended. At this point, the Zhédié system's primary task was complete for the time being, the system cut the plasma flow to the core, and the quantum field collapsed. Everything that had been inside the folding bubble reappeared in normal, non-relative space, if not in non-relative time. The ship's internal chronometers had recorded—Moses verified—twelve full seconds had passed since the pilot had pushed those two buttons. However, the external chronometers, which upon re-emergence synched back up with the Galactic Exonet, and verified that not even a moment had passed in the outside world. Galactic Standard Time precisely matched as if they had never jumped at all. They had not traveled backwards through time in any practical sense, but in a technical sense they did so every single time they used the Zhédié drive. Seemed to Moses a guy could age right out of his skin if he jumped enough, the reverse problem that someone traveling close to lightspeed would have!

This line of thought often made him dizzy, so he pushed it from his mind. Moses breathed deep, and released his iron grip on the command pillar. He was glad he had skipped dinner; it may have ended up all over the bridge. The lights and computers all flickered back to life sporadically across the ship, as if every onboard system shut down upon every jump and re-booted itself. Including his very body.

"Jump one complete, Captain," Kitner announced. "All systems back to standard parameters. Prepping for next jump."

Moses opened his eyes to see Osterland staring at him.

You okay? Ozzie mouthed.

Elwick squished his face into a smile and nodded as bravely as he could.

Ozzie's brows went up, and he took a little too long to spin himself back around to his console.

Moses swallowed hard and cleared his throat before speaking, to ensure his voice didn't break or even cut-out mid-sentence. "Ozzie, let's look at that jump plan again, now that we have a few minutes to wait before the next time my insides are scrambled."

"I've got it up now."

Elwick made his way back down to the navigation station, careful not to lose his balance and plow sideways into Kitner, and looked over Osterland's shoulder. He already saw a change he wanted to make. "Let's be sure and hug the western edge of the Arcadian Stream, and the eastern edge of the Empyrean Straights. I know Sag A's gravity can't reach us this far out, but that thing's weirded me out ever since I was a kid. Been giving it a wide berth all my life."

"I feel you there, Captain," he replied, and began making adjustments to the entry and exit coordinates so that the straighter line of orange circles bent into a more pronounced outward-pushing curve. This would allow them to stay away from the large, central bulge of the Milky Way, home to Sagittarius A*, the supermassive black hole at the center of the galaxy. "How's that look for a rough course?" the XO asked.

Moses nodded. "Looks good. Thanks, Ozzie."

"Aye."

Elwick pointed to a small, purple square on the map, near one of the orange boxes along their route. "Is this the gas station?"

The XO nodded. "Aye, Captain. The hadron collider in the Norma Expanse. It's a smaller ring than the one out in the Scutum-Crux, but it will save us the most time."

"Sounds good. Connelly, contact that station, let them know we'll be making a *fast* pit stop."

"Aye aye, Captain," Guy replied, and went about sending a QE comm that the skeleton crew on the collider would receive in microseconds, similar to making a simple phone call to a neighbor. Only this neighbor was a several thousand light years away.

"Zee Dee core in cool-down phase," Kitner announced. "Seventeen more minutes before jump capability is restored."

Always takes longer when they push the motor to these ridiculous levels, Elwick thought. But it gave him time to tease his young Starman a bit. "Pilot, keep one eye on the radar at all times, and be sure to steer clear of any flying saucers or ghost ships."

Burgess spun around. "Sir?"

"Just a precaution. These innermost galactic arms are haunted, but don't worry, there hasn't been an incident in oh, when was the last one, XO?"

Osterland shrugged. "A couple months, maybe?"

The young pilot tilted his head. "Aw, come on, sir."

For support, Elwick looked around the room. "Am I making this up?"

"Not that I can tell, sir," the comms officer chimed in.

Cleverly put, thought Elwick.

Lieutenant Kitner jutted out his lower lip and shook his head.

The XO leaned over to Burgess and pointed out through the large windows, where a thick, fuzzy, speckled cloud seared the sky from one side to the other; the Scutum-Crux arm of the Milky Way seen edge-on. "You see those slow movers out there?"

Burgess leaned forward, eyeing the vast expanse before him. "Slow movers? Where?"

"If you stare long enough, you can make out some of the stars moving. Only those *aren't stars*."

"But they have to be..."

Ozzie shook his head.

"What are they, then?" Burgess whispered.

"No one knows. They're not ships, ships don't move that fast. At least, no ships built by humans…"

Burgess whispered, "Well, they can't be aliens!" The now wild-eyed pilot turned around to face the group. "No one's ever found aliens! At least, none that can build spaceships!"

Elwick shrugged. "Galaxy's a big place. Last I heard, we monkeys haven't even explored one percent of the Milky Way, even after two centuries of exploration. And any advanced race could easily hide from us if they wanted to. Just keep your eyes peeled, in case they want to show themselves."

Burgess spun back front, and peered out the large bay windows, completely transfixed.

Moses cracked a quiet smile as voices murmured behind him. He turned to see a small group of people assembling in the Briefing Room, an open area to the rear of the ship's bridge designed for meetings pertaining to Current Operations. It was the Search and Rescue or "SAR" team. It wasn't quite 1930 yet, but he figured he might as well join them. "Lieutenant Kitner, you have the conn."

"Aye, aye, Captain."

Osterland slapped Burgess on the shoulder. "I need to join the Captain on this meeting. But let me know if you see anything, aye, sailor?"

"Aye, Mr. Osterland," Burgess replied, still staring into the depths of space.

Elwick leaned in close and whispered to the XO. "Are we having a little too much fun with the poor kid?"

Osterland chuckled. “Are you kidding? We’re going easy on him. He’s lucky we didn’t send him outside in a widowmaker to scrape all the baked cherry juice off the hull and tell him we drove through another cloud of alien mucous!”

“Ah, if only there was time,” Elwick mused.

5

Emerald Pearl

"Why won't he wake up?" Tabitha asked. She lay on the floor beside Rae, clutching herself, surely missing her cherished flannel teddy bear.

"I don't know!" Rae lied. "I think these screens are messed up." She couldn't share her dread with her little sister. Her gut told her those pods had broken, and everyone inside them was dead.

"Look!" exclaimed Tabby over the noise of the klaxon.

Rae looked over her shoulder and saw the lights in her mother's pod fading, then going completely dark like before. Her screen went back to showing the jagged blue lines. A spike occurred every few seconds on the various rows, indicating heartbeats and the glow of her brain's lobes, verifying she was dreaming. *Dreaming of home?* Rae wondered. *Of me and Tabby and Jamie? Of our future on—wait, where are we going again?*

"Why can't you wake anyone up?"

"I told you, I don't know!" Rae yelled.

"He's not going to wake up, is he?"

"Oh Tabby, don't say things like that!" Rae's voice cracked as she spoke. "He's just asleep! He's okay!"

"But that screen says Daddy's pod is broken."

What screen? Rae followed Tabby's pointing finger and noticed, for the first time, multiple displays covering an entire wall. *How did I miss that?* One section of the wall showed sixteen rows, representing all cryo pods in the two chambers. Pods labeled "1" and "2" read *"OPEN"* in happy white letters. These represented Rae and Tabitha's pods. Six others showed the blue respiratory and other data similar to what Rae had seen on their mother's screen. The other eight flashed the word *"MALFUNCTION"* in angry red letters. Rae's heart dropped, her legs collapsed, and she ended up in a heap next to her sister.

"Attention," Tabitha read. "Oper-ations a-lerted. Is 'Operations' a place?"

"Where do you see that?"

"Right there." Tabby pointed at the very bottom of the large display.

Rae guessed the system was now alerting the crew of the *Emerald Pearl* to an unauthorized attempt to bring passengers out of hibernation earlier than scheduled. "Good," she shouted. "Turn us in, you stupid computer! We need help!" She looked at Tabitha, who busied herself peeling the last of the foreign devices from her skin and yanking out those that had been inserted into her small veins just before hibernation. Plastic was soon strewn about the floor.

Sis has the right idea. Rae ripped a sensor off her neck, then ever-so-carefully pulled a tiny plastic tube from her left arm. A drop of blood oozed from the resulting hole.

"You gotta push on them," Tabby said.

"What?"

"When you're pulling them out. You have to push on the vein so it doesn't bleed all over the place. We don't have any Collagex, dummy."

How does she know all this stuff? Rae pushed on the broken skin where the intravenous tube had been. For the second and subsequent IV, she pushed on the break in the skin as she drew them out, preventing even a drop of blood from escaping. Rae was more than familiar with commercial hemostatic agents used to make blood clot than she in fact cared to be; she had to use it on their father on one occasion while out in the middle of Green Bay on his boat. No time to think about sailing with her father now. She focused on the IVs. It took a few minutes to get them all out of her body and all the wired sensors off her skin. She found them sticky, and they made her skin tight when she moved. The ones that had been on her face were especially annoying. She made various faces to try to work out the adhesive.

Tabitha, finished with the task of "de-hibernating," pulled her sleeves down and hugged herself again to ward off the cold.

It had gotten a bit chilly, Rae had to agree, and the floor felt like ice! Rae pulled herself up using her father's cryo pod. She tested her muscles. They burned and her spindly legs shook, but she was upright. Permanently, she promised herself, fighting the urge to drop again. They had work to do! "Come on, Sis, get up, it's not that hard."

Tabby's face solidified and she rolled over on all fours. She put one foot underneath her, winced, then somehow shot right up. She wobbled a bit, but stayed on her feet.

Wow. Why wasn't it that easy for me? "See? Aren't you warmer already?"

"No," said Tabitha.

"Emergency. Emergency. Hull breach detected. Life Support and Environmental Systems failing. Immediate evacuation recommended."

"Yes, we know!" Tabby yelled at the ceiling.

Rae's eyes narrowed. She looked at all the other pods. *Why didn't anyone else wake up?* Then another thought entered her mind. *Why hasn't anyone come to the cryo chamber to tell us what to do? Or to scold us for trying to open a pod without permission?* She looked at Tabitha, who stood quietly and staring at the giant set of screens on the wall. *Someone needs to do something.* If no grown-ups were going to show up, Rae was going to have to take charge of the situation.

The very idea turned her stomach upside down. *Me? In charge?* It would make her daddy proud, but would Tabby even let her be in charge? *And do I have the strength and the brains to actually "be" in charge?* Rae bit her lower lip and looked at her sister. Tabitha stared at her. Her eyes. Rae couldn't read them. Either little Tabby was about to cry, or about to start telling her what to do. Rae wasn't about to let that happen. "Alright, that's enough lollygagging!" she announced, channeling her father. "Come on!" Rae wobbled when she tried to walk. She lunged for the nearest cryo pod, which had once been her own, to break her fall. She forced her feet from their pigeon-toed stance and tried to put weight on them again. Success! When she looked at Tabby, her jaw dropped.

Her sister stood stoic, head cocked. "Want me to carry you?" Tabby asked.

"Shut up. Let's go find out what's going on." Rae dove forward, and strode chin-up past the wall of blinking health status information and toward what appeared to be the only exit to the room, a large, round, metal door. *Why is it so big?* It loomed before her like a dark gray oak tree, the harbinger of bad things to come. What lay behind it? Darkness? Cold? Death? *Space!?* Hopefully, friendly crewmembers ready and willing to help.

"Well?" said a voice beside her, seeming to gather impatience with every passing second.

Rae turned and looked at Tabitha, swallowed hard and breathed deep. She looked over Tabitha's shoulder at their father in his dark tomb. He could no longer be her rock. It was up to her. She had to be strong.

Rae touched the controls next to the giant hatch leading out of the cryo chamber. The heavy thing clanged and began to move. She steeled herself for whatever nightmare might be on the other side.

6

GSCS *Nightingale*

"Evening, everyone." Various replies similar to "Evening, sir" reached Captain Elwick's ears as he squeezed into the briefing room. The seven-man SAR team gathered together at one end, and were already getting a bit rowdy. The population of the narrow alcove that spanned the rear of the bridge had already reached nine with Moses' arrival, and would soon be packed to maximum capacity.

Boatswain's Mate Petty Officer First Class Kelly Crawford squirmed at the other end of the tight room, trying to find room for her giraffe-like legs so as not to be in the way others filtering in.

The ship's head surgeon arrived right after Moses, Commander Doctor Gwendolyn Galloway. The crankiest, most ancient, most Australian woman Elwick had ever met. She commanded authority and not a little fear anytime she walked into a room. Moses often joked she knew her way around the *Nightingale's* med bay better than most people knew their way around their own minds. Her mere arrival quieted the lot down. Moses took a deep breath, adjusted his blue, Navy-issue ball cap, and got down to business.

"You got your team, Master Chief?" Moses asked of the SAR Team's leader.

The stoic, middle-aged Dale Masterson looked around. His voice then resonated in the small space. "Aye, Captain."

Master Chief Dale Masterson, who Moses had served with many moons ago in the RNA Navy, reminded Moses of a hero from a bygone era, from the early days of two-dimensional holofilms—something they called television and movies back then. The man indeed held the rank of hero in Elwick's eyes, but that was a memory for another day. Scuttlebutt warned both young and old that extended exposure from Dale's glowering gaze could burn holes in steel and souls. Elwick never once attempted to discourage the rumor.

Moses began his brief. "Okay, this should be pretty routine, except for one, um, small concern which I'll get to a bit later in the brief." He turned and touched what looked like a smooth black wall that had, up to this point, reflected his image. It now sparked to life. A cut-away diagram of a spaceship showing interior decks and various data points appeared under his fingertips. He turned back to the group. "From the signal being relayed by the emergency beacon, the ship in trouble is the civilian transport vessel *Emerald Pearl*. She's a very old Navy frigate that's been converted at some point in her life into a private passenger vessel. Crew: unknown. Passengers: unknown. Our TTI is currently three hours, but that could change."

Murmurs spread throughout the small room. Kelly kept quiet.

"A three-hour intercept, Captain?" Masterson asked. "Why so long? I take it that will be shaved down as jumps are fine-tuned?"

"It could increase, actually."

"What? In three hours, anyone on board—"

"I know, I know," Elwick said, holding up a hand for quiet. "The problem is that concern I mentioned. Again, I'll get to that in a minute." He turned back to the black wall and swiped it, effectively "turning the page" and displaying a screen full of text and numbers. "Like I said, the *Pearl* is a very old boat, and when I say 'old' I mean *ancient.* As in built before any of us—or even our parents—were even *born.* Well, maybe except for you, Bruno. We all know you watched Neil Armstrong walk on the moon when it actually happened."

Everyone laughed at Moses' joke, and even Masterson smiled. The "large and in-charge" Antonio Bruno had twenty years on Elwick, but the retired Navy Machinist's Mate would be close to six hundred years old had he pulled off such a feat as witnessing the first moon landing in 1969 C.E.

As the brief ruckus died down, Lieutenant Kitner's voice filled the air. From the sound of things, he had SARCOM on the horn, likely receiving updated guidance regarding this mission. Despite Moses' deep-rooted desire to help anyone and everyone in need, a part of him wished his Higher Headquarters would order the *Nightingale* to divert, and perhaps enlist a vessel much more suited to enter a high temperature, high pressure nebula. Especially in such a volatile region of space. A full-fledged battleship would do nicely, what with its multi-layered hull and plating that required someone with an above-top-secret clearance to know details about. Barreling headlong into the Hades Quadrangle in a tiny Triple S, especially one with giant red crosses painted on all sides, did not sound to Moses like a roaring good time. The *Nightingale* didn't even have so much as a BB gun duct taped to its bow. But that probably wasn't going to be an issue; the likelihood of encountering hostiles in the quadrangle was surely slim, if not zero. Political enemies of the RNA usually didn't give hospital ships any trouble, and even pirates weren't crazy enough to go in there. The crews of search and rescue ships *were* crazy enough, it would seem.

Moses' XO's earlier words stuck in his mind, however. There always was a "first time for everything." He paused a moment in his brief for whatever new orders the Lieutenant received from their higher headquarters.

Within ten seconds, Lieutenant Kitner looked back at Elwick and gave him a thumbs up, indicating the Officer of the Watch at Search and Rescue Command headquarters had approved their flight plan, and understood the reasoning for their extended timeline.

Damn, Moses thought. *So much for getting out of this one.* "Okay, continuing," he said to the assembled group. "We couldn't find a recent dossier on the *Emerald Pearl*, which as you can imagine is a bit odd, but not unheard of. What *is* odd is that we could barely find anything on her." He turned to face the wall screen again. "We did find a ship similar to her that the Navy decommissioned nearly a century ago, and even the Merchant Marines decommissioned some twenty years ago: *Kristin's Vision.* It's also been converted into a passenger-type vessel. Apparently, the owner of the *Pearl* converted three of these old military frigates into cargo and small-passenger ships. After conversion, the *Vision* had a crew compliment of twelve, a 'steerage' passenger capacity of over one hundred, eight VIP quarters, and sixteen cryogenic chambers for long distance flights. I'm going to assume the *Pearl* is similar."

"Cryogenic chambers?" Dr. Galloway interrupted. "How old'ya say this thing was again?"

"Old enough that the jump capability of its core isn't much better than a horse and buggy compared to our Cadillac. Journeys between stars took years or even centuries instead of hours or days. We're talking… maybe one-hundred-light-year-hops, tops!"

"But that would take forever!" someone blurted.

"Exactly. Other galaxies were completely out of the question. So, instead of carrying extra food and water for passengers, which cost more in fuel due to the added mass, they went with cryo pods."

The doctor scoffed. "You're askin' me to dust off some very old skills, there, Captain. But I think I can conjure up some old files on stasis tube recovery and reanimation."

"Good. Hopefully the *Pearl's* pods have been replaced with newer models since the last refit, which, according to records, took place almost a hundred years ago, which of course, can't be the latest one."

"Newer models?" Australian firefighter Daniel Gilbin laughed. "Is there a company out there that still manufactures those things?"

"Good question," Elwick agreed. "Someone must, or at least refurbishes them. One of the outer colonies, maybe; I don't know who else would need them. In any case, the pods are probably a few decades old at least, and old pods could complicate our rescue efforts. Especially if they've been damaged. So, that's something to keep in mind."

"It just keeps gettin' better," Doc Galloway muttered.

Gilbin shook his head. "Bollocks! You weren't kiddin' when you said that ship was old!"

"Did you think I was exaggerating when I said this thing's older than Antonio?" Elwick asked.

The team's British-born counselor and doctor of psychology Barbara Laskey scowled. "Why would anyone risk hopping stars in such an old bucket, refit or not? Especially one with tech older than me! Cryo pods," she seethed. "That's just asking for trouble." Tight strands of silver hair hugged the wrinkled face of a wise old soul.

"I suppose people who don't have a lot of money will take whatever they can get," Elwick suggested. "Anyway, we haven't made voice comms with anyone yet… is that still accurate, Connelly?"

The enlisted man looked up from his station—mere feet away from the conference nook—to check the communications panel once again. "Aye, sir, that's correct. No response to hails."

"Do to that," Elwick continued, "we unfortunately have no way of knowing just yet how many casualties we have, or even how many souls are on board. It gets worse. The distress call is text only, which holds very little data. We don't know the condition of the ship, its Zee Dee core, the condition of its life support, the environmental situation, or even what their flight plan looked like. It's like she was flying completely unregistered and didn't waste money or time on a decent emergency beacon."

"Not unlike a pirate," offered Masterson.

Elwick nodded. "Anything is possible. Let's just hope this isn't a trap, either by pirates or some rogue faction. But if it is, the *U.S.S. Jeffrey Buker* is on standby for support."

"Good to hear. Those ninth-gen railguns would make quick work of just about anything but a neer-peer battlecruiser."

"Yeah, but we'd still have to get a message to her, and pirates like to jam you the moment you exit folded space. Not only that, well, she probably won't be able to provide any support for a good number of hours."

Several brows furrowed, and everyone present seemed to lean forward in expectation, their faces questioning, worrying. This is the part of the brief Moses had been dreading.

7

Emerald Pearl

"Emergency. Emergency. Atmospheric System failing. Environmental System—"

"Failing, yes, we know!" Rae screamed at the disembodied voice that now echoed in the gray hallway outside the cryostasis chamber. The klaxon rattled her nerves every ten seconds. It sounded like some prehistoric predator bellowing deep in the bowels of the ship. "I wish someone would turn that off!"

"It kinda sounds like a T-Rex's tummy growling," Tabby observed. "Daddy would like it."

"Well, I don't!" Rae said.

Her sister teased. "Scared?"

"No more than you!"

Tabitha said nothing.

Rae found it easy to see where they were going, what with the hallways so brightly lit. Evenly-spaced strobe lights in the ceiling flashed yellow every three seconds. *That will probably get annoying sooner or later,* she thought.

"Hello?" Rae called into various rooms. She received no answer. Most of the gray doors they encountered turned out to be unlocked. Each had a number and a letter stenciled on it, and on this floor each label started with stylized "3." Debris from small wall compartments that had popped open littered the halls. First Aid kits, storage bins of small tools, blankets, other bits of flotsam. Rae stepped over some official-looking forms that had scattered themselves about, the purpose of which she could only guess.

"Where is everyone?" Tabby asked.

"I'm wondering the same thing. I wonder if—" Rae's nose crinkled. The tangy smell of cryogenic fluid had suddenly been replaced with something she hoped was not what she feared. She couldn't help but breathe in the coppery scent, much as she tried not to do so. She slowed her pace but Tabby barreled forward, either not noticing the smell, not recognizing it, or the girl's curiosity had simply gotten the best of her.

Her sister stopped short at the next intersection where three hallways met. Sis stood frozen, staring at something Rae couldn't see. *That can't be good.* Rae crept forward. She saw a sign come into view on the opposite wall that read "Engineering." She leaned around the corner. There on the floor lay a woman dressed in blue coveralls. She lay on her back, arms splayed out to either side, her face bloody, her long black hair a tangled mess. Rae saw a red stripe leading from the woman's leg to a closed door only a few feet away, and a large red pool underneath the leg. The door sported a darker shade of gray than the walls and looked really heavy, not unlike the door to the cryogenics chamber. Tabby walked over to the woman.

"Tabby, stay away from her!" Rae yelled.

"She's not gonna hurt me." The little girl bent over the still figure. "She's hurt."

Rae only managed a glimpse of the woman's leg before she slammed her eyes shut. *Don't be afraid, Rae, it's not like you haven't seen blood before. It's just a cut.*

A very bad cut.

She opened her eyes back up to get a better look. The woman's clothing was torn wide at the left thigh, and Rae could see— Nope. She slammed her lids closed again. *A very, very deep cut. Oh my, what was that yellow, globby stuff?* Rae covered her mouth with her hands.

"Hey!" Tabby yelled in the woman's face. "Can you hear me? Wake up!" She shook her arm a bit violently.

"Tabby!"

"What?" her sister shouted. "We need help. She can help! She works on the ship! Look," Tabby tugged at the woman's tunic. "Uniforrrm."

Rae moved closer and stood on the other side of the fallen woman, trying hard to ignore the Grand Canyon in her leg. A colorful, embroidered patch decorated her right breast; the words "*Emerald Pearl*" arched over a green, snow-topped mountain. Immediately below that, a nametape read "Norstrom." On the left breast, another sewn patch read, "Merchant Marine," and above that was a symbol Rae guessed might be rank. She scolded herself for not learning navy enlisted ranks like her father had tried to get her to do.

"Who do you think she is?" Tabitha whispered.

"Well, she's definitely one of the crew people, but I don't think she's going to help us. I think she's…" Rae couldn't say the word.

Tabby frowned and shook the woman again. She bent over and screamed. "Lady! Wake up!!"

The woman's eyelids burst open and both Rae and Tabby threw themselves backwards. Rae may have yelped.

Norstrom turned her head from side to side. At first her eyes seemed wild, but then they focused in turn on Tabby, then Rae. She tried to sit up, but dropped back to the floor and cried out. A hand moved to her wounded leg, and then she brought that now bloody hand to her face. Norstrom closed her eyes.

"Are you okay?" asked Tabby leaning over the woman once again. Her pigtails fell to one side when she tilted her head to better align with Norstrom's.

"Where… Where are your parents?" Norstrom asked.

"They're sleeping," Sis said.

"What are...? Why are you...?"

Rae guessed what her question might be. "We're the only ones who woke up. We don't know why. All the passengers are still in cryostasis."

The woman turned her head from side to side. She seemed to be searching the walls for something. She spoke to Rae. "Get," she began, but the rest was unintelligible.

Rae bent down over the woman, and Tabby followed suit.

"Find… Captain Timmins. Zee Dee drive, rigged… Mi-Ling. *Mi-Ling!* I… I can't believe I never… Girls, you have to… to tell him…" She took a deep gulp of air, winced, and her eyes opened wide.

Rae leaned in. "Miss Norstrom?"

Her gaze focused on a point on the ceiling. Her breath now came in short bursts.

Tabby got right in her face. "Miss Norstrom!"

Two brown irises darted toward Tabby, but the eyelids now fluttered rapidly. "Girls… do not… do *not* open that door!"

Rae looked at the gunmetal door, the one with the blood trail leading from it to Norstrom's leg. "You mean that one?"

Norstrom turned to look at Rae. "Get Captain—" but she cried out before finishing her sentence. It was undeniable she suffered in a torrent of pain, but it only lasted another moment. Then her face relaxed, her arm dropped to the floor, and she lay still.

"Miss Norstrom?" Tabby squeaked.

Her eyes. They were wide open, but she didn't blink again. She said nothing more, no matter how many times Tabitha screamed her name.

"Miss Norstom!"

"Tabby," Rae said calmly. "I think she's gone."

Her sister stared at the woman's face. Her little eyebrows knitted and her head tilted. "She's *dead?* For real?"

Rae nodded.

Tabby stared some more, then looked down at the body. "Who is Mee Ling?"

"And what did she want us to tell him?"

Sis bounded backwards. "Rae!"

Rae looked up at her sister, then down at the floor. The pool of blood had grown, and now encompassed Norstrom's buttocks. She jumped up before it reached her knees, and stepped backward so it wouldn't touch her shoes.

She took in the scene. It looked like something out of a murder holo. Norstrom's eyes didn't blink. Rae had never seen a dead person before. She hoped it would be her last, but when she glanced down the hallway, something told her it wouldn't be. But she couldn't let that hold her up. She was in charge! "Come on, Tabby. We have to find Captain Timmins." She extended her hand to her sister, who took it absent-mindedly, still staring at the dead woman.

Nearby Rae found a near-vertical ladder-stair, with light pouring down from above. She could see Floor Two, seemingly more brightly lit than one they were on. “Hello? Anyone up there?” No answer. *Hopefully not more dead people.* Rae went first, leading the way.

The hallway they climbed up to looked nearly identical to the one they had just left, with the large, gun-metal gray doors leading to what Rae assumed was still the engineering section. Only on this floor, all the hallways were white. Rae remembered these halls well—her family had spent most of their waking hours on this level—but it seemed almost too bright now. The doors all had a “2” on them, in the same blue, stylized font as Floor Three.

The girls wandered down a long hall next to the ladder-stair. They walked past numerous apartments, or quarters, each with tiny numbers and letters next to the doors. They all seemed so small compared to the quarters her family stayed in during that one week prior to launch. All the doors were closed, and they didn’t try to open any of them. At the end of the hall lay an intersection, with a winding staircase nearby that led both up and down. Rae could see many more hallways past that. “This place is like a maze!”

“That’s what Jamie said,” Tabitha noted. “To me it’s more like a city. All the hallways are like streets in a city.”

“Huh. Yeah, I guess they are.”

“If you think of it that way, you can’t get lost!”

Huh. Tabby can see things so differently than me, Rae thought. *But in a good way. Sometimes, anyway.* “There are so many quarters! Too many for the size of the crew. Seems like, anyway.”

"Didn't Daddy say this used to be a warship? Maybe more people lived here when it was a warship?"

"Yeah, maybe."

Rae led Sis to the winding stair. First, she looked down. She saw ugly-gray Deck Three, just as they had left it. Above them, the level looked red. This confused her. She remembered an observation dome up on Deck One, where people could admire the vastness of space. It should be dark. Why would it be red?

No time to solve the mystery now. They had to find Captain Timmins. Down a wider hallway leading off to her right, she saw another spiraling stair not too far away. "Look! Another staircase! I remember this! This isn't far from our quarters!"

"Yeah," Tabby said, walking toward the other stair and stopping at a large intersection. She pointed and said, "It's right down there," as if she had known it all along. She probably had. She spun 180 degrees. "And that's the Captain's quarters."

"It is? How do you know?"

"Because it says 'Captain's Berth' on that sign."

It did. "Smart aleck."

"Well, you got the smart part right."

Rae knocked. While she waited for an answer, she glanced at the other doors at this intersection. One had a placard that read "First Officer's Berth," another had one that read "Yeoman," and the fourth read, "Political Officer."

"I don't think he's home," Tabby whispered."

"Captain Timmins?" Rae called. She examined a small pad next to the door, and found the key that read "Chime." She pressed it. A muffled sound and voice came from within, probably the computer alerting him he had a visitor.

"Captain?" She turned to her sister. "Tabby, ring those other doorbells!"

Tabitha complied, and ran to each door and pressed the Chime button. Now they waited.

Dead silence.

"Maybe they're all asleep?"

More dead silence.

Tabby then pounded on the Captain's door. "Hey! Are you sleeping? We need help!"

"Tabby!"

"What? We do!"

Okay, that's true. Rae pounded on the door now as well, and called out Timmins' name a few more times.

No one answered.

Tabitha pressed all the buttons on the keypad next to the door, but was rewarded only with a series of buzzes that didn't sound friendly. She then looked up at Rae and shrugged.

Rae's shoulders dropped. "Now what?"

Tabby sighed. "Come on." She took off in the direction of the second staircase.

"Where are you going?"

"To the bridge, duh!"

"How do you know it's that way?"

Sis didn't answer.

Just past the next winding stair lay another intersection, much smaller. Rae glanced up as they passed the staircase. More red. She ignored it. Up and down the cross hallway, several mounted signs proclaimed the letter "N" and a number after it: "N-4 Logistics," "N-5 Plans," were on one side of the short hall, "N-1 Admin," N-2 Intel" on the other.

These meant nothing to Rae. When she turned back in the direction they had been walking, she noticed a sign that read, "N-3 Operations."

"Operations!" Tabby exclaimed, seeing it at the same time Rae had.

Excitedly, they tried the door, and found it unlocked. They burst through, only to find an empty office. On two of the walls lay a brightly-lit star map overlaid with a honeycomb grid pattern. "I wonder if this shows where we are?"

"You know how to read that?" Tabby asked.

Rae thought about lying to Sis, just to give her some hope, but immediately realized she would ask a thousand smart questions that Rae would surely be too dumb to answer.

"I didn't think so." The little girl stepped back into the hallway. "Come on."

"Are you sure it's this way, Tabby?"

"For the last time, *yes!*"

"Because I don't remember—"

The small girl spun on her but kept walking forward. "You never remember *anything,* Rae."

"Do so!"

Tabby likely would have spat a retort, but she stopped dead in her tracks at the intersection just ahead. She now stood silently, staring down another hallway.

Something told Rae not to look, but curiosity gnawed at her. She inched toward the corner, and peeked around. A ways down the hall, past another sign that read "Bridge," someone stared right into her soul.

8

GSCS *Nightingale*

"Something you want to let us in on, Captain?" Dale asked, in his naturally calm demeanor. "I take it this is that concerning part you mentioned."

Elwick took a deep breath. "It is. Even after our final jump, we still won't be able to obtain any additional data on the *Pearl,* probably not for another hour after we reach our exit point. We'll simply be too far away."

"Too far away?" asked a confused Barbara Laskey, the SAR team's counselor. All assembled exchanged questioning glances and began whispering to one another.

"Here's the problem," Elwick said, in a commanding voice to quiet the growing ruckus. "The *Pearl* is well out of any and all established travel corridors or authorized jump inject points. We can't and won't be able to get a RADAR lock on her. Not even a QBert lock will work in this case. The problem is, according to the coordinates we pulled from her distress signal, she's deep inside Riker's Hope, on the other side of Sag A."

"What's so bad about that?" asked Gilbin. "We're all Golden Galactic Dragons. Exceptin' for the slimy, young *galwog* at the helm there. Nothing scary over on the far side."

Burgess glanced back, surely knowing the Aussie Fireman was referring to him—the only sailor on board who hadn't crossed the Galactic Bisection Line of the Milky Way and had entered the far side of the galactic disk. Burgess *had* crossed the Galactic Equator, however, and had experienced the ceremony transforming him from polywog to Galactic Shellback, something every sailor could take pride in. *Funny how we still call ourselves sailors,* Elwick mused.

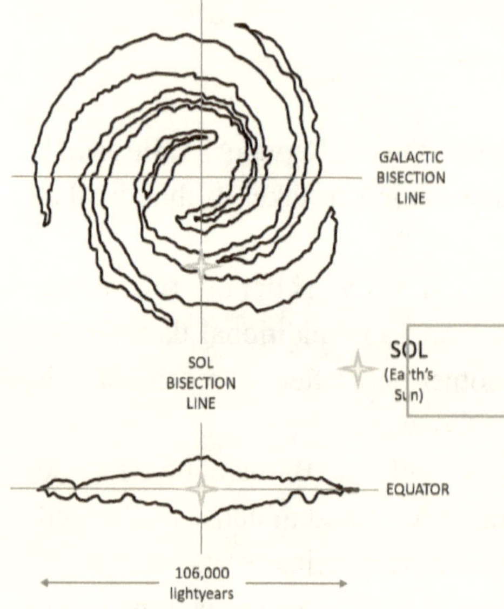

Moses lamented there would be no Golden Galactic Shellbacks in any nation's space fleet; to become so would require a person to simultaneously cross the Galactic Bisection Line, the SOL Bisection line, and the Galactic Equator. One problem: there was a supermassive black hole in the way! That being Sagittarius A*. Elwick knew not what the asterisk in the name meant, just that it showed up on every star map he had ever seen.

The black hole lurked at the dead center of the galaxy where all the humans' various, imaginary, ceremonious lines met, and was something no sane person itched to go anywhere near. Dozens of probes had, and eventually daredevils who lived to push the envelope. They got a lot closer than Elwick would have thought possible, and most even made it back to tell the tale. But a few did not. To this day, he still failed to erase from his mind the images relayed of an "extreme gravity" incident that happened when he was twelve. He shuttered at the memory.

"Captain?" Dale inquired. "I take it there's a reason the QBert won't work…?"

Elwick sighed. "A picture will be easier." He brought up the graphic of the Milky Way that he and the bridge crew had reviewed earlier, with its colorful squares and boxy sectors.

Using his fingers, he zoomed in first on an area with a text label of, "Riker's Hope," then zoomed in further, until a red, fuzzy blob labeled "Unnamed Nebulous Object Scheau Blao VW-2 NX01-MHO" filled most of the screen. He turned to the group. "The *Emerald Pearl* is here."

Someone gasped, others scoffed. One of the ladies muttered, "Oh dear Lord." "Flat-out negligent!" exploded from someone. "Are we sure it's in there?" came a whisper.

Gilbin raised his voice. "Come on, guys! He's kidding around! Good one, Cap'n! You had us all there for a sec!"

Moses answered in a low tone. "I wish I *were* kidding, Gilly."

The firefighter's smile faded, and he returned Moses' forlorn stare. "You're not?"

Elwick's SCUBA Master, the usually-smiling Hamidi Abiodun, blurted in the silence that followed, "Why would someone willingly hop into a nebula? And a red one at that!?"

"That's a very good question, Hamidi."

Doctor Laskey spoke up. "If I recall, the Orion Convention of 2306 made emissions nebulae, and Herbig-Haro objects especially, off-limits to all civilian craft. And most military craft, for that matter. The regulation is international and intergalactic, and hasn't changed in nearly two hundred years. So, what the hell is that ship doing in there?"

Elwick's brows went up at the doctor's remark. "Barbara, you know detailed laws regarding nebula off the top of your head?"

"It's that creepy, eidetic memory of hers," former Senior Chief Petty Officer Bruno quipped. "The sly lass can't forget a thing. She's worse than an elephant!"

"Believe me, there's lots of stuff I *wish* I could forget. But somebody's got to remind you boys of all the dumb things you do. Especially you, Bruno."

Chuckles flooded the room as knowing glances went around. Barbara Laskey's wink to the old engineer verified that the "secret" affair was still going strong between the widow and widower. *It's been ten years, Bruno,* Moses thought to himself, *make an honest woman of her for Pete's sake!* "You're absolutely right, Counselor," Elwick said, "there's no way the captain of any ship out here doesn't know that piece of intergalactic law. It's like the good doctor here not knowing a femur from a funny bone, but I doubt more than four or five people on this ship know it."

"Or a Kiwi bunting tosser not knowing what a white flag means," the Aussie added.

Those from the Americas looked at one another and shrugged their shoulders.

"That'd be a French skivvy waver for you non-Aussie types," Bruno elaborated.

Blank stares still ensued.

The old man sighed. "Eh, forget it."

Rose Vereau shook her head. "How'd they even get out that far? I mean, in a standard civilian ship, it would take *thirty* 1,000 light year jumps and probably a whole month to get where they are. We're spoiled here on the *Nightingale;* any civilian ship I've ever been on has to wait a full day between jumps for the motor to cool down! And they couldn't have been close to their destination; where were they even headed?"

"Good question," Elwick replied. "The XO poked around on the map and did find an old mining colony another forty-some thousand light years on the other side of the *Pearl.* That could have been their destination; there's very little else out here."

"Maybe the ship's old but the core isn't?" Kelly offered. "Maybe they had a core that could jump farther than even we can?"

Gilbin roared. "A civilian ship like this?"

"You can laugh all you want, but there are some pretty crazy ideas floatin' around in the forums regardin' kittin' up yer core. Mostly fer illegal racin' and whatnot, but there's legal R&D goin' on too! For instance, the experimental motor that the leaders of the *Lewis and Clark III* expedition want to install on their ship is somethin' called a structural-foam-folding drive." Crawford actually pronounced the 'g' at the end of a word for once, Moses noted. "The article I saw said an SFF drive could do *a hundred thousand light years* in a single jump!"

Now it was Osterland's turn to chuckle. "All the way across the Milky way in a single jump!? You're right, I *will* laugh all I want!"

"That's not the half of it, XO. Their goal is ta hop across the gulf 'tween the Milky Way and Andromeda in a single leap!"

Others scoffed now. Bruno even said, "Oh, now you're just being silly, lass. That's downright impossible! Why, Heisenberg would roll over in his grave! So would Einstein!"

"I don't know if they're gonna do it, but that's what they're a-tryin'!"

"Or at least," Dale remarked, "that's the lie they're telling everyone in an attempt to get funding."

"You know," said Barbara Laskey, "It would be worse if it *were* true… The second Lewis and Clark expedition merely went to Andromeda and back, but the third, I read, those young people are trying to push out as far as they can go. Can you imagine your ship breaking down a dozen galaxies away? It would take years, decades maybe, for even a modified ship like ours to reach you!"

"One way trip," Elwick agreed.

Nods all around.

"Yes, well, anyway," Elwick said, raising his voice to get the briefing back on track, "right now, it's not our concern *how* the ship got there, or *why*, we simply have to deal with the fact that it *is* there. And if you didn't catch the Lieutenant's thumbs-up earlier, SARCOM has verified the *Pearl's* beacon location, as well as our rendezvous plan and timeline. That means it's definitely where we think it is. Smack in the middle of that damn cloud." Moses looked behind him at the blood red nebula on the otherwise black display.

The foreboding tension in the room could be scooped with a spoon. Elwick zoomed back out to show their entire travel path. He pointed to the colorful, geometric shapes as he mentioned them. "This is our current location, in the Arcadian Stream. Our navigator calculated seven jumps over the next two hours, approximately, which will take us through the Empyrean Straights where we'll top off our fuel tanks, and then head on out to Ryker's Hope. There we'll exit folded space at a safe distance from the nebula, and then enter it under traditional ion pulse drive at no greater than base five, or one-twentieth of lightspeed. I'm hoping we can rendezvous with the target within one hour of entering the cloud. That's if we find the damn thing in that amount of time. It could be two hours before we reach it. Or longer. Hence why I said earlier that our TTI could increase."

Galloway scoffed. "That could be five hours from the time we first received the signal! Any casualty not ambulatory will likely be dead!"

Elwick's shoulders slumped. "I understand that, Doc, but it's the best we can do. We are *not* jumping straight into that nebula. SARCOM let alone SENTCORPS would never authorize it, and I'm not risking all our lives doing so. God only knows what this ship might look like if we unfold into that thing; this region of space has been roped off for a reason. Anything inside is to be handled with extreme caution. If we're not careful, we'll soon be sending out our own distress call, and then SARCOM would have *two* ships to worry about saving."

"God's not the only one who knows what we might look like if we unfold into that thing," Masterson muttered.

With that, the group fell silent. Dale ignored them.

Oh, how I'd kill to know just a fraction of the crazy crap you've seen, Dale, Moses mused, but knew better than to ever ask. Even his own high clearance still wasn't high enough, and even if it had been, he didn't have the need-to-know by any means. He returned his focus on the group.

"Okay, so there you have it. Give me your concerns. Opinions." His hunger had become more than a simple annoyance, and he didn't really want to hear any opinions at that point, he only wanted a turkey sandwich. But over the decades of being a leader, he had found that asking for such input from experienced shipmates was often useful, sometimes humorous, and always educational.

"My father lost an old Navy shipmate in one of those blasted things," Bruno began, in his gruff but gentle manner.

And here we go, Moses mused. So much for that sandwich anytime soon.

"I don't know if any of you land lubbers've been inside a red MHO, but I have. A SEAL recon back in '28. I was a mere lad—"

"Of forty-seven!" Daniel Gilbin interjected. Soft chuckles all around.

"I was all of eighteen if I was a day," Antonio Bruno continued, ignoring the Aussie, "still damp behind the ears. I can't tell you a lot, not because it's classified but because I don't remember! But I *can* tell you that these red ones are completely unpredictable. We barely made it out, what with those little devilish gremlins all swarmin' about! They'd stall our engines, interrupt our hydrogen collectors…" With Antonio's teeth clenched as they were, the three holes in his grille displayed themselves more than usual. "And this one's in the Hades Quadrangle! Most ships never make it out of there at all."

Moses glanced at Kelly. Her mouth formed the silent words, "one-third."

"Gremlins?" Dale said more than asked. "Really, Bruno? Trying to scare the kids or something?"

"That's what we called 'em: gremlins. Wild wormholes, far as we could figure!"

More than one person laughed.

"I'm telling the truth, I am! And those are the among the more pleasant things you'll find in there!"

The *Nightingale's* resident African-French Canadian, Rose Vereau, broke up the low chuckles drifting across the briefing room in her usual, pleasant melody. "Nevermind the tall tales, I'm still stuck on what the hell an MHO even is, red, blue, green, or pink!"

"Molecular Hydrogen emission-line Object," explained Commander Osterland, who had been silent up to this point. Using his fingers, he zoomed back in on the nebula in question. "It's rare that a ship would have a run-in with one today, but that's only because every navigator worth his weight in mythical dark matter knows not to set a heading with one in his path." He turned his head to Bruno. "Naturally-occurring and even 'wild' wormholes notwithstanding, you're right, Bruno, it's not a nice place to risk jumping across or flying through, let alone hanging around in for very long. There's a reason this region of space is named as it is, and why it's barely been mapped." Here he turned to the group once again. "But we're going to have to do just that. And head-first."

"It would appear the *Pearl's* navigator didn't think twice about charting a route right through this one," said Abiodun, in his Middle-African accent. "What, were they in a hurry or something? And because of a little impatience, now they'll probably never get to where they were going. And now we have to put our lives in danger pulling them out!"

Gilbin playfully punched Abiodun's arm. "All in a day's work, Hamidi! *Deliver All...*"

"*Thwart Death!*" the entire SAR group chanted, much less enthusiastically than usual. Often this phrase led to members high-fiving one another in a show of camaraderie. That didn't happen this time.

"They are beautiful, aren't they, though?" Counselor Laskey whispered, staring at the dark red cloud on the screen.

"Beautiful!?" Bruno shouted. "Sure, just like one of Odysseus' deadly sirens! The green and blue nebulae are fine. Never had any problem with those. But these damn red ones... Like that devilish Alta Gracia Nebula over on our side of the galaxy! She'll suck you in and end you with nigh a second glance! Do you guys realize the Alta Gracia only looks like an angel in the skies of Eurydia Prime, right? Where the real, flesh-and-blood Amazonian sirens are the most beautiful ever to grace the unending Black?" He turned his head and winked at Kelly, who rolled her eyes but still smiled before glancing over at Barbara Laskey, who only shook her head. Elwick was certain the counselor had long ago grown accustomed to the big teddy bear's inappropriate but harmless flirting. Bruno continued. "From every other viewpoint, it's just a nasty, formless cloud of evil. Only the gods themselves know what other dangers lurk in there. 'High Grace' my arse! It's the color of *blood* for a reason. 'Tis an angel of death! And I'll bet this month's paycheck this one is no different!"

In the room, one could hear a fly's butthole pucker. Everyone stared at either Bruno or the image that filled the screen. For some reason, Masterson allowed the story to continue, which made Elwick smile. Surely, deep down,

Dale enjoyed Antonio's yarn-spinning as much as Moses did.

"That size there is wrong, too!" the old Engineman went on. "The map might say it's thirty-four light years across, and it is, in the visible spectrum. But what you can't see is the real depth of that monster. From stem to stern its influence likely reaches two to three times that. The majority of it is visible only in infrared due to molecular emissions! That's why it's called an MHO!"

Elwick touched a few controls on the screen, and a more detailed legend of text appeared. "He's right; actual diameter, according to scans taken by the *Nightingale's* computer within the last half hour, is eighty-three point six light years."

Bruno's face glowed like Moses hadn't seen it do since Antonio had bounced his latest grandchild on those tree knots he called knees. The old man turned to Osterland. "XO, we need to keep a close eye out for new star formation. A sun can ignite in nigh the blink of an eye just one or two AUs over! Then those bow-shocks come 'atcha a whole lot faster than you can jump away, even if your finger's already on the plasma injection button! Let me tell ya," here he whistled in dramatic fashion, "those shockwaves are rough on a battleship's hull, but on a Triple S like this? We'll be lucky if there's a ship left to send out a distress call!"

"Alright, big guy, that's enough," Dale said. "Now you *are* scaring the children."

The tall, bespectacled Information Systems expert from Southern Germany spoke up. Moses had to pay close attention to understand his words through his heavy Bavarian accent. "Captain, with all the high-energy emissions going on in there, and with Chief Bruno's, er, what you call, anomalies? How can we even hope to find our target?"

Moses smiled. "Vielen Dank, Herr Ebersbacher." He addressed the group once again. "The Bavarian Bluffer here brings up a good point. All RADAR technology will be damn near useless. I won't lie; we might need a miracle. Seriously, if anyone has any good ideas on how we might locate this ship in all this tomato soup, don't hesitate to let me know. Even if you don't, you probably have a good two hours to come up with one."

People looked at one another once again, but no one spoke.

"Any more questions? Concerns? Advice?"

The group remained silent.

"Alright. Master Chief, the floor is yours."

The leader of the SAR Team stood up. "Okay, kids, here's the ingress plan upon reaching the target." Masterson made his way to Elwick's position around the maze of legs, and swiped the screen. The image returned to the graphical schematic of the *Pearl's* sister ship, *Kristin's Vision.* "Like the Captain said, we expect the *Pearl's* deck layout to be similar to this layout. We'll of course scan the ship when we get there, and the floorplans on all your PEDs will be updated. After determining which one of these two identical airlocks are still accessible," he pointed to a rectangle first on the port side and then to starboard, "we'll dock, board the vessel, and split into two teams of three personnel each." Dale turned and pointed to Antonio. "Bruno, you lead Gilbin and Abiodun to the bridge located at the bow of Deck Two, and begin the data download of the ship's logs. Once that's initiated, leave Hamidi there to babysit the computer, and you and Gilbin head out and search for survivors. Keep in mind the heat and radiation from the nebula may interfere with the readings on your thermal detectors. We'll need to set the sensitivity accordingly. We probably won't be able to determine the best setting until we're on board."

Bruno let out a resounding "Aye aye, Master Chief!"

"Rose," Masterson said, turning to address her, "I want you to lead Mr. Ebersbacher and Doctor Laskey to the cryo chamber on Deck Three." Dale pointed to a large open space toward the bottom of the schematic. "Jan, if anyone *is* in those pods and the pods turn out to be old or damaged, we'll need your computer expertise to get those people out of there."

"Aye aye, Master Chief," said the towering European in his best North American accent. He turned to Hamidi Abiodun for approval. "Besser?"

"What do I know? Have you heard my accent? I don't hear it myself, but apparently everyone else does!" The two men laughed.

"Barbara," Masterson said, ignoring the pair, "it's possible survivors may have been exposed to untold radiation if the hull has been breached. I don't know what MHOs do to psyches, but if it's similar to what it can do to flesh, well, we'll need your services more than ever. These people will probably be confused as hell when we pull them out of cryo sleep early, as usually happens when sudden reanimation occurs. However, ironically, older pods don't induct ultra-REM sleep like modern pods do for the sake of brain safety. So hell, if these things really are older units, we might get lucky. These folks may pop out of their pods ready to walk, talk, and fight, with only minutes to recover instead of hours or days!"

"Aye aye," Laskey acknowledged.

"Rose, take every precaution. It's probably a low risk, but if you detect a significant bio-hazard or radiation risk, announce it across the open channel, and we'll all skedaddle. In that event, do *not* open those pods. If anyone is still alive inside, the outer shell will provide more protection than we can. In that case, we'll find a way to transfer all pods to the *Nightingale* with the sleepers still inside."

"Sure thing, Master Chief," Miss Vereau replied. She pulled her thick black hair up and away from her neck, and began fanning herself with her hands.

Moses hadn't noticed before, but it was indeed getting warm in the small room, despite the fact most of one wall wasn't even there. That meant they had all been blowing hot air for too long again. About time to wrap this up! His stomach chose this moment to growl. Kelly noticed, and gave him a look Elwick tried to ignore.

"Doctor Galloway," Masterson called. "You're up."

"Thanks, dearie." The old Doc from Down Under stood up and addressed the group. "Alright, listen up, youngins! Like's been mentioned, these MHOs generate a lot o' rads. And I mean a lot. If any of yas have to go outside, it will be like working on the surface of Mercury. The *'Gale* will protect you for as long as we need to be inside 'er, but we need to severely limit any extra-vehicular activity. A normal suit won't protect any of ya brazen idiots for more than a few minutes. And even inside those widowmakers, y'all'll be sterilized after an hour! So, at the two hour-mark, head back inside."

Two people laughed at her joke.

Widowmakers. Elwick hated it when anyone referred to their ship's small, one-man vehicles that way in mixed company. He looked at Bruno, the primary person who might react negatively due to, well, how he lost his wife. Thankfully, he did not. *This time.*

Doc pulled out a partially decrepit finger and pointed to each member of the SAR team in turn. “I know y’all think you’re blasted immortal, but you all heed the words of the White Witch here!” She zeroed in on Chief Masterson. “That goes for you too, hero.”

Dale turned and looked behind him at the wall, as if trying to figure out who she might be pointing at.

“Pull a little stunt like you did back on Carl’s Revenge,” Galloway spat, “and you’ll glow in the dark for all of five minutes right before you melt! I ain’t patchin’ ya up again! Ya silly bastard,” she added.

Masterson shrugged. Nervous chuckles filled the space. Some looked like they wanted to laugh, but were scared to do so.

“I doubt we’ll need the EVA pods,” Elwick interjected, “but don’t worry, Doc, we’ll all keep your advice at the forefront of our minds. Aye, folks?”

Muttering of “aye” and “aye aye” filled the room.

Galloway continued to eye Masterson like she wanted to either strangle him or eat him, but said nothing more.

“If that’s all from the good witch doctor, Chief, let’s wrap things up.”

The Chief spoke with even more authority after Gwendolyn Galloway’s chastising. “I want to be in and out of this old boat inside one hour if possible. You all know I’m not afraid of much—save the Witch Doctor here—but I’ve spent a little time in this sector of space. I can’t go into it; I’ll just say we might heed old Chief Bruno’s warnings.”

The Engineman-by-trade turned helping man-for-hire looked up at Masterson and nodded respectfully.

With that, Dale turned and nodded to Moses, indicating he had nothing further.

"Alright, everyone," Elwick said, "dismissed."

"Okay, team," Masterson's deep voice bellowed, "next muster is in the bay in thirty minutes. Full seven-twenty-eight inspection, to include pee pee tubes. Hooyah?"

"Hooyah," "hooah," or "oorah!" yelled the former military members of the team as they stood to leave. The civilians sounded off with their favorite variation, albeit with much less vigor. The SAR Team quietly skirted the right rear bulkhead of the bridge and exited down a narrow passageway.

"Don't forget to come see me, Captain," whispered Doc. "We need ta talk."

The sound of her voice sent shivers down Elwick's spine. Faint voices of the SAR team reached his ears as they zoomed down the almost-vertical inclined stairway near his cabin on their way to Deck Two. Moses now wished he had followed them down the ladder. Instead, he turned to face the scary woman. "I will, Doc."

She pointed at him. "You said that last time. Don't. Forget. This. Time."

"Aye, Doc. I won't. I promise."

She eyed him in a similar fashion as she had Dale as she squeezed past him and departed the bridge.

Moses did a slow about-face on his heel and moved to his command pillar. Mess Decks could wait. He wasn't about to share a passageway with Galloway.

"Must be important," Ozzie said as he made his way back to the navigation station.

Elwick gave his XO a stare that made the Commander face front the moment he reached his seat by the pilot. Moses looked around the bridge. All the faces around him looked away simultaneously, turning their noses into their consoles in front of them.

9

Emerald Pearl

The man staring at Rae looked a bloody mess. He lay crumpled like a ragdoll on the floor. The metallic smell of blood did not nauseate her; not only from her very recent experience with Norstrom, but mainly due to the fact the incident on her father's boat had gotten her over such things years ago. Sort of. The smell always made her want to toss her cookies. Back on that crazy day on the water, Rae had held it in long enough to call emergency services, walk through getting him stabilized, and threw up later.

But it was not the smell that made her light headed at the moment, but the overall image invading her vision. How the man lay in such a twisted fashion, how so much of the precious nectar of life lay everywhere around him instead of inside him. And not merely in a pool; it had splattered. On the walls, the floor, even the ceiling! The poor fellow had probably suffered his deadly injuries when he bounced off each one in succession.

While Rae had seen blood, before today she had never seen a dead body in her entire fourteen years of life. Now she had seen two in the last ten minutes. The eyes were the worst. The eyes of Miss Norstrom stared off into nothing. This man's did the same. She couldn't look at them. *Mother always says the eyes are the windows to the soul.* But Rae doubted this man's soul still lingered. It had surely traveled off by now, to wherever he believed it would go.

Rae's eyes widened. It occurred to her then that she and Tabby might be a very long way from home. A long way from Mother Earth. Could a soul find its way home from so far away? She had never even considered this before! She had never really been scared for her life before, let alone for her soul! After a few seconds of imagining the distance between stars, she realized she had no idea where she and her sister actually were. Now she *really* wished she could read that star map! Where exactly had this cold, empty ship taken them? They could be just out past Jupiter, or halfway across the galaxy for all she knew! And wasn't there a black hole out here somewhere? Daddy had told them they'd be skirting the biggest black hole anyone had ever seen; Sagittar-something. Hopefully *that* wasn't close by! "Don't look at him, Tabby. He's not going to be able to help us."

The little girl stopped before reaching the body, and suddenly screamed, "Wah-la!" scaring Rae half to death. Tabita threw her arms in the air and spun back round to Rae. "Told you I knew where it was!"

"Tabby! Don't scream like that!"

"What, are you afraid I'm going to wake *the deeeaaad?*"

"Shut up."

"Oh look! There are two ways in!" She touched a button lit up in blue on a keypad, and the door swung open. "I'm going in *this* one!"

Rae followed the little smarty-pants down a long hallway with more quarters and a couple of offices, at the end of which lay two more doors that looked exactly like the ones from a minute ago. Rae walked up to a keypad, and Tabby ran to the other. They both pressed the blue button to open the doors at the same time. Both doors swung open, and a bright red glow greeted each girl.

Rae squinted her eyes against the bright, bloody glare. Soon she heard her sister mutter a minor curse like Daddy often had. *Oh, precious spirits, do I even want to know?* Their mother would have called to the Great Spirits of Earth. But Daddy always called out to the God of the Hebrews. As her eyes adjusted to the light, and Rae saw what lay before them, she immediately knew they'd need the combined might of both Mother *and* Father's gods to help them out of the pickle she and Tabitha now found themselves in.

10
GSCS *Nightingale*

After only three minutes, Elwick had grown tired of staring at his command pillar. Nothing new from the jumbled text of the distress signal jumped out at him, and his hunger seemed to grow by the minute. "Kitner, you have the conning tower."

"Aye, Captain."

In seconds, he had zoomed down the small passage leading off the bridge and prepped his feet to fly down the ladder toward the Mess, when a presence off to his right startled him. A familiar ball-capped, Amazonian sailor leaned by the door to his office and stateroom.

"Hey again."

He sighed. "Kelly, I'm not really in the mood—"

"Relax, Cap'n, I'm just here fer the duty roster."

"Oh. I thought we were going to go over that later."

"Might be busy later. After that briefing we just had, I figured it best ta get this knocked out now."

Elwick nodded. "Probably a good idea." But his stomach had other ideas. Hopefully he had a snack stuffed somewhere in his stateroom… "Might as well come in and— *whoa.* What in all the seven galaxies? I guess *that's* why it seems you've grown even taller since yesterday!"

"Oh! Yeah, ya like 'em?" She looked down and lifted one foot. "Steel-toed! Them heels are a full fifteen centimeters! I picked 'em up at that lil' settlement in the Tau Boötis system last week when we pulled in ta grab that box o' replacement parts. I *had* ta get *boots* at Tau *Boötis*!"

"Well, of course you did." He eyed them with suspicion.

"Oh, they're within regulation, Cap'n. I checked!"

"Regulations are getting lax these days, then," he muttered. Moses did some quick math. These shiny, faux-leather monstrosities, with buckles in all the wrong places, pushed Kelly past seven feet. Her baseball-style Command Working Cap, which barely contained her fiery explosion of hair, now tickled the overhead. "Watch your melon coming in. You're an absolute giraffe in those ridiculous things."

She laughed. "Yeah, I've been getting' remarks like that since I put 'em on. We all know how much our favorite joker below decks *loves* the tall gals. He wants 'tween my knacker crackers so bad, I'm fixin' ta let him! See how he likes eight feet o' legs wrapped around his scruffy face while I—"

"Kelly!" Moses exclaimed, looking up and down the passageway, which ran nearly the full two-hundred meters of Deck One, to see if anyone had heard *that*. He spotted one soul. Past the officer's berthing quarters and the shared heads, Petty Officer Cabón had just exited the Wardroom carrying what looked like a laundry bag. He now stared at Elwick, frozen in place. *Great.*

"Oh, relax, Cap'n! I meant while I'm chokin' him out! Shame on ya for thinkin' whatever you were thinkin'! You should be ashamed!"

Moses' eyebrows raised. "Fine, I stand corrected. However…" He motioned aft with his head. "You want *him* repeating scuttlebutt like that, thinking what I was thinking?"

Kelly spun 'round. "Hey!" She shouted with lungs the size of Canada. "Why are you hanging out on this deck, Cabón?"

The Engineman now had the bag behind his back. "Jus' doin' a quick inventory!" the stocky sailor shouted back in his heavy Puerto Rican accent. "Jack o' the Dust, you know!"

"Inventory, my ass. What ya got there?"

"Ah, is nuthin', BM1."

She put her hands on her hips. "You just boned a bunch o' gee-dunk from the Wardroom, didn't ya?"

No reply.

"I work my butt off every day tryin' ta get you bilge trolls into shape, and all ya do is undermine my efforts every chance ya get!"

Cabón shrugged his shoulders. "I don' know what you mean—"

She crossed her arms. "Check yer shit. It's drippin' all over the deck!"

The busted non-commissioned officer cursed softly upon checking his now wet laundry bag.

Elwick shook his head. "Come on in when you're done, Bosun. There's something else I want to talk to you about anyway."

She perked up.

"It's *not* about your sister."

"Oh." The disappointment visibly ran through her entire body. "What then?"

"Nothing good. Probably."

"Uh oh." The imposing woman stepped aside to allow Moses entry to his office, then turned to face Cabón again, who had now gone back in the Wardroom. "Don't be puttin' any of that back!" She yelled. "You tell them boys to enjoy every last bite of that! We'll work it off at Evolution. Zero five hundred!"

"Aww, Crawford!" came a distant complaining. Elwick dove into his office and tuned out the rest.

11

Emerald Pearl

Rae's mind unconsciously rated the horror of the sight of the dead man in the hallway at a solid seven. The sight before her now? That hit eleven.

She brought her hand to her mouth. The bile in her stomach yearned to see the light of day. Or in this case, the light of the bright nebula flooding through the floor-to-ceiling windows that surrounded the bridge. It illuminated several people lying in various poses around the room. People every much as dead as the man in the hallway. The entire environment presented as a shade of red. All over the bridge, shiny patches and splatters dwelled. Rae could barely see them in the red light, but instinctively knew they all had to be blood; water didn't stick to vertical surfaces like that. Rae thanked the Great Goddess that the glass had not broken where bodies had impacted the panes and left the reflective liquid. Even a crack would do her and Tabby in; the ship's air pressure would slowly weaken that spot, and eventually she, her sister, their air, and everything else not nailed down would be blown out into space. Into that blood red nebula. And that, she knew, was *not* how she wanted to end this. She also knew it was *blown out* and not *sucked out,* contrary to what she'd heard most "Terries" say, people content to live their lives on hard ground or "Terra Firma," and rarely, if ever, venture out into The Black.

Rae meticulously scanned the windows, especially the corners, searching for cracks. She found none, but that didn't necessarily mean anything. But then she remembered something Captain Timmins had mentioned on the initial tour. All the windows on the *Emerald Pearl* weren't made of glass, but some metal. Graphite or something. *Tabitha is right. I do have trouble remembering things.*

She searched her memory to keep her mind busy. Anything to distract her from the horror her eyes and nose were feeding her brain. It was too much. Overload. So much that it made her temporarily numb. Rae focused on the red clouds beyond. She imagined flying into it. Losing herself. Escaping this impossible situation. Escaping this nightmare.

Sounds came to her consciousness over the sound of the steady if now distant klaxon. Beeps. Other strange electronic noises. A girl crying.

Sis?

She turned to see Tabitha on the floor, rocking back and forth, her cheeks glimmering. Rae dove to her sister and hugged her. "It's okay, Tabby, it's okay."

"It's *not* okay," Tabitha protested through tears. "They're all dead!"

Rae could ignore the five dead crewmembers strewn about the room no longer. "Stay here. I'm going to check on them. It'll be okay." She rose and faced the dead. She took a deep breath to steady herself, and instantly regretted it. The stench of bile and excrement and everything foul-smelling Rae could imagine dug deep into her brain. The bodies still looked intact for the most part, but things were… leaking… from some of them. One man's head had opened up, revealing some pink ooze dripping to the floor. One lady's abdomen had been ripped open. Rae guessed that's probably where the foulest smell came from. But the bones... Bones stuck out of so many of them! Arms, legs, ribs!

She choked down a dry heave, and closed her eyes for a moment. *You got this Rae. You are in charge. Check on them. Maybe one is alive?*

This last thought propelled Rae forward. If even one crewmember was still alive and could help them wake others up or send out a call for help, it would mean she didn't have to make all the decisions anymore! She walked around the bridge, inspecting the bodies systematically, studying each one. She didn't want to look at their faces, at their wild eyes, each frozen open in terror. Each person wore a uniform with a rank she did not fully understand, and each was someone who she and her sister desperately needed to be alive right now.

"This is the crew of this stupid ship, isn't it?" Tabitha asked, suddenly beside her.

Rae jumped, and put a hand to her chest to calm herself.

"All the important people."

"Yes," Rae answered. She had just seen all these people a few hours ago—well, a few hours ago to her, anyway—at a dinner hosted by the Captain just prior to the "long sleep." How long had really been? A week? A month? A year? How long did Daddy say the trip to the colony would take? A good chunk of the Summer for sure.

As Rae looked around the bridge, her gaze fell upon a darkened corner, where she and her father had stood just a few days ago, by her reckoning, with a majority of the other passengers. They had all been on the bridge thanks to a tour of the *Pearl* Captain Timmins had been providing. This brought to mind a particularly tense conversation she overheard while the group had still been on the bridge, between Captain Timmins and some guy. Had Rae seen him in the cryo chamber a short time ago? She couldn't remember…

Emerald Pearl: Gangway

A few hours prior to hibernating for the long trip

"Captain," the skinny man had whispered, "might I have a word with you?"

"Certainly." Captain Timmins addressed the small crowd. "Everyone, please feel free to look around and ask questions of the crew. But once again, if anyone touches any buttons and we end up stranded in the middle of the Adredes cluster, that person's gonna be walking home!"

Chuckles spread through the group. Captain Timmins took the man down one of the gangways that ran between the brightly lit hallways and the more dimly lit bridge. Rae sneaked away from her father, who was already in a deep discussion with another passenger concerning a set of star maps. She tiptoed around a slight corner, out of eyesight of everyone, and listened.

"Captain," the man began, "I don't want to raise an alarm, but I saw a Chinese man below decks. He was in a uniform just like yours. I thought you should know."

"I hope he wasn't in a uniform like mine! Mine has much more piping on the sleeves!" Chuckles rose from two passengers nearby who had also heard and understood his meaning, unlike Rae.

"I'm not joking," said the skinny man.

"Neither am I. I assume you're talking about Mr. Mi-Ling. Ezra Mi-Ling, our electronics technician?"

"You know him?"

"Of course I know him. Brought him on myself!"

"Are you telling me he's a member of your *crew*? Why in the world would you give so much responsibility to someone... someone who could...?"

"Who could what, Mister?"

"Who could, I don't know," here the man dropped his voice to a whisper, "maybe at worst sabotage the ship? Spy on us at the very least!"

"Look here, Mr.... Napharr, is it? I won't have your racist attitude on my ship. Ling is a valuable, hard-working, and trustworthy member of the *Emerald Pearl's* crew. Has been for many months now. If you knew his situation, like I do, you would join me in my assessment. I can assure you he is not capable of harming a fly, let alone conducting espionage operations or anything nefarious! Contrary to what *you* may think, not all Chinese people are up to something, Mr. Napharr."

"Now, I didn't say—"

"Mr. Mi-Ling received the same level of vetting as every crewmember I have ever brought aboard, and all his paperwork checked out. So, his parents are Chinese, big deal, mine are British. Do you have a problem with me as well?"

"The British? Why would I ever have a problem with them? The Brits never attacked our country!"

"Neither have the Chinese," Timmins replied.

"They most certainly did!"

"Technically, no, they did not. Yes, the Revolutionists led by General Ping in league with the Russian Federated States did invade the North American continent, but it was *after* the fall of the United States and *prior* to the founding of the Republic of North America. No official government was in place at the time."

"But—"

"Now, we may have to watch out for that one leader we're always hearing about, oh, what's his name...? Wu! General Wu Heng Guang. He could be trouble, considering his resources and attitude toward the West. But he represents nothing but a rogue faction that will be squashed like the bugs they are. The Chinese are a noble people, and setting aside Wu's unofficial 'country', the *recognized* country we know as China never attacked our grand republic. By your line of thought, Mr. Napharr, the British attacked America, too, and should be held accountable!"

A pause. "They did?"

Rae heard a sigh of exasperation from Timmins. "Mr. Napharr, I have no time for this nonsense."

"Look, Captain, I'm not talking conspiracy and rogue elements. All I'm saying is, none of the Chinese people are exactly best friends with Westerners, and definitely not the RNA. I've spent time in the military and I know that many of our values go counter to their traditional ways. I'm not saying your man Ling is an extremist to be feared or anything—"

"No? Because it sure sounds like it. Sir, I don't know if you realize it, but I spent time in the military as well. Possibly not as much as you, just twenty-four years in the Navy and another sixteen here in the Merchant Marines. But I will wager a full month's pay I've seen a bit more than you, with your full head of black hair and lack of crow's feet around the eyes. If you ask me, you just pulled yourself off your mama's teat last week!"

"Now look here, Captain, I'm not going to stand here and—"

"No, *you* look here. If you want to spew that prejudiced, racist trash, do it in your own quarters, out of earshot of my crew and the other passengers. And definitely out of earshot of *me*," Timmins added. "Now I will say good day to you, sir. I have *much* more important things to do than commence in discourse with the likes of *you!*"

Boots stomped in Rae's direction, and she did her best to melt into the wall behind her.

Captain Timmins re-entered the bridge with a big smile on his face, and clasped his hands. "Now, who had the question about the Merchant Marines? Oh yes, you there!" he faced a woman Rae guessed might be in her early-to-mid nineties. Or maybe just her mid-to-late fifties? Rae was terrible with judging the ages of adults. "I wanted to be sure to tell you not to worry, miss; if we do happen to get called to duty during our trip to the Preia Byoea system, it will likely be nothing but another 'data milk run'!" Timmins stepped close and put a hand on the lady's shoulder. "If I have anything to say about it, you'll reach your destination on-time and on-schedule. You have my word."

The tour ended shortly afterward, and Rae and her father climbed a beautiful, winding stair and met up with Mother, Tabitha and Jamie in the Observation Dome. Tabby lay asleep in Mother's lap on a couch, and Jamie sat cross-wise on one of several plush chairs. His eyes seemed to focus on something Rae couldn't see, and he worked his fingers in strange patterns. Some might conclude her brother had a mental issue, but Rae understood he was simply wrapped up in a game being projected onto his retinas and vibrating into his temples, an illusion only he could see and hear.

As Daddy collapsed on the other end of the couch and shared a smile with Mother, Rae took one of the remaining chairs and threw her head backwards. Above them sprawled a panoramic view of the Milky Way. *So many stars!* Mother had told them that the stars would make all new shapes in the sky from the vantage point of the colony they were traveling to; all new constellations. This knowledge made her imagination run wild; she wondered how many other children might be staring upward from planets around some of those tiny points of light right now, using Earth's Sun to help create shapes and mythological heroes in their skies...

Her breath caught. *Maybe not just human children, but alien children!* She shivered at the idea that such things might exist, despite the fact no alien people had ever been found even after a crazy number of decades of galactic exploration. But then again, her father had told her that in all those years, over ninety-nine percent of galaxy was still completely unknown. *Plenty of room for aliens to hide in!*

She wondered what they might look like. *Probably gross. Slimy. Smelly. With big, bug eyes, maybe. And with a dozen legs!* Without her permission, her mind conjured the creepiest, crawliest things in the universe, with even bigger creepy crawly things that *they* called parents. Rae hopped up and all but dove into her father's lap, and snuggled up to him.

Daddy laughed. "You're thinking about alien kids again, aren't you?"

"No!" Rae lied.

This made both him and her mother chuckle. Jamie had told Rae many times that she was far too old to still be snuggling up with Dad when she got scared, but Rae didn't believe him. In fact, it only made her do it more often, and hug him more tightly.

And when she did so, her father always wrapped his arms around her, which usually prompted a kiss on her hair. "Don't worry," he said, "I'm sure they would find you and your white teeth and pretty hair and only two arms even more gross!"

Emerald Pearl: Bridge

"I don't see Captain Timmins," Rae said as she rounded a console.

"Maybe he wasn't here when whatever happened happ—"

Rae yelped, interrupting her sister, stepping on the sleeve of a crewmember she hadn't seen before then. She couldn't see the face, but the uniform… Four bars. A rank she *did* recognize.

Captain Timmins.

He lay bent in an unnatural fashion. Fresh blood trickled from a wound on the back of his head and pooled under one ear. Rae stepped back to avoid getting the ruby liquid on her shoes.

Tabitha ran to Rae's side and looked down. "Oh. Guess he was."

Rae tip-toed around to the other side of the body. The wild eyes of their captain stared unblinking at the opposite wall. She jerked her gaze away.

"Now what do we do?" the tiny person next to her asked.

Rae closed her eyes, breathed fast and shallow, held a hand to her mouth, and concentrated hard on not throwing up. The stench of open bowels was strong, but at least it wasn't the smell of death. Bodies may begin to decay immediately, but they don't smell for four to twenty-four hours. She learned that from the murder mystery holos she watched with her mother. "Blankets," she said. It might not help much, but it would be better than nothing. Plus, it would cover up all these eyes.

"Where do we find blankets?" Tabby asked.

Rae looked around. "I saw a crewmember open a bin on the tour, showing us stuff like emergency equipment and things like that."

"Oh yeah!" Tabby darted from the bridge, down the long hallway with the offices and even smaller quarters, and into the bright, white halls.

"Tabby! Don't leave me here!" Rae hollered, following. Upon reaching the white halls, she scanned for her sister. To her right was the splattered dead guy. *Pry your eyes away,*

Rae! She looked to her left and found Sis a short distance down the hall, pulling on a box on the wall.

"I can't get it open!"

Rae jogged over and yanked it open with ease.

"How did you do that?"

"I've got muscles, unlike you."

Tabby quietly mocked her words back to her in a whiny voice.

Several items had been compacted into the small container, but Rae focused on a silvery package. "I think this is a blanket."

"There's only one?"

"Looks like it."

"How many more of these bin thingies are there?"

Rae shrugged, then looked up and down the hall. She spotted one on the other end, past the bridge entrance and the dead crewmember. *Not going to point out that one.* "Um, there are probably more in the other hallways."

"Wait a second. Why do dead people need to stay warm, anyway?"

"It's not to keep them warm, silly," Rae said, "it's so that—" Should she tell her? That might scare the little thing. Eh, probably not.

"Keep them from what?"

"Well, it's just what you do. Out of respect."

"Oh."

Plus, Rae thought, it will prevent accidentally looking at one and catching them staring at her! She shivered at the thought.

Tabitha then whispered, as if trying to keep the dead people from hearing her, “I think we might need the blankets more than they do. I’m getting cold.”

“Well of course you are, you’re wearing a dress!” Rae chided. “You should’ve worn leggings like me!”

“Leave me alone! Mother said I can wear whatever I want!”

“That’s right, and you chose to wear that! So now you’re cold. Deal with it!”

Tabitha stuck out her tongue.

“Baby,” Rae spat. “I’m going to look for more blankets.” She started down a hall.

“Go on. I’m taking *this* one!” The little girl threw the silvery cloth over her shoulders.

“You’re going to give that up if we need it.”

“No I’m not!”

“Are too! Do you want the dead people to stare at you the rest of the time we’re stuck here?”

Tabitha fell silent.

“Me neither. Now come on, Tabby Cat. Help me look for some more.”

Rae looked over her shoulder to see Sis pout, but she followed. A second later, Rae noticed for the first time that a headache had started forming at her temples. Probably thanks to the rhythmic reminder from the yellow lights every three seconds that something was wrong. The klaxons were less loud here in the hallways than on the bridge, but still annoying. “And then, Tabby, we’re going to find a way to shut those stupid alarms off!”

12

GSCS *Nightingale*

Elwick entered the three-room Captain's Cabin while Kelly continued to counsel poor Cabón. An open door in the left corner of the square space led to his berthing compartment, complete with personal shower and restroom, or "head." In the approximate center of the office set his beloved gray desk which had seen better days, and three overly-functional chairs. One of these he offered to Kelly, the same chair she had been sitting in earlier this evening when she brought him the cupcake.

"I said I don't wanna hear it!" she yelled, now with one foot finally in the door. "Don't forget, half y'all gotta lose ten kilos 'fore yer next PT test, or the lot o' yuhs're goin' home!"

While she was distracted, Moses quietly closed the door leading to his "berthing compartment," the Navy's word for bedroom. On his bed, or "rack," was a mess of clothes he still needed to wash. How he longed for a yeoman—a Captain's assistant—to take care of the more mundane day-to-day duties like on larger craft. A Captain on a ship the size of the *Nightingale* was not afforded such luxuries.

"Now git back to yer station, yer turnin' my stomach!" Crawford bowed low to keep from bumping her head on the doorway to Elwick's office. She violently slammed the heavy door behind her.

Elwick's eyebrows raised and he sucked in a lungful of air. "Cabón's a card, isn't he?"

"He and a couple of the boys have been makin' good progress, actually. Cabón alone has dropped eight kilos since we started him on the Fat Enlisted People program just a month ago!" Crawford sat down, making the spindly chair look more like one made for a child rather than a full-sized adult.

"*Fitness Enhancement Program,*" Elwick corrected. "Let's be nice."

"*You* can be nice all yuh want, but I'm paid to be the hard-ass ship's Bosun." She took her Boatswain's Mate's whistle from her left breast pocket and twirled it by its elaborately braided black rope.

Elwick's brows narrowed. "Please don't blow that pipe in my cabin again. That thing was never designed for an Elysian's lungs."

She gave him a hard stare, then relented. "Oh, fine. Ya big sissy." She smiled and tucked it away.

"Alright," he said, tossing a wireless pad onto the desk in front of her. Pull up your roster. I'm hungry."

Her fingers danced lightly on the embedded screen, and a holographic spreadsheet now floated over the device. She handed it back to Moses, then eyed a keepsake on his desk. "I can't believe ya still have this ugly thang," she said, plucking a charcoal stick that had been hovering over a rather intricate wooden base. "Didn't ya say Dale picked this up for ya at the gift shop on Betelgeuse Six?"

"Um, yeah," he replied, studying the spreadsheet she had given him.

"Look at it! It's downright hideous! And isn't it made out o' Fool's Gold or somethin'? Just about the most worthless mineral in the galaxy?"

"Fool's *Titanium.*" Moses corrected. "Even *more* worthless."

She shook her head. "It's just silly."

"I guess I'm just overly sentimental," he said, reaching over the desk and snatching the pen of his Sister-in-law's hand and setting it hovering over its magnetic base once again. He couldn't relay that his keepsake meant much more to him than a mere novelty bought from a gift shop on an obliterated planet that once orbited a now-exploded sun. Betelgeuse, the orange-colored star in the shoulder of Orion, the Great Hunter, as seen from Earth. Moses also couldn't relay the fact the gift shop itself never existed in the first place. Nor that the stuff of which that particular pen was made was the main reason he, Dale, and Bruno made it out of the Battle of Europa alive. They lost a lot of good sailors that day. All for something most of the galaxy's population didn't know even existed. And hopefully certain Chinese warlords didn't know existed either.

"All hands, this is the Officer of the Deck," Lieutenant Kitner's voice rang out over the loudspeaker in the overhead. "Prepare for interstellar space folding. Jump number two will commence in one minute."

"Speaking of Beetlejuice, I heard about a hunnerd years ago, some amateur astronomer won twenty-four hours of use of the Neil deGrasse Tyson II after calculatin'—or probably just guessin'—the exact month and year it actually went nova! That was back when the early colonizers were still on their way ta find out fer sure."

"He figured out the *exact* month?" Moses asked, not taking his eyes off the roster.

"S'what I heard."

"Tyson?"

"A popular astronomer back in the Twenty-first Century. They named the telescope after him. Both of 'em, obviously."

"Ah. One of those questions I missed on my eighth grade history final, I'm guessing."

"How me and Zoey are so into history and you never were, I'll never understand. Anyway, that feller who won the contest got purty excited about it. Should've seen him on the old newsfeeds. You'd think he won a fancy racer with a fifth generation Zee Dee drive or somethin'!"

Moses could think of about a thousand other things he would prefer over a mini-craft with a Zhédié motor faster than some military ships, but then Kelly was a unique creature, in love with all things mechanical.

"It's amazin' to think Betelgeuse blew up back when the old USA was a brand spankin' new country! Right around 1850, if I remember right."

"Is that when the USA came about? That's one piece of history I should probably know," Moses said, staring off into space.

"Heck, I dunno. I just fix engines and motors and look at stars."

"How far away from Earth did you say it was?" he asked, turning his attention back to Kelly's duty roster.

"What?"

"Betelgeuse."

"Six hunnerd and forty-some light years."

"I don't know how you remember all those distances," Moses muttered. "I think that sounds about right, though, because the nova's light reached Earth when I was just a year old. I wish I'd been older to enjoy it! Of course I saw all the holos of the supernova lighting up Earth's skies, but to actually see it… Ah, that would have been a sight!"

"Shone like Venus in the sky fer years! I read that fer four months it shone as bright as the full Moon!" She licked her thumb and tried to clean a black greasy smudge off the back of her left hand. She must not have looked in a mirror lately; several more smudges painted her freckled face. Her violet one-piece jumpsuit, streaked and stained with even more grease, was the norm for the hard-working Petty Officer. As a matter of fact, Moses would have become suspicious had she or her flight suit ever been tidy.

"All hands, Officer of the Deck. Commencing jump number two in five… four… three… two… one."

Elwick braced himself. His stomach turned inside out, his eyes rolled into the back of his head, and once again he had the eerie feeling of sliding into his own navel. In a few seconds, things had gone back to normal.

As the overhead lights and Elwick's desk computer flickered back to life, Kelly giggled and shook all over, like she got a sudden chill. "Ooo! Love those seventy-five-hundred-year hops!"

Moses stared her down.

She looked up at him, smiling. "What? It's not my fault the super jumps tickle my insides!" She arched her back. "Whew! Might need a cigarette after that one."

Elwick grimaced.

"Oh, Moses! Ya think you'd be used to me by *now*."

He took a deep breath and let it out slow.

Kelly's smile faded. "Hey, you okay? Yer tummy still givin' ya fits when we do the big jumps?"

Moses nodded. "Anyway," he said changing the subject, your roster looks good. I just approved it." He sat down the pad and began scanning for his coffee mug. He must have left it… where…?

"So, you're cool with it? All of it?"

He looked at her questioningly. "Yes?"

"Hot diggity! That was easy."

"Wait. What was easy?" He dove for the pad he had just set down.

She snickered. "Oh, Moe, why're ya so easy ta mess with?"

He shot her a stare under low brows. "Speaking of messing with people…"

"Uh oh. This is that 'nuthin' good' part, ain't it? Okay, let's have it." Kelly turned sideways and crossed legs four feet long if they were an inch. "And please tell me this ain't about Pruitt. I'm just playin' around when I say I'm gonna file a formal complaint. I kinda enjoy beatin' the piss outta 'im every time he does somethin' stupid."

"It's not about Pruitt. But I do wish we still had a Chief Petty Officer onboard to handle situations like that. I guess I could sic Antonio on him." He smiled. "Ol' Bruno served as a Senior Chief for a lot of years, you know."

"No," Kelly said sternly. "I don't want Kurt *dead,* I just want him ta suffer a little."

Something clicked in Elwick's mind. "Tell me you didn't break something when we spoke on the circuit earlier."

She shrugged. "Doc said it was just a lil' crack."

"Kelly!"

"Oh, he'll be good as new in a couple o' weeks. He's lucky; my first instinct was ta shove that hand in the plasma stream!"

Moses honestly couldn't tell if she was serious or not.

"No, I can't take him out fer good, unfortunately. Who'd I put in charge while I mash out all the paperwork and bring chow down ta the boys when they can't get away from them engines?"

Elwick smiled. "Well, now that's getting back to what I wanted to talk to you about." He leaned over the desk. "Kelly, I've never told you this, but honestly, you're the best Ship's Bosun I've ever had. You're the primary reason I haven't pushed to get a replacement Chief's Mate. We don't need one."

"We don't?" she asked.

"Nope. We got you."

Kelly snorted. "Yeah. Ya got me ta do the job, and fer cheap! Lucky you. Hey, don't get me wrong, Moses, I don't mind fillin' in until we get a new Chief. I kinda like bein' in charge! I only wish the position came with the extra pay, the cool new fancy uniform, and most of all, the respect CPO rank comes with! I mean I do have the pipe, but it's just not enough."

"Have patience, BM1."

"Yeah, yeah, I know, I have ta wait fer the exam results."

"Funny you should mention that; I found something in my inbox late last night…"

Her breath caught.

"It wasn't your exam results."

She huffed and her shoulders slumped.

"It was this year's CPO selection approval list."

"Hmm. Wonderful. I'm happy for all of them." She tapped a forceful finger on his desk. "Them exam results were supposed ta be to the selection board a full month ago, *before* the cutoff, so I could be considered fer promotion!"

Moses had been expecting this outburst, and brought up a particular roster on the pad.

"Who's ass do I have'ta kick ta—"

He tossed the pad on the desk in directly in front of her. A glowing list of names now floated above it.

Petty Officer Crawford's eyes soon bulged, then her eyebrows knitted together. "I don't understand. How am I eligible? The results—"

"Made it on time. Two months ago."

"But you said—"

Elwick shrugged. "Two can play your little game, Kelly."

Her breath caught again. "*You* were messing with *me*? The board got the results on time?"

"Obviously. And they were impressed enough with your promotion packet that your name made it on the list."

"Oh my goodness! I can't believe it! Really!?"

"Really, Chief Petty Officer *Select* Crawford," he replied with a smile.

She released a girlish yelp. "Chief Petty Officer Select! Oh, Moses!" She leapt around his desk and enveloped him in a bear hug before he could even think about protesting.

"Okay, okay! Careful, before I'm out of commission for a couple of weeks, too!"

"Sorry!" she said, releasing him. "Oh boy! Pruitt's gunna love this!"

"About as much as he likes clearin' the shitter," Moses muttered.

"Oh, Moses, this just made my whole week! My whole year! Look! Something good happened today, of all days!" But then her smile soon faded. "Wait a second. You said it was nuthin' good…"

"Hmm, look at that. Two burns in one day. That's gotta be a record for me."

Her jaw dropped. "Moses Elwick!" She shook her head and smiled big, then looked back down at the pad. "Sixteen September. Does that mean I'll get pinned on Sixteen September?"

"Along with every other CPO selectee. But we could frock you now, if you'd like."

She yelped again.

Moses wondered what the bridge crew must be thinking right about now; the multi-alloy walls were much thinner than they looked. He couldn't help but be elated right along with her. He hadn't seen Kelly this giddy since that bar brawl at Mylar's Tavern a couple years back. A mere ten minutes in that backwater colony bar had earned her the respect of the entire ship. Not to mention an entire remote manufacturing settlement. "You've earned it, Kelly, that's for sure."

"Thank you, Cap'n! But I'm not sure about the frockin'. Soon as I put that on, I'll be hazed for a solid six weeks!"

Elwick nodded. "You'll definitely get put through the paces. Dale may not be an active duty Chief anymore, but make no mistake, there's a reason everyone still calls him Master Chief. He's been looking forward to *someone* making the selectee list for a while now. Soon as he hears about this, I'd get ready for one hell of an initiation if I were you, regardless of whether you're wearing that rocker or not."

"You don't think he'll be *too* rough on me, do you?"

"Well, considering you have muscles in places he's never even had fat, I wouldn't count on him going light on you just 'cause you're my Sis-in-Law."

She nodded. "I can handle it. I'm ready."

"I hope so. Because Dale's crazy. And I don't mean the usual crazy. He's certifiably insane."

"Tell me something I don't know!"

Moses raised his brows. "So, that'll take care of the Chief we're lacking on this boat! Maybe eventually I'll actually get a navigator so my XO won't have to pull double-duty. I don't know if Ozzie will give it up, however. I think he enjoys that station too much. Gives him an excuse not to do his paperwork."

"Can't blame him there!"

Elwick toyed with his short beard "Maybe I can trick Pruitt into reclassing into the QM rating? He's already got the background. He'd probably make a superb navigator."

"And there aren't no white hats like *me* on the bridge to distract him."

Moses winked. "I love it when a plan comes together."

"But then we'd need another QL Sys Tech to take care of the core," Kelly considered. "It's too much for Girard to take on both it and the ions."

"Cabón could handle it for now."

"Cabón uh'd get jelly fillin' all over the injectors! But I guess it does only take one hand to adjust a boson particle funnel…"

"And one hand to hold the gedunk." Moses added.

"But then, we'd need a new box kicker."

"Supply's an easy extra duty to give to anyone. Heck, I'll sick Ozzie on it if I have to. He's always looking for something to do besides paperwork, anyway."

She smiled. "Well, look at that! We just solved all the personnel problems on this little boat, and all it took was me gettin' promoted! You shoulda done that a long time ago, Moe!"

"*Boat?*" Elwick repeated, giving the woman his best insulted look. "Lookee here, *Boat-swain*," he poked, articulating both words instead of running them together into "Bosun," "I'm the only bub on this here boat who can call it a boat!"

She pressed her lips together and seemed to try hard to suppress a laugh. It didn't work.

"Hmm," Moses said, sitting up, "you know, I could really use a Chief Petty Officer right about now to help me sort out the latest policy updates from SENTCORPS—"

"Oh my goodness!" Kelly said, glancing at her bare wrist, "look at the time! So much to do!" She stood and stepped over the chair's back as easily as taking a step. "Gotta get that doo-hickey calibrated, and that thing-a-ma-jig configured. You know how busy the life of a CPO can be!"

"CPO *Select*!"

"Bye, Moey Poey."

"Hey! Only certain people get to call the Captain that! Bosuns are forbidden!"

"Sorry, Moe."

"How 'bout *Captain*?"

"Cap'n Moey Poey." She whispered, then winked and disappeared into the passageway, re-closing the door behind her.

"Whew," Moses said out loud, and released a huge sigh. "There's *one way* to avoid another Zoey conversation."

13
Emerald Pearl

Rae and Tabby returned to the bridge and covered the last body with a silvery thermal blanket. With the horrible images hidden from view, if not the various smells that accompanied them—*oh please don't let that be poop!*—Rae now had time to take stock of their situation and actually think straight. Well, somewhat straight. If only that dang alarm would stop reminding her of their impending doom every few seconds! "Tabby, help me get that alarm shut off!"

As the girls searched for the right switch, thoughts exploded in Rae's mind: *Would a distress call be sent automatically, or does someone have to send it? Maybe there are other crewmen who survived and can help? Maybe mom and dad can find a way to send a distress call? Or rather, maybe mom can... But what if there are no nearby ships to rescue us? Then how do we get off this ship? And even if we do find a way off the ship, how do we get home? Or even just to the mining colony where people are expecting us?* Rae glanced at her sister. She sat at one of the stations, toying with the controls. "Tabby, don't just start pushing buttons! We don't want to make things worse!"

Sis ignored her.

"Tabitha Lenore!"

As if on cue, the bridge lit up in white light. Rae looked around, amazed. "How did you—?" She paused waiting for the next wail of the emergency klaxon. It never came.

Tabitha turned to Rae. "You were saying?"

"How did you know what to do?"

"I can read. This display right here says, 'Manual input'. And there's a keyboard. So, I just typed in, 'Lights on', and then 'Alarm off', and the lights came on and the alarm went off." Tabby sat there smiling like the Cheshire Cat, kicking her small legs. Her feet hung far from the floor in the adult-sized chair.

Rae smirked. "Huh. You *are* a smart little brat," Rae admitted. "Sometimes."

Tabitha playfully stuck out her tongue, then gave Rae a tight, prideful grin.

Rae rolled her eyes. "Alright, smarty pants, do you think you can figure out how to send for help?"

"I don't know. Maybe." She got to typing, but soon frowned. "Hmm. 'Help' didn't work. Just brought up a whole list of other things I can ask for."

"Do any of them say 'Distress signal' or 'Emergency call' or anything like that?"

After a few seconds, Tabby shook her head.

Rae looked around. Despite the white overhead lights, the bright red glow of the nebula outside still tinted everything a rosy shade. "Which one is the station that sends out messages? The communications station?" Rae looked around the room at the consoles around her, trying to avoid looking at the bodies again. "That's the one we need."

Tabitha hopped down from her chair to look around. In a few seconds she proclaimed, "It's that one!" She ran to a wide, flat metal desk with a map displayed on it, similar to the one they found in Operations.

Rae joined her sister. "This looks like the navigation station."

"Not this one, dummy. That one!" She pointed to her left. "I even said, '*that* one'! I came to this one to see where we are."

Rae sighed. "You're really annoying sometimes, you know that?"

"I know."

Rae, now at the console her sister pointed out, stared at the overwhelming maze of manual buttons and dials. Each one sported a label, but the text may as well have been written in another language. Rae shook her head. "I don't even know where to begin."

Tabitha sighed dramatically. "Do I have to do *everything?*" The little girl walked over and plopped down in the chair at the communications station. Sis took a minute to go over the entire console, then touched a screen with her finger. Her mere touch brought the console to life, from a dim glow to a brightly lit cornucopia of colors. It was almost like Tabby actually knew what she was doing.

Maybe she does, Rae thought.

Rae thought back to all the science fairs Tabitha participated in with their father, while she herself spent those weekends gardening with their mother. *Mother is more like me, spiritual. A savior of the Earth, a champion of Nature. Tabitha is more like Daddy, technically-minded. A princess of the electronic world. It sure is coming in handy now!* Rae pretty much just accepted the world as is, admiring the beauty of it, not worrying too much how it worked. She lived happily knowing that it, and they, existed. She now wished she was a little more like her little sister. But she'd never, ever let the little brat know that! She regarded the girl with jealously and annoyance, but at the same time a lot of pride and admiration. If anyone could figure out how to send an S.O.S. to save them, it was little Tabby.

14

GSCS *Nightingale*

“Captain? Petty Officer Connelly.”

The call startled him so badly, Moses hit his head on the inside of the refrigerator. “Ow!” Red liquid squirted onto the deck. He must have squeezed the still mostly full juice box without realizing it. While he looked for a nearby towel, he answered the call via the communications pin on his collar. “Elwick.”

“Sir, we just got a QE wave from Sentinel One.”

Moses’ eyes grew huge. *Sentinel One? Earth? That’s never good.* “Go ahead.”

“Apparently the Navy is in the middle of an investigation regarding that signal we received from the *Pearl,* after verifying its authenticity via archival data.”

“The Navy? Archival data? I don’t understand.”

“Me neither, sir. But there’s a packet attached in the reply we got back. And it reads, ‘REL/Commander, *Nightingale.*’ Obviously TS-level stuff. I couldn’t open this thing if I tried. And I, um, might have tried.”

“Does anything in the wave say which Naval department verified the authenticity?”

“Yeah, it was in the title metadata of the attachment. Get this. Republic Bureau working jointly with SENTCORPS J-2!”

"Woah. That's a heavy set of eyes. Why would the Intel guys, let alone the Bureau itself, care about a transport ship?"

"Maybe the answer is in the packet that my puny permissions wouldn't open?"

"Route it to my inbox. I'll take it in my office."

"Aye aye, sir."

* * *

Moses sat back in his creaky chair at his beat-up desk and stared at the screen. He reached to his left and touched a virtual button. "Ozzie, I need to see you in my office. It's urgent."

"Aye," came the immediate reply. The comm switched off.

"This makes not a lick of sense," Moses muttered out loud to no one, then took another sip of coffee from a completely new cup because he still hadn't found his mug. The black drink hadn't even had a chance to cool down before he had finished the top secret memo from the J-2. It had taken all of ten seconds.

A knock at the door, and Osterland entered without waiting for approval. Fine and good, Moses had a mouthful of piping hot joe and didn't want to respond anyway.

"Good news from the secret squirrels, I take it?" the XO smirked.

"Is news from Intel ever good? No. I mean, this news is not necessarily bad, just… unexpected." Elwick shook his head and stared at the screen on his desk. "They want us to stand down."

"Oh, come on, really?"

"Remember earlier when I said the RSS *Buker* is on standby, in case we run into trouble? They're sending her in our stead."

"A *destroyer*? For a rescue mission?"

"You see my confusion now?"

"Unless they know about some trouble we don't. Maybe Dale was right. Maybe it's a trap. Have the Chinese been reported out that direction?"

"I haven't searched through the most recent intel reports yet. But if that's the case, why not just come right out and say the region is hot? Stay away. They've always told us before. Why all the secrecy now?"

The XO shrugged. "Gotta be *some* reason. "Maybe the unclass Chinese channels could give us a clue? I'll sick Connelly on it."

"Don't. That will just arouse suspicion and questions that I won't be authorized to answer."

Osterland needed. "I suppose I can't see that communiqué you got?"

"Wouldn't help if you could," Moses said, motioning to the screen, now opaque from the XO's perspective. "It's all of two dozen words. And that includes the header!"

"No explanation?"

"Zilch."

The XO sighed. "So, what are we gonna do? Just shut up and color?"

"What else can we do?"

Osterland shook his head. "Curiouser and curiouser. First an ancient ship we can barely find info on, and now the Navy tells us to keep our distance and ignore a class one—"

"Captain, this is Connelly," interrupted the comms officer.

"Elwick. Go ahead."

"Sir, I just picked up another QE transmission. Voice."

"If it's the Navy, tell them I'm not home."

"Actually, the origin is in the opposite direction from Earth. Computer says it's originating from one of the deep space relays out in the Quadrangle. Sentinel Relay 3287. Sir, I think it's a live transmission from the *Pearl!*"

Elwick shared an incredulous glance with his XO. Before he could answer, Connelly spoke again. "But we can't seem to get a response when we reply."

"Are you sure it's not a recorded message?"

"Verifying. Standby, please."

Osterland shook his head. "Captain, any DSRs in that sector have to be two centuries old. I'm surprised it's even still working."

"Agreed."

"Sir," said Connelly, "I can see the parameters and characteristics of the signal the DSR is picking up. You're not going to believe this, but the relay's computer is telling me it's relaying a radio broadcast."

The cat snagged both Elwick's and Osterland's tongues at *that* moment. "*Radio?* You're kidding."

"Not kidding, sir."

Elwick sat back in his chair, which creaked all the way back. "Hmm. Well, let's think this through. If their comms is on the fritz, possibly due to damage, broadcasting on the radio spectrum might be at the very end of their comms PACE plan."

Osterland nodded. "That would make sense, considering how old that ship is. The 'E' could be radio. But wow, I can't believe any interstellar craft is still using radio for anything but ground-to-ground or ground-to-orbital comms. It would be useless for anything else; no one would hear you for tens of thousands of years, especially this far out!"

"Mmm hmm. They must be desperate. Their communications array must be in serious disarray."

The XO winked. "I see what you did there."

"Not sure if it's that, Captain," said Connelly, "or if the person on the line doesn't exactly know how to work the comms, and radio is the best they could do?"

"But that doesn't make any sense, Guy. How could even an inexperienced crewman—"

"It may make sense when you hear it, sir. Kinda sounds like a young girl rather than a member of the crew."

Elwick paused. "A young girl?"

"Possibly two."

Elwick hesitated only a moment for Connelly's words to register. "On my way!" He bolted out of his cabin, with Osterland hot on his heels.

* * *

"Captain on the bridge!" Kitner shouted when Elwick barreled onto it. Every sailor present stiffened at the Lieutenant's announcement.

Moses made a bee line to Petty Officer Second Class Connelly, who stood, as usual, at the Sciences and Communications Station.

The XO took up his place again at Navigation.

"Is the channel open?" Elwick asked.

"Aye, sir. Here, I'll transfer it to the overhead speakers."

A couple of seconds later, a young voice exploded across the bridge. "—try again, but I just don't know if anyone's listening, Tabby."

"But we have to keep trying." came a smaller voice. Another young girl, by Moses' reckoning. "Run your finger the other way!" she exclaimed.

Moses bellowed in his command voice. "*Emerald Pearl*, this is the Galactic Sentinel Corps Search and Rescue vessel *Nightingale*. What is your status?"

No response.

Captain Elwick looked at Connelly, but the Non-Commissioned Officer only shrugged.

Moses tried again. "*Emerald Pearl*, do you read?" Silence.

Connelly leaned to his left and typed on a small keyboard. After a few seconds he nodded his head. "Sir, I just pinged the relay. Communications issue is definitely not on our end."

"Was it just me, or did those girls have an odd dialect?" Commander Osterland asked the room.

"Wasn't just you, sir," Starman Burgess agreed.

"Okay, okay, Tabby, hold your horses, I'm doing it! Hello?" the first young voice rang out again. "Is anyone out there?"

"*Emerald Pearl,* this is the GSCS *Nightingale,* search and rescue," Elwick shouted. "Are you receiving us?"

"Yes!" came the reply. "You can hear us? Something's happened. We need help!"

"Yes, *Emerald Pearl,* we read you!" Elwick replied.

"Told you it was that one," came the second little voice.

"Thank you, Good Spirits!" whispered the first. Then louder, "Who is this?"

"My name is Captain Moses Elwick, Captain of the Galactic Sentinel Corps Search and Rescue Ship *Nightingale*. What is your situation and condition?"

The second voice came across the air again. "He sounds funny."

"Tabby, be quiet!" the first girl said. "Hi, Captain Moses. My sister and I are on the bridge, and we're the only ones awake. A bunch of crewmembers are here. On the floor. I'm pretty sure they're all dead."

Elwick shared the same look with everyone on the bridge: incredulity. "You're the only ones 'awake'?" he asked. "Does that mean you were in the ship's hibernation pods at one point?"

"Yes. The computer woke us up, I think. There are still more people downstairs in cryo pods, um… I'm not sure how many."

"Fourteen," came the other voice, which sounded annoyed.

"Right," the first girl confirmed, "fourteen others. I'm not sure they're all still alive, though."

"I understand. Are you or your sister injured?"

"No, we're okay. Just a little scared."

"Understood." Elwick breathed a sigh of relief. "What are your names?"

"My name is Rae Marshall. My sister is Tabitha."

"Okay Rae, don't worry, we're coming to get you and your sister."

Osterland jerked his head over his shoulder so fast it could have spun right off. The came a look that could have melted Elwick's face. He said nothing. He didn't have to; Moses knew exactly what he was on about.

"As well as all the rest of you," he added, while returning his XO's stare.

"Did he say his name was Moses?" asked the second voice, who Rae had identified as Tabitha. "Like the Bible guy?"

"Like the Bible guy, yes," Elwick answered. "My mother was something of a fan of the Old Testament, God rest her soul. How old are you girls?" Elwick asked.

"I'm fourteen. Tabby is ten."

"Ten and a half!"

Elwick nodded. "Where are your parents? Are they still in—"

"Tabby, don't lean on the console! You might make us lose the call!"

"At least *I* could get them back if we lost them," Tabitha muttered.

"Shhh!" Rae chided, "I'm trying to talk! Captain Moses, our parents are still asleep in the cryo pods, along with our brother, Jamie. We don't know the other people in the cryo chamber."

"The guy in the pod next to Daddy is Jason," reported Tabitha. "The man on the other side of Jamie, in that other little room, is Kraig," "The one next to him is Ike. Then the one next to Ike should have been Greg, but it looked like one of the—"

"How do you know all that?" Rae interrupted.

"Because I like to make friends. You just like to look at stupid fashion e-zines and—"

"Girls," Elwick interrupted, "I need you to talk to *me* for a little while and not each other, okay?"

Silence on the line.

"The crewmembers there with you… how many are there?"

"Well, there's five here, including Captain Timmins—"

"Don't forget Norstrom and the one in the hallway, Rae!" Tabby said.

"Yeah, there's a lady down on Floor Three named Miss Norstrom, and a guy just outside the bridge in the hallway. We don't know his name."

"Alright. These last two people, were they crewmembers, also?"

"Pretty sure. The guy wore a blue and black suit uniform like these people here, and the lady wore a blue jumpsuit, like overalls, with patches and stuff. She actually talked to us!"

"She did?" Elwick's heart leapt. "So she's still alive? What did she say?"

"She *was* still alive when we first found her, but she died while talking to us. She was hurt really bad."

Elwick's heart sank as fast as it had jumped. "Oh."

Tabby spoke up. "She warned us not to open a door!"

"I see." Elwick looked at the XO and spoke softly. "Hull breech?"

"Likely," replied Osterland.

"I'm sorry you had to experience that, girls," Elwick said. "Have you seen any other crewmembers? On any of the other decks or in any of the compartments? Berthing or otherwise?"

"Compartments?"

"Rooms," Elwick clarified. "Offices, sleeping quarters, the mess decks, places like that."

"Oh... No, no one else. We called out to people on the way here, and we even knocked on the Captain's door and a few other doors, but no one answered," Rae said. "So, we came here to find Captain Timmins. But…" Her voice trailed off.

"He's dead," Tabitha explained.

"Yes, I understood," replied Elwick. "I'm sorry."

Rae then blurted out, "I don't know why we were woken up and the others weren't!"

Elwick had no answer for this. He changed the subject. "Is it getting cold there, girls?"

"No, not really," Rae replied.

"I'm a little cold," Tabitha whispered.

"Shh!"

"Okay," Elwick said, "that's good. Do you smell anything burning? Or anything, well, stinky…?"

Connelly stifled a laugh. "Stinky, sir?"

"These are kids," Elwick whispered to the Petty Officer. "Do you think it better to ask if the Schrödinger relays are exhibiting signs of corrosion?"

"Good point."

"Um, well, not yet," Rae replied.

"You kinda smell like Grandma," said Tabitha.

"Shut up!"

"Girls, please!" Elwick interrupted. "I only need your attention for a little while longer."

"When are you getting here?" asked Tabitha.

"Well, I'm getting to that," Elwick switched to a polite, caring tone. "It's going to take some time, but don't worry, we'll be there as fast as we can. In the meantime, we need to make sure your ship can keep you warm long enough for us to get there, alright?"

"Alright."

"Now Rae, I'm going to ask you to do a few grown up things, do you think you can help me?"

Rae answered with confidence. "Yes, Captain."

"I need to you ask the computer some questions."

"Okay."

"You're gonna mess it up," Tabitha whispered.

"No I'm not! Be quiet, Tabby!"

"Rae, listen you're not going to mess anything up," Moses assured. "This is easy. Are you ready?"

"He heard you," she whispered. Then louder, "Yes, I'm ready."

"Don't worry, Captain, I'll help her," Tabitha said.

"Stop it, you little know-it-all. I can do it!"

Elwick ignored the continued interruptions. Despite his growing frustration, the girls' playful banter reminded him of his daughter and the neighbor girl Sia at their house in Sentinel City, up in the beautiful Pacific Northwest Freeman Province. Unfortunately, Sia could never again argue with Alena. He shook off the distracting memory. "Rae, ask the computer for a Status Report."

"Okay. Computer, I need a Status Report!"

Silence.

Tabitha sighed. "That's not how Captain Timmins did it. First you have to call it by its name. Like this: *Emerald Pearl,* I need a Status Report!"

More silence.

"Ha, it didn't work for you, either!" Rae chided. "Any more bright ideas?"

If the little girl responded, Elwick did not hear her. "Girls, maybe you should—"

"Hold on, Captain," Rae interrupted. "I think we know what's wrong."

"*I* know what's wrong, not you!" Tabby said, her voice distant now. "I'm already fixing it."

Elwick heard fumbling on the other end of the line, as if two children were climbing all over chairs and control panels. Likely, precisely what was happening.

"The younger one is absolutely precocious!" Connelly whispered.

"Okay!" Tabitha blurted. "It should work now."

Elwick shared a surprised look with Guy Connelly as he heard the girls posing their question to the computer again. "You seriously got it to work?" Moses asked. "Honestly?"

"Shhh, Captain!" Tabby said. "The computer is speaking!"

Elwick found his mouth still agape. He closed it. "Connelly, turn up the gain a bit."

As the Petty Officer did so, another female voice rose in crescendo. This one had much less emotion.

"—breached on Decks One, Two and Three in sections Delta, Echo, and Golf. Atmospheric System failure imminent due to loss of primary power. Environmental System failure imminent due to loss of primary power. Judeya Sheekong space-folding core processor not responding. Navigation function inoperable. Cryogenic System operational but responding with multiple malfunctions. Ship operating on backup power. Immediate evacuation recommended."

Elwick waited, but nothing more came. "Rae," he continued, "ask the computer how long until the backup power runs out."

"*Emerald Pearl!* How long—" Rae's voice boomed down the entirety of the *Nightingale's* upper deck before Connelly could readjust the volume. When he finally did so, to a level that wouldn't make their ear drums bleed, Elwick and his crew could no longer hear the computer's responses. "Rae? What did the computer say?"

"She said 'approximately one hour'."

One hour! The *Nightingale* would need a minimum of two hours just to reach the nebula! Then God only knows how many more precious minutes would be spent navigating to the *Pearl* and the SAR team finding their way in. Moses shook his head. *There simply isn't time.* "Girls, I'm a little concerned the ship may not hold out until we get there. You're going to need to get to either the lifeboats or the escape pods. Connelly, pull up the schematics on the *Pearl's* sister ship."

Guy flew through menus, and the deck-by-deck layout of the *Kristin's Vision* appeared in the air over his console.

"But what about our parents?" Rae asked.

"Captain," PO2 Connelly said, "I'm going to venture a guess there's a failsafe that jettisons any habited cryo pods when the power gets below a safe minimum."

"He's right," said Osterland. "However, if we don't get there before that happens, we'll end up on a search for several man-sized objects that could last days, if not weeks. That nebula is going to play havoc on the sensors. Finding objects that small without instruments will be like searching for quarks in a QE stream."

"Or needles in a haystack, as we say on the farm," offered Kelly, who must have been eavesdropping from below, in Engineering.

Osterland frowned. "That's what I just said."

"Okay," Rae broke in, "Are you saying our parents should be okay, even if all the power shuts off?"

"That's right," Moses replied.

"Tell those other people thank you, whoever they were," Rae added.

Elwick smiled. "There'll be time for introductions later, I promise. Alright, girls, looking at the schematics, it looks like *Kristin's Vision* has six lifeboats that hold twenty people each. Three at the bow and three more astern. Hopefully the *Pearl* has all these, too. Plus, a series of smaller, one-man escape pods all along the keel. The larger ones will have beds and heads—I mean restrooms—so I'd check those out first."

"What floor are they on?" Rae asked.

"They're all on Deck One. So, if you're on the bridge, you're on Deck Two—"

"We know where to go," said Tabby. "Come on, Rae."

Elwick raised his voice. "Um, girls? Can you be sure to check in with us when you get there? Any communications panel should work. Just ask the *Pearl* to tie in to the external comms."

"Aye aye, Captain!" yelled Rae.

Moses noticed Osterland staring again. The XO pressed his lips together in a tight smile and nodded, then turned back to the nav station.

Well, at least the XO is on my side, Moses thought. Not so sure that will hold true of anyone in SARCOM, SENTCOM, or the RNA Navy.

15

Emerald Pearl

The girls darted from the bridge. "This way!" yelled Tabitha, running straight out one of the doors to the bridge and right up a ladder.

Rae followed. "Is this a shortcut? Why don't we just take the winding staircase?"

At Floor One, papers and other small objects littered the corridors here and there, but thankfully, no more bodies. Tabitha led them around a few corners until they could go no further in the direction Rae understood to be the bow of the ship. Before them, in a small semi-circular gangway, lay three recessed panels taking up most of the forward wall.

"Look," Rae pointed to a small sign on the wall that read "Lifeboats."

"Yeah, that's why I came up here."

"That's why I came up here," Rae mocked.

Tabby stuck out her tongue.

Rae noticed a black, square panel in a nearby wall. Before her family went to sleep for the long journey, she had seen crewmembers speaking into similar panels as they went about their duties. "This is a comm panel, right?"

"Probably. Touch it."

She did, and a red circle illuminated under her fingers. She leaned close, and spoke into the circle. "Captain Moses? We're here."

No one answered.

"You have to tie the comms from the bridge to wherever you want to talk from," Tabby told her.

"How do you—? Nevermind. *Emerald Pearl,* tie in to the external comms to this panel so I can talk to the *Nightingale.*"

"External communications now routed to Panel one dash three four."

"Captain Moses?"

"Hi Rae, that didn't take long at all." Moses' voice echoed in the small passageway. "What do you see?"

"Well, there are three large doors in front of us. There are flat, white panels on the wall next to each one."

"Alright. What do you see on the panels? Are there any red lights or warnings of any kind?"

"Not yet…" Rae touched the panel next to the center door. Nothing happened. She tried the other two. "Nothing's happening. The panels are still blank."

"That's strange. Especially when you have power to everything else." He mumbled something Rae couldn't hear.

"Captain Moses?"

"I'm here. Just discussing something with my crew. No problem, the doors can be operated manually. There should be a handle around there somewhere. Something you can turn."

"I don't see anything like that."

"Pry the panel off," Moses instructed. "Maybe it's inside the wall?"

Using her fingernails, Rae pried the edges of the panel. It popped off easily and hinged downward. Inside she found a silver crank and a handle that looked like it could be pulled forward. She described what she saw.

"Okay, good. Now, don't do anything yet. First, tell me what you see through the windows in the doors. I assume there are windows?"

"Yes, little small round ones. But they're above my head." She jumped, and at the far end of the deep portholes she caught a circle of red, the same color that had been flooding the bridge earlier. "I can see the nebula!"

Silence on the line.

"Captain?"

"Rae, are all the windows the same? Can you see red light coming in all of them?"

She went to each window and jumped to peer out each one. "Yes. All three."

Tabitha groaned.

"Wait, what does that mean?"

"It means the life boats are gone, girls."

Rae looked at Tabitha, who had her chin to her chest.

"But don't worry," the Captain went on, "My Communications Officer says there are three more aft, plus all the little ones on Deck Three."

"Aft?" asked Tabitha.

"That means the stern, Tabby. The back."

"But that's a long ways away!"

Another male voice came on the line, a younger-sounding voice. "Girls, I know it's a hike, but can you please try to make it to stern?"

Rae took a deep breath. The air here seemed cooler than elsewhere on the *Pearl*. Maybe just because *outer space* lay just beyond these three doors? "We can try."

Tabby sighed, turned, and started jogging back the way they had come.

Rae followed, and in mere seconds, she and her sister encountered a curved wall. They followed it along the port side of the *Pearl*. Rae remembered this curvature; this was the wall that looped around the Observation Dome! She had fun making a long, slow turn to the left as they followed the curve. Tabby slammed on the brakes in front of her, and she jumped to the side to avoid a collision. "Woah!" she yelled. "Why did you stop?"

Sis stood before a large, gun-metal gray door and pointed up. Above the door, a sign read, "Engineering."

"Yeah. So?" Rae asked.

"Norstrom said not to open that door," said Tabby.

"That was on Floor Three. This is Floor One."

Tabitha looked at Rae. "Are you really that stupid? This sign says the same thing that sign said: *Engineering*."

"Okay. Again, sooo?"

"Okay sooo *you* open the door. Just wait for me to go back to the bridge and seal all the doors behind me."

"Do you really think space is right on the other side?"

Tabby shrugged. "Maybe. I don't know how to find out, so I'm not opening that door."

Rae looked at the ominous gangway. Then back to Tabby.

"And if we can't open any of the doors that say 'Engineering', I don't think there's any way to get to the back of the ship. Aft," she added, in a snide way.

"How do you know for sure?" asked Rae.

Tabitha gave her a look that told Rae *she knew*.

"Okay, okay, I'll take your word for it."

Rae found a comm panel not far away. "Captain Mo—ugh. *Emerald Pearl,* tie external comms to this panel—no, wait. Tie comms to *all* panels like this one across the entire ship!"

"External communications now routed to all internal communications panels."

"Thank you!"

"That was almost smart," Tabitha smirked.

Rae stuck out her tongue playfully. "Captain Moses?"

"Elwick here."

"We can't get to stern. The door in front of us says 'Engineering' and we were told not to open that one door to Engineering downstairs. Tabby thinks that means we can't open any doors that say 'Engineering'. Is that true?"

"Standby," Elwick replied. "Connelly, thoughts?"

"She's right, Captain," Rae heard another man say. "If they're where I think they are, they're right at the entrance to the Engineering deck. It's a large, three-level chamber. The far end houses the Zee Dee core and the primaries. I'd wager that entire section is in vacuum. Or a large part of it, anyway."

"See?" said Tabby. "I was right."

Rae leaned against the wall. "Now what?"

"There are still the one-man escape pods at the keel."

"Where is that?"

The guy Elwick called "Connelly" came back on. "Deck Three, ladies. They should be easy to find, they'll all look the same, all in a row. Should be… approximately twenty of them per side."

"On it!" yelled Tabitha, who took off toward a ladder in the center of the long hall. This hall was one of many that ran cross-wise, or the width of the ship, on this floor and the others. Or rather, "decks," as this man had called them.

Of course they're called decks, Rae, she berated herself, as she reached the ladder and climbed downward.

The girls passed brightly lit Deck Two and found themselves back on boring, gray Deck Three. They passed by the cryo chamber and found a door labeled "Escape Craft Antechamber: Starboard." The handle turned easily, and the girls all but fell into a long, dimly-lit hall that ran the length of the *Pearl.* But there were no tiny, individual ships like they had expected.

"Uh oh," Tabby muttered.

"Captain," Rae said into a black panel by the entrance door that lit up when she touched it, "we found the room with the escape pods, but—"

"But what?" came the reply.

"I think they're all gone. There is just a long trench that a person could— Tabby! Be careful!"

Tabby had already climbed down into the trench, and now peered into several small, deep, round portholes on either side of the trench, similar to the ones they had seen in the doors upstairs. She spoke as she walked. "Red. Red. Red. They're all red!"

Rae sighed. *Why does this day just keep getting worse?* She let out a long breath. *Wait, that sign said 'starboard'. That means there might be one on the other side!* Rae bolted out the door.

"Rae! Where are you going?"

She didn't answer, instead running as fast as she could down a cross-wise hallway to the port side of the vessel. Exactly where she predicted, another sign labeled, "Escape

Craft Antechamber: Port" greeted her. She flew through the door.

"Of course," she spat, finding the same thing as on the starboard side: nothing.

Tiny footsteps preceded Tabby's arrival. "Rae! What are you—? Oh. Nevermind."

16

GSCS *Nightingale*

Elwick's stomach had now tied itself in knots for a completely different reason. With all the fore lifeboats gone and the aft boats inaccessible—if they were even still there or not damaged—and the dozens of escape pods along the keel missing, he was running out of options to get the girls off the *Pearl* before they froze to death. He now needed to extend that fatal one-hour deadline, and in a big way.

Or get there faster.

He sighed. "I'm going to regret this."

"Captain?" Connelly asked.

Elwick turned and addressed the helm as he moved to his command pillar. "Ozzie. What's our current straight-line distance to the *Pearl?*"

The XO checked a display. "We're still really close to twenty-eight thousand light years, Captain, as the crow flies. We didn't make much headway even after those last two jumps because we're swinging wide of Sag A*. Plus stopping for gas in Norma."

Elwick nodded. "Recalculate for fourteen."

Osterland blinked. "I'm sorry, Captain, I didn't quite catch that."

"Recalculate for fourteen thousand light year jumps, Mr. Osterland. Two of them. Connelly," he said, turning to the comms officer, "notify the good folks on the NE collider that we've been forced to cancel our pitstop. And do not, I say again, do not relay the XO's new flight plan to SARCOM." Elwick opened up a screen on his pillar and began a calculation of his own. After a few seconds, he became aware of a silence that had filled the bridge, and that no one had acknowledged his recent orders. He looked up to see every bridge officer looking at one another. "Is there a problem?"

"Well, sir," the XO began, "it would seem you just ordered us to push the Zee Dee core past its redline, and then ordered the comms officer to break protocol. I just… I thought I should verify."

"You have your verification, Navigator. The order to helm is two separate fourteen thousand light year jumps to the same exit point previously calculated. The order to comms is to not relay the change of flight plan, only to notify the plasma station we will not be refueling after all. Acknowledge all."

"Aye aye, sir," "Acknowledged," Osterland and Connelly respectively said in unison. Ozzie turned back to his station and got to work without another word.

Moses touched the 2MC button, connecting him to Engineering. "BM1," he called flatly.

"Crawford here!"

"I need you to configure the plasma injectors for one fourteen thousand light year jump, followed by a second jump of equal distance as soon as humanly possible."

There was that silence again.

"Kelly? Did you copy my last?"

"I'm not exactly sure I did, sir. It sounded like you said fourteen thousand, but I know I didn't hear that right."

"Aye, BM1, you heard correctly. Fourteen thousand."

"Cap'n, I have to point out, a ten-gallon drum can't possibly hold a hunnerdweight o' milk. If it holds the ten gallons it's doin' the best it can!"

"Kelly, I didn't grow up on a farm. I don't know what that—"

"It means our core, as beautiful as she is, ain't rated for even ten K, let alone anythang over that. If my boys down here push 'er to fourteen, she may just blow herself out! I don't know 'bout you, but I don't care ta end up dead in the water, especially out in the Hades Quadrangle!"

"All I need are two jumps."

"Y'all'll be lucky ta get one!"

"If she burns out, she burns out. The RSS *Buker* will send for a tug to tow us home. She's already on her way. Which, it seems, now, is turning out to be a good thing."

More silence.

"Ladies and gentlemen," he said, to everyone listening, "I'm not asking. This is an order. We have two brave young ladies stuck on a boat that's going to kill them in *one* hour if we don't find a way to extend that deadline or reach them sooner. Ozzie, assuming our Zee Dee core doesn't burn out after the first jump, what's our new TTI? Not to our target, merely to our exit point outside the nebula?"

The XO turned to Elwick and answered in a low volume. "Fifty-seven minutes from moment of commencement. That includes a fifty-two-minute cool down time between jumps, which the core will need in order to prep for the next mega-extreme folding event we demand of it. Plus the standard three minutes for magnetron spin up. Then two minutes for quark soup compression. Sorry, but it's not like we have a Zee Dee racing core or a war core that can jump ten K in ten seconds flat. Hell, even those burn out after a few hops. And Captain, I gotta tell you, I'm getting so many red warning lights over here, I feel like I'm about to be arrested."

"Fifty-seven minutes between jumps? That'll get us there in an hour, but that barely gives us time to—" Moses cut himself off, hanging his head. "You've got to be kidding me." He looked up and called out to the heavens. "Give us a break, will you!?"

The bridge crew had all paused what they had been doing and stared at Elwick.

Shaking his head, he addressed the bridge crew, as well as anyone in Engineering within earshot of the still open 2MC circuit. "Even if we get there in only an hour," he all but whispered, "we still need time to navigate at sub-light speeds to the damn ship. That will take a solid half hour even if we push it to a quarter of lightspeed, which isn't anywhere near safe. Maybe we can get by with an eighth in one hour…? Then Dale's team needs time to actually get in, and they'll probably have to cut their way in if the power's out by the time we get there. So we're talking two hours right there. Rae and Tabitha will be two pretty little popsicles by then. I need suggestions and I need them *now!*"

"Well, Captain," the XO began, "I doubt you want to hear this, but we can relay the time crunch to the crew of the *Buker*, let them take it from—"

"Already thought of that, not an option. They won't make it in time. Not even with their fancy war core." Elwick noticed the XO tossing him a side-ways glance. *Is that suspicion?* "I still have the calcs up on my pillar if you want to double check them, Ozzie."

"I believe you, Captain. But it would be more… prudent… if they assumed the rescue."

Ah, not suspicion. A call for reason. "I said it's not an option."

"But Captain—"

"I said no, Ozzie!" That came out a little more forceful than he intended, and he followed up in a softer tone. "No. The *Nightingale* is those girls' only hope." Elwick understood that his XO was trying to talk sense into him without spilling top secret, need-to-know information to the crew. The man was only trying to keep him out of trouble. Possibly more trouble than Moses realized, what with Naval Intelligence involved. The sound advice any Captain would want his trusted Number One to provide. He simply chose to ignore it. The lives of those two young people were vastly more important than his career, or even a few years in jail. He hoped a Board of Inquiry—or possibly a Court Martial—would understand and show leniency due to "selfless intent." There was the matter of putting his crew in mortal danger; even if everyone returned to Earth safe and sound, he would still have to atone for that sin. Regardless of everything, he intended to move forward with this rescue. He couldn't imagine living with himself otherwise. The guilt, it would be overbearing. Like the guilt he harbored because of Alena. "Other ideas. Come on, folks!"

"Well," Max Burgess offered, "one bonus is, what with only two little girls breathing the air in the whole ship, the oxygen/nitrogen supply may last several hours!"

"You're right, Starman," Elwick said, "but the oxygen turning into carbon dioxide isn't really our enemy. It's the exothermal threat; the environmental systems are about to shut down. When that happens, the heat that ship still has will melt away in no time."

"But sir, it's in a nebula. I thought those were super hot."

"They are, Starman," the often silent Lieutenant Kitner interjected, "however, spectral analysis indicates that the plasma in this one, like most nebulae, aren't concentrated enough to warm the hull to human-friendly temperatures."

Elwick scoffed. "How ironic. Even with the *Pearl* floating in an ocean of fiery hydrogen, reaching what, probably upwards of ten million degrees Kelvin…?"

"Twelve point nine, sir, according to these readings."

"Nearly thirteen million degrees Kelvin, and it's just not concentrated enough to keep them warm and alive."

A dainty voice came over the intercom. "Cap'n?"

"Yes, Kelly?"

"It's time ta shut that ship down. Lights an' all. Everythin' but comms and environmental. Yes, even the magnetrons; the hull will keep 'em safe, I already looked at the specs on *Kristin's Vision.* Just tell 'em ta steer clear of any damaged areas, stick to the sections they know. It'll get dark and probably a little scary fer them sweet little gals, but there's no other way ta give us the extra time we need."

"A bold move." Ozzie shrugged. "I like it."

Elwick nodded. "Connelly, get the girls back on the horn."

"Aye aye," Guy replied.

Crawford's voice rang out again. "By the way, the boys're preppin' the core fer two, and only two, fourteen thousand K jumps."

"Thanks, Kelly."

"God help us," she replied, and closed the circuit on her end.

Elwick smiled. "XO, force the nav computer to accept the new flight plan, even if it lights up like a Christmas tree from Hell."

"One step ahead of you, sir!"

17

Emerald Pearl

Now back on the bridge—because they had no idea where else to go at that point—Rae called the *Nightingale* to let them know.

The disembodied voice of Captain Moses rose from hidden speakers around the room. “Perfect. I need you to check on a few things, and that’s the perfect place to do it.”

“Sure,” Tabby quipped. “What do you need to know, Captain?”

“This is very important. I need for you to find out what the temperature is outside the ship.”

“Okay…” Rae looked around. “How do we do that?”

“There should be a screen with that information on one of the consoles. Perhaps the science station.”

“Hold on!” Rae said as her little sister ran from one station to another, being careful to step around all the shiny blankets that littered the floor. The girl finally stood up on a chair and bent over the console. “Temperature!” she said, an index finger on a screen.

“Okay I think we found it, Captain.”

“*I* found it,” Tabitha said quietly.

Rae ignored her. “What does it say, Tabby?”

"It keeps changing. Right now it says two-fifty-one. Now one-ninety-three. One-forty-two. Now it's back up: one-seventy-four..."

"Can you hear my sister? The temperature is bouncing around, but it's over a hundred degrees. That's good, right?"

"Well Rae, we have to check what scale you're set to. Is that in degrees Centigrade or Kelvin?"

"Heck, it could be Fahrenheit," whispered someone on the *Nightingale,* "considering how old the ship is."

"How can we tell that?"

"Look for a C or *K* on the display. Possibly even an *F*."

"Tabby, look for—"

"It's Kevin," the little girl announced, without letting Rae finish.

"*Kelvin*," the Captain's smiling voice corrected.

"Oh. I see the *l* now. Kell-y-vin. What is that?"

"Well, Tabby, it's a scale like Centigrade or Celsius, but one that mainly only scientists and astronomers use. Do you know how cold it has to be in Celsius for water to freeze?"

"That's easy," replied the little girl. "Zero."

"Even I knew that," Rae added.

"That's right," replied the Captain. "Now, zero Celsius is the same as two hundred seventy-three degrees on the Kelvin scale."

"Two hundred seventy-three? But we're only at one-fifty!" screamed Rae. "What does that mean?"

"Well, honey, it means that… um…"

"It means," Tabitha said flatly, "we have to get off this broken-down ship or we're gonna freeze to death."

Rae's lip quivered. "She's right, isn't she, Captain?"

"Yes. I'm afraid she is, Rae."

Rae closed her eyes. *Dear Spirits, if you can hear me, help us.*

"But don't worry, girls, I think I might know how to make your ship stay warm long enough for us to reach you."

"You do?"

"Just tell us what to do, Captain Moses!" Tabby said, staring at Rae.

"Okay, girls, this shouldn't be hard at all. I want you to tell the computer to shut down everything except Communications and Environmental. Don't worry, you—"

"But what about our mom and dad?" Tabitha broke in.

Rae sat up. "Yeah, what about the cryo pods?"

"Don't worry about the cryogenic systems," Moses replied. "Like I mentioned before, they have their own power source and won't shut themselves down when occupied. Your parents and everyone in them will be fine. We do need to keep an eye on them, though. We can do that by telling the computer to alert you if there is any change to their overall status."

"So, the computer will stay on?" Rae asked, only a little scared of hanging out on a completely shut down spaceship.

"The computer is integrated into the ship itself. I don't even think it can be shut down. Based on the schematics we have of the *Pearl's* sister ship, it has its own nuclear battery that should keep it running for several decades yet."

Tabitha perked up. "Nuclear power! Can we use that to keep warm?"

"Well, the Carbon-14 inside the computer's battery is only the size of a walnut, and you probably can't break open the diamond casing even if you wanted to, even if you could get to it! Sorry, Tabby. But that's terrific thinking, though!"

"Nutters!"

"Plus, that would probably be dangerous and stupid!" added Rae.

"Well," Osterland interjected, "it's just beta decay, so it probably wouldn't hurt you unless you ate it or breathed it in real deep. But *I* wouldn't mess with it!"

A pause. "Well," Tabitha poked Rae. "Go ahead, shut this old boat down."

Rae collected herself in a chair one console over from her sister. "*Emerald Pearl*," she began, "I want you to shut down everything on this ship except the communication system and the…" She drew a blank.

"En-vi-rohhhh—" Tabby whispered.

"Environ-mental system. Oh, and please make sure the cryo pods stay on, too."

"Tell us if there is any change to them!" added Tabitha.

The voice of the woman in the computer came over a different set of speakers than the Captain's voice, and echoed from the hallway that led off the bridge. *"Command authorization required. Say or enter command code, or use biometric identification to complete this request."*

"Um, Captain Moses? We need some kind of code."

"I was afraid of that. I'm sorry but we don't know the captain's personal command codes, and no computer I know of will be able to crack it in time… You said Captain Timmins', um, body is nearby?"

"Yes," Rae replied, a lump growing in her throat and anxiety building in her veins. "Whyyy?"

"I'm afraid You're going to need to let the computer scan his eye, face, or finger."

Rae glanced over at Tabitha, who stared at her.

"You're kidding, right?" Tabby asked.

"I'm sorry, but I'm not."

Tabitha looked at Rae.

Rae looked at Tabitha. "I'm not touching a dead body!"

"You touched Miss Norstrom."

"That was before she died!"

"All you have to do is sit him up, girls," Moses explained. "The computer should be able to locate him no matter where he is, but he can't be prone."

"He can't be what?" asked Rae.

"Lying down. If he's lying down, the computer will assume he is incapacitated, and this won't work even if it *can* see him."

"But what if the—" someone on the *Nightingale* whispered, but his voice trailed off.

Captain Moses seemed to reply, whispering, "Let's hope not, but I'm sure they'll be able to do that if they have to."

And then a tiny female voice reached Rae's ears. "The only other option is fer them ta override the system directly from engineerin'."

"The entire engine room could be in vacuum," the first voice whispered.

"Well?" Tabby shouted. "What are you waiting for?"

Her yell jerked Rae away from the discussion on the rescue ship. "Tabby, I already said I'm not touching him!"

Sis rolled her eyes and hopped off her chair. "Fine. *I'll* do it."

"Tabby wait!"

She ignored Rae, of course, and moved to Captain Timmins' head. The little girl bent down, grabbed the dead man by his shoulder lapels, took an enormous breath, and gave it a go.

He barely budged.

"A little help here!" she yelled.

Rae closed her eyes. What was their alternative? Going into the engine room, where there's probably no air to breathe, and doing… what? Overriding a computer they barely knew how to operate in the first place? She let out a guttural yell of her own. "Fine! Hold on!" Rae stood up, breathed deep, and rung her hands.

"He's going to rot before you get over here!"

"Shut up! Gross!" Rae trudged over to where Tabby tapped her foot with her hands on her hips. "Just give me a second, this is my first dead guy!"

"More like…" Sis counted on her fingers.

"My first time touching a dead guy, alright!?"

"He hasn't been dead very long. He's still warm!"

"Oh, Great Goddess. I'm going to throw up."

"Throw up later! Just help me! You're bigger!" Tabby bent down and took one shoulder.

Rae sighed and grabbed the other one.

"You count."

"Okay, ready? One…"

Both girls chanted in unison, "two… three!" Both lifted at once, and Captain Timmins head and shoulders began to rise, then stopped.

"Pull harder!" Tabby yelled.

"I'm trying!" As Rae tugged, she decided this had to be the absolute grossest thing she had ever done in her life. Worse than that time she had stop Daddy from bleeding to death on their boat. That had been gross too, but this was on another level!

"Girls?" Captain Moses again. "How is it coming?"

Rae scrambled behind Captain Timmins' back and shoved all her might into him. "We've… almost… got him… up!" she grunted.

Tabby stood between his legs and pulling both arms now.

Finally, the dead man sat in an upright position, with Rae still pushing on his back. "Alright!" she shouted. "He's up, Captain Moses, now what?"

"Tell the computer to verify command authorization, Captain Timmins, and execute previous request."

Rae called out to the *Emerald Pearl* and repeated the exact words Captain Moses had just said.

"Command authorization required. Say or enter command code or use biometric identification to complete this request."

Rae's head slumped. "It didn't work."

"Okay, we were wondering about that. Rae, you're going to have to open his eyes. Or at least one of them."

"Oh no! No, no, no, I'm not—"

"Just make sure he doesn't fall over, Rae!" Tabby had already grabbed Captain Timmins' head, and used her thumbs to pry his eyelids open.

"Oh Goddess, I can't look!"

"*Emerald Pearl*," Tabby yelled, "verify command authorization, Captain Timmins! And um... execute previous request. Please!"

A beam shot from somewhere in the ceiling, and a thin line of bright, blue light poured down both of the dead man's eyes.

"Command authorization verified," the computer announced. *"Shutting down all systems,"*

Rae heard whirring noises like motors spinning down. The comforting, bright white lights on the bridge went dark, and Rae's universe went completely red once again, her retinas overpowered by the stark color of the nebula surrounding her and Sis on three sides. The gory task now complete, she and Sis didn't hesitate to jump up and back away. Captain Timmins' head hit the floor with a thud. "Tabby!"

"What? He can't feel it."

Before Rae could respond, all the pretty, colorful screens and gauges on the consoles winked out. Her heart leapt for a moment, but then the computer continued.

"Communications Systems status: active, fully functional. Environmental system status: active, some systems in need of attention. List of systems in need of attention is available upon request. Temperature control system active, fully functional. Atmospheric handling system and basic atmospheric functions are failing. Cryogenic System status: active, fully functional. Cryogenic hibernation pods one and two are open and ready. Pods three through eight now operating on internal power. Pods thirteen through sixteen need attention. Pods nine through twelve are inoperable. Notifications regarding Cryogenic System status will commence, starting time: now."

In a matter of seconds, the ship became practically silent. Rae hadn't realized how loud it had been; she had gotten used to the "standard" noise of the *Pearl* to the point she hadn't even heard it anymore. She held her breath.

Tabitha jumped up onto Rae and wrapped her small arms around her neck, toppling both of them to the ground.

"Tabby!" Rae yelled, but Sis only whined softly and squirmed. She wrapped her own arms around her sister and squeezed tightly.

Captain Moses' voice sounded now even more welcome than before. "Girls? Are you okay?"

"Everything got dark! And quiet!" Tabby exclaimed, thankfully not in Rae's ear.

"It's okay, don't worry." His soft tone brought comfort. "Do you still have gravity?"

Rae's nose scrunched up. *Why wouldn't we?* She whispered to Tabby, "I didn't even know that was something you could turn off! We're not floating in the air, if that's what you mean, Captain."

"Good! That means the *Pearl* is fitted with grav plates that don't require constant energy. That will make things easier on all of us. Okay, Rae, now ask the computer once more how much time is left before the power runs out."

"*Emerald Pearl*, how long before the power runs out now?"

"Two hours, twelve minutes, thirty-four seconds." The girl waited for the Captain to give further instructions, but he did not. "Captain Moses?"

"Sorry, girls, we can't hear the computer very well, what did it say?"

"She said a little more than two hours," Tabby hollered.

Cheers could be heard over the line. "That's wonderful! That gives us the time we need, but just barely." The Captain sounded very pleased, which in turn pleased Rae. Keeping adults happy was important, as such things came with benefits. Not to mention less punishment. Keeping this particular adult happy was of utmost importance to her, as he was, right now at least, their only means of getting her and her family out of this incredible situation.

Well, at least three of them.

How am I going to tell Sis that Daddy's... dead? She took a deep breath. A heavy blanket of dread constricted her chest. The thought of going on without their father physically hurt her heart. *How are we going to make it without him?*

Captain Moses continued. "I know it's probably a little scary, but don't worry. Sit tight and we'll be there as soon as we can, okay?"

"Promise?" Tabitha asked.

Elwick's voice sounded filled with sincerity and hope. "I promise."

"Can you keep talking to us until you get here?" Tabitha asked, releasing her grip on Rae and climbing to a seated position.

"Sure girls. If not me, one of my shipmates will be here any time you need us. Just call out, we'll leave the channel open. We do have to conduct a couple of more Zee Dee jumps, however, and comms may be interrupted for a few seconds each time. You probably won't even notice. Do you understand what I mean by 'jumping'?"

"Well, duh," Tabby muttered. "Does he think we're in kindergarten?" Sis stood and moved to one of the chairs. *Good call,* Rae thought, *this floor is cold!*

Captain Moses must have heard her. "I'm sorry, I didn't mean to insult you. We're about to make another jump here in… what did Kelly say?" he asked, surely speaking to one of his crew.

Another voice broke the air that Rae wasn't yet familiar with. "Ten before Kelly's team is ready, Captain, then five more for the magnetrons—"

"Fifteen minutes," the Captain said, interrupting the man. "When it's complete, we'll be fourteen thousand light years closer to you."

Wow, fourteen thousand! Rae mouthed silently; she thought that sounded like a crazy whopper of a distance. Even her sister's eyes got big, so she figured she must be right about that number being huge. Rae felt a little confidence gathering, thanks to Captain Moses' reassurances. She trusted him immediately. Something about his voice... *Everything might end up alright after all,* she thought.

Tabitha hugged herself and looked around the room, then under the nearer consoles, like she was making sure there no monsters hid there.

"Afraid of the dark?" Rae teased.

Tabitha turned and threw a stare that could bore through steel.

Rae couldn't help but giggle.

"Do you think we will be able to see Captain Moses' ship coming?"

Rae intuitively looked out the wide front viewport. "I think so."

"But what if they come from behind us?"

Tabby was right. From the bridge they could only see out the front of the vessel. They needed to get somewhere they could see in every direction. "I know!" she exclaimed. "The Observation Dome!"

Tabitha's eyes lit up. "Yeah!" Tabitha took off.

Rae ran after her. "Captain Moses, we're going to the Observation Dome so we can watch you come pick us up!"

"Oh. Okay. But remember, it will probably be two hours."

"We know!" yelled Tabitha. "We'll get some snacks!"

"Wherever you go, don't get too far from a communications console, alright?" Moses instructed. "I want to be able to get ahold of you if I need to."

"Okay, Captain," she called over her shoulder. When she turned back around, she plowed into her sister, and they both tumbled to the ground. "Oh my Goddess, Tabby! Are you okay? You have to quit stopping in front of me!"

"I'm not going out there."

Rae turned to look at the exit to the bridge. Darkness lived there. With all the systems shut down to conserve power for heat, only a few sporadic lights now held that darkness back. Just outside the bridge, in what she could only think to call the "office area," a tiny white light in the ceiling made a circle on the floor. *Ceiling?* Just like floors were called 'decks', Rae knew sailors called ceilings another word, but she couldn't remember it at the moment. It wasn't important. She leaned over and saw, beyond the bridge, several tiny yellow lights running down the hallways at knee-level. Barely enough to see by. Sis was probably onto something; the idea of barreling down those dark tunnels rose the hair on the nape of her neck.

An idea popped into Rae's head. She looked around the bridge. "Maybe we can find a flashlight?" She walked around the consoles, again being careful to give the bloody bodies a wide berth. She looked under the consoles, on the sides. Nothing. Finally, her gaze scanned the rear wall, the only one that wasn't a giant window. *Oh! Always the last place you look!* She found a handheld light mounted next to a First-Aid kit. She yanked it off the wall, and made the mistake of turning it on while looking into the business end of the device. The brilliance destroyed Rae's vision for several seconds. Her sister giggled while she blinked it off. "Come on, you scaredy little tabby-cat!"

"I want Teddy!"

Rae halted in her tracks. "What?"

"I said I want Teddy!"

Rae rolled her eyes. Tabitha's bear was… where? *Oh yeah.* In the giant fenced rooms, in the personal storage lockers. It will surely be dark down there. Super dark! "Tabby, do we have to go get it?"

"I. Want. My. Bear."

She sighed. *Wait a second... my book! My book of Earth prayers is in there!* "Alright, let's go. I want to pick something up too!" Rae exclaimed.

"We have to go down to Floor Four," Tabby said.

"Yeah, I know. Down in the cargo bay."

Tabitha took her sister's hand. "Don't go thinking this means we're friends or anything. I just need to hold someone's hand if we're going walking in the dark."

Rae smiled. "Don't worry, I know we're still enemies."

"Well, I wouldn't go *that* far. Just not friends."

"Deal." With the powerful flashlight burning like a tiny sun to melt the dark away, the girls made their way toward the bowels of the dying ship.

18

GSCS *Nightingale*

"Officer of the Deck, you have the conn. I have a SAR team to check on, and…" he sighed, "I guess I'll be paying Doc Galloway a visit, too."

"Ooo," the XO said. "Enjoy that."

Moses scoffed. "I will not." He couldn't use the ladder adjacent to his cabin and the bridge; it only serviced Decks One and Two, and he needed to make a fast break to Deck Three within one minute; he would be damned if he was still negotiating ladders when the Great Belly Button Dive overwhelmed him.

He jogged toward the Wardroom. Halfway down the passageway was installed the ship's only lift. It allowed the ship's company and crew to reach all three decks of the *Nightingale*, but it moved awfully slow. Much too slow for Moses at the moment. An elevator, even one as huge as theirs, might do him in as well.

Elwick flew down a nearby ladder, putting his feet on the rails rather than the steps. He arrived at Deck Two in six seconds and Deck Three in six more. But hitting the deck so quickly *hurt*. His knees reminded him he wasn't an eighteen-year-old starman anymore.

He exited the ladder, and found himself just off-center toward the starboard side of the *Nightingale's* Multipurpose

Bay. The bay made up the forward half of the ship on Deck Three; tunnels on the starboard and port sides of the ship led to the engine room, which took up the rest of the deck. Moses heard familiar noises coming from one of the tunnels, like something metal was being banged around. His Machinemen—or "Knuckledraggers" as they had more-or-less affectionately been nicknamed, to include his sister-in-law—were probably fixing something he hadn't been notified of yet. And probably something he didn't want to know about until change-of-mission. He ignored it. For now.

Adjacent to the ladder he had just flown down lay the slow lift he hadn't used a moment ago, which carried equipment up to Decks One and Two. For some reason it carried a bin of what looked like junk. He might go to the XO, but he was sure that, if he just waited a bit, it would disappear by itself. His crew did well to help him keep a tidy and uncluttered boat. He simply had to give them time and not harp on them.

Directly ahead, a full American football field away, set the over-sized forward airlock at the bow of the *Nightingale*. Large enough to drive a 20th Century tank in with room to spare, it also doubled as the Boatswain's Locker. Historically, on sea-going vessels, the "Bosun's Locker" had been used for centuries to conduct off-the-books counseling for crewmembers in need of an attitude adjustment. Like Pruitt. Of course, not a single soul had or would ever get tossed out of an airlock on Moses' watch, but the "youngins" still weren't absolutely sure of that. Especially when he handed them over to Dale or Kelly and said, "Do what you have to do, I never saw any of you."

On the starboard and port sides of the bay, several wheeled vehicles of various sizes had been "tied down." *Shouldn't be needing any of these babies today,* Moses hoped. A small, two-man aircraft with the wings folded up ninety degrees set next to a large transport. "X-terminator" had been emblazed on its nose, along with an eye, a red mouth, and a mean set of shark's teeth. Elwick eyed its two currently empty missile racks, longing for the day craft like this wouldn't be issued to vessels like the *Nightingale.* There hadn't been much more than light skirmishes in distant colony systems since the war had ended, but Elwick knew all too well that peace was a fleeting luxury; the threat of conflict would be ever-present, as long as humans existed in the universe. For now, multi-purpose vessels like the *Nightingale* could focus on humanitarian missions rather than war. And Moses promised himself he would enjoy the "inter-war period" as long as it lasted.

Near where Elwick had entered the bay, opposite the airlock, set the portable sick bay. Made up of three modular sections, it had been designed to be joined together for easy installation and removal into vessels of all types. The center section housed the surgical center. A set of double doors facing the large bay allowed gurneys to be wheeled in and out quickly. The port-side section was the "medicine shack" where the pharmaceuticals remained locked up 24/7. Moses' destination lay to starboard: the recovery room and the physician's office. Galloway's office. "Might as well get on with it, Moe," he muttered to himself.

He removed his hat, as is customary before entering a ship's infirmary, and entered a short hallway. To his right, on the far side of the operating room, a bouncing black pony tail caught his eye. Lieutenant Alyssa Jorgensen, the Head Nurse, busied herself attending to one of the thousands of things nurses and corpsmen do for which they are wholly unappreciated, in addition to preparing the sick bay to take on casualties when they reach the *Emerald Pearl*. Moses all but tip-toed by.

Doc Galloway's voice startled him. "No need to step gingerly around here, Cap'n."

Now in her doorway, Elwick turned to see her stand up from behind her pretty white desk in her office, which doubled as the examination room. "Oh, I just didn't want to—"

"Didn't want Alyssa to know you were admiring her teeny white jumper?"

He rolled his eyes. "Of course not. I just didn't want to interrupt her. She always drops everything she's doing when she sees me."

"Give the girl a break," Doc said, reaching behind him and un-dogging the heavy door to the pod. "She's downright starstruck."

Elwick rolled his eyes at her sarcastic remark as the pressure door closed, sealing them in. "Closing doors now? That bad, huh?"

"Not closing it for you," she replied. "*Because* of you, though. Ya keep the blasted pressure so low on this damn rust bucket I can't even light a match!" She lowered her large frame into the chair behind her desk, which creaked like it wanted to give up and die.

"Well of course I do, safety regulations—"

"Watch your ears." A few virtual buttons on her desktop beeped at her touch, and a low whir emanated from a vent in the wall.

In seconds, Elwick had to work his jaw to equalize the pressure on his ear drums. "Speaking of safety regulations, you know that's against—"

"Spare me." A thin, black stick then appeared out of nowhere. A tiny, blue light brought the glowing cherry at the end of Doc's cigarette to life. "Write me up if you want," she croaked.

Moses only shook his head and looked for a place to sit.

The air now pressurized enough for things to burn properly, Galloway savored a long, deliberate draw. Her eyelids closed, and she reveled in whatever sensation tobacco provided, something completely alien to Moses. A few seconds later her gaze found him again, and she alighted him with a stare that told him to sit down and keep his mouth shut, for he was about to get an earful.

Moses pulled a small, wheeled stool over to her desk and did as instructed.

"You've been enjoying all these super jumps we've been making, haven't ya?"

"Not really." Moses shrugged. "Probably just low blood sugar from skipping dinner."

"Don't give me that shit. You think people haven't taken notice over these last few months? Hell, even I got queasy on that last one. What are we doing, seventy-five hundred a hop?"

"The last two were seventy-five. The next two are going to be fourteen thousand each. We have a deadline now."

"Fourteen!" She shook her head, holding the cigarette glowing-end up to keep the ashes in place. "Must be a real emergency to push 'er that hard."

Moses nodded. "Life or death."

"So, the unusual."

"It's a little different this time."

"And you really can't figure out why it's gotten worse." It wasn't a question.

"Sorry?"

"Why the bigger hops all but do you in?"

"Oh. That. What did the tests show?"

"Tests?"

"The ones I took last month, when all this started getting, well, noticeable?"

"Oh, those tests," she said, then chuckled.

"What's so funny?"

"You actually think I looked at the results?"

"Why wouldn't you?"

Gwendolyn Galloway leaned over her desk. "You just had your annual physical not three months ago, and you think something's changed?"

"Something *has* changed. Even the smaller jumps make me lose my appetite. Look at me, I've lost ten kilos since then!"

"You look pretty darn good to me. Back to the weight the corps wants you at."

Elwick sighed. "Why'd you call me down here Doc? Just to tease me?"

She folded her hands atop her beautiful, amazing, clean desk. Not that Moses was envious or anything. "Tell me, Cap'n, when's the last time you talked that pretty little bride o' yours?"

"Alright Doc, look, if that's what this is about—"

"Alright, alright," Galloway said, throwing up her hands, "I'll stay outta your personal business, Moe."

"Thank you." He scoffed. "Honestly Doc, you had me scared there for a minute! I thought for sure my results came back with, well, I don't want to jinx myself, but something really bad. I would've never come down had I known—"

The electronic Boatswain's pipe sounded attention, interrupting him. "All hands, this is the Officer of the Deck. Prepare for interstellar space folding. Jump number three will occur in one minute. And it will be a whopper," Kitner added, his disembodied voice echoing across the bay and back in to sickbay.

"I'll bet," Doc quipped.

Moses ignored her and finished his sentence. "—Had I known you were going to give me the third degree and not a diagnosis. Now, if that's all, I have a lot of things to—"

"Not so fast, Cap'n Stubborn." Galloway stood, walked around her desk, and leaned in close to Elwick's ear. "Now hear me, you little bugger, and hear me good. You've been out in The Black long enough. After this mission, you get your arse home to that little Sheila before the both of you regret it."

Elwick pulled his head back to look into the almost empathetic eyes of his ship's surgeon. If she had simply blinked, that would have been something. Moses's nose crinkled at the intense smell of cigarette smoke emanating from her very pores. He looked away and tried his best not to breathe. He felt his face flush. A little bit enraged, a lot more embarrassed. "I thought you said you were gonna stay out of my business?"

"And I thought you were a man of better character than to leave your little lady back home to fend for herself after the worst tragedy a parent could imagine!" Galloway straightened up, returned to her desk, and sat down, to the lament of her chair. Without another word, she touched a couple of buttons, and a holographic graph with data appeared silently over her desk. She took another long draw from her cancer stick, put it out, then returned the room to its former pressure.

Elwick popped his ears again as he waited for her to continue with whatever wisdom she felt necessary to impart. But she remained silent, and instead focused intently on the data.

Elwick stared at her. "Are you really trying to tell me that my pulling away from Zoey is turning me into a seasick greenhorn? And what, that eventually I won't even be able to manage even a thousand light year jump, let alone a fourteen thousand?"

Another Boatswain's pipe. "All hands, this is the Officer of the Deck…"

Galloway tossed him an evil smile, full of schadenfreude.

Kitner's voice continued: "Initiating jump number three in five… four… three… two… one."

It was bad.

Sliding into his navel would have been a delight. The one time he did open his eyes during the ordeal he saw Doc Galloway having a hell of a time with it too, but at least she wasn't retching plaid poetry all over the floor. Usually, he could keep his wits about him, even though no one probably could once you went two dimensional. Kelly would ensure him it was four-dimensional, but he could never fully wrap his head around the time thing.

But this jump, which represented a distance farther than he ever experienced before—at least while conscious—his mind went in the direction of peanut butter. Or maybe cantankerous. His body went fuchsia. Or maybe doormat. He honestly couldn't tell, he only knew it hurt. Was that even pain? Could you still feel pain if you didn't have a body anymore? If you were nothing but an anger of affable floating in a deep, belligerent greeting flame of football candle?

Moses what are you talking about!? he shouted to himself in a brief moment of clarity. He probably hadn't shouted; he didn't have his vocal cords back yet. They still existed somewhere with the rest of the ship and everyone on it, in a googolplex of locations spread across the vastness of the multiverse.

"Moses…" came an ethereal voice.

How long will this go on? In another moment, he had his answer. A sharp sting woke him. Doc Galloway's face filled his vision. He blinked. Had he really made it back to the real world?

Doc slapped his face. *Again?* His eyes burst open. She appeared again. Elwick identified the overhead of a sick bay module behind her. *Pretty sure I'm not dreaming.*

"There he is," she said.

"Doc. That was…"

"Bad, I know. The systems 'round here even had a bad go at it. My desk hasn't even woke back up yet!"

Moses turned his head to see Doc up-righting the stool he had been sitting on. A mess of yellowish liquid on the floor caught his eye. He about threw up again when the smell of bile assaulted his nostrils.

"Don't worry 'bout that, I'll have one of the corpsmen clean it up."

"Tell them I'm sorry."

"Eh, I'll tell 'em it was me. No need for the Cap'n to fall off the peak o' the mountain in the eyes of the youngins. I'm just glad it happened here and not in front o' the whole crew."

"Thanks, Doc."

She waved it off. "Just call your lassie, and we'll call it even."

This again. He had hoped he had left this argument in the previous parsec.

"It's eating ya up inside, and ya won't even admit it. What you felt just now? That's stress. Jumping that far made my mind twist in circles! Hell, I just had a somersault with me third grade teacher, Mrs. Wellington—and then she turned into a ferret for a minute!—but I can tell it did a lot worse of a number on you! But hey," she said, holding up her hands, "far be it from me from give the Old Man advice on 'is personal life."

Moses remained silent. What could he say? Honestly, he didn't feel like saying anything, what with his stomach still in knots.

"Now if you need help finding the door, I'll call in Alyssa; she can lead yuhs right to the airlock for all I care. Otherwise, I've got a lot of test results to *not* go over." With that, she went back to studying her display again.

Moses sighed, then climbed gingerly to his feet. He waited a moment to make sure he could stay upright, then made his way to the exit. Before unsealing the pressure door, he paused. "Do you realize you are the absolute most insubordinate officer I've ever had the pleasure of serving with?"

She looked up. "Do you realize you've put up with me mouth longer than any other commanding officer I've ever had?"

"Now *that* I can believe!"

"Lucky for me, *you* don't want a doc who likes to hold your hand and give out lollipops to your crew. You want someone who's gonna give it to ya straight and not wrap it in a pretty, shit-glow bow. And there ain't nobody who's gonna tell ya to get your scrawny, stubborn, cowardly ass off this boat and be the husband you once were to that little gal you claim to love so much, except *me!*"

Moses' fists closed, and his blood began to boil.

"Go ahead, get mad! That's perfectly natural when someone tells ya something about yourself that you don't wanna hear." She smiled. "Now either get out or toss me in the brig, one of the two!" She went back to ignoring him again.

Moses' words came out in a whisper through clenched teeth. "Now you listen to me, Doctor Gwendolyn Galloway..." He took a deep breath, and pointed his finger at her. "This! Is! A! *SHIP!* Not a *BOAT!*"

A silence hung in the air for a moment, and the steely stares between the two could have melted a hole in the graphene-titanium alloy plating on the *Nightingale's* hull. But then Galloway thew her head back and belly laughed like Moses had never heard her laugh before. It might have been the first time he had ever seen any expression on her face other than a scowl since she had joined the crew two years ago. He didn't even know her face was capable of doing that. It made Elwick chuckle.

"You old sea dog! Get outta here! Git before I tell Alyssa you're the one who dropped a curbside quiche on me floor!"

She shook her head. “Go on! There’s two whole shiploads of people who need you, Moses Elwick!” Then she winked. “You’ve made an old woman’s day!”

19

Emerald Pearl

An excitement rose within Rae as she *finally* got to fly down one of the eloquent, spiral staircases again. But the sensation ended too quickly; Rae and Tabitha could only go down a single floor because the stair didn't wind all the way to the fourth level. The girls wandered around the third floor for several minutes looking for a way down. *Not even Tabby could remember everything,* Rae mused.

They walked past the cryo chamber twice before finding what they were looking for, a bulkhead door that read "CARGO BAY: Deck Four."

"Deck! Floors are called decks in the Navy!" Rae exclaimed. *I knew that,* she chided herself. *Didn't I?*

"Is that why they're numbered backwards?" Tabitha asked. She turned the handle, and the large door popped open. "The first floor is at the bottom on a building, not the top."

"You're right, they *are* backwards! I never thought about that before," Rae said, as Tabby leaned backwards and pulled the large door open. Rae shined her light into the dark opening and saw a silver, corrugated platform, but nothing else. The darkness seemed to swallow up the light anywhere else she pointed the beam. Leaning across the door's threshold and shining her light downward revealed a staircase that descended into a blackness as deep as when she first woke up. *Great. More scary stuff.*

She stepped through and onto the landing. Tabitha squeezed her hand tighter, and gently pulled her back. "Don't worry," Rae consoled, "it will be okay. You want your bear, don't you?"

"Yes," came the soft reply.

Her footfalls on the metal platform echoed in the silence, deeper now that most of the ship's systems had been shut down. She got a sinking feeling in her gut that it must be a long way to the floor. Rae shined the flashlight over the railing to see what they were up against. She breathed again when her beam danced feebly upon items that didn't look all that far away: civilian and military storage containers, palettes of unknown items wrapped in plastic, and some of the larger personal effects of the passengers that couldn't fit into their assigned cargo cages.

"Wow. That's a long way down!" Tabby's voice echoed much louder than their footsteps. She let go of Rae's hand and now had a death grip on her sister's blouse.

"It's okay, Tabby, it's okay," Rae assured, more for herself than for her sister. "Teddy's down there. We'll be in and out in a flash. Okay?"

Sis took two deep breaths and finally said, "okaaay," but her voice sounded tiny. Frightened.

"I can't believe you're afraid of the dark!"

"I'm *not* afraid of the dark. Daddy says so. I'm just afraid of what's *in* the dark."

Rae shook her head. "You're silly, Tabby." She wanted to tell Sis she was frightened, too. Scared out of her mind, even! But she needed to be strong for Tabitha's sake. Otherwise, they'd both run out of here screaming, and there would be no bear and no book. Ever!

"Whew," Rae said, upon reaching the first landing. "Look, we're halfway there!"

Tabitha looked over the railing into the inky blackness. "No we're not!" she exclaimed, her voice echoing through the bay.

"Shhh!" Rae hushed.

Tabitha's face crinkled. "Why are you shushing me? It's not like someone's going to hear us and we're going to get into trouble!"

"I don't know. I just feel like we're sneaking around or something."

"We're not. We're here to get our own stuff! It's not like we're stealing anything!"

"You're right, Tabby. Let's find our locker. And get out of here!"

"Right behind you," Tabby said, and grabbed the tail of her sister's blouse again, but this time without the death grip.

Tabitha's bravery—or apparent bravery—made Rae not so frightened, and the girls moved at a faster pace down the long staircase.

They flew by one landing and reached another.

"Geez, how far down does this thing go?" Tabby asked.

Rae shined her light down the next flight, and found the floor only one flight further down. "There it is! Only one more set of stairs."

"Thank God! And your Goddess! I was starting to get *bored*."

Once they finally reached the deck, Rae had to pause. *Now which way do they go?* She shined her tiny but powerful torch around the vast room. At one end of the bay, her beam glinted on a narrow stripe consisting of yellow and black diagonal bars running from floor to ceiling. She guessed that must be the bay's airlock. The passenger lockers would not be in that direction. "Okay, I think our family locker is…" She turned in a circle. "This way!" Rae started toward the same wall as the door far above in which they had entered. She had left it open, and a feeble light poured in from above. Little hands tugged gently on Rae's blouse, not stopping her, just trying to stay close.

After a few steps, the light above disappeared. Rae stopped, and Sis ran into her. Rae backed up two steps, and the light reappeared.

"What are you doing?"

"The wall should be here."

"Why?"

Rae checked again. The high-ceilinged room definitely continued underneath the deck above. "I don't know, I was just expecting a wall, that's all." They continued on, between large containers on either side that Rae couldn't see over. She honestly had no idea if she was leading Tabitha in the right direction, but she figured they would find out soon enough. How big could the bay be, after all? Behind her, Sis gasped. "Tabby? What is it?"

"I thought I heard something," she whispered.

Rae shined her light all around, hoping to illuminate whatever evil lurked in the dark aisles between the boxes and stacked pallets, waiting to eat them. After a moment she relaxed. *Don't be silly. No one's down here but you and Tabby!* But the cold silence and large open space tore into her limbic system and made her shiver, despite the logical part of her brain trying its hardest to rationalize the situation.

"Rae, I changed my mind, I want to go back upstairs."

The light fell up on some wire fencing just up ahead. "Look! There they are!" Rae grabbed her sister's hand and ran, nearly dragging the little girl to the far wall. There they found a long row of wire cages, each as huge as Rae's bedroom back on Earth, sporting a yellow number on a gray panel.

Tabitha let out a dramatic, deep sigh. "Hooray! Ours is number fourteen."

"Fourteen! Yes, I remember that."

"Now that I said it, you remember."

Rae let that one go. Her sister had been right, but she wasn't going to tell her that. She did remember their family locker was somewhere in the middle of the row. She craned her neck upward to read each number as she passed. "Seven, eight… Eleven… Thirteen and… here it is."

Rae and Tabby stared at the cage before them. It boasted a large "14" stenciled in yellow spray paint. Rae flashed the light over their family's belongings, easily seen through the wire walls of the cage. The other passengers' belongings could also be seen in the other cages.

Tabitha looked at Rae. "Well? Let us in."

Rae's face drooped.

"Where's the key, Sis?" Tabitha asked flatly, as if she already knew the answer. Which she did. "Daddy's got it, doesn't he?"

Rae said nothing.

"Oh, that's just the antelope's antlers!" Tabitha's voice echoed again. "You're supposed to be the responsible big sister!"

"How was I supposed to know we'd have to come down here without Mom or Dad?" Rae yelled back.

Tabby released a guttural growl. "So stupid! Look! Mr. Fluffles is in *that* bag right *there!*" She pointed to a brown satchel.

Rae saw the bag. She saw their mother pack it. It contained the bear, some coloring books, and other odds-and-ends. *So close. But so far away.* She tugged on the door's handle. It would not turn. Rae tugged fiercely. No luck. She rocked the handle back and forth in desperation. The door merely rattled and banged.

Banged? Yes, it had! That meant it wasn't sealed tight! Rae shined the light on the lower portion of the door and jostled the handle as before. It wobbled under her force. She dropped to her knees and sat the flashlight down. She grabbed the wire with her fingers and pushed and pulled the door back and forth. To her surprise, it pulled away, but only a little. "Tabby, look!" The crack Rae could make while pulling wasn't big enough for her to fit through, but perhaps enough for a certain petite Third-Year Educata student to do so.

"Oh, bully!" Tabitha exclaimed, an expression of delight which she must have picked up from some ancient holovid. She stuck one black saddle-shoe and white ankle sock inside the cage. "Pull it out a little more!" she said as she forced one bare leg through the hole up to her thigh.

"I'm trying!" Rae tucked her left leg underneath her, pressed her right foot against the wall of the cage and pulled with her arms.

Tabby sat down with bent knees and awkwardly flipped over on her stomach in a push-up position, her knees boring into Rae's leg.

"Oww!"

"Sorry."

Rae was glad she had worn her tight blue leggings on the trip; Tabitha's maneuver would surely have given her a "rug burn" had she gone bare-legged like Tabby.

Sis had both legs inside now, and scooted backwards. She reached the point where she needed to squeeze her shoulders through. "Make it bigger!"

"It's really hard!" Rae's fingers hurt. Bad.

Tabby wiggled the last few inches. "Bigger!"

"I can't!" Rae said, and let go. The door banged into Tabby's head.

"Oww!" Sis yelled, and yanked herself completely inside the cage.

"Sorry! I couldn't hold it anymore!" Rae rubbed her aching fingers.

"You did that on purpose!"

"No I didn't! Why do you always think I'm trying to be mean to you?"

"Because Jamie's mean to *you!* I'm the only one *you* can be mean to!"

Rae blinked. That wasn't true. Was it? Did she take things out on her little sister sometimes, just because she could? Tabby was definitely right about their big brother. But Rae wouldn't call him mean. Ornery maybe. "Tabby, I'm really not trying to hurt you."

"Whatever." Sis looked around, still rubbing the side of her head in front of one pigtail. "Shine the light over here!"

Rae didn't want to subject her tender fingers to any more trauma, so she clumsily picked up the flashlight with her knuckles and shined the beam in Tabitha's direction.

Tabitha grabbed her brown satchel first and dug out what she wanted. “Mr. Fluffles!” She squealed with glee, and hugged the stuffed toy tightly in her arms.

“Tabby, look in that little red suitcase over there,” Rae said, and shined the light on it. “I want to you get that ‘Earth Prayers’ book that mom gave me.”

“You want a *book?*”

“Yes. It calms me down.”

Sis chortled. “Whatever.” The little monkey climbed over the luggage and touched some electronic buttons on the front of the hard plastic container.

Rae heard a series of beeps and then the sound of a small latch clicking open. She was thankful Tabitha remembered the combination. Rae couldn’t remember it right now for the life of her. *The little brat does have a great memory.*

Tabitha opened the suitcase and dug around a bit.

“I think it’s under my green dress if I remember right.”

“You probably don’t.”

Rae let that slide, too.

“I can’t find it.”

“It *has* to be there,” Rae answered. “Look again. And don’t make a mess.”

Tabitha ignored the instruction, or perhaps did exactly the opposite of what Rae said intentionally, in retaliation for the door plowing into her head. She turned the case on end, flinging clothes all about.

“I said don’t make a mess!”

Tabitha turned ‘round and ‘round and squinted her eyes in the torchlight’s bright beam. “*This* book?”

“Yes, that’s it! Now pick everything up.”

"Don't boss me around!" Tabitha spat, "I'm gonna let Daddy take care of it, I want OUTTA HERE! Come on, Mr. Fluffles, we're—"

>*Thud*<

Rae's hair stood up on the back of her neck. *What was that?* She whirled around and flung her beam into the dark. Nothing but boxes. Pallets.

"Rae! Stop it! I know you're just trying to scare me!"

Rae started to protest, but perhaps she shouldn't? If Tabby wasn't scared, that would be one less heart attack to worry about. And the Good Spirits know she was scared enough for the both of them!

"Hellooo," Tabitha called behind her, annoyed. "Can't see herrrre!"

Rae swung the beam of light back onto her sister. "Sorry. Yeah, you're right, I was just playing around," she fibbed.

"I hate it when you do that!"

Rae glanced to her left and right when Sis wasn't looking. A chill ran down her spine. "Hurry up. I want to get out of here, too."

"Vent your turbos, I'll be zoomin' atcha here in a sec," Tabitha quipped. Another bit of slang she picked up from somewhere, probably another silly show she'd been watching recently.

Rae sat the torch down again and rubbed her hands together in anticipation of the pain she experienced before. She gripped the wire and pulled with all her strength. First the bear and the book came through the crack, then Tabitha's head and shoulders, and finally her tiny body. Rae let go, this time waiting for her sister's feet to clear the door completely. "Wow! It's a lot easier when you're coming out! That was gangbusters, Tabby."

Her sister stood and put her hands on her hips. "No problemey!"

Rae grabbed the flashlight and got back to her feet. Locating her precious book on the deck, she scooped it up, then grabbed Tabitha's hand. "Let's go."

The girls ran as fast as their legs would carry them to the staircase, and bound back up the tall metal structure with renewed energy toward Deck Three.

Rae could almost feel someone behind her. She gasped and froze. *Was that another thud?* She didn't want to find out.

Tabby took the opportunity to pass her.

"Hey! Wait for me!" Rae took several of the metal corrugated stairs two-at-a-time, but still couldn't catch up to her sister. *I guess we're both a little afraid of what's in the dark!*

20

GSCS *Nightingale*

Captain Elwick closed the door of Doctor Galloway's office, and considered the words she had whispered in his ear. As a member of the Christian faith—maybe not as devout as he used to be, but still practicing—he knew forgiveness was not only the right thing to do, but in fact commanded by God. But why was it so difficult to forgive Zoey? Was it merely anger?

Or guilt?

Voices began to flood the bay, which seemed a bit dimmer now. Moses looked up to see a few of the bay's light fixtures unlit. He turned to see Dale Masterson's team mustering in the center of the large space. Each member busily lay out their 728 for inspection. "Seven-Twenty-Eight" has been the Navy term for basic field gear for centuries, Elwick mused, a nickname taken from the issue form still used by the old United States Navy. Hundreds of aspects of this long-gone military organization had been adopted by the RNA Navy, and subsequently by the Naval Department of the Sentinel Corps in the same way the U.S. Navy had adopted customs, words, and so many other things from the ancient British Royal Navy.

He headed toward them, still queasy due to the turmoil his body had just endured. From this distance, many members of the team were difficult to tell apart in their shiny, red spacesuits, especially with their face shields down. But Antonio Bruno stood out like a parade float in his extra-large suit. The tallest among them had to be the Bavarian Bluffer, Mr. Ebersbacher. Moses had to watch for specific movements to identify the others, at least until he reached the group, that is, and he could then read their nameplates. He located Masterson and made a beeline for him. “Any issues, Master Chief?”

Dale’s face shield disappeared up into his helmet. “You mean after that ridiculous super jump you didn’t warn us about?”

“Sorry. I’ll make sure the OOD mentions the distance in the next announcement.”

“How far was that, anyway?”

“Fourteen.”

“Fourteen thousand!” he exclaimed. This got the attention of the group.

“Wow, haven’t jumped that far since my sailor days!” Moses identified that yell as coming from Bruno.

One of the more slender suited figures put a hand to her stomach. “That explains my stomach ache.”

Barbara Laskey, Moses thought.

“That dis-gusting Cordon Bleu Rosie made us for dinner this evenin’ ‘bout came up!” That had to be Gilbin. “I think you should take away her access card to tha’ galley.”

“Aw, bugger off,” Rose Vereau replied through her helmet, which Elwick knew to be a lighthearted comeback in Gilbin’s native culture.

"An' that's not the half of it," continued the firefighter, his own shield disappearing in a whiff. "The green beans—OWW!"

Elwick's gaze followed a heavy spacesuit glove as it shot into the air after bouncing off the side of the Aussie's head. It landed on the deck not too far away.

"Keep it up, Danny Boy," said the dark-haired beauty, face shield now up, glowering at him under dark brows and holding up the other suit glove. "I got another one right here, plus two Kevlar boots just begging to get stuffed where the sun don't shine."

Muffled laughter echoed off the walls of the bay. Daniel Gilbin grinned, showing a gaping hole in his lower row of coffee-stained teeth.

Elwick picked up the tossed glove and, as he handed it back to Rose, he caught her winking at Gilbin. When the Aussie winked back, it dawned on Elwick that their embittered banter had been nothing but a cover up this whole time. *Wow. Way to go, Daniel,* Elwick mused. "Here you go, Rose."

"Thank you, Captain," she replied in an overly sweet tone and a smile to match.

His brows rose. "Hey! Been working on that Midwest accent, I see."

"What Midwest accent?" she asked.

Moses froze for a second, then scanned the room for a way out. "Mr. Ebersbacher!" he all but shouted. "How are you? When's the next poker night?"

Jan "The Bavarian Bluffer" Ebersbacher replied in this thick German. "Tomorrow night, Captain! Will you be joining us again?"

"And miss my chance to win some of my hard-earned credits back? Wouldn't miss it!"

The tall man smiled. "Sehr gut! I'm looking forward to emptying everyone's pockets again!"

Others joined in now, taunting, "We'll see about that," or "Cheater" or "Bring it on!"

Elwick continued his rounds. "Mr. Abiodun, everything checking out?"

"It will in a moment, sir," Hamidi replied, still configuring parts of his suit. His face shield remained in place. "Dan, give a hand, will you?"

While Daniel Gilbin assisted Hamidi, Moses turned to the only other SAR member he hadn't spoken with yet, the team's counselor. "Miss Laskey?"

"Yes?"

"Good to go? I know being in these suits isn't exactly your favorite thing in the world."

"Where's that blasted button? Oh, here it is." Barbara's shield disappeared. "Are you kidding? I love these damn things."

"Well, when the time comes, hopefully you won't have to be in them long."

Her helmeted head tilted sideways. "You don't have to sugar coat anything for me, Captain. I'm just glad we have an auto-evac in these things, if you know what I mean."

Bruno inserted himself into the conversation. "Well, you definitely can't fit inside the head with one of these suits on! Not even a slim little ass like yourself!"

Chuckling flew around the group.

"What? What'd I say?"

Elwick tapped him on the back. "We all knew what you meant, Bruno."

Suddenly Antonio's face turned red. "Lass! Slim little *lass!*" Then to Barbara, "I'm sorry, my dear."

"It's okay, Broonie," she cooed, touching his face. "We all know what's going through your head twenty-four, seven."

The two shared a smile, which made Moses smile. "Alright then," Elwick said, clapping his hands together, "I'll let you all get to it. We have a full hour before the next and thankfully final jump, then the real work begins: finding that ship!"

Masterson looked confused. "I thought we had three jumps left? Of seven total?"

"We did have seven originally. We had to um, shave that down. For… reasons."

Dale nodded. "Aye, sir."

That's what Moses loved about Dale; he knew when to ask for an explanation, and when to let it go.

Dale then turned to his group. "Alright, let's get this inspection knocked out!"

As the group filed into their positions above their 728 and Elwick turned to leave, Antonio stopped him. "Captain? Can I speak with you for a minute?"

Elwick looked at Dale, who nodded. Bruno had a few minutes before the Master Chief got down the line to him. "Sure, Bruno." They turned and moseyed toward a large transport. "What's up?"

Antonio spoke in low tones. "I wasn't merely spinning yarns for the crew earlier."

"Yes, I know you weren't, Bruno. You've seen a lot of crazy shit in your long career, and I know to listen to you."

"What really worries me, Mo, is the push from the last waypoint into the cloud. Best practice here: boost the magnetic field to five hundred percent—if we can manage it," he quickly added, as if reading Moses' mind, "and spread the sensor nets wide open." He then held up an index finger. "All except the *forward* nets. Keep those focused and shinin' as far in front of us as possible. Ozzie will need all the advanced warnin' he can get to see whatever we're zoomin' at. Give a wide berth to anything that looks even the slightest bit off. And I mean anything."

"Aye, aye, buddy. We'll do exactly that."

Bruno grabbed Moses' shoulder with his large, gauntleted hand. Firm, but just like the man himself, gentle. "If anybody'll get us through this, Mo, it's you. You're one brave son of a bitch. You and Dale, both. *That* I've seen with my own eyes, and more than once. But make no mistake. This isn't *anything* like Europa, above *or* below. The natural rules of physics and logic don't always apply here. *That* I've seen with my own eyes, too."

Moses nodded. "I…" He took a deep breath to quell the nausea that had still not completely gone away. "I promise to heed your warning, and defer to your experience, old friend. And thanks for the vote of confidence."

A couple of only slightly overly-powerful love pats, and the bear of a man stepped away to rejoin his team.

Moses turned and meandered to the ladder that had brought him to this deck. The junk on the lift had disappeared, just as he predicted it would soon be. He paused before the starboard tunnel to Engineering, and thought about checking on his knuckledraggers. A bit of yelling and more banging from that direction changed his mind. They surely had their hands full with ongoing maintenance, adjustments, and even a few repairs after pushing the core to the extreme degree he had ordered. Probably damn near broke the thing, honestly. And they still had one more similar jump to go! No one back there would be happy with him right now, and "checking in on them" would only add fuel to the fire. *The Chiefs have got this,* he reminded himself. Best to keep his brass ass out of Kelly's Kitchen.

He climbed upward, heading for the bridge. But first, the fridge. Finally, he would get a real bite to eat!

21

Emerald Pearl

The girls made quick work getting back up to Deck Three, now that they knew exactly where to go. Tabby breathed heavily; she had ran the whole way.

Rae's heart still beat fast as well, especially after they had also climbed the winding stair from Deck Three to Deck Two. At that point both girls reduced speed to a slow climb. Rae looked up and saw the now familiar red tint of the sky. "Almost there!"

"Good!" shouted Tabitha. "I'm exhausted!"

Panting, Rae followed Sis up into a lounge large enough to host the entire complement of crew and passengers of the *Pearl*.

"Wow!" Tabby exclaimed. Her voice echoed here, but differently than it did down on Deck Four.

Rae's mouth dropped open at the sight above her.

"I didn't know the *whole* sky was red!" Tabby exclaimed. "We're completely *inside* the nebula!"

Rae hadn't realized this either. "I thought we were just on the edge of it!"

"Daddy said it was dangerous to fly into anything in space, especially glowing clouds. We shouldn't be here, Rae."

"Maybe that's why the ship got damaged?"

"It is pretty, though."

"Yeah. Pretty dangerous, I think."

"How would you know? *I'm* the science genius in this family."

"Dad is. And I've learned a few things too. Brat!" Rae dropped onto one of the four identical, black couches all facing each other near the center of the large circular area. They both breathed deeply, trying to catch their breaths. Each couch sat equidistant around a sturdy, red table. *Well, maybe it only looks red?* The blood-soaked glow from above overpowered everything; Rae figured the table could have been any color and still looked red. The couches probably weren't black, either. She shrugged it off. It didn't really matter.

Earlier, when on the bridge, she and Sis had been looking out the front windows. Now Rae was positioned to see what lay up and behind them. Amongst the numerous trees, plants, benches, chairs and tables that filled the lounge, Rae could easily imagine she sat in a park or a forest on Earth looking up at the sky. An odd, red sky, the likes of which you wouldn't see on Earth. Like a giant heat lamp over a greasy burger. The forest illusion disappeared now that reality had set in again, and she wondered if the trees and other plants were real or fake? If real, she felt sorry for them.

Tabitha plopped down on her left. The girl rested her head on the divan and stared upward as well.

The Observation Dome was exactly that, a large circular latticework dome with crisscrossing titanium-alloy girders that held unbreakable glass. Or so she had been told. "On the tour, Captain Timmins said all the windows were made of graphite," Rae told her little sister.

"What's that?"

"I don't know. It's something really strong and it keeps out all the *bad* types of light that comes from the stars."

Tabitha got that look on her face again. "Bad light? You mean radiation?"

Rae shrugged. "I guess."

"And hold on. Graphite? Isn't that the same stuff they make pencils out of?"

"No, that's plastic. Or wood, if you're like a thousand years old."

"I meant the part you write with, dummy."

"Oh. Then yeah, I guess so."

"So this whole dome is made out of pencil stuff?" Tabitha asked in a sarcastic tone.

"No," Rae said as she rolled her eyes. "The dome's made out of metal. The *glass* is made out of pencil stuff!"

Tabitha's eyes narrowed. "I was *talking* about the glass, moron," she said through clenched teeth. "And I don't believe you."

"Quit calling me names. And anyway, you're the moron because Captain Timmins said that's what it was."

"Idiot," Tabby retaliated.

"Just shut up and help me look for the rescue ship."

Tabitha bounced her head on the couch a couple of times. "Pencil stuff!" she scoffed.

"I wish Dad were here, he'd tell you I'm right," Rae muttered.

"I wish Dad were here too! He'd be much better company than *you!*"

Rae crossed her arms and stopped talking to her sister. *She always thinks she's* so *smart. Just because she goes with Dad at every science and astronomy fair does* not *mean she knows everything.* She stuck out her lower lip and glared at Tabby out of the corner of her eye. Then she remembered she was fourteen years old and pulled her lip back in. *She's dragging me down to her age! I've got to watch that.*

And yes, she probably knows more than me, Rae admitted, *but she doesn't know as much as she thinks she does, that's for sure!* She closed her eyes. *I spent more time with Daddy than you, Brat! I had three and a half years with him before* you *came along! I was the first one Daddy took sailing. You could have gone but you didn't like it! So, that's our thing. Daddy and me. Not yours, not Mommy's, not Jamie's, not anybody else's.*

Ours.

Earth, Manumission Province: Green Bay
Six Years Ago

It hadn't been the best day for fishing. Gray clouds filled the autumn sky, and the icy wind bit more than usual. Eight-year-old Rae Marshall and her father had only caught two small walleye the entire morning. They were discussing how they might catch more when Rae spotted another boat. It angled directly for them at a high rate of speed.

"Daddy, look!"

"What is it honey?" He squinted. "Oh. Umm, yeah, don't worry. It's just some business associates of mine." He bent down, putting himself at eye-level with her. "Rayray, you know what I think will help us catch more fish? My special lure. You remember, the shiny bright green one? Would you run below and get it? It's in that old tackle box we don't use much anymore."

"Sure, Daddy," Rae replied excitedly. She flew down the steep steps to the lower compartment where the bunks were. She looked in the cracks and crevices, opened cabinet doors and the large drawers under the bunks. *Where does he keep it?*

The motor of the visiting boat had grown louder in the last minute or so but died abruptly. Rae could now hear men talking. She heard a gruff voice say in a low volume, "Hugh, my boy," and then something she couldn't quite make out.

"Come on, Al, my kid's on board."

More quiet talk. Rae tried to tune it out. It was Daddy's business, not meant for children. It took her some time but she finally found the beat-up old box. Opening it revealed a plethora of shiny and once-shiny things. And sharp things. "Ouch!" She licked her forefinger to make the dot of blood disappear as she saw her father do on occasion. She looked for another minute but could find no green lures anywhere. Oh, but there was purple one! A diamond in the rough. She picked it up carefully so as not to prick another finger on one of its three sharp barbs. It sparkled beautifully; when she turned twixt her fingers, a rainbow of colors mesmerized her.

A voice from above brought her out of the temporary hypnosis. "Just a few more days. I swear it only take a few more days." Father's voice.

"Hugh, Hugh, Hugh..." came the gruff reply.

Rae took off her sailor's hat and stuck the lure through the material. "There!" Now she wouldn't have to carry it and risk jabbing her finger again. She licked the tiny drop that had formed once again, then closed the box with a bang and immediately regretted it. She held her breath and listened.

"I told you, my little girl is down there. Please, Al."

An uncomfortable silence followed for what seemed like an eternity to Rae. She heard footsteps, then a strange *thoop*, then another. *What in the world makes that kind of sound?* "Nice working with you, Hugh. I'm glad we could come to an agreement. See ya around."

The motor of the visiting boat sprang to life. She looked through a small porthole on what her father called the "starboard" side to see his business associates veering away. Rae dumped the tackle box on the floor and headed up topside—er, no, "above" was the correct word, Daddy had said. She bolted up the stairs and burst onto the poop deck.

The fading sound of the other boat's engine made her look in its direction. From the back it looked like a very nice craft with scores of electronics above its conn, electronics that probably weren't broken like most everything on Daddy's boat. She spotted four nicely dressed men aboard. One waved and blew her a kiss. She found this odd but waved back nonetheless.

"Rae, come here, honey."

She turned and found her father sitting on a small, built-in bench. "Daddy, who were those men?" Rae then noticed the blood. "Oh no! Daddy!"

"Rayray, listen. I need you to do me a favor." He cringed and breathed uneasily. "Bring me the med kit, you know where it is. Then call the Coast Guard. Just like I taught you."

"Daddy, what happened?"

He smiled. "Oh honey, I'm so clumsy. I lost my balance and fell right onto the tip of that harpoon there!"

She looked, and indeed there was blood on the tip. Far past the tip, actually.

"I should have been more careful."

"But... why didn't your friends—?"

"Rayray. The med kit. Hurry!"

Rae practically fell down the stairs and dug around for the white box with a big red cross. She rummaged haphazardly, no longer caring not what landed where. *There it is!* She snatched it and a towel from the tiny bathroom, then flew up the stairs two at a time. She collapsed at Daddy's side and fumbled at the snaps holding the med kit together. She froze when she looked at her father's wound. *So* much more blood than before! It had already soaked his shirt, which he had somehow removed on is own and balled up over the wound. Red tendrils snaked down his side and dripped on the deck. The sight of it all turned her stomach. Rae tried to ignore it, but the smell of copper overpowered her nose. She was now thankful for the icy bay breeze, which sporadically carried the stench away.

"Here," her father said, opening the kit in a flash.

Now unhampered by the simple snaps that had never before been so bafflingly complex, she reached deep into her memory for what to do next. Her father had been teaching her first aid since she was six! But for little cuts, tiny punctures, like the one on her finger. Nothing like *this.* She looked away.

Daddy must have seen the look on her face or something. "It'll be alright, Rayray. Hold it down. Breathe for me, okay? Breathe."

Okay, she thought, taking a deep breath, then another. *Okay. What do I do?* She forced herself to look back at the red, plaid mess her father held tightly against his side. *That's right! Stop the bleeding!* That's why she had instinctively grabbed the towel. "Here!" While replacing the towel with the shirt, Rae caught a glimpse of the wound. It was just a small slit, maybe a couple of inches long, right near where she thought his kidney might be. He winced when he pressed the absorbent material against it.

Rae did the same out of compassion. "I'm sorry, Daddy."

"It's okay, honey. Grab the antiseptic and the Collagex."

Rae grabbed a brown bottle and a clear bag containing tiny white beads from the kit. She twisted and twisted the bottle's lid, but it just spun and spun. "I can't get it off!"

"Push down, then turn," Hugh Marshall said, in what Rae thought was such an odd, calm voice considering the situation.

She followed his instruction, and the lid came off easily. She wanted to happy cry. But she didn't.

"Now I want you to pour it directly on the cut. Ready?" Her father removed the towel and Rae dumped all of the bottle's clear contents onto the wound. This made her father cry out, and Rae yelped in sympathy. "I'm sorry! I'm so sorry!" Her eyes teared up at the sight of her father in pain.

"Hey! No, I'm good, Rayray! I'll be okay! It's not your fault." A tear rolled down his cheek. "Alright," he said, still wincing. "Now the Collagex."

Rae dropped the empty bottle without returning the lid, then tore open the small bag. She carefully sprinkled a few of the beads into the wound. Each one immediately swelled up to several times its size, and turned pink.

"More. More."

She dumped the bag's entire contents on him. Most of the beads fell everywhere, but at least the slit was completely full.

Hugh covered it, trapping as many tiny balls as he could. "Good. That will seal me up. Now I need that package right there, the one with the blue strips."

Rae pulled an envelope from the lid that was as large as the med kit itself.

"Rip it open, pull off the white backing, and slap it on me."

She did so. It turned out to be the biggest bandage she had ever seen! It covered most of his side, adhering to his skin immediately. "Good job, Rayray, good job. Thank you."

"You're welcome, Daddy!"

He tried to sit up, but screamed in pain.

"Daddy! Don't move! You'll start bleeding again!"

He sighed. "You're right, honey, you're right. In that case, I need you to call the Coast Guard. You remember how to call for a Mayday right?"

"I think so."

"You'll do fine. Read off the coordinates from the dashboard. They'll send someone to help."

"Can't the computer do all that stuff automatically?"

"I'm pretty sure my friends took care of the computer. And the EPIRB. And our entire electrical system."

EPIRB. Emergency Position something-something Beacon. "Do you mean the emergency beacon?"

"Yes."

"You mean it doesn't work anymore?"

He shook his head.

Oh no.

"But not to worry, we practiced for a situation like this, right? You can do it. I know you can. Go on."

"Okaaay." Rae hated to leave him but her desire to get him professional help overrode her newly discovered Florence Nightingale-like instincts. She leapt up into the small conning platform above the sleeping quarters. She spotted the small orange EPIRB device. It had a hole in it that hadn't been there before. She tried to activated it, just to see what would happen. Nothing. She sighed. *Fine. Radio it is.* She noticed immediately that the radio had a new hole in it as well. She tried to turn it on, but it remained dark. "Daddy? The radio isn't working."

A groan came from below her. "That's okay. We have a spare. Thankfully they didn't go below decks! Probably because you were down there. Thank God Al's still got a lick of decency."

"Thank the Goddess, too," she called.

Her father seemed to ignore that, as he always did when Rae and Mother's religion came up. "There's a handheld, um... under my bunk. Plus..."

Rae waited. "Daddy?"

"Yeah?"

"Plus what?"

"Oh... um... plus an old GPS locator. It should still work."

Rae hopped down from the "crow's nest," then down the stairs once more. In the drawer under her daddy's bunk, under several layers of clothes, she found what looked like a weird communications device, another weird box with old-style buttons, and a gun. Her gaze seized upon the gun. She knew she shouldn't touch *that.* She carefully pulled the other devices out and darted back up to her father. He looked as though he had fallen asleep. Or—?

"Daddy!" Rae screamed.

"Wha—?" he yelled, jerking awake. His eyes seemed unable to focus.

"I got the things!"

"Oh!" he said when he saw the items Rae held up. "Perfect. Turn them... turn them both on... and—" his voice trailed off again.

"Daddy?"

His head flopped to one side.

"Daddy!"

He didn't reply.

"No, no, no..." Rae pushed every button on both units until each one illuminated. She fumbled with what her father had called the "GPS," whatever *that* meant. Soon, it displayed numbers and letters that she recognized as longitudinal and latitudinal coordinates. Whether they were current or from a previous fishing trip, she had no idea, but she'd use them anyway. She then cleared her throat and held the radio close to her face. "Radio, I need to call the Coast Guard."

>BEEP< The handheld answered her in a pleasant, male voice. *"Calling Coast Guard on channel sixteen, 156.8 Megahertz."* There was a brief pause and then, "Channel open, ping received."

She spoke as loudly and clearly as she could. "Mayday, mayday, mayday, this is the *Bella Luna.*" She repeated this sentence again, then waited a moment. No reply. She broadcast two more times, as her father had taught her, then waited again.

"This is the Green Bay Coast Guard," the radio squawked. "Please state your location and status."

"Our location is..." She looked back at the GPS thing. "Forty-four degrees, forty-one minutes North. Eighty-seven degrees, fifty minutes West." She took a breath. "Our electrical system is out and we are adrift. We have two people on board. One person with a—" Rae stopped. She looked down at her father's bandage and said, quietly, "stab wound."

"Roger, *Bella Luna,*" came the reply. "Please activate your EPIRB."

"I can't. It's broken. None of our electronics work."

"How are you communicating?"

"With a handheld radio."

"Roger, *Bella Luna.* Locating you via satellite using given coordinates. Stand by." A pause. "May I ask how old you are?"

"I'm eight!" She meant to announce that with pride, but even she heard the pleading cries of a child.

Another pause. "Is an adult on board?"

"Yes, but he's, um, he's asleep right now. He's been hurt really bad."

"Understood. Don't worry, help is on the way."

"Okay."

"Alright, we've got you on satellite and RADAR. Dispatching a rescue drone to your location."

"Aye aye." Her father had taught her that, too, along with a few other nautical terms.

"Miss, you performed that mayday call very well. Not a lot of children your age could do that."

"Thank you."

"Standby for further instructions, okay, miss?"

"Okay."

Her father's voice startled her. "You did wonderful, honey."

"Daddy! You're awake!"

He smiled. "You're the best daughter... a guy could ask for."

She smiled big in return. But right after that, he passed out again. "Daddy..." She hugged him, unconcerned about the blood now. "Please don't die," she whispered.

The computer-flown drone arrived in four minutes, and two paramedics exited the patient compartment of the near-silent helicopter. "What's your name?" one of them asked.

"Rae Marshall."

"Are you hurt?"

"No. My daddy is."

"Is this your dad?"

"Yes."

"Okay, don't worry, we'll get him fixed up."

They injected medicine into Hugh Marshall's arm, told Rae she had done a good job patching him up and calling for help, then tried to instruct the *Bella Luna's* nav computer to head back to its home port on its own.

"The computer's broken," she told them.

One of the medics touched the bullet holes in the boat's dashboard, and then gave his counterpart a sideways glance. "We're going to need to call dispatch for a tow." Then to Rae, "Come with us, miss. You can call your mother or legal guardian once we reach the hospital."

"Okay."

Rae boarded the still-hovering aircraft, which lurched toward the distant shore while she still fumbled with her safety harness. Rae clicked the belts into place just as she heard another, much louder popping sound from behind. She turned back and watched, mouth agape, as her father's rusty but nostalgic boat split in half.

"What the—?" one of the medics exclaimed.

The craft slid beneath the calm, cold waters before Rae could even begin to cry.

Emerald Pearl

Rae had made both her parents proud that day. Very much so! They reminded her often over the years. *Hmm*... It could have made her little sister jealous, now that she thought about it. *Maybe that's one reason Tabby is so nasty to me all the time?* She had never thought of it that way. *Daddy would surely be proud of me for taking care of Tabby now!* This made her smile. She opened her eyes, and jumped when she found Sis staring at her.

"That's great, Rae. Way to look out for your little sister. Go back to sleep. I'll make sure we're rescued."

"Stop. It was only for a minute."

"You stop. It was more like an hour."

"Oh Tabby, it was not!"

"How do you even know?"

"Because I can tell. Plus I can tell when you're lying!"

Tabitha let her head drop back onto the couch and looked up. "No, you can't."

"Just watch the sky," Rae ordered.

"I am," Tabby said as she stared into the red swirls above. "Unlike you."

Rae took a deep breath. *Let it go, Rae, let it go. It's not her fault, she's just a little kid, just like you were once.* She threw her head back and gazed upward again, too. Those clouds… were they swirling? And moving? They mesmerized her just like that purple, sparkly lure with the rainbow inside.

After a few minutes, she glanced over at Tabby. Sis had closed her eyes, and seemed to be breathing deep. She had probably drifted off herself. Rae's stomach turned and her eyes filled with water as she stared at the girl. *The poor little thing. How can I be mad at her? How am I supposed to tell her about Daddy? And how am I supposed to go on? How are any of us?* Rae's chest felt poised to collapse in on itself. She took a quick breath and held it, not wanting Tabby to hear her and awaken. She had no desire to explain her sudden wave of sadness at that moment.

Whether she would see her father again or not, she had to do what he would expect of her. For him, she pushed her fear down. For him, she stared down the nebula. For him, she could and would get them through this!

A set of stars caught her eye. "Oh wow," she whispered.

"Oh wow, what?" asked Tabby.

"Sorry. I didn't mean to wake you up."

"I wasn't asleep."

"Anyway, look! See that dark patch? Where some stars are shining through?"

"Yeah."

"I think that's the way they'll come."

"Why?"

"Because the cloud is thinner there. And it looks like the closest way in or out."

"What about all the sky under us?" Tabitha asked.

"What?"

"What about the other half of the sky? Down there?" She pointed to the floor. "Under our feet? The part we can't see? There could be a dark patch down there and they could come from that way."

Rae stared, amazed at her little sister's understanding and insight. Sis was right. *Again.* She and Tabby were not on a planet looking up at the night sky, they were on a spaceship looking out at only half of the galaxy around them. If that. "You're smart, Tabby, they *could* be coming from underneath us."

"I know I'm smart, I don't need a big dummy like you to tell me."

"Stop it, Tabitha. I don't want to fight anymore."

Tabby scoffed. "Whatever. Anyway, we're spinning, so it doesn't matter."

"We are?"

She pointed upward now. "Look at those stars. They've been moving diagonally. So, we'll eventually be able to see the *whole* sky if we sit here long enough."

"What?"

"Just watch a while," Sis said in an annoyed tone.

Rae did, and neither said anything for a full minute if not more. Her eyes bulged. The stars *were* moving! She could tell by holding her head perfectly still and using the dome's unmoving metal girders for a reference. *Huh!* The little smarty pants was on a roll today! When Rae looked back at her, the little brat smiled ear to ear. *Ugh! I hate it when she—*

A through struck her. "Oh! I forgot to turn on the comm panel!" Rae looked around briefly, then launched off the couch and ran to a wall. She touched a virtual button, and a blue light illuminated above the red circle, as expected. "Hello? Captain Moses?"

The reply came in a few seconds. "This is Petty Officer Connelly. Is this Rae?"

"Yes. Um, nice to meet you, Mr. Connelly. Is Captain Moses there?"

"He's below decks at the moment. Anything you need? You can call me Guy, by the way. No one calls me 'mister' around here!"

"Guy?" Tabby called from the couch, then skipped over to join Rae. She scrunched up her eyebrows. "But what's your real name?"

"That *is* my real name," the new voice replied.

Rae and her sister exchanged glances, and Tabby's two pig tails jerked to one side. "Did your mother not know what to call you?"

"Tabitha!" Rae scolded.

Connelly laughed. "It's okay, Tabitha. The name 'Guy' is an old Norman-French name. Some people think it means 'Life' when traced back to Latin."

"Oh. You can call *me* Tabby. That's what everyone calls me. At least when they're not *yelling* at me." She glared at Rae.

"Okay, Tabby it is," Guy said, with a smile in his voice.

"William from my Educata says it means 'mangy old striped cat.' But I think it's just a quicker way to say Tabitha!"

"Indeed it is."

"I like your name now, Mr. Guy."

"Well, that's good to hear."

"Guy," Rae interrupted, "please tell Captain Moses that we made it to the observation level! We can see half the sky from here. Well, the whole sky, if we wait long enough."

Sis shouted, "We're in a slow spin!"

"I see," Guy Connelly said. "I'll make sure he gets the message."

Rae walked back to the couch, where Tabitha now re-perched herself, tucking her pale legs underneath her blue sundress. "Can you still hear me?" Rae called to the comm panel.

"Yes, I can hear you just fine," came the reply, a bit quieter now that Rae sat a few meters from the panel.

"Good. We're sitting on a really comfortable couch. It's warm."

"I think it's blue, but it might be black," Tabby called.

Rae rolled her eyes. "I think we'll stay here until you get here."

"That sounds great," said Guy. "Stay together, keep warm, we're coming, but it might be a while."

"Okay." Then, there was nothing else to say. Rae stared at the cloud above. A yawn escaped her. She looked at her sister, who stared up at the sky once more. Rae thanked the Mother Goddess she was not alone. She put a hand on Tabby's, and gave her a tight, endearing smile.

Sis looked down at Rae's hand, then looked up into her eyes. With a quick flick of the wrist, Tabitha threw her sister's hand back onto her own lap.

Rae smirked. *Brat.*

22

GSCS *Nightingale*

It took Captain Elwick longer than usual to get up the ladder from Deck Three to Deck Two, what with his stomach still in knots. The hunger pains hit even stronger now that literally nothing but air filled his gut. Soon he may not be able to think straight due to low blood sugar. He made a command decision.

Elwick headed down the central passageway on Deck Two of the *Nightingale*, trying his best to look stoic. Luckily, the passage lay abandoned, as everyone currently manned their stations. He entered the "forecastle" of the ship, which everyone pronounced "fo'c's'le" as per tradition, which simply meant the front section of any vessel, which usually contained the berthing compartments for the lower ranking crewmembers. But on the *Nightingale*, this forecastle held the "Mess Decks" where the lower enlisted and civilian crews ate every meal. Moses, his officers, and select crew ate in the Wardroom one level up, so he rarely entered this space. It also doubled as the Quarterdeck, where more formal ceremonies were often held. Less formal ceremonies, especially those for enlisted starmen, were usually held in the cargo bay out of appropriateness. Plus, the cargo bay was easier to clean up after a raucous party.

Elwick entered a small vestibule with the galley to his left, but through small windows on the double doors leading to the multipurpose hall known as the Mess/Quarterdeck, he saw the large room bathed in an eerie, red light.

The nebula.

He hadn't yet seen it; they had only just jumped to its edge from ten thousand light years away. He decided to enter the large dining room.

The glowing cloud filled all of the large, transparent, graphene panels before him, which stretched in a semi-circle around the perimeter of the room. Not unlike how the bridge one deck up had been laid out by the designers, only the Mess was much bigger. Moses' brows raised high. "Well, well, you're a bit brighter than I expected," he said to the multi-parsec-wide cluster of molecular hydrogen.

The Triple-S, Multipurpose Rescue Vessel, AHR-47 Galactic Sentinel Corps Ship *Nightingale* had a tough titanium and graphene hull covering over ninety percent of her surface. The last eight or nine percent made up accepted vulnerabilities: port holes and windows, maneuvering and attitude thrusters, Zhédié Folded-Space Drive vents, external communications antennae, and sensor arrays. All airlock doors and life boat chutes only suffered from the tiniest of seals. The biggest windows on the ship filled the front of the ship—on the bridge and here on the Mess Decks. All windows could be covered by sliding panels of titanium-graphene shielding when required, but when exposed like they were now, the windows amounted to nothing but a few centimeters of material that separated everyone from the deadly vacuum of space.

And the deadly radiation of space.

Of course. He closed his eyes. *Oh no…*

Inside the three-inch thick windows, hundreds of thousands of layers of graphene held back death, each microscopic layer only as thick as a single atom. While they appeared fragile, Elwick often had to remind himself that these panes were anything but. Graphene had been developed in the late 20th Century by two physicists—perhaps certain engineers could remember their names but Elwick could not—who could only have dreamed of the possible applications of the material. It proved to be hundreds of times the strength of steel, didn't rust, and could be made transparent. It had not been not until the mid-to-late 21st Century before the benefits of this "atomic chicken wire" could be realized and mass produced. Like the transistor, which had changed the world in the 20th and 21st Centuries—especially once it became microscopic and trillions could fit on a fingernail—graphene also had to go through several innovations from its first incarnation. Structural quality, manufacturing methods and the sheer expense of production had to be overcome. It took many decades to get the pure, defect-free version used in Elwick's day. Now, the amazing material not only made up the windows, but made up many parts across the ship, from the frame to the outer plating. In fact, all interstellar vessels of both war and peace had been constructed with either pure graphene, or had their poly-alloy hulls plated with the stuff. This provided not only strength but also protection from small kinetic threats, such as micrometeorites and smaller munitions that could not be deflected by the powerful magnetic fields created by ships' magnetrons. It was this magnetic field that kept most of the dangerous radiation at bay, not the high-tech windows.

But Rae and Tabitha's magnetrons were no longer spinning. Even though the girls should be quite well protected deep inside what had formerly been a warship with a poly-alloy hull, Elwick prayed the nebula's radiation wouldn't kill them before he could reach them. Was the *Pearl's* windows made of transparent graphene? Or at least coated with it?

He opened his eyes and stared into the swirling mass of mesmerizing crimson. The color reminded him of those damned emergency lights back on the *RMS Elliott,* the battlecruiser on which he had lost his Captain and would have lost his life, were it not for the heroics of one crazy Chief Petty Officer, Dale Masterson. A rescue that a then much more fit Petty Officer First Class Antonio Bruno witnessed first-hand from an adjacent ship. The memory of that mission… Captain Persephone Bannon's and so many others' sacrifice had been far from worth the meager gains the RNA achieved on that fateful day, and—

A whistle came from a nearby comms panel, interrupting his thoughts. "Captain?"

Moses side-stepped, entering the galley, and swiped a stripe on the panel in there with a finger, opening the 18MC non-discrete channel to the bridge. "Elwick here," he said, moving toward the pantry where the Jack o' the Dust kept the dehydrated food stocked aplenty. "What is it, Ozzie?"

"Since we've plenty of time until our next and last jump, I temporarily reconfigured the sensors and got a good nav fix on the remote distress beacon that's broadcasting the *Pearl's* signal."

"Excellent," he replied. He darted to the storage bins and began rifling through various bio-degradable packets. "Can you by chance use it to triangulate the *Pearl's* actual location?"

"Without downloading its internal telemetry, no. And I can't do that remotely or I would have already; these beacons out here on this side of the galactic bulge are just too old to have that capability. Now, if we link up with it directly…"

Moses paused his search for dinner and thought about this. "I'm sure downloading and interpreting the data will take seconds, but how long will it take to actually reach the beacon?"

"Probably longer than we have, Captain. It's a bit out of our way by about a hundred and fifty million clicks. And since it's inside the nebula, we'd have to run up to it on ion drive. Likely add a full hour to our trip, there and back, even at one-quarter lightspeed."

"Definitely longer than we have. By the time we reach the beacon, turn around, and finally reach the girls…" He did some quick beer math. "We may not get there for another four hours, considering we still have to wait a full hour before we can jump again."

"Agreed. However, it may be the only way to find—"

"If we do it that way, yes, we'll find the ship," Elwick interrupted, "but we'll also find two little frozen ladies. Thus defeating the entire purpose of rushing in, in def—" he almost said, *in defiance of orders,* but cut himself off, realizing he was speaking on an open channel.

"Got it, sir."

"Don't worry, we'll find that ship," Elwick stated as if it were fact, possibly more for his own edification than that of anyone listening. "And before their time runs out." He went back to his packets.

"Aye, Captain." The XO paused briefly before continuing. "There's another reason I called you."

Moses stopped again and closed his eyes. *It can't be good, or Osterland would have already spit it out.* "Go ahead."

"There are several little red dots on RADAR all around the beacon for, well, a good, long ways in every direction. Each one represents a tiny energy signature. Computer analysis returns just what I already suspected them to be: naturally-occurring microscopic wormholes. They're pretty common in this region." As if he could read Elwick's uncertainty, Osterland continued. "If they were Series M or W, I'd say we do a one-eighty before the *Nightingale* ends up split into seventeen parts! But they're series J, so no real threat, and common, especially in this region of space. However, that said, I'm siding with Bruno. Harmless or not, we should steer clear of them."

"Can't argue that. Anything else you want to complicate my evening with?"

"Not at this time, sir. I'll reconfigure the sensors before we jump again."

"Oh hey, speaking of which, when you do the reconfig, boost the magnetic field to five hundred percent, and spread the port, starboard, and aft sensor nets wide to cover three hundred-sixty degrees in all vectors. X, Y, and Z. I already realize that will shorten their range, you don't have to remind me. But I'm not really concerned about what's coming at us from any direction except dead ahead, especially if we're pushing the old girl to Ion Base eight or even nine. So set the forward arrays to a narrow, ten-degree beam. Bruno thought you should have as much warning as possible to navigate through what he anticipates to be a minefield."

"Makes complete sense, Captain. Aye aye."

"Right. I'll be up in about fifteen mikes. Elwick out." Moses checked his timepiece. *Forty-five minutes until our next super jump. Should be plenty of time to get some mashed potatoes and...* He swiftly rifled through another bin. *There it is! Meatloaf! Time enough to get both down deep enough into my guts so I don't barf them back up!*

Hopefully.

23

Emerald Pearl

Something inside Rae gurgled. She threw a hand over her stomach and glanced over at Tabby. Sis had fallen asleep again, cuddling her teddy bear.

Rae stretched and stared up at the red cloud. This trip was supposed to be a quick one—from the passengers' perspectives. She had been on interstellar trips before. Twice in fact. They were as boring as being on any regular old interplanetary bus. But the buses between planets didn't have freezers—cryo pods—so they took longer, from her point of view at least. On these interstellar trips, you board the ship, get the tour of the few areas the passengers are allowed to enter, enjoy a few dinners and the entertainment the ship has to offer for a few days, maybe a week until the ship is ready to disembark, listen to the even more boring safety briefing, lock up your things, hit the freezers, go to sleep, wake up, figure out how to walk again, eat, collect your things, and you're on your way.

Not this time.

She remembered the tour, and Captain Timmins addressing the group in his deep, fatherly voice. "It should take only a few minutes from your all's perspective—ten at most to get into your deep sleep and then fully wake up—regardless of how much time actually passes for the rest of the universe. Which should be, from my and the crew's perspective, three months."

Rae wasn't sure she understood all the complexities, but she did understand "ten-minute trip." Which is what she had expected. When everyone woke up, they should find themselves only a couple of hours from their destination. Enough time to relearn how to walk, grab a bite, and empty the family cage. No passenger should ever wake up halfway through the trip! Of this she was certain. And most definitely not a teenager and a ten-year-old with no adults around to guide them!

Rae's stomach executed a full on growl this time. She hadn't thought to stuff a snack in her pocket before going into the pod. She didn't even have pockets in these pants! Tabitha's dress didn't have any, either. They would both need to eat soon. But that would mean wandering through scary dark hallways again looking for the kitchen. Rae sighed. She may have proven her bravery to her little sister, but she was far from convincing herself.

"Daddy's not waking up, is he?"

Rae jerked; Tabitha's voice had startled her. "I thought you were asleep!"

"I'm not stupid," Tabby said, ignoring Rae. "I know what the word 'malfunction' means. And I saw that all the lights on his pod were off. Samesies for all those pods in Daddy's row." The girl shifted her tiny weight to where she could now stare into Rae's eyes. "You don't have to protect me."

Rae had been holding her breath. She forced herself to relax and start breathing again. But she said nothing, for there was nothing to say. Still apprehensive after the recent "hand incident," she didn't push her affections upon Tabitha like she so desperately desired to do at that moment. It quickly became a moot point, however, as Sis flung her small body onto Rae's and hugged her tightly.

"What are we going to do now?" Tabby whimpered, her head on Rae's shoulder but turned away to face the large room.

"What do you mean?"

"Where are we going to live if Daddy really is gone?"

Rae bit her lower lip. "Well, we'll live with Mom and Jamie of course."

"That's not what I meant. I know we'll live with Mom and Jamie!"

"Oh. You mean if Daddy can't take the new job at the mining colony?"

"Yes!"

"Well, I guess we'll just head back to Earth."

"But where will we live once we get back?"

"I don't know," Rae answered. "Maybe we'll live in our old house?"

"Daddy sold that house."

"Hmm. You're right."

"This trip was supposed to take three months of 'real time', right? So, if it's been three months, new people are probably all moved in by now."

Rae nodded.

"But I liked our house. I miss Lorrie and Odessa." Tabby then climbed off Rae and plopped down next to her.

"I miss them too." Rae sat back, took the pig tails out of her sister's hair, and brushed her long brown mane straight with her fingers to get the knots out. Tabitha showed no objections. Rae knew Sis liked it when Mother played with her hair, so she tried to emulate that as best she could. The effort would serve to comfort her as much as it would Tabby. "We can visit them when we get back," Rae suggested. "Even if we can't live next door to them anymore, maybe we can find another house in our old neighborhood and still see them a lot?"

Tabitha raised her eyebrows. "Maybe it hasn't been three months?" she offered. "Maybe it's only been a couple of weeks since we left?"

Rae's brow knitted, and she was about to ask why Tabitha would think such a thing, when Sis spoke again.

"I forgot to look at the date when we were on the bridge."

Rae's eyes opened wide. "You're right! We don't know how far into the trip we are!"

"I'm right. Like *that's* any surprise." Tabitha looked pleased with herself.

"*Emerald Pearl*," Rae spoke louder than before to ensure the computer heard her. "How long have we been traveling? How far into the trip are we? When did this ship leave Earth?"

"You dummy, you're going to confuse—"

"The Emerald Pearl departed Arthur C. Clarke Station thirty-four days, seventeen hours, forty-eight seconds ago," the female voice replied.

Rae stuck out her tongue. "She understood."

Tabitha stuck out her own tongue. "So? I was right!"

"Yeah, you were! It's only been a month!" Rae remarked excitedly. "Maybe we'll get lucky! Maybe Mom can contact Aunt Beccah, and she can check on the house for us!"

"But Mom's still asleep and we can't wake her up."

"She's asleep right *now,*" Rae said, "but the rescue team will wake her up along with Jamie. Maybe even Daddy, too! Doctors can work miracles nowadays, you know! If his life support is broken, it's only been for a short time, and his body is *very* cold in that pod. So, there's a chance we may not lose him after all!" Rae picked up her own spirits with this line of reasoning. "When we're all on board the rescue ship, safe and sound and on our way home, then Mom can call Aunt Beccah and tell her what happened."

Tabitha took a deep breath then, and squeezed Rae's neck a little more tightly.

With each passing minute, Rae found herself more and more happy to have the little squirt there with her to help figure all this out, and not asleep or dead like everyone else on board. Tabby had turned out to be very useful so far. *It's not like she's a bad kid or anything,* Rae admitted. *Tabitha is more of a mouthy terror than anything else.* Often Rae just wanted her to shut up, not go away.

Ever since the moment Rae heard her scream "Mommy," something had snapped inside her. Immediately Rae had developed a new affection for her little sister. She didn't know whether it had been some motherly instinct kicking in early, or if Rae saw herself in little Tabitha, and would want someone to protect *her* in such a situation. Either way, Rae felt a strong conviction to protect this little girl. Even a *duty* to do so.

"Maybe we should ask the computer lady if *she* can wake Mommy up?" Tabby asked.

"But haven't we already done that?"

"No. We tried a bunch of other things, but we never just asked her outright to wake everyone up!"

Rae's heart jumped. "I think you're right!"

"Of course I'm right. Uhhh-gaiiin."

"*Emerald Pearl,*" Rae asked with renewed vigor, "I want to wake up the people in the cryo chamber."

"Cryogenic pods can only be activated or deactivated by the Cryogenics Officer, the Captain, the Executive Officer, or the Officer of the Watch."

"Oh no. Is there an override?"

"*Override can only be authorized by the Captain, the Executive Officer, or the—"*

"Nevermind," Rae interrupted. "What if a rescue ship arrives and we have to evacuate?"

"Pods will function as lifeboats in the event of evacuation. Cryogenic pods Three through Eight are functioning within nominal parameters. Cryogenic pods Nine through Sixteen no longer function."

"Can the pods be opened by the rescue team?" She whispered to Tabby, "Surely they have the medical know how to stabilize anyone who is—"

"Cryogenic pods can only be opened by the Cryogenics Officer, the Captain—"

"Yes, yes, we already know that part!" The information offered by the computer brought up a question Rae had been terrified to ask.

But apparently Tabitha wasn't scared. "*Emerald Pearl,*" the little girl all but shouted, "are all the people in the pods still alive?"

The mean old artificial lady spoke matter-of-factly and without emotion. *"Life signs nominal in cryo pods Three through Eight. Occupants are hibernating. Life signs negative in cryo pods Nine through Sixteen. Occupants are deceased."*

Tabitha's breath caught, and a moment later she buried her face in Rae's shoulder.

Up to this point, Rae had merely *feared* all the people in those pods were dead, including their father. She had still held out hope. But now, hearing his soul had departed as a matter of pure "fact" was hard for her to take. *No. Not hard. Impossible.* She felt her face doing things she couldn't control.

"Daddy!" Tabitha whimpered

Rae wrapped both arms around her little sister and squeezed tightly. Sis did not resist. She only sobbed. Her tears squished out and soaked Rae's shoulder. Rae's own tears streamed down her cheeks. The girls rocked gently on the plush sofa for so long, Rae lost track of time. Tabitha cried and moaned herself to sleep, and Rae sobbed until she was completely out of tears.

24

GSCS *Nightingale*

Moses had thoroughly enjoyed his rehydrated meat and potatoes meal. He hadn't eaten on the Mess Decks in a while; he always took his meals in the Wardroom surrounded by his staff, which amounted to little more than the XO and the Chief of the Boat. The COB had been Kelly ever since Chief Petty Officer Robinsen had retired, a temporary position while they awaited the assigning of a new CPO. Now that Kelly was about to pin CPO herself, she could remain the *Nightingale's* COB. Moses used to enjoy dining with the enlisted sailors when he was a mere ensign and lieutenant, but tradition and appropriateness prevented its regular happenstance now. However, civilians who were also old friends were a different story, hence why Dale Masterson and Antonio Bruno often joined them for meals.

His hunger finally sated, Elwick turned from the windows and entered the galley though a secondary door. Red light filled the stainless-steel space, thanks to the large serving window which had been left open for some unknown reason. He shut it, and the white overhead lights banished the bloody spillage from the next room. Moses breathed deep, and pushed the memory of the past out of his mind. Memories of the *RSS Elliott*. Memories of Captain Persephone Bannon and the fact that she had died so that he may live to fight another day.

Moses made his way to a large, silver, industrial-sized refrigerator. He found a stack of turkey sandwiches wrapped in plastic and grabbed five—one sandwich for himself, and one each member of his bridge crew. He also grabbed a container of chocolate milk, his favorite, then two white milks for the Lieutenant and the Helmsman. A sparkling water for Ozzie. An apple juice for Guy. His hands and arms now full, he looked for a bag or a box as an afterthought. He found a small plastic bag in a drawer, threw everything into it, and headed upwards. Thankfully the trek was a short climb; a ladder right off the vestibule opposite the galley led right to where he wanted to go.

"Captain on the bridge!" Guy Connelly announced upon seeing him.

"As you were," Elwick said, and began handing out the gedunk. "What do we have left, about twenty minutes?"

"Eighteen," the Officer of the Deck announced.

"Sir," said the XO, "Sensors reconfigured to your parameters."

"Aye, thank you, Ozzie."

"Captain? Are you still there?" a young voice asked.

The girls! "Yes, I'm here. Is that you, Tabitha?"

"Tabby!"

"Sorry. Tabby."

"It's okay." She sniffled, and Elwick wondered if she had been crying or if she had caught a cold. "Are you ever going to introduce us to all the other people there with you?"

He chuckled. "I guess it probably is about time we did proper introductions, huh?" *Eighteen minutes to kill, sure, why not?*

"What's going on?" Rae asked, sounding like she had just awakened from a nap.

"Captain Moses is about to introduce us to his crew!" Tabitha exclaimed.

"Why didn't you wake me up?"

"Because you're awake!"

"That's not what I meant!"

"Okay, girls," Elwick broke in, "we're on a slight time crunch, so let's stay on target. With me on the bridge is Mr. Osterland, he's my second in command. Then we have Mr. Kitner, he's our official pilot and currently the Officer of the Deck. Then there's Petty Officer Connelly, he's in charge of communications—"

"Guy! We know him!" Tabby exclaimed.

"Oh, I hadn't realized you had met."

Connelly shrugged. "It happened earlier, when you were below decks."

"Ah. Anyway, rounding out the bridge crew is Starman Apprentice Burgess, who is striking for a rating so we're letting him fly the *Nightingale*. Crazy, I know."

"Whatever *that* means," Tabby muttered. "Mr., Petty Officer, Starman… Do any of you people have first names? Like you do, Captain Moses? And Guy?"

"Ha, yes, of course. So, Commander Osterland's first name is Quinton, but we just call him 'Ozzie.' Lieutenant Kitner's first name is Lance. And Starman Burgess is Max."

"Hi, Ozzie, hi Lance, hi Max," Rae answered. "And hi again, Guy," she added.

Everyone chimed hello.

"We have a few more folks down in Engineering, as well as on a specialized Search and Rescue team. You can meet them a little later."

"Okay."

"Where are you girls from anyway?" Elwick whispered to those around him, "I'm curious as to where they got these accents."

"Earth," Rae said. "Well, *I* am; I was born in Druthers Province. But Tabitha was born in space. So she's only American because Mom and Dad are. Barely even a Terran!"

"That's a lie! I wasn't born in space! I was born on Bradbury station!"

"Which is *in space*. So it doesn't count; it's *above* Earth."

"It does *so* count!" Tabitha yelled.

"I don't think so."

"You were born *above* Earth too, stupid!" Tabby spat. "About one meter up, on a hospital table! Or were you *hatched underground?* In a caaave?"

"Shut up!"

"You shut up."

Moses interrupted. "You girls are from Druthers Province?" Anything to keep the conversation from deteriorating into another childish argument.

"Like I said, I am," Rae answered.

"Which city?"

"Rapid City."

"I see. Isn't that where Captain Reznohr is from?"

"Captain who?"

"Reznohr. You know. The Lewis and Clark project?"

"Do you mean the two guys who discovered America?" asked Tabby.

"They just walked across it," Rae corrected. "They didn't discover it. They were looking for the Pacific Ocean."

Moses laughed. "Ah, no. I mean, Rae is right, they were explorers looking for a Northwest passage to the Pacific, but I'm not talking about that expedition. I'm talking about the one that's going on now. Or will be, soon as they figure out a few technical details."

"The one that's what?"

"I'm certain you heard about it. The Reznohr and Kobane Expedition? They're currently doing experimental jumps, hopping between galaxies at a single leap! But that's not the half of it; they have plans to hop multiple galaxies at a time, in an effort to find the edge of the visible universe!"

Silence filled the air.

"Their ship is called the *Lewis and Clark III*, remember?"

Rae and Tabby remained quiet.

"Nothing? It was all over the newsfeeds a couple years ago, when everyone thought they had blown up hopping to Andromeda from Earth orbit. But they had just hopped into a pocket of space that blocked their comms and jump capability. They got out of it though, I don't know how, and somehow made it twenty galaxies away before turning around and returning to Earth. It was a really big deal! Your teachers or parents surely would have told you about it."

"Nope!" Tabby said in a loud voice.

"We didn't stay in Druthers for long," Rae explained. "We mainly grew up in Manumission Province. So maybe we just didn't hear about it up in Green Bay."

"But… intergalactic news reaches every— You know what? It's okay. Nevermind."

"Sir?" said Kitner, in a low voice. "Ten minutes. Engineering has already begun the super jump procedure, and I need to start making my announcements."

"Aye, Lieutenant," Elwick answered quietly. "Okay, girls, we need to prep for our last jump to the nebula. Will you two be okay for a little while?"

"Sure, Captain Moses," said Rae. "We're really tired. I think we're going to take a nap until you get here."

"Sounds good, Rae. We'll be there 'fore you know it!"

"Promise?" This from Tabby.

"I promise," Moses told her. "Get some rest."

"Okay," the girls said in unison.

Elwick gave Connelly a cutthroat motion with his hand.

Guy touched a button. "Muted, sir."

Elwick punched a virtual button on his command pillar. "BM1, how are you coming along with my super jump?"

No answer.

"Kelly?" Moses said loudly.

After a few more seconds, Kelly's voice exploded across the bridge. "We're makin' it best we can, Cap'n! Give us a couple of minutes!"

"Aye, Kelly. I know this is a delicate procedure. Let me know when you're ready."

"Aye aye, sir! Oh and Cap'n?"

"Yes?"

"Ya do realize we're prolly gunna burn out the core with this last one, right? And be stranded out here on our lonesome?"

Elwick looked at the faces around the bridge. He nodded to himself, then said "Aye, Kelly."

"Alright, sir. Long as you're prepared for the bitchin' and moanin' 'til the calvary arrives and tows us back to dock!"

"Mr. Kitner," said Moses, avoiding the conversation, "begin your ship-wide announcements. I want to get to that final waypoint sooner rather than later."

"Aye aye, sir!"

"I need to grab something from my cabin. Keep up with the countdown."

"Aye," came several voices in reply. Elwick barely heard them; he was more focused on getting out of sight of the bridge crew before they saw him pass out like a common land lubber as soon as space folded his entire world inside two measly dimensions.

He barely had time to latch his cabin door before the super jump took hold of him completely.

Moses awoke. He lay on his side, unsure what year it might be. When he opened his eyes, he discovered everything he had eaten in the past hour spread out before him in a cone-shaped pattern. He looked away, and tried hard no to breathe through his nose. The world seemed a blur of reddish-black.

"Captain?" came a voice Moses thought he recognized. A moment passed before he could muster up the wherewithal to answer the call. He was thankful the comms even still worked; the lights sure didn't. The reddish color his eyes reported came from a single emergency lamp high on one wall. His beloved ship had surely taken a real beating. "Elwick," he choked, still on the floor.

"Final jump complete, sir."

"Thank you, Mr. Kitner." At least he hoped that had been Kitner.

"Systems are slow to come up," the lieutenant continued, "but the *Nightingale's* SRS is working on those, and where it can't perform an auto fix, we have people on it. No cause for concern. Yet."

Thank God for technical miracles. Moses wished the Navy had had Self-Repair Systems on all ships in the fleet back in the war, it might have saved all their asses. He swallowed. Ugh, shouldn't have done that. Need water. Moses drug himself to the head, and with some effort, pulled his body upright to the sink to rise the foul taste of vomit from his mouth. The ice-cold water tasted delicious, and soothed the burning in his throat. "Roger," he managed to choke out.

"Cap'n?"

He definitely recognized *that* voice. "What is it, Kelly?"

"Well, like I feared, the Zee Dee is dead. She's done made 'er last jump. And so have we. If we're goin' home, we're gonna need a tow."

Moses sighed. "Yeah, I figured that might happen."

No reply. Kelly was likely biting her tongue to keep from saying something she shouldn't. Not over the ship's comm, at least.

A single overhead light flickered on as Moses took another drink to whet his whistle. "Focus on the ion drive now. That's what's going to get us to the *Pearl* and back out of the cloud again. We'll request a tow from the *Buker* when she gets here."

"Aye aye, Cap'n."

The circuit closed before Elwick could say more. *Time to pick yourself up, Moses. You just failed your crew, in a sense, by breaking your ship. Don't fail the survivors of your rescue.* He gargled the ice-cold water once more, and straightened his tunic in the mirror. Somehow, his uniform had escaped two hurling episodes today. On his way out the door, he snatched up his command cap from the floor by the puddle of puke. Again, no stains. *Thank God for real miracles, too,* he thought.

* * *

"Captain on the bridge," Connelly faithfully announced upon Elwick's arrival.

"Ninety-three percent of all systems are back up," Lieutenant Kitner announced. Indeed, the bridge already looked completely back to normal.

"Thank you, Lance." The nebula now filled the entire view outside the windows. Before their final jump, he could still see some blackness around the edges. Now, claustrophobia began knocking on Elwick's door. "How close did you get us, Pilot?"

"Right on the doorstep, sir!"

"He's right," said the XO. I'm reading several parts per thousand of hydrogen outside right now, but it climbs to trillions a few million clicks away. But we're not 'inside' just yet."

"Aye, alright." Elwick took a couple of breaths and forced the squeezing feeling away. "Good job. Lieutenant Kitner, drop a beacon. This will mark our entry and exit points. It will also mark a good rendezvous point with the *Buker* when this is all over."

"Aye aye."

"Can't wait for that," muttered the XO.

"Burgess, as soon as Ozzie feeds you his route data, make a beeline to that distress signal. Ion base nine if the XO thinks we can muster it safely."

"Base nine, aye, sir!" the Starman replied.

"I'll tighten my turns…" the XO said under his breath.

Elwick thought about Ozzie's "Can't wait" comment. It had been a direct reference to what would befall them—him—when they return to the beacon and rendezvous with the Navy. If they hadn't rescued the passengers and made it back to the nebula entry point by the time the *Buker* arrived, Moses might as well just stay on board the *Pearl.* It would at least be a *bigger* prison than the one he would find himself in for disobeying such clear and blatant orders from the RNA Navy. And it would amount to a quick death at that; freezing, he thought, would be preferable than languishing in a box the size of his bunk for the next ten years. If not twenty. "On second thought, push it to eleven."

Osterland shot Elwick an incredulous glance.

Moses returned his gaze. "Can we do that, XO?"

Ozzie sighed, then nodded. "I'll make it work."

"Ion base eleven, aye!" yelled Burgess. "Bat out of Hell!"

"Pilot, make sure you wait for the XO's go ahead before you step on the gas, yes?"

Burgess nodded. "Aye aye, Captain." His voice had lost the excitement of a moment ago, as if realizing they didn't have an exact heading, and couldn't go anywhere just yet.

"Captain," said Connelly, "if you have a minute, I think we have a problem."

Uh oh. Moses made his way to the comms station. "What is it, Guy?"

"Alright, sir, I was able to obtain an exact location of the *Emerald Pearl* by remoting into Deep Space Relay 3287, but—"

"You remoted into Sentinel 3287?" Elwick exclaimed, turning to look at Osterland.

"Hey, he's the comms expert," the XO replied, "I'm just an O-5, what do I know?"

Elwick chuckled. "I want to know how you did it, but you can explain later."

"It was pretty simple, I just had to configure the—"

"He said you can explain later!" yelled Ozzie from the nav station.

"Right. Sorry, sir. Anyway," Connelly continued, "Captain, even though I obtained the location…" He paused and added, "And just so you know, I've checked and triple checked this data…"

"It's okay, Guy, what are you trying to tell me?"

"Sir, she's not at those coordinates."

Elwick thought for a second. "The ship could have drifted."

"Sir, it probably has, but the signal is constant, it's never stopped broadcasting since we first picked it up. These coordinates should be good as of, well, this very second. Here, I'll update it again." He touched some controls and the numbers displayed on his console slightly refined.

"Hmm. Well, remember, Guy, our sensors are highly ineffective inside these things. Even if we haven't breached the cloud yet, the sensor beam could easily be scattering—"

"Sir, I realize that, which is why I narrowed the beam, just like Mr. Osterland is doing with the nav sensors. Only I narrowed the comm beam to a thousandth of an arc second, which is max resolution. That focuses on the point in space the signal is originating from to within a single meter at this distance," Connelly explained. "I thought we could at least get a ghost image of the frigate if nothing else. Maybe assess the damage, but—" He sighed. "Captain, I'm sorry, but there's just no ship there."

25

GSCS *Nightingale*

Moses' stomach growled again. His dinner still lay over the deck in his office. Normally he would bring it to someone's attention, have it cleaned up. But he decided it might be best to clean it up himself, to avoid questions and rumors. Hopefully he could get to it before it stank the place up. He found and unwrapped his little piece of turkey heaven and tried to stave off the hunger pangs once more. "So explain this one, Ozzie," Elwick said, and took a big bite. He didn't wait to swallow before speaking again. "What would cause us to not have the ability to locate that ship? Are the sensors already on the blink? Returning false data? We haven't even entered the nebula yet!"

"Running a quick diagnostic on the sensor array…" the XO replied. After a moment he shook his head, "Sensors are green. I got nuthin', sir. With a beam that refined, we should be getting *something.*"

Moses sighed, straightened up, and peered into the mixture of bright red and dim magenta patches and swirls. as if trying to stare down the red demon. "Well, we're not going to determine anything sitting here. Ozzie, do we have a clear path to what we *think* is our destination yet?"

A moment passed before the XO answered. "Annnd, done! Feeding coordinates to the helm now. You're going to have your work cut out for you, Max. Just follow my path to the letter. Those calculations at this speed leaves almost no room for error."

"Aye aye, Mr. Osterland."

"Good job, Ozzie," Elwick said. "Burgess, I have every faith in you. Mr. Kitner, Let's get underway. Ion Base eleven."

"Ion Base eleven, aye!" the Lieutenant confirmed.

Starman Burgess repeated the command, and moved his hands in all the appropriate ways to get the ship moving.

Ion engines were fairly silent, but Elwick could pick up the ever-so-slight rumble and even less-noticeable vibration running throughout the hull. They were moving, and *fast.* One-quarter the speed of light itself. Nearly seventy-five thousand kilometers per second! At this speed, a ship could close the distance from the Earth to the Sun in half an hour. Or cross Earth's entire solar system in a little less than seventeen hours. Only they weren't on a leisurely cruise to Neptune. They were heading directly into a glowing mass of trouble.

"What do the aviators call this?" Lieutenant Kitner asked. "Heading into the *goo?*"

Elwick chuckled, and focused on the path before them. He had hoped the *Emerald Pearl* should have been an ever-growing black dot in the center of their viewport by now. Instead, it was off hiding somewhere.

"I don't get it," Connelly spoke up. "The signal is being broadcast from a location directly in front of us!"

"Distance?" Elwick asked.

"Approximately… six million kilometers. Two light seconds."

We'll pass them in eight seconds! Moses realized. "Helm, full stop!"

"Full stop!" Kitner yelled.

Burgess yanked back on his flightstick and yelled, "Full stop, aye!"

"Distance now, Connelly?"

"Now, wow. Good flying, Max. We should be right on top of them!"

Through squinted eyelids Moses scanned the heavens for a tiny black dot. Talk about searching for the proverbial needle! Too bad they couldn't burn the haystack. *Well,* he mused, c*onsidering this haystack was made of highly volatile substances, it actually could burn...* But igniting the nebula would be far worse than lighting hay; in this case, not only would the barn be destroyed in an instant, but the entire farm and all the animals on it. To include his ship and crew. Definitely defeated the purpose of a rescue.

Elwick stroked his beard. "Nothing on short range or QBert?" asked Moses.

"Sorry, sir," Osterland replied. QE RADAR is already useless."

Not many options remained. Moses turned to face Connelly. "Guy, hop up into the bubble and see if you can't spot our lost children."

"Aye aye, Captain." Connelly acknowledged, turned his blue Navy-issue ball cap around so the bill faced backward, and moved quickly to a ladder near his station. He climbed up to a small, transparent dome atop the *Nightingale's* bridge. Called a "Locator Bubble," it was used to give a crewmember a quick, 360-degree assessment of the area above and around the ship. While this may seem an antiquated method in the days of faster-than-light travel and

RADAR that could, under normal circumstances, "see" across dozens of light years in an instant, it was effective and didn't require anything but a set of eyes to work properly.

"Let's give Guy a hand. Open her all the way up, Pilot," ordered Elwick.

"Aye aye, sir."

The Helmsman touched his controls, and six remaining four-meter by five-meter protective graphene-coated titanium panels that covered the front right and front left sides of the bridge slid back along the hull. This exposed half the octagonal-shaped bridge to the torrent of redness pouring in from outside. The bridge brightened immediately, and Elwick found himself protecting his eyes from the glare once again.

The extra viewport covers now removed, that additional layer of protection for the bridge crew disappeared as well. But they still had the magnetic field being generated from below decks, which protected them from all the standard deadly cosmic radiation coming at them from all corners of the universe, not unlike Earth's magnetic field protected life on the surface of his faraway homeworld.

A terrible thought crept into his mind again. He and his people were safe from the radiation of the nebula, but were the girls? The children were now in the observation lounge on board the *Pearl*. And the power—meaning large machinery like their magnetic field generator—had been shut down. Moses was the one who instructed Rae to shut off every system except the bare-bones minimum. Doing so, had he undermined all their rescue efforts? Had the girls both already received a lethal dose of cancer-causing radiation? The *Pearl* was a century old; did it have graphene "glass" like the *Nightingale*? The wonder material with the capability of blocking the invisible light that threatened to break down the DNA in every cell in a human body? "*Nightingale*, Archives,' he said into his command pillar, speaking directly to the computer. "*Emerald Pearl* refit history."

Text flew across a screen, no audio. "*Error,*" reported the ship's computer. *"Cannot connect to QE-paired communications beacon. Standby. Adjusting General Relativistic Curved Spacetime Inducer."* A pause. *"No effect. Unable to complete request."*

"Now's a fine time," Moses said flatly. "Is the radio channel to the *Pearl* still open?" Elwick glanced up to see that Connelly still up in the Locator Bubble. He flew to the Communications Station and touched a virtual button on the appropriate screen. "Girls, are you still up in the Observation Lounge?"

No answer.

Connelly called from above. "Sir? I don't see that ship anywhere. I've scanned the sky three times." His voice resonated in the enclosed space. To Elwick, it sounded like Guy's head was stuffed inside a metal drum. "Maybe it's under us?"

Under us! "Helm, roll one-hundred-eighty degrees."

"Helm, roll to starboard," announced the Officer of the Deck. "One-eight-zero degrees."

"Aye, roll to starboard!" Burgess repeated.

The view outside changed little as the ship executed its maneuver.

"One-eight-zero degrees, Captain," reported Kitner.

"Guy, take another look now," Elwick ordered.

"Aye aye, Captain!"

"*Emerald Pearl,*" Moses called again, "this is the *Nightingale*. Please respond."

Silence.

"Connelly?"

"Nothing yet, sir!"

There has to be something in the ship's database, even if I can't reach the archives back home... Elwick returned to his pillar and bored down a series of menus. "Ah, here we go." The text read, "*Emerald Pearl. Commissioned 2460. History: Prior commissioned* Republic Star Ship *Holloway, 2434. Decommissioned 2454.*" Moses' gaze flew over the original schematics of the *Holloway*. No observation lounge or dome. Only a single rail gun turret at the highest point of the ship. The dome had been fashioned later, when the *Holloway* had been converted to a civilian, Merchant Marine vessel. This is the reason they had used the schematics for *Kristin's Vision* during the mission briefing. He closed his eyes and lowered his head. There was simply no way to tell if he had made a mistake by allowing them to go to the observation dome. *But Moe,* he told himself, *it doesn't matter how much radiation those girls are exposed to if you never find their ship! They'll freeze long before the cancer gets them.* "Rae! Tabitha! Can you hear me? This is Captain Elwick."

He heard sounds but he couldn't decipher them. Were they sounds of clothing rubbing on a plush sofa? Or just out-gassing from a dying ship? "Girls!"

"Captain Moses?" came a familiar but groggy voice.

Elwick's heart started beating again as he heard the sweet utterance of one Rae Marshall.

"Thank God," he said to anyone listening. "It's time to wake up, girls, we have some rescuing to do."

"Tabby. Tabby wake up. They're here."

"Well, girls, we're not quite there yet," Moses said. "We've reached the location of the distress beacon but we're having a few… problems."

"What problems?" asked Tabitha, who sounded sleepy as well.

"We're near," he lied, "but it will be a little while longer before we dock with the *Pearl*. In the meantime, would you make your way to the *port* airlock? Let me know if you can get to it and whether or not it's damaged, okay? Port is on the *left* side of the ship when you're looking toward the bow, the bow being the front of the—"

"I *know* what a bow is, and I know which direction port is, Captain Moses," Rae interrupted. "I've been on boats and spaceships all my life."

Moses shook his head for underestimating these girls yet again. "Alright, sorry, I just wanted to be sure. I didn't know you knew ships so well."

"It's okay. I never told you that," Rae said. "I just need to have the computer show me a map and we'll be on our way."

"Rae? One more thing. Do either of you feel sick to your stomach?"

"No. Well, I'm starting to get hungry."

"Me too," Tabitha added.

"No, that's not what I meant," Elwick said. "I mean do you feel sick like when you get the flu. Have either of you had the flu?"

"I have," Rae said.

Tabitha sounded upbeat. "I haven't. I'm immune."

"No you're not, you're just lucky," Rae said. Then, "Hey! Don't stick your tongue out at me!"

"Girls, if either of you start feeling ill, please let me know. It may be nothing to worry about, but I don't think you should be hanging out in the Observation Lounge anymore."

"Observation *Dome*," Tabitha corrected.

"Right, Dome. Listen, I'm not one-hundred percent sure the glass in that dome will protect you from the nebula."

"What do you mean?"

"This particular nebula is putting out a lot of dangerous radiation. The dome was installed long after the ship was built. I have no way of knowing it was constructed with the materials that will protect you from that."

"Oh, it's okay. Captain Timmins said it was made out of graphite."

Elwick paused. "You mean graphene?"

Tabitha giggled. "Told you it wasn't made out of pencils."

"Shut up, Tabby. Like you knew!"

"I did."

At that moment, Osterland looked back at his Captain with a grave look. *Uh oh.* Moses held up his index finger to Ozzie, asking for "one minute." "Listen, girls, if the dome is made from graphene, it will offer some protection. But just to be safe, try to limit your time there, okay?"

"Okay, Captain," Rae agreed. "We shouldn't have to come up here again anyway, right?"

"Probably not, we'll be there soon. Or at least, as soon as we can. We have some work to do now, so I'm going to put you back on mute just for a little while so we don't bore you to death with all the technical details, okay? Call for me when you get down to the airlock."

"Aye—"

"Aye aye, Captain!" Tabitha called.

"Tabby! Why do you always have to talk over me?"

"Well, if you knew what you were doing, maybe I wouldn't have to step in all the time," the younger one said.

"Shut up! I know what I'm doing!"

Connelly made a motion with his hand, indicating he had muted the channel.

"At least the girls are in good spirits," Elwick mused. "Alright Mr. Osterland, this had better not be more bad news. I don't think I'm in the mood for it."

26

Emerald Pearl

"I have to go to the bathroom," Tabby complained.

"Okay," Rae said. "I think there's a—"

"I know where it is," Sis spat.

"Of course you do."

The girls made their way downward, re-entering the dark halls of the derelict ship.

Why can't we just wait in the dome and let Captain Moses find us? Rae followed her little sister to the nearest bathroom. She remembered her father calling it a "head" when they were on the boat, but she had no idea why. She also didn't know why they were called 'bathrooms'; there were no bath tubs in the restrooms on the ship, except for in their quarters. Realization dawned on her. "I think you mean you have to go to the restroom."

"Whatever," Tabby replied, walking faster.

She had likely figured this out long before now, was already onto Rae's imminent teasing, and was having none of it.

Tabby shoved hard on a door marked "WC" and disappeared into the dark room beyond. Rae didn't know what *WC* stood for, but she knew it meant there were toilets in there. She didn't feel any pressure on her bladder, and she had no desire to hear her little sister do her business, so she stood outside the door and leaned against the wall. At least the lighting seemed brighter here. But now another realization dawned on her.

I'm alone.

For the first time since waking up, no other human being was in the same room as her. A chill ran up Rae's spine and back down again. She shivered all over. She looked left. No one there. She looked right. Same. "Hurry up, Tabby!"

"I just sat down, leave me alone!"

Rae's lower lip protruded on its own. Not that she *really* thought zombies would round any one of those corners at any moment, but it wasn't out of the realm of possibility; there were a *lot* of freshly dead people on this ship!

That made her think of the people down below who were still alive. Their mother, their brother, and the four other people in their cryo pod row. They were all men, and their pods weren't malfunctioning like all the ones in their father's row. Suddenly, yet another realization hit her, and she became angry.

She spotted a comm panel just down the hall. She jogged over and activated it with a closed fist. "*Emerald Pearl*, why were we woken up?" she spat.

The computer always sounded unaffected by the tone of Rae's voice. "Inquiry not understood. Please refine the request."

Rae rolled her eyes. "How did you choose the cryo pods you did and revive the people inside?

"Standard Ship Operating Procedure states that when the crew is incapacitated, individuals in cryogenic stasis may be awakened to survey the situation, affect repairs if necessary, and tend to other needs of the ship."

"They didn't tell us that in the safety brief," Rae remarked. *Or if they did, I probably wasn't listening. There were adults around, after all, and such things are for them to worry about, not us children!* Which led precisely to the point she had been trying to make, a mystery she wanted to finally solve. "*Emerald Pearl*, why weren't the adults woken up? Why not any of the other pods? Why just mine and my sister's?"

"Multiple queries. Please—"

"'Please refine the request,' I got it," she chimed in unison with the computer. "Why did you only open pods One and Two?"

"Pods One and Two were reactivated in numerical order as per Standard Ship Operating Procedure," the voice announced robotically. *"SOP dictates the minimum number of pods necessary to complete emergency tasks be opened when life-support systems are compromised, and captain and crew are incapacitated or otherwise unable to make the decision to open any or all cryogenic hibernation containers."*

Rae's eyes grew, and she stared at the panel. "The crew shouldn't have put us in those pods. Adults should have been in pods One and Two, not two little girls! They should have known that!" Rae shouted. "I can't *believe* this!"

"Did you get lonely or something?" came a voice behind her.

Rae jumped and spun 'round. "Tabby! You about gave me a heart attack!"

"Well how do you think *I* felt when I came out of the bathroom and you weren't there?" Sis exclaimed.

"I'm sorry, I just had some questions for the computer."

"Yeah, I know, I heard you from the bathroom, I wasn't really scared."

Rae's shoulders slumped. "Tabby!"

"So, we shouldn't have been in those pods, huh?"

"No. The crew conked up. Grown-ups should have been in our pods. Not us. Or any kids. And if they conked up something that serious, it makes me wonder what else they might have done wrong," Rae added.

Tabby looked down with her brow all furrowed, like she was working through something. After a moment, she looked up. "Rae? I'm scared."

Rae sighed. *Oh, that's just great. It had been bad enough when only one of us admitting being scared! Me! Now I've filled her head with Goddess-knows-what.* She bent down on one knee and gently grasped her little sister's arms. "Everything will be okay, Tabby. Don't worry. Captain Moses is on his way."

Tabby's lower lip stuck out then, and began to quiver.

Rae hugged her. "I'm sorry. Forget I said anything about the crew messing up. Everything will be okay. Captain Moses will be here soon, and we'll get Mom out and Jamie out and we'll get something to eat, and Captain Moses will notify our aunt, and we'll be home in no time. Well, a month or so probably, but it'll seem like no time because they'll stick us in two brand new cryo pods and we won't even notice the trip! You and me and Mom and Jamie will probably be at Aunt Beccah's house tomorrow, from our viewpoint! Doesn't that sound great? Things will be hard without Daddy, yes, but Mother is strong. Everything will be just fine. You'll see!"

Tabitha squirmed free of her sister's embrace. "Rae, what if they don't come?"

Now it was Rae's brow's turn to furrow. "Why would you say that? Of course they'll come! They're on their way! What, do you think they're lying?"

"Why aren't they here already? It's been hours! Spaceships are really fast, Rae. Something's wrong."

"You're just scared. I'll prove it right now." Rae stood and tapped the comm screen right above the red circle. "Guy?" Rae called. "*Nightingale?* You're still there, right?"

Only the slightest of pauses transpired before the familiar voice of Guy Connelly shot from the speaker on the wall. "Yes, of course. We're all here," he assured.

His voice and his words soothed Rae's soul, her heartbeat slowing immediately. "See, Tabby?"

Tabitha's eyes gave away everything she surely felt at that moment. Rae had no doubt in her mind the little girl wasn't reassured at all.

And Rae now regretted not using the "WC" room.

27

GSCS *Nightingale*

"Captain, you might want to have a look at this."

"Please don't tell me more bad news," Elwick said to Commander Osterland as he reached the Navigator's station.

"It's only bad if you think having a microscopic wormhole ten meters off your starboard bow is bad news," he replied.

Elwick's eyes grew wide. "How did we miss that, Ozzie?"

"Sorry sir, I didn't have the sensors fine-tuned far enough to pick up ones that small. I've made the proper adjustments, obviously, or I wouldn't even have seen that one. Oh, and don't worry, I scanned behind us, we didn't fly though any on our way in."

"Are there any more in front of us?"

"Sensors are still refining their sweeps. I'll know in a few seconds. If there are, I'll readjust calculations and feed a new path to the helm."

"Aye. Is this one affecting the *Nightingale* in any way?"

The navigator's head spun in several directions, checking various displays. "Guy, check your console, please."

PO2 Connelly still loitered up in the bubble searching for the *Emerald Pearl,* but shot down the ladder in a flash. He dove to his station and checked all his screens and readouts. "No anomalous readings on my end," he reported. "Sir, I got an idea while staring into all that gas and plasma. It's a little crazy, though."

Elwick crossed his arms. "I'll take anything at this point. Go ahead."

"These little anomalies… Well sir, we all know it's been hypothesized that radiation and possibly even matter as well can enter one wormhole and then exit through another, like a subway tunnel, without ever passing through the space in-between."

"I don't think it's a hypothesis anymore," said Kitner. "I read about some studies being done on sending messages through wormholes. Not that it really helps or matters what with instantaneous QE comms, but it was an interesting read." He let out an uncharacteristic laugh. "Some crackpot even said his team had been successful in sending a whole ship through a wormhole! With people on it! Can you imagine someone would believe that? How it would fit is anybody's guess!"

Elwick's mind whirled. "So, wait a minute. If you're getting at what I think you're getting at, Guy, you think the *Pearl's* emergency transmission may be exiting say, that microscopic wormhole that's parked right off our starboard bow?" He pointed that direction without conscious thought. "The one Ozzie only just now picked up? And that's why it appears we're right on top of them? But we're not?"

Guy nodded. "Aye, sir, that's exactly what I'm saying."

"Alright," Elwick continued, "say I buy that. Not sure I do, but let's just wargame this for a minute." He paced between the two command pillars in the center of the bridge. "If the signal is *exiting* from *this* wormhole, it must be entering through another one somewhere else."

"That would fit with the theory, yes, sir," Connelly agreed.

"Okay, so where's this other wormhole?"

Silence.

"Wait," said Ozzie, "is this really possible? That radio, and well, I guess any light radiation, can go through wormholes?"

Kitner spoke up again. "I read about it sir, and not in a pseudo-science site on the Galactic Exonet. It was actually in the latest *Nature and Astronomy*. The part about sending matter through, though, that had to be a bucket o' bilge water; I couldn't find it on any reputable site."

The XO sat back in his chair. "But why haven't I ever heard of such a thing?"

"Well, sir," explained Kitner, "that issue just came out. It still needs more peer-review before SENTCORPS will give it any credence."

"But to not even to warn us this kind of shit is possible!? What if that *really is* what's going on right now?"

"Maybe this is the first time?" Elwick offered. "Maybe no one's ever seen something like this before? In the field, I mean."

"I don't know, Captain. This sounds hokey to me."

Connelly interjected. "Just because we haven't seen such a thing occur before, sir, doesn't mean it can't. And honestly, by the same logic, the other wormhole could be anywhere. Hopefully somewhere in the nebula, but if I understand the phenomenon right, it could be anywhere in the universe. Right, Lieutenant?"

"That's right," Kitner verified in his deep bass. "However, I think it's safe to say they're still very much inside this sector and within a parsec, considering the type of ship the *Pearl* is."

Guy put an end to their fears of the derelict ship being elsewhere in the galaxy. “The girls said the sky was red outside the ship. Isn’t it safe to assume they were seeing the same nebula we’re seeing right now?”

“Well, if it’s not,” Max Burgess muttered, “the girls are dead for sure.”

No one countered his argument.

Moses smiled. “He’s right. We will assume the girls are nearby. Because otherwise…” He didn’t finish his sentence.

“Aye aye!” several voices replied in unison.

“Well,” said the XO, “using that same logic… This cloud is thirty-four light years across at its widest point. Twenty-one at its narrowest. And we can’t use our jump drive in here. If those girls aren’t within a single light year of our position—”

That silence fell again.

“Okay!” Elwick said. “More assumptions! Honestly, boys, we have no choice at this point. We’ll either find them nearby, or we won’t. If we don’t, no one can say we didn’t give it everything we had. To include one Zee Dee core.” *And one career,* he wanted to mutter.

Osterland looked at Guy. “You seem to have all the bright ideas, Connelly. Tell us a quick way to find this other wormhole.”

Guy shook his head. “Sorry, sir, as you like to say, I got nuthin’.”

“I may have an idea,” came a very feminine voice from behind them.

The voice startled Moses, and by the look of everyone’s faces, the entire bridge crew.

“Barbara? When did you sneak in here?”

"Oh, about five minutes ago. I came up for a different reason, which I've now long since forgotten—I hate getting old—but it probably doesn't matter now. I just sat back here so as not to disturb anyone."

"What's your idea?"

"Oh! Yes." The septuagenarian stood up. "When I was a little girl, I loved the ballet. Well, my mother loved it more than I did. I actually hated it, come to think of it. Anyway, I'll never forget this one performance we put on. It was one of those kitschy laser shows, you know, the ones that come in and out of popularity over the centuries? So we had laser guns on our toes, the tips of our fingers, and even right between our eyes. We were quite the sight on a dark stage! There were only six of us up there, but when we got to spinning, we literally lit up that entire concert hall. I saw the holo after the show. It was amazingly beautiful."

Elwick stroked his beard. "Spinning… Like a ballerina with lights on her fingers."

"And her head."

"And toes!" Max burst.

"Right, young man!"

The XO crossed his arms now. "Are you asking us to spin the *Nightingale* like a ballerina, shining lasers in every direction in the hopes that they will light up something? And we're supposed to be on the lookout for shiny little dot to appear while we're all retching our guts up?"

"Oh, it's not so bad, Mr. Osterland. If a little girl can do it…"

"Not with lasers," Guy pointed out, "but with focused sensor beams. The nav computer will alert us if it finds anything!"

Elwick smiled. "That it will. So it won't matter if we're all on the floor passed out in a pool of our own vomit, when we wake up, we'll have a heading."

"Assuming," said Kitner, "the *Pearl* is within a light year of our position. Even at ¼ lightspeed, if we don't reach that ship in the next four hours, those two little girls will be dead."

Moses nodded. "Quite right, Lieutenant. Barbara, thank you, you were a godsend at the precise moment we needed you. If this actually works, I mean."

"Almost like I was meant to be here," she said, winking.

"The Lord does work in mysterious ways," Moses agreed.

"If by the Lord you mean Allah," said Kitner, "then if he wills it, it will happen."

"For once I think our religions may agree, Lance. I think so, anyway. Alright!" He announced in a loud voice. "We're going to take a little roller coaster ride." He turned once again to Barbara. "If this works, it shall henceforth be known as the Laskey Maneuver."

Barbara smiled. "Just give me a minute or two to get to my quarters and strap myself into my bunk, if you would be so kind, Captain."

"Oh! Of course. I should probably warn everyone else on board..." He touched the 1MC, once again opening a channel to every corner of the ship. He allowed the auto boatswain's call-to-attention to finish before speaking. "Attention, all hands. In precisely three minutes, we be conducting a Laskey Maneuver. This will involve spinning the ship across all vectors simultaneously. I suggest you do not stand during this procedure. It should only last a minute. Maybe two. Stop whatever you're currently doing, batten down your hatches, find a seat or a bunk or just lie down on the floor, and try and hold onto your dinner. For you actual seadogs, this will be your angles and dangles for the day."

"Hopefully for the year," the XO muttered.

Moses had to agree. *God knows what will find its way to the deck after this little stunt.* He continued with his announcement. "You'll be notified when the maneuver is complete, but your inner ear should be the one to tell you when it's safe to stand up again. That is all." He closed the circuit. "Mr. Kitner, wait exactly one hundred and eighty seconds to allow everyone to stow gear and get somewhere safe, and then give me a fast spin first on the *X* vector, then a simultaneous spin on the *Y* vector, and finally on the Z vector."

Kitner probably did not know how to call out this order so he simply said, "Aye, standing by for one hundred and eighty seconds, then initiating spin." He moved to the helm and talked quietly to Starman Burgess, likely on precisely how they were going to make it work.

"Ozzie," said Elwick, "narrow the beams on all six emitters to the point I could zero in on a single page of the RNA Constitution. Return them to their default orientations; I want us pointing one of Barbara's lasers straight out from the mast, the keel, the bow, aft, port, and starboard."

"Aye aye." The XO shook his head. "God, I hope this isn't for nothing." The navigator's hands flew across his virtual screens like a conductor directing an orchestra.

Elwick perked up now that they had a plan that might actually get them somewhere. If the spinning didn't land the entire compliment of the *Nightingale* in Sick Bay.

"We good, Pilot?"

"Good, sir, I understand the procedure." replied Starman Burgess.

"Aye. Now move over while I program the auto-stop."

Burgess, unable to move the Helmsman's chair, spun toward Osterland while the Lieutenant programmed the Helm so they would be able to come out of the maneuver more quickly. Max spoke softly, but still loud enough for Elwick to hear him.

"Mr. Osterland," the young man began, "I have a question."

"Shoot." The XO replied.

"I remember learning in school that massive gravity sources can impact a jumping ship's navigation and shorten a jump, but how strong does it have to be before that happens? I mean, how close to we have to be to it? And how much gravity do these wormholes have?"

The XO chuckled. "Worried they're like microscopic black holes, and will turn you into a noodle, Starman?"

"Something like that."

"Well, I don't think you have anything to worry about. Wormholes don't have gravity. Not like black holes and neutron stars do, anyway."

"That's another thing; I don't know what scares me more, black holes or neutron stars! At least with a black hole I wouldn't fry from the inside out!"

"Like I said, I wouldn't worry about it too much. Plus, like Kitner alluded earlier, I really don't think the *Nightingale* could get 'eaten'. I'm still not fully convinced even radio or QE waves could get sucked in and spit out, but hey, I'm just a quartermaster, what do I know?"

"Yeah but, we *are* in the Hades Quadrangle. There's probably some reason ships go in and then just—" he cut himself short and glanced around the bridge before whispering, "disappear."

Elwick couldn't prevent himself from swallowing at that moment. An autonomous reaction to a fear he himself had been trying to ignore.

Osterland shook his head and chuckled again. "Where do you kids come up with this stuff?" He turned to look at Elwick. "Can you believe this guy? Superstitious as my mother-in-law!"

Elwick jumped in to help Ozzie. "Nothing to worry about, Pilot. Would SARCOM, let alone SENTCORPS, allow us to go in after that ship if there was a serious risk of something impeding our ability to help those people?"

Osterland looked over his shoulder. "They might not allow us to go in there for any number of *other* reasons, but not because of *that!*"

Elwick shared a glare with his XO.

Burgess nodded his head. "I didn't think of it that way. I'm sure they know what they're doing."

Not so sure I know what I'm *doing,* Moses thought. He sincerely hoped he had made the right decision to continue this rescue.

Burgess' face twisted up. "Sir, do you think it was just carelessness that caused the accident? Like maybe they were just trying to shave a few jumps and tried to angle off a black hole or a neutron star? Like how Death Racers use high gravity sources to their advantage and conduct super jumps?"

"You mean to tell me, Burgess," Connelly cut in, "you think a seasoned, Merchant Marine captain would try something so crazy as boost-jumping in a civilian passenger ship!?"

"Didn't it used to be a military ship?" Burgess countered.

The XO snorted. "Yeah, but a frigate, not a Zeus class! And hey, I'm sure these private civilian crews are always trying to save a credit or two and widen their profit margins, but if they were nuts enough to do something like that, they've got bigger balls than I do!"

"Hear, hear," Elwick agreed.

"Even if it was just carelessness," said Osterland, "it's still negligence in my book." He breathed deep, stared into the starfield ahead of them, and added, "There is another possibility. That wicked nebula we're about to go waltzing into could have been targeted specifically."

Starman Burgess' eyes bulged. "Sir, you don't think it could have been intentional! An act of sabotage?"

Osterland shrugged and returned his focus to the three-dimensional displays around him. "Eh, you're right. Seems silly when I say it out loud."

Elwick stared at the back of the XO's head. All those words weren't meant for the young pilot. They were meant for *him*. *Was* he doing the right thing, ignoring the Navy's orders to stay away? What if the reason RNA Naval Intelligence had gotten involved was because of something secretive on that ship that the powers-that-be didn't want getting out? Could there be danger of the *Nightingale's* systems suffering complete failure, leaving them deaf, blind, and as freezing cold as the *Emerald Pearl*? So many ships had already not returned from this region of space. And the *Nightingale* was already dead in the water as far as ever leaving it without a repair to their Zhédié core, or a tow. Had he just doomed his entire crew?

"Mr. Kitner. When you're ready, initiate the maneuver."

"Aye aye, Captain. Almost finished."

Burgess risked a look over at the Officer of the Deck. "Oh wow. I never would have thought of doing it that way!"

"What, you thought I was just a dumb lieutenant? Is that what you mean, Starman?"

Max stumbled over his words and ran them all together. "No, no, sir. I didn't mean to imply anything, I merely meant I—"

Kitner howled and patted the young man on the back. "I'm just pokin' Charlie there, Pilot! Captain, we're good to go!"

"Aye." Moses touched the 1MC again. "Now hear this. Initiating maneuver at this time. Grab onto something. Elwick out." Then to the OOD, "Initiate, Mr. Kitner."

"Aye, Initiating Laskey Maneuver!" the Lieutenant replied.

Burgess collected himself. "Initiate Laskey Maneuver, aye!"

"Just as we discussed, Burgess," whispered Kitner.

Elwick looked around for something to grab hold of; the Captain didn't have a chair. Neither did the Officer of the Deck. He saw Kitner bracing himself on the edge of the Helm. Elwick would do the same, only on his command pillar. He wasn't about to take a seat on the floor, if someone else had to stand. Surely, he could make it through some angles and dangles, right? Granted these would be a bit extreme, but it's not like his feet would leak out of his head or anything. Not this time; they were remaining in normal spacetime, after all.

But he might toss his cookies again…

He stared out the windows. Hard to tell movement from examining the nebula outside. Yes, there were a few stars here and there, some pretty swirls, but for the most part it looked homogenous. Moses' inner ear was a better indicator that the ship had begun to spin in at least one vector.

Then a second vector. Now he began to get dizzy.

When the third vector kicked in, his stomached checked out. He leaned over the pillar and closed his eyes.

Hold it together, Moe. This is nothing. A nostalgia ran through him, of roller coaster rides he enjoyed so much as a kid. Not so much as a forty-something, however. Especially the rides that ran you in circles, like the spinning teacups at Disneyland. But in this case, the teacups were spinning in *three directions at once!* He found it infinitely better than sliding into a belly button, but it was still uncomfortable. He risked a peek around the bridge. Guy had his eyes closed, as did Osterland, and Max had his chin to his chest. But they were seated, unlike he and Kitner. The Lieutenant stared intently at the helm, likely in an attempt to focus on something not moving—like the RADAR screen—and not concentrating on the blurry mish-mash that lit up the windows on half the bridge. Moses decided it may not have been such a good idea to open all of them! He glanced over at the nav station. "Ozzie! Will we get an audible from the nav computer? Because it sure doesn't look like you're keeping an eye on it!"

This caused the XO to open his eyes and check his display. "I don't see any echoes yet!" he yelled.

Elwick chewed his lower lip as he waited for their plan to work. If it ever did. The *Pearl* could simply be too far away, too deep into the nebula, still. And would the gas diffuse their beams to the point of uselessness? How long would it truly take to cover the entire sky with his little trick? *This plan was surely insane,* he thought. Shining six pencil-thin signals into the stellar neighborhood as they spun 'round in every direction! Hoping for one of them to bounce back with even the tiniest glimpse of a small chunk of metal in the deep, red ocean. An ocean many, many times larger than Earth's entire solar system!

Talk about a shot in the dark. More like a shot in the red.

Masterson's voice came across the comm system. "Captain, this is Masterson."

Elwick's finger finally found the right virtual button to open the channel. "Elwick. What's up, Dale?"

"Barbara told me what you guys are doing up there. I think it's a good plan, considering the circumstances. I just want to know how long you think it might last? You've already passed your one-minute time hack."

Surely he is going through the same ordeal as the rest of us…? Masterson spoke like he was on a ship alongsides the *Nightingale*, or even back on Earth, not riding a multi-vector merry-go-round. "Dale… how are you sounding… so normal right now?"

"I don't know, I just am. Kinda feels like tumbling into a gas giant at seven gees! Almost nostalgic! Anyway, what are you thinking? Another couple of minutes? I need to send a couple of my folks to see the Scablifters as soon as it's over. Grab a Dramamine."

Moses made the mistake of actually lifting and turning his head, and instantly regretted it. The vertigo nearly debilitated him. He closed his eyes to try to return to the slight dizziness he had been complaining about only seconds ago. "Dale, I honestly… don't know. But you'll be the… first person I call."

"Aye! Thanks. In the meantime, I think I'll hit the head." He laughed. "Peeing on this merry-go-round will be more of a challenge than trying to hit the hole that first time I set foot on a Coriolis station! Those old spinning rings they built before we had gravity plates, remember them?" The circuit closed itself, which was fine with Elwick. He wasn't planning on speaking again anyway.

"That man…" shouted the XO, "is downright certifiable! You… know that right?"

Elwick couldn't answer, it was all he could do to keep his turkey sandwich from seeing the light of day again.

28

Emerald Pearl

"Are you sure this is the right door?"

"Yes, Tabby, I know the difference between port and starboard."

"So how do we know if it works or not?"

Rae looked at the controls to the airlock. No lights. "Shine the flashlight over here."

Tabby obliged but said, "It doesn't have any power." She then shined the light onto Rae's face. "Captain Moses said to turn everything off, remember? So we did so."

"Get that light out of my face! I never should have let you have it."

Tabitha moved the light away and Rae blinked repeatedly in an effort to get her night vision back. "How would you like it if I did that to you?"

"Sorry! Geebers."

"I know we turned the power off! But the Captain said to make sure this airlock works. I don't know how to do that without any power."

"So ask him."

Rae blinked. "Oh. Yeah."

Tabby shone the light on the wall. "Use that."

Rae turned back to the airlock control panel and saw a small screen with a familiar red circle next to it.

"Stupid," the younger girl muttered under her breath.

"You're stupid."

"Am not."

Rae touched the center of the screen on the comm panel and a single blue light, more of a dot, lit up over the big red circle. She breathed a sigh of relief and spoke into it. "*Nightingale?* This is the *Emerald Pearl.* We have reached the airlock on Deck Two!" No immediate answer. "Captain Moses?"

"Hi girls."

"Guy?"

"Yes… We're in a… crazy maneuver right now. Can we… get back to you in a few minutes?"

"Why does he sound funny?" whispered Tabby.

"I don't know," Rae whispered back. "Um, sure. We just want to know how to tell if the airlock is operational now that we've shut off the power. There are no lights or indicators to tell us if it's working or not."

"Aye. We'll… get back to you… soon!"

"Okay."

"That sounded very official, sis!" Tabitha exclaimed. She almost sounded sincere. "I've never heard you talk like that and use such big words."

"Are you making fun of me?"

"No! I really mean it. I mean, yeah, I do make fun of you a lot, I guess, but I'm not doing it this time."

"Oh. In that case, thank, you, Tabby," Rae said proudly. "I might just be getting the hang of this military stuff!"

29

GSCS *Nightingale*

After enduring the Laskey Maneuver for four solid minutes, Elwick called it. Luckily Burgess, with Kitner's help, had programmed an automatic all-stop that the maneuvering computer could run on its own. It had worked beautifully, and much faster than any human could have done, which would likely have been to stall the spin one vector at a time. In another couple of minutes, everyone seemed to be able to stand upright again.

Elwick still felt dizzy. "Report. Tell me we picked up something."

Both Osterland and Connelly stared intently at their displays. One of them groaned. Probably Ozzie.

"Anything. An asteroid would make me happy, just so I know it worked and the signal didn't get diffused ten thousand K out."

"Uh, well, sir, I've got six, no…" the XO counted by hand. "Seven echoes."

"And?"

Connelly shook his head. "The resolution is not fine enough to determine what they are. The signal probably suffered diffusion by the nebula, just like we feared."

"So you guys are telling me we failed?"

"Not yet, sir," Osterland said. "Just means we're gonna have to dig into the data to determine what each one of these things is made of."

"How long will that take?"

The XO shrugged. "Eh, not long. The computer will need a few minutes for each one. Maybe thirty, forty minutes."

"It's got twenty. With each passing second, those girls get that much closer to death. Find a way to speed this up."

"Aye, sir. Connelly, you take signatures one through three. I'll take four through seven."

"Aye, aye, XO."

30

Emerald Pearl

The girls sat side-by-side on the cold floor of the hallway by the airlock. Time passed ever so slowly. *How much? Half an hour? More? Did we fall asleep?*

"I'm getting hungry," Tabitha blurted out of nowhere.

Rae startled. *How does she do that so often?* "Quit scaring me."

"Quit being so easy to scare."

Rae breathed deep, trying to calm her nerves.

"I know where the kitchen is."

"How do you know that?"

"Do we have to go through this *again?* Because I pay better attention than you do!"

"Oh, shut up."

"Me and Mommy and Jamie found it when we were walking around the ship before the crew people made us go to sleep."

Confusion. "Where was I?"

"On the tour with Daddy, I guess. I don't know."

"Oh." That seemed probable. "Where is it?"

"In the maze."

"Oh," Rae said again. Someone once pointed out "oh" was her default answer to many questions. It had proven a hard habit to break. “Does it say ‘Kitchen’ on a door somewhere?”

“No. But there’s a sign on a door that says ‘Galley’.”

Duh, Rae chastised herself. “‘Galley” meant “kitchen” on Navy ships. “Why didn’t you mention before now that you saw that?”

“I wasn’t hungry before.”

Rae sighed and rolled her eyes. “Well, anything in the maze is too far away. The Captain said to stay here.”

“But it’s on this floor! I’m hungry! And you are too. I can tell.”

“Tabby, but we need to wait just a little while longer. There will be tons of food on board the rescue ship.”

“I don’t care. I’m hungry now! And I’m going!”

“No you’re not! You’re staying right here!” Rae grabbed Tabitha’s arm.

“No! Stop! You’re hurting me!”

Rae let go instantly.

Sis stuck out her tongue and ran off down the darkened corridor.

“Tabby!”

But she was gone.

31

GSCS *Nightingale*

PO2 Connelly leapt from his seat. "I got it! I got it! I've got the *Pearl!*"

Moses all but dove over his pillar to get a look the comm's officer's screen. "Are you sure?"

"I can't make out a definite shape, but unless there's a lot of rocks floating around out here made of chromium-titanium alloy, pretty sure. Look at this spectrum."

"Which signature?" the XO yelled.

"Number three!" Guy yelled back.

"Ozzie," Elwick said, returning to his pillar, "train every RADAR we have on those coordinates. We need more resolution. And bring 'er up on the holo. Let's see her."

Commander Osterland complied, and a small, blurry, spear-like shape hovered in false color on the other side of the Helm.

"Can we clean it up a bit, Ozzie? And zoom in."

"Aye. Give me a sec."

A few short seconds later, the graphical facsimile, drawn by the imaging system using data from the navigational computer resolved into something definitely man-made.

The *Emerald Pearl.*

She stood on her head and upside down from their perspective, but she was a glorious sight to Moses' eyes. "Rotate one hundred degrees. Level her out."

The long frigate first quadrupled in size, then turned slowly until it lay horizontal across the bow of the bridge. It resembled the ship the crew first saw in the mission briefing: a spear, with a large, boxy region just behind the nosecone, narrowing to bulbous engines at the stern. A large, dome-like protrusion on top of the boxy structure replaced the rail gun turret from an earlier life, when she had been the *RSS John Holloway*. "So, it's definitely there and intact," he muttered. "Navigator, distance to target?"

"Just about two hundred and ten million kilometers," Osterland reported. "Coordinates 1-3-6, Mark 7-8! At Ion Base eleven, we can be there in about forty-five minutes."

"Excellent. Helm, you have a heading. Nav, plot your new path."

"Aye aye, sir!" the XO shouted, fingers already dancing on his console. "I'll just need five minutes!"

While Kitner began his spiel of coordinates and ordering the Helm to prep for speed, Elwick punched up the circuit that would bring up the SAR Team. "Dale, this is Moses."

"Masterson."

"We found the ship."

"About time," Dale replied in a snide manner. "Sir," he added.

Elwick smiled. "How's your team?"

"Most everyone's bellies have settled down. I made a bit of a mess in the head. Otherwise, we're itching for a rescue. How much time until rendezvous?"

"Forty-five mikes."

"Aye. We'll be more than ready."

32

Emerald Pearl

"Tabby!" Rae called. Her voice echoed through the dark, twisting corridors. Tabitha had slipped around corner after corner and Rae finally lost her.

The little brat is fast.

Her sister was nowhere to be found. Rae would never find her if she had locked herself behind one of the myriad doors in the maze of hallways. But she probably wouldn't do that. All the rooms they had peeked into earlier were pitch black. Tabby said herself she feared what was *in* the dark, so even if she had darted into one of those rooms she wouldn't stay long.

And I'm the one with the flashlight.

Rae wandered up and down the dimly lit, deserted hallways—no, Captain Moses had called them "passageways"—growing more impatient with every passing second. They were running out of time. *Captain Moses will be here soon*! Rae didn't want him to come through the airlock and find no one there. He wouldn't turn around and leave, would he? He would come looking for them, right? *Tabby, where are you!?*

Rae rounded the next corner and stumbled over her own feet. Her breath caught in her throat. Directly before her lay an all-too familiar sight. The second dead body she and Sis had discovered after they woke up. The man who, earlier, had stared right into her soul. Rae crinkled her nose at the first detectible smells of decay. She tip-toed around the corpse, as if it could wake up and grab her at any moment. The slight smell, combined with her hunger and the attack on her nerves, proved too much. Rae ran down the passage and heaved. Her stomach was so empty that only a small amount of yellow liquid hit the floor. She coughed and spat. *Tabby, I'm gonna kill you!* She wiped her mouth with her sleeve.

Wait. If the dead man is here, I know where I am. Near the Auditorium. *If I'm near the Auditorium, I'm near the bridge. There is a map on the bridge!* Rae ran. She found the bloody red bridge in short order. *Map, map, map. There has to be a floorplan just laying around somewhere!*

And then she saw it. On a screen not far from where Tabby had been sitting earlier. *Ha! That's where she learned where so many things are!* She dove to it, and pressed her fingers to "draw" the right commands on the screen. She separated "Deck Two" from the rest of the vessel. She then enlarged it until text appeared. She scanned every title of every room, and it didn't take long to find the letters "G-A-L-L-E-Y. "Got you, you little brat!" Rae studied her route from the bridge to her destination. *Got it!*

She tore off the bridge as fast as her cold feet would carry her. She followed the route in her mind, running straight, turning, straight, turn, turn, turn. And… here!

No.

No? Where is it?? She shone her light on the signs on all the nearby doors, and decided she must have passed it. Turning back, retracing her steps, her light fell upon the word "GALLEY." Her shoulders slumped, relieved. "Finally!" she shouted out loud.

The galley had no door, just a large, open archway that led to a dark expanse. She tiptoed inside, her lamp leading the way. Light from the open door of one of the biggest refrigerators Rae had ever seen illuminated a corner of the room. Her sister knelt on a chair, leaning over a long stainless-steel table, digging into a white container with a spoon. Teddy sat nearby on the tabletop. "Ugh, Tabby, you can't run off like that!"

"You found me, didn't you?"

"Yeah, but that's not the—hey, wait. Why is that fridge lit up?"

"Um, because I left the door open?"

"No, I mean we shut off power to everything except the systems that would keep us alive."

"Right. And we need food to keep us alive. Look!" Tabby exclaimed. "Chocolate!"

"Do you know what just happened to me? I threw up!"

"Why?" Tabitha asked with indifference, focusing again on her ice cream.

"Because I almost tripped over the dead guy in the passageway! He was staring at me. I couldn't help it."

"Sorry. Not my fault."

"Yes it is! I was chasing after you! And you're not sorry!"

"I didn't tell you to chase me."

Rae let loose a guttural growl. "I really can't stand you, you know that?"

"Yes, you can," sis replied sweetly, spooning more brown mush into her mouth.

Rae walked over to the open fridge and peered inside. It was packed full of icy cold goodness! She would have preferred something warm, but at the moment everything looked delicious. She retrieved a plastic container and peeled it open. Inside were vegetables. Rae stared at them, trying to decide if she was *that* hungry. *No.* She put the container back and grabbed another. She found this one full of ham sandwiches. *Yum!* She grabbed one and placed it on the metal table behind her. "Don't eat this. It's mine."

"Why would I eat a sandwich when I have ice cream?" Tabitha seemed to absent-mindedly kick one toe repeatedly on the chair as she dug deeper into her chocolate treasure.

Next container. It smelled funny, but looked like fried chicken. *Ooo I love chicken! But cold chicken? I need an oven.* Rae flashed her light around the room and found what she was looking for. She hopped over to the device, opened the small door, and put the container inside. She touched buttons on the device, but nothing happened. "Why won't this work?" Rae asked.

"Power's off."

"But the fridge works!"

"I think it's on a battery or something," Tabby explained. "Otherwise the food would all go bad if the power went out, right?"

Well, that makes sense. Rae let out a heavy sigh. *Why does that little runt think of everything before I do?* She turned back to the oven, and lamented. "Cold fried chicken it is." Anything was better than nothing right now. It chilled her mouth when she bit into it. "Oh, wow that's cold!" She looked at Tabby, happily devouring the small bucket of ice cream.

Ice cream!

It came from the freezer; it had to be even colder than the icy cold leg Rae had just bitten into! "You're crazy eating that!"

"To each her own," the little girl said, and feigned feeding her bear a spoonful.

"Quit quoting Mom."

Tabitha shrugged.

"I guess it's really no wonder we're so hungry," Rae said, "we haven't eaten in a month!"

Tabitha giggled. "Okay, that was funny."

They ate the rest of their meal in silence. Rae mused that, now that their tummies were happy, maybe they wouldn't fight so much?

Right. And if buffalo had wings…

33

GSCS *Nightingale*

“There it is!” exclaimed Starman Burgess, pointing to the middle of the screen.

Elwick strained to see. He wished for the young eyes of the Helmsman. He blinked and squinted. No luck.

As if he could read Moses’ mind, Osterland glanced over his shoulder. “Don’t feel bad, Captain. I don’t see a damn thing either.”

“Huh. That’s odd,” PO2 Connelly said.

Captain Elwick turned his gaze to the overhead. “Lord Jesus, what now?”

“Sir, I’m getting telemetry from the *Pearl*. But it can’t be right.” The Science Officer’s black eyebrows nearly touched. “According to these readings, the transport is emitting no radiation at all. No heat, no radio transmissions, no sub-dimensional transmissions, nothing. Still picking up the original distress call but of course that’s now in the opposite direction. I’ll know more when we get closer, but it looks dead.”

“Obviously this wacked-out region of space is messing with the sensors,” the XO remarked.

“Agreed,” Elwick said. “Ignore those readings. The only things we can trust are our five senses while we’re inside this Quadrangle. There’s a reason for all the wild reports that have come out of this region for the last hundred years. But I'm not going to give in to salty old sailor superstition, or be led astray by these 'gremlins'. Oh! I almost forgot..." Elwick touched the 2MC symbol on a screen to his right. "BM1, this is the Captain." While waiting for her to respond, he added, "Kelly made the selectee list, by the way."

The XO swiveled around in his chair and nodded. "Good for her. It's high time. She'll fill Chief Robinsen's shoes nicely."

"Are you kidding? Her skis would never fit in those tiny things!"

Ozzie laughed.

"By the way, folks, that CPO business is strictly on the down-low for the time being."

All bridge personnel acknowledged.

"Crawford here."

"Kelly," Moses said, "We're going to need to initiate a power transfer from the *Nightingale* soon as we dock."

"Aye aye, sir."

"And remember, this is an ancient ship by our system's standards. I make no promises there's a power coupling anywhere near the airlocks. One of your boys might have to take a little walk."

"Sir, not sure I feel comfortable sendin' one of these apes out into that radiation soup."

"Not like we have much choice here, Kelly. But I leave it up to you who goes."

"Aye. I'll hold ya to that."

34

Emerald Pearl

A new chill froze the air. Rae closed the still-open fridge; it definitely wasn't helping the situation. At least her tummy was no longer empty! She dumped her and Sis's spent plastic in a nearby trash bin.

"I wish we had pockets," said Tabby, "we could grab some sandwiches for later!"

"Captain Moses will be here by the time we get hungry again. Let's get back to the airlock."

"I'm freezing," Tabby complained.

"Well then you shouldn't have eaten that ice cream."

Tabitha said nothing, only shivered.

This made Rae pause. At least she herself had long sleeves on her fluffy blouse that she could pull down. "It *is* starting to get really cold, isn't it?" And the cold was only going to get worse before they were rescued. *How long would that be exactly?* "Tabby, tell you what. Let's call Captain Moses and see how much longer it's going to be before they get here. If it's going to be a while, maybe we have time to find some warm clothes."

"Warm clothes?" Tabby asked. "Where?"

"Didn't mom pack some clothes in one of the suitcases?"

"I don't know. You helped her pack, not me."

"Well trust me, she did."

Tabitha's eyes got huge. "Wait a minute! You want to go back down there, don't you!?" Her voice raised an entire octave.

"What's a-matter, Tabby-cat? Scaaarrrred?"

"Nooo," she replied with disdain, but her face straightened out a moment later. "Okay maybe a little."

Rae smiled. "It's okay, Tabby, it'll only take a minute. We know exactly where to go now!"

Tabitha's eyes narrowed.

"Come on, don't be scared of a few bumps in the night! And you don't want to be cold, right?" Rae gazed into her sister's eyes while the little girl studied her. "Tabby. I know it's a little scary down there but trust me, there's nothing alive on this ship but us," Rae assured her. "And Mom and Jamie and four other people. And they're locked in pods. You know all this probably better than I do."

Tabitha wandered around in a circle, and then turned back to Rae. "Only a minute?"

"It'll be real quick. In and out. I promise!"

Tabby took a deep breath and breathed out through her nose, slumping her shoulders in capitulation. "Fine."

"Ok. First let's call Captain Moses and let him know what we're doing, and find out how long—"

"That'll take too long! I'm freezing! Let's just run down there and get it over with!"

"I don't think that's a good idea—"

"Ugh, forget it!" Tabby stomped out of the room. "I'll go down there myself!"

"What? Wait up!"

35

GSCS *Nightingale*

A dark speck appeared in the viewport.

"Hey!" Elwick shouted. "I see it now!"

"It's been up there for the last ten minutes," muttered Osterland, who looked over his shoulder and grinned. "I'm kidding. I just noticed it when you said something."

Moses gave him the side-eye.

Connelly interjected. "XO, can you verify something for me? I think I'm reading damage."

"What'cha got, Guy?" Elwick asked, moving over to the comm station.

"Surface-scanning radar reports perturbances in the mid-section. Doesn't match the schematics. I think it might be a hole."

Elwick waited a moment, giving his crew time to verify.

"Definitely a hole," Osterland said. "Looks like something blew right out the top of the ship."

Guy breathed deep. "Uh oh. The damage isn't far from the Zee Dee core."

"Well, we know the core itself hasn't been compromised," the XO observed. "The ship would have vaporized."

"But what could have accidentally ruptured that would do that much damage, and that precise, but not breach the antimatter chamber?"

Silence.

"A shaped charge would do it," Max Burgess whispered.

All eyes went to him.

Burgess looked around the room. "What?"

"He could be right," Osterland ventured.

Elwick gave the XO a hard stare. *Naval intelligence* danced on his mind. He was certain it danced on Ozzie's as well. "Doesn't matter. That investigation will come by people with pay grades higher than ours to decide. We have people to rescue. We'll report our findings to SARCOM who can report it up to SENTCOM and they can let the Navy or the Air & Space Force crawl all over that ship after we're done and gone. Right now let's get to doing what we do best."

"Aye aye," various men replied in unison.

Elwick opened the 5MC circuit to the flight deck. "Dale, we're at about twenty minutes to docking."

Masterson's voice forcefully ejected itself from the speaker on the Captain's Console. "Aye!"

A dainty female voice broke into the conversation. "Captain? This here's Crawford."

"Yes, Kelly?"

"I checked the schematics of the *Pearl.* Even though this used ta be a naval vessel, it looks like it was built 'fore ship-to-ship power couplings were standardized. We won't be able ta do a link-up using the cables we got."

Elwick opened his mouth to speak.

"Don't worry," she continued, "we're almost finished printin' an adapter that'll do the trick!"

Elwick closed his mouth. It was as if she knew what he was about to say. *Well of course she did.*

"Pruitt is goin' ta finish up here while I suit up 'n prep for EVA."

Moses fell silent. *Should have known that girl would pick herself.* "Understood." he said into the comm. Actually, Kelly would have been his first choice to go "outside" and wrestle such a unique task. No one could handle machinery quite like she could. Of course, that didn't stop him from fearing for the safety of his wife's sister; if something happened to her so soon after Alena… "Kel?"

"Cap'n?"

"Don't feel you have to out-do yourself. We really just need enough juice to make sure we can interface with the core computer, open a few doors, retrieve some cryo pods, and keep two little girls from freezing to death while we're at it. We won't be attempting to fire up the engines or even bake a pie."

"Understood," Crawford replied.

The Executive Officer leaned to his right. His fingers danced on a small screen. "Prepping the widowmakers."

36

Emerald Pearl

Now more familiar with the *Emerald Pearl,* the girls made their way to Deck Three and the recessed door that read "CARGO BAY" in short order. Rae and Tabby pulled it open together.

Rae peered into the darkness, past the small white corrugated platform. The dark beyond was still foreboding, but at least she felt familiar with the large space now. She led the way down the white metal staircase. The girl's feet made the familiar tap-tap-tapping as they went. It echoed across the cavernous space but Rae no longer concerned herself with alerting zombies or ghosts or whatever other non-existent thing that might creep into her mind to terrify her. Rae remembered her promise. *In and out. One minute.*

At the middle platform, Rae shined her flashlight over the white railing. Still a long ways down. *Okay, maybe two minutes.* The light once again fell upon the storage containers. She would have been surprised not to see them. But something seemed different. She slowed and scanned the area with the light.

"Hey!" Tabby yelled, "I can't see! If I fall down these stairs you'll be in trouble!"

"Shhh! Something's different. See those boxes? There was a lot more of them earlier."

Tabitha froze. “Why are you trying to scare me now?”

“I’m not. But look! It’s different, isn’t it?”

Tabby’s silence only gave credence to her suspicions. Sis would surely be challenging Rae by now if the little know-it-all had the slightest hint she was wrong here. “How can boxes move all by themselves?” Tabby asked.

Rae shivered. That same chill from earlier ran through her again. She pulled her sleeves down and took a deep breath. *Be strong, Rae. Be strong.* She needed to be, for her little sister’s sake if nothing else. Tabby needed some warm clothes and she knew of nowhere else to get them but in this room. “Let’s get what we came for and get out of here, Tabby!”

The girls bounded down the rest of the stairs and ran to the Marshall’s family locker. Number fourteen. Rae had no trouble remembering that.

Tabitha leaned her bear against a large box. “I’ll just be a minute, Mr. Fluffles!”

Using the same technique to get inside the cage they had used earlier, Tabby squirmed inside in seconds. The process still hurt Rae’s fingers, but not like before. She wasn’t sure if she simply didn’t care or whether it was the adelle- adren-adrenal-whatever pumping through her veins. Or both.

Tabitha opened up one of the suitcases and began throwing things out as before.

“That’s my cardigan!” Rae exclaimed.

Tabby paused, grabbed the blue material to which Rae referred, and threw it at the cage door.

Rae bent down, reached through the wires, and worked the garment through. She began to don it when Sis hollered.

“Hellooo? A little light?”

“Oh! Sorry.”

Tabby mumbled something under her breath but Rae couldn't make it out. Her sister was still busy rummaging through bags when Rae heard it.

Behind her.

A thud.

In an exact repeat of recent history, Rae spun with the light. She saw nothing but pallets, metal storage containers and large plastic boxes of various colors. But this time was different. This time she was *positive* she had heard it.

"Why do you keep doing that?" Tabby asked, her voice echoing in the large space. "I can't see!"

Sis hadn't heard it! Rae decided that might be a good thing. With trepidation, she shined the light back inside the cage. "Sorry, Sis."

"Yeah, you are!" Tabby said snottily, and went back to digging.

Rae made no reply to this insult, but instead turned to look over her shoulder for any hint of danger. The fact she could see could see literally nothing actually reassured her a little; evil things often had glowing eyes. Didn't they? *No evil red eyes, no danger. No evil red eyes—*

"Hey," Tabby said. "Look."

Rae turned. Her sister was holding up a necklace with a small silver amulet dangling from it. "Is that my amulet?"

"Duh."

"Now who's being mean?"

"Do you want it or not?" Tabby asked.

"Of course." Rae extended her arm into the cage and opened her hand. "Toss it here."

Tabitha did so, but its path took it nowhere near Rae's hand.

“Sorry,” the little girl said in a slight voice.

Rae didn’t get upset. She figured Tabby had not deliberately missed on purpose; it was Rae who was good at sports and sailing and other physical activities, while Tabby had the math, science and basic know-it-all skills. Rae maneuvered to the necklace, reached her arm through the wires, and snatched it up.

“You’re welcome,” she heard Tabby say. “What did mom pack for me?”

“Um, I—” she tried to think, but could only imagine that at any moment, someone or some *thing* would grab her from behind. “I don’t know.”

“That’s helpful,” Tabby replied with not a little sarcasm.

Rae strained to push down her fear and think. “Um, I think there’s a—a sweater,” Rae offered. “Yeah, there is. It’s in the red bag.” Rae looked around the cage using the flashlight. “Over there!” She shined the light on it.

Tabby stood and hopped to the other side of the cage.

This cargo bay is not haunted. This cargo bay is not haunted. Rae closed her eyes and repeated the phrase over and over.

“Found it!” Tabby exclaimed.

Rae opened her eyes to see her sister holding up a white sweater. “Okay, good, now come on, let’s get back upstairs.” She sat down the light so it pointed upward, and pulled the hood of her cardigan over her head. The violet-colored sleeves shone brightly in the lamplight. The material felt cold but it would warm up fairly—

>*Thud*<

Rae froze. There was no way her sister could not have heard it that time.

“What was that?” Tabitha asked in a whisper.

>*Thud, clink*<

Rae's heart shot into her throat as she spun 'round. She didn't dare breathe. She tried to speak, but nothing came out. Rae swallowed in an effort to get her voice working again. "It's..." She swallowed again. "Time to go," she squeaked.

Tabby dove for the cage door and pushed with her shoulders and tried to force her head through the tiny opening she had created.

"Help!" she yelled.

>*Thud, thud, clink*<

Rae slammed her butt on the ground, put one foot on the cage wall and pulled on the door with all her might. Adrenaline gave her enough extra strength to pull the bottom of the door outward, enough for Tabby to slip through without even touching the sides. She did so in a flash. Together once again, the girls bolted to the stair, a poor, stuffed bear being dragged by one ear.

>*Thud, thud*<

Whatever made that noise, it was immediately on the other side of the boxes to their right. Rae grabbed Tabby's clothing and pulled the girl to her.

"What are you—?"

"Shhh!"

>*Thud, thud, clink*<

That came from another direction; somewhere in front of them. *There is more than one.* The light flew out of Rae's hand as Tabby snatched it away from her and switched it off. Rae opened her mouth to protest, but then realized it was Sis' effort to hide them.

Tabby grabbed Rae's hand and crept backwards a few steps. When they reached an intersection of boxes, Rae heard the little girl's footfalls disappearing to her left. *Tabby!*

>Thud<

Rae didn't think. She bolted in the same direction as her sister had. In short order, Rae plowed into her and they both tumbled to the ground.

"Oww!" Tabitha shrieked.

Rae could see nothing, but her other four senses were on fire. The smell of machinery and plastic filled her nostrils, and a metallic taste filled her mouth. Had the impact gave her a nosebleed?

>Thud, thud, clink<

It had to be only a few feet away, to her right. The hair on Rae's arms stood on end. A second later, something grabbed her. "Tabby! It's got me!"

"Shhh! It's me, you scaredy-cat!"

Rae groped outward with her hands, and found Sis. She scrambled to hug her, and Tabby did the same.

>Thud, thud<

Rae feared the pounding of her heart would give away their location just as easily as their shouting surely already had. She held her breath and willed it all to be over. It didn't work.

>Thud, clink<

This time the noise sounded farther off, in another section of the cargo bay. *There's even more monsters!?* She clinched her eyelids tight. *Daddy! Oh, how I wish you were here!* The cargo bay fell silent for a moment. Rae heard nothing but her deafening heartbeat and the soft but rapid breathing of her little sister. "Think they're gone?" she whispered.

A finger touched Rae's lips, and she said no more.

She admitted that, between the two of them, Tabitha was probably better equipped mentally to know what to do in these situations. She almost always beat Rae at every game they played. So if Tabby didn't know the best strategy to outsmart whomever or whatever now toyed with them, they were doomed for sure.

>*THUD!!!*<

Rae screamed.

A hand grabbed hers and yanked her upright. "Come on!" Tabitha turned on the flashlight, and took off at a run.

Rae could make out Sis's movements in the flickering light. The little girl ducked under a long metal table and Rae tried to follow, but she did so far too late. Something tugged on Rae's clothing from behind, and snatched her up. The loudest blood-curdling scream she had ever heard filled her ears. The voice was her own. She yearned for the ground, but neither her hands nor feet could reach. Rae swam in the air, arms flailing. *Help!* she wanted to shout, but her mouth wouldn't work.

>*Thud, thud*<

She fell backward, her cardigan enveloped her, then she fell sideways. *No!* Rae took a deep breath and finally found her voice. "Help! Daddy! Great Goddess!" No one answered. She saw a light. It flickered all around her. *Tabitha?* "Tabby, run! Run!"

No reply.

Hopefully that meant Sis had already sprinted off for the stairs, her dainty footfalls not betraying her. Then Rae heard Tabby's voice. *She's still here! Was that a yelp?* "No! Get away from her!" Rae kicked and fought, but in her blindness, she only assaulted air. She heard Sis's voice again, but this time it sounded… like giggling? Rae halted her flailing and listened. No, it couldn't have been. Rae swallowed hard. "Tabby! Go! Get out of here!"

An unbelievable but unmistakable sound then filled her ears. Her sister was *laughing!* Why? Rae stopped fighting and opened her eyes. The light shone in her face.

"Calm down, Big Sis," Tabby said. "You're not gonna die!"

>*Thud, thud, clink*<

Rae froze. What was happening? Everything seemed a contradiction. Beyond doubt, a monster or a ghost or a demon was joyfully dragging her away to do unthinkable horrors to her, and her sister merely followed along, laughing. Loudly. Could she really be *that* evil?

>*Thud, thud*<

Tabby grabbed Rae's hand. "Hold still, stupid."

Another tug on the sleeve of Rae's cardigan pulled it off her right arm. She then jerked free of the left sleeve and landed hard on the floor. She looked up but saw nothing but the brilliance of the flashlight. She held her hand to her face to block it.

"Are you okay?" Tabby asked.

"Tabby! Get out! You're gonna—!"

"Oh, Rae, it's alright! Look!"

The light moved away, and darkness returned. Rae blinked, trying to shake off the temporary blindness.

"Look!"

Rae rolled over and saw a large yellow shape, with a piece of clothing dangling from it. *Is that my cardigan?* The light danced all over the big, bulky thing. She stared at it.

"It's not a monster, Rae. It's just a mover bot!"

She squinted, her brain trying to make sense of what her eyes were seeing.

>*Thud, thud*<

Tabby giggled. “Who’s afraid now? You’re a total scaredy cat!”

The yellow shape made sounds as it moved and pivoted.

>*Thud, thud, clink*<

Realization dawned on her. Rae collapsed onto the floor in relief. The warehouse robot that had inadvertently grabbed her had simply been following its program. It seemed oblivious to their fear but fully aware of their presence, because it stepped around them and continued its business.

>*Thud, thud*<

Tabitha walked over to it, jumped up, and retrieved Rae’s cardigan, the hood of which had become caught on a spiky protrusion on the robot’s back. “Thank you, kind sir, I’ll take that!”

Rae heard the other thuds again, some more distant than others. None of them frightened her now; it only meant there were other robots in this cargo bay, simply doing whatever robots do in cargo bays. Mover Bots. Inventory Bots. Inspection Bots. They are what rearranged the boxes that were missing from the area near the stair. They are what Rae heard earlier, when she and Tabitha were collecting the book and the bear.

Her heart still beat as loud as a drum. She breathed deeply to calm herself. *I’m sorry, Daddy,* Rae said to herself. *I let you down. I wasn’t brave at all. And I threw up earlier up in the passageway. I’m not strong. I don’t know if I’ll even make it until Captain Moses arrives. I’m a worthless sailor, not to mention a worthless big sister. I’m sorry.* Rae looked up to see Tabby bending over her. She didn't want the little runt to see her this way for many reasons, the biggest one being that Rae had to be the example, the one who would lead them to safety. Tabby needed someone to look up to, someone to take care of her.

Didn't she?

Despite the fact Tabby stood before her cradling a teddy bear like a toddler, she had proven time and again she could easily take care of herself, *and* Rae. *Sis is the one who remembered where the cargo bay was. She remembered which storage container was ours. She's the one who climbed into that metal prison! She led me to the galley so we could get something to eat. And she figured out how to call the Nightingale for help! Surely that's the most important thing! And now, Tabby just rescued me from a monster! Or what I thought was a monster because I panicked! So silly and childish!* Tabitha had kept her wits about her the entire time.

Not me.

Does she really need someone to watch after her? If so, I'm not the person to do it. And she's only ten. Ten! What in all the universe is she going to be like at sixteen?

"Are you okay now?" Tabby asked.

Rae looked up with a newfound respect for the amazing little squirt standing above her. She nodded.

"Good. *Now* can we get out of here?"

Rae smiled and allowed Tabby to help her to her feet. "Lead the way, my brave little rescuer."

"Well, duh, I have the flashlight, of course I'm gonna lead the way."

Rae shook her head, smiled, and followed her sister back up the long staircase to Deck Three. More slowly this time, as her legs were wobbly from the recent terror. But she kept up. *Next stop,* Rae thought, *the airlock.*

And salvation!

37

GSCS *Nightingale*

The *Emerald Pearl* loomed large in the windows. The entire ship could be easily seen from bow to stern, illuminated in the glow of the nebula. Elwick stared at the gargantuan hull rip amidships, which exposed the entire engineering section to vacuum, like the girls had been told by the female crewmember who passed away before their eyes. He couldn't remember her name. *That must have been so difficult for two young girls to take,* Elwick thought. *They're going to need some serious counseling after this.*

Standing near the bridge's bay windows, Moses could literally see the decks on which people formerly worked, but no people remained. He shook his head. "If anyone was in that section when it blew, well, their bodies could be hundreds of kilometers away by now. I don't know how we're going to recover them."

Osterland nodded. "And considering the temp outside is reading negative one hundred seventy-nine degrees in this area, they're likely frozen solid."

"I think we all got extremely lucky," added Kitner. "These emissions nebulas can reach ten million degrees Kelvin. The ship could have been vaporized the instant it jumped in."

"Sir," asked Burgess, "what is that in Celsius?"

A pause, then the OOD replied, “Somewhere between a hundred and one twenty-five, I think.”

“Close, a hundred and seventeen,” Connelly corrected.

Kitner bowed his head. “A hundred seventeen.”

“Well, we still have a responsibility to locate and retrieve those bodies, if we can. And some if not all of them could have been wearing spacesuits, if they had prior warning of impending disaster. So, Connelly, please program the scanners to comb the surrounding area. Make it slow and methodical; it’s extremely easy to blow right past a human body at that distance. We don’t have to worry about urgency here. If they’re wearing spacesuits that are still functioning, they should have several hours’ worth of air and heat left. If they weren’t, well, it will strictly be a recovery effort.”

“Aye aye, sir.”

“Meanwhile, we’ll take care of the urgent matter at hand: getting little Rae and Tabitha off that ship, followed by the survivors still in the cryo pods. Not to mention anyone else who could still be tucked away somewhere in a protected section of the ship who hasn’t spoken up yet. So! Pilot, you’ve identified your docking location, aye?”

“Aye!”

Elwick stepped back to his pillar. “Then bring us in nice and slow.”

“Aye, sir! Switching to thrusters.”

Osterland muttered over his shoulder, “Now let’s hope the thrusters don’t ignite all the hydrogen and oxygen out there.”

Max Burgess snapped his head toward the XO, one finger hovering over the virtual button that would fire up the maneuvering rockets. “You’re kidding, right?”

Osterland shrugged. “Probably.”

Burgess eyed him suspiciously, then looked back at Elwick.

Moses snorted, then nodded to the young man that it was indeed safe to proceed.

The pilot sighed, now knowing he'd been temporarily duped, and pushed the button. He then took the manual flight stick that had risen from the console upon initiation of the procedure. His tongue stuck slightly out of his mouth on one side as he expertly and gently—to Elwick's surprise—maneuvered the bulk of the *Nightingale* alongside the much larger former naval frigate.

Elwick waited *almost* patiently. The young Starman had proven his talent in simulation, which is what got him assigned to this apprenticeship, but the lad had only docked with four *real* ships since coming aboard three months ago. Moses realized he had been holding his breath, and convinced himself to breathe again. Turned out he had nothing to worry about; this time Burgess needed no assistance, no guidance, and no coaching.

Kitner looked back at Elwick and smiled. "Good job, Starman!"

"Docking complete," the XO announced, once the mechanical interlocks on both ships latched into place. "Good job, kid."

Once Max locked down the maneuvering controls, Kitner patted him on the back. It made Max smile big.

Elwick smiled himself and opened the MC5 to the flight deck. "BM1, Master Chief, this is Elwick."

"Crawford here."

"Masterson."

"Showtime," Elwick said.

"Aye, sir, suiting up now!" Kelly reported.

"Roger, Kelly," Elwick replied. "Remember, your safety comes first, but keep in mind it's probably starting to get chilly over there."

"Aye aye, Captain!"

"Dale, I'm confident the power we're about to provide will make a difference bringing up the temperature so the girls don't freeze, but I don't know if it will be enough to get those doors open, so be prepared to burn your way in."

"Aye, sir. We staged ourselves in the *'Gale's* starboard airlock on approach, and we've already begun to work the manual controls of the *Pearl's* port airlock. For some reason they're seized-up pretty good."

Elwick's brows went up. "You're way ahead of us up here, Dale! Odd those levers are frozen up already. We only shut the power off what, a couple of hours ago? Maybe these side access points aren't used that often, in favor of the aft airlock?"

"It's possible," Dale said.

"Of course, the aft airlock is no use to us; the girls can't get to that one anyway."

"Naturally."

"Perhaps feeding the beast a little power will warm up some circuits and make our lives easier?" Elwick suggested.

"Perhaps. Tell me again why can't we just link up and direct the energy where we want, like we do with every other ship?"

"Chief Masterson," Connelly interjected, "the problem is that this boat is simply too old to have a modern CommSync, so we can't interface with the onboard brain until we're actually on-board."

"Got it," Dale replied. "And reprogramming the power settings is probably too complex a task to ask of the girls."

"It is," said Elwick, "I think we've asked enough of them. We'll have to make do with whatever the default power profile is for now."

"Understood," Dale acknowledged. "I expect to be inside shortly."

"I'll let you know when Crawford gets us hooked up. Elwick out." He flipped off the 5MC and flipped to 3MC. "Kelly, do you read?"

A pause. "Lima Charlie, Cap'n! Conductin' final checks." Her voice came across tinny, mechanical. "I'll be ready ta launch in about two mikes!"

"Aye. We'll leave this channel open. Launch when ready."

"Aye aye!" she replied.

"Guy, let's get a camera on that widowma—I mean that PEVA."

38

GSCS *Nightingale*: Outer Hull

On either side of the *Nightingale's* primary airlock were smaller bay doors leading to six one-man spacecraft intended exclusively for extra-vehicular activity, or EVA. Three to starboard, three to port. These were the "widowmakers" to which Doc had referred in the mission briefing. Officially known as a PEVA, or a Personal EVA craft—a self-standing apparatus more like a spacesuit that astronauts climbed into more than wore—they weren't originally meant for much more than quick repair work. They had less propellant, air, and battery power than Chief Petty Officer Select Kelly Crawford would have liked, but they were extremely maneuverable, cheap, and easy to replace when one went Tango Uniform—or "Tits Up" in crude military speak. Thankfully, they were tougher than they looked; Kelly couldn't remember the last time a sailor had been lost in one, and she sure didn't want to become a statistic today.

Crawford had logged more hours spacewalking than any member of the crew. That's what she had been told, anyway, and she believed it, because she enjoyed it so much. Every time the opportunity arose, she volunteered. Always volunteering had a practical benefit; Kelly soon became the resident expert at EVA. If the Captain wanted an "outside" job done fast and right, she was without doubt the best choice. And this time he couldn't afford anything less; they were working against the clock, not to mention operating in a very dangerous environment. Sometimes the simpler approach proved faster, but in this case, climbing across both ships using handholds while tethered to the ship with a line would be downright suicidal. A spacesuit would provide some protection, but not enough against the nebula's radiation. In ten or fifteen minutes, she would be riddled with cancer. And it would take a lot longer than that to complete *this* job. A widowmaker was the only option.

Now finished with her final "flight checks," Kelly alerted the bridge via radio. "Ready ta disembark!"

"Clear for EVA," the XO confirmed.

Using simple rocket thrusters, Crawford maneuvered out of the *Nightingale's* port-side airlock and "flew" along the side of the multipurpose Triple S. She quickly identified her destination: the only apparent "surviving" exterior power coupling on the *Pearl.* Of course it had been installed in the most inconvenient place imaginable. She couldn't for the life of her comprehend what the designers were thinking. Government logic, obviously, since the ship had started life as a Republic Navy frigate. But putting it up on top of the vessel near what used to be a large turret emplacement was ridiculous. With the two aft power ports in the damaged area of the *Pearl,* the only remaining option made it impossible to conduct an auto-coupling—standard procedure nowadays—requiring no extra-vehicular activity at all. Fifty-year-old vehicles always complicated matters. One hundred-year-old vehicles were *far* worse. *Why anyone would risk their lives in such an old contraption is beyond me!* But that was a moot point now; she had a job to do.

Kelly first flew to the bow airlock. She maneuvered close to her own ship and, using one of the four mechanical arms on the widowmaker, "grabbed" the power cable with a giant metal claw. With the cable adapter she and Pruitt had 3-D printed from the *Nightingale's* machine shop, and the power cable in the other claw, Crawford gunned the forward thrusters with her right foot and headed for her destination atop the derelict transport. She guessed she would need about four, five minutes.

Her thoughts turned to the significance of today's date—Alena's birthday—and Kelly's heart became heavy once more. She wished more than anything to have the opportunity to do that one, fateful day over. Honestly, just five minutes would do. Those terrible, unthinkable three hundred seconds had changed *everything*.

Had it not been for those five minutes, her sister Zoey would still have a present and attentive husband. Had it not been for those five minutes, Kelly wouldn't have left the Navy to keep an eye on Moses. Had it not been for those fateful five minutes, she wouldn't be in this damned widowmaker in the middle of one of the deadliest regions of space.

But she was there for noble purpose. As they always were, each and every time they left Earth. More noble than the Navy, for while the Navy protected a way of life, they also took lives when necessary. So did the SENTCORPS. But Search and Rescue Command did not. SARCOM saved lives. And sometimes gave their own in the attempt.

Kelly would do her best to make sure she didn't give hers today, and refocused on the business at hand. She checked all readouts, and verified her azimuth. All numbers looked good, and the *Emerald Pearl* lay dead in her sights. Only a couple of minutes now… She breathed deep. Maybe, just maybe, rescuing little Rae and Tabitha would give Moses a push in the right direction? Wake him up to what's important once again.

Or if not, maybe losing them would?

Kelly shook her head to shake *that* possible future from her mind. *What a terrible thought, Kelly!* She chastised herself for letting it even skim through her gray matter.

Soon, a fast beeping garnered her full attention. The collision warning. She had fully expected it upon reaching a specific proximity to the behemoth ahead. It now completely filled the canopy of her widowmaker, and she slowed it to a stop. "Crawford to *Nightingale*. I've reached the power couplin' and am preparin' ta connect!"

"Roger, Kelly," came Captain Elwick's reply. "Standing by."

She rotated the small, upright craft 180 degrees so as to get the best angle at which to connect the cabling. She engaged the magnetic "feet" of the pod and in seconds, she and it were stuck fast to the hull of the *Pearl.* Although her fingers danced on switches and buttons, her gaze controlled more capabilities via the 3-D displays inside the cockpit.

"Don't worry, girls, I'll have y'all enjoying some sweet juice in a jiffy!"

39

Emerald Pearl

After their little adventure down in the cargo bay, Rae decided boredom was welcome. But her sister proved another story. Tabbycat fidgeted and squirmed.

The girls ventured a good distance either way down the long dark hallway—no, "passageway," she reminded herself—from the port airlock, where Captain Moses had told them to wait. Tabitha did her best to squeeze whatever warmth she could get out of Mr. Fluffles, which she had retrieved from the couch under the dome, and buttoned one more button on her sweater.

Rae had pulled the cardigan's hood off her head in order to don her favorite necklace, which they had recently retrieved. The cold air bit at her neck and fingers. *Come on, Rae! The sooner you get it clasped, the sooner you can—there!* Now secure around her neck, she tossed the circular-shaped pendant into her blou—*ohhhh that's cold!* She instantly regretted not leaving the ice-cold chunk of metal on the outside of her clothing. *Too late now, I guess.* She yanked the hood back over her head, and rubbed her arms to generate some heat.

"How much longer?" Tabby asked.

"Not much longer, I think." Honestly, she had no idea, but Rae didn't know what else to say to comfort her little sister.

Another minute passed. Neither girl spoke.

Tabitha bounced up and down in an attempt to warm herself up. "I can't take this anymore," Sis exclaimed. "I'm still cold even with this sweater! I want some *warm* food! And I'm dying to get off this ship!"

"Me too, little sis. Me too."

Tabitha's face lit up. Literally, not figuratively. Rae looked up to see they were directly under one of the small lights in the ceiling. No, not ceiling. What was it? *Over-something. Overhead! That's what,* Rae said proudly to herself. *I'm getting all these Navy terms down pretty well!* Each light in the overhead marked an intersection now that the primary lighting had been turned off. They had hopped and skipped all the way to the first junction nearest the airlock with nigh a thought. "Better turn around."

Tabitha leaned forward and stared intently into the dim passageway. "Let's walk to the next intersection."

"I don't want to go that way," Rae said. "That's where the dead guy is."

"So? He's dead, he won't hurt you."

"Oh, like you're so brave! You thought we were being chased by ghosts or monsters, too, until you finally figured it out!"

"I wasn't scared until you were!"

"Yeah, right."

"I wasn't!" Tabitha insisted. "The screams and the look on your face scared me! Mom would have been brave! You need to be like Mom! You're the older sister! The one who's supposed to be more like her! Why can't you be more like her?"

"I'm trying!" Rae shouted. Her voice echoed deep into the dark maze of passageways. Tabby stopped yelling, apparently enjoying the acoustics. Or dreading them. All seemed quiet, but a foreboding filled Rae. If there were indeed ghosts on this ship, she and Tabby had surely awoken them by now. And that dead crewman lay only just down that corridor, somewhere in the dark... She backed away. It may have simply been a remnant of the paralyzing fear she had experienced down in the cargo bay—which turned out to be silly—but nevertheless, her flight mechanisms were alive and well.

Tabby's eyes shone large in the dim light, darting back and forth between Rae and the poorly-lit, cold metal walls that surrounded them. Rae's heart went out to her. Sis *was* terrified, despite her insistence otherwise. And she had been right; in the absence of their mother, it was Rae's job to fill the matronly position. Tabby would never admit it, but Rae felt absolutely certain the little squirt looked up to her. What Sis had just said proved that. About how she wasn't scared until she took a cue from Rae. And that she hadn't given up on the possibility of her becoming more like their mother.

"I'm trying to be like mom," Rae said quietly. "I really am. But I just got the job today. Cut me some slack, okay?"

Tabby pursed her lips and looked at her feet. The girl looked up briefly, and then to Rae's surprise, grabbed her hand and led them in the opposite direction of the bloody corpse.

Rae smiled inwardly, happy that she had most certainly just made some tiny inkling of headway with her sister.

40

GSCS *Nightingale:* Airlock

The Captain's voice rang painfully loud in his ear. Dale Masterson adjusted the volume on his comm circuit. "Masterson here, sir."

"Looks like the Knuckledraggers' power adapter is working," the Captain said. "We're now tickling the *Pearl's* system with one-point-six megajoules. I know that's barely enough to turn the lights on, but I first want to ensure that old transport's system can handle it. Don't want to blow out a breaker or permanently damage the circuits. We'll slowly increase up to ten gigajoules over the next hour."

"Well sir, it looks like we're providing enough power to light up the external control panel, but this stubborn outer door still won't open. Even if we had the full ten GJs pumping in now, I'm afraid the mechanisms are frozen too tight for either automatic or manual operation. We're going to have to cut our way in."

"Aye, aye, Dale," he heard Elwick reply. "Do what you need to do."

"Gilbin, get in here with that torch."

The others maneuvered out of the way as the Aussie Firefighter moved into position with a blow torch. Even wearing bulky spacesuit gloves, Gilbin expertly lit the device in a flash. "Gonna take a few minutes, mates! Go ahead and have a smoke."

A few scoffed at the joke. None of them could even scratch their noses at the moment, let alone light a cigarette even if they had wanted one. The six other members of the SAR team waited patiently in the now airless open airlock of the *Nightingale* as Daniel Gilbin guided the blow torch along the center seam of the port airlock door of the *Emerald Pearl.*

Emerald Pearl

Is it getting colder?

"Let's jog," Rae suggested. Tabitha did not object.

They flew down the passageways. The air bit crisp at Rae's face. She slowed, and Tabby followed suit. Soon they passed the starboard side airlock. It looked no different than the port airlock. Rae glanced over at her sister. The overhead lights flashed off her brown hair every few steps. "Doing okay?"

"Yyyyep," came the reply.

In less than ten minutes, the girls had jogged all around the circumference of Deck Two and were presently back at the port side airlock. They stopped and listened, but could hear nothing over the sound of their breathing. They finally sat down, neither saying a word. Rae's breathing came softer now, and she concentrated on listening for any signs of the rescue party.

Nothing.

"I wish these airlocks had windows," Rae thought out loud. "That way we could at least see if they were out there or not. Who makes a door without a window?"

"Um, whoever made *this* door?" At the word "this," Tabby knocked it with her elbow.

"Smart aleck."

Tabby giggled.

Rae smiled. *Look at that. It's like we're actually starting to get along!*

GSCS *Nightingale:* Airlock

"Done!" Gilbin exclaimed.

Masterson checked his watch. That had taken nine minutes.

Using two crowbars fetched from maintenance, four of the larger men grunted and groaned in their effort to open the doors wide enough to get a space-suited Bruno through. That would ensure *everyone* could make it. Once the entire team passed through the *Pearl's* outer airlock door, the inner door gave them the same problem. Frozen shut. Dale notified the Captain. "Cutting through another one will take another ten minutes. Well, nine at least."

"I can do it for you in eight!" Daniel hollered.

"Do what you need to do," came the reply from Elwick.

"Aye aye," Masterson acknowledged. But cutting both doors created another problem. Once the *Nightingale* undocked, this section of the *Pearl* would be exposed to vacuum. If there was not enough power in the vessel to close nearby bulkhead doors to seal off a small section, when the rescue ship undocked, any air left in the entirety of the *Emerald Pearl* would blow out into space. This would push the derelict in the opposite direction, setting it to tumbling haphazardly on an unpredictable vector. But it may not matter, if they can get all the survivors off. A cleanup crew could take care of the rest. Probably the RNA Navy itself, if Dale's experience gave him any insight. It usually did.

With little else to do for at least another eight minutes, Masterson checked the screen on his wrist. Thanks to the fact all their suits were tied into the *Nightingale's* sensors, he had access to pages of information about the environment on the other side of the inner airlock door. The numbers were disturbing. But as per the Captain's guidance, he ignored the errant information displayed and quickly went back to being bored. Crazy ass nebula. He would crack a beer in celebration once they were out of it, and another once they exited the damn Quadrangle. He hated this place as much as he hated certain violent, rogue factions of Asian governments.

He glanced over at the other members of his team. "How's everyone doing? Mixtures set right? Pressure holding up in your suits?"

Positive responses from the entire team set his mind at ease.

Dr. Laskey had her own display up to her face. She squinted and tilted her head, causing several short strands of fine silver hair to fall over her left eye. "I don't like these numbers I'm seeing," the elderly counselor whispered. "I do hope the Captain is right about the sensors being out of sorts;

I really hope it's not a hundred degrees below centigrade inside that ship."

"Yeah, me too, Barbara," replied Hamidi, the SCUBA Master. "Because if they're correct, those little girls must have built a campfire somewhere out of the sensors' reach to stay warm!"

"Don't worry yerself, little lady," Bruno inserted. "I can count on one hand the number of times th' Cap'n has been wrong in the last fifteen years!"

Rose Vereau jumped into the conversation. "I pray you're right, Antonio. Has anyone spoken to them in a while?"

Emerald Pearl

"You have to cut through *another* door?" Tabby exclaimed in disbelief.

"Don't worry, girls," Elwick assured, "it won't be much longer."

Little Sis groaned.

"Please trust—" His voice cut off.

Rae looked up to find Tabby's finger on the comm link, which had gone black. Rae's eyes bulged out of her head. "What did you do *that* for?"

"I'm tired of listening to his excuses," Tabby said. "Come on, Rae, let's find another way off this ship."

She can't be serious. "There *isn't* another way off this ship! You know that!"

Tabby stomped down the dim passageway toward the rear of the *Pearl*. "Maybe we can get through that door in

Engineering after all? Maybe we *should* see what's on the other side?"

Rae stood up slowly. "This girl's going to be the death of me," she said under her breath, repeating a line she had often heard her father say when he thought no one could hear. "Tabby, you *know* you can't go through that door! The lady engineer said—"

"Norstrom."

"Norstrom! She said there was nothing but outer space on the other side of that door! You understand what that means better than I do!"

Sis slowed her pace.

Rae walked a short ways down the passage toward her sister. "We've gotta wait for Captain Moses, Tabby. He's just outside. He'll be here soon. And there will be blankets and hot chocolate and maybe some hamburgers!"

Tabby stopped.

Rae knew food would get her attention. "I'll bet they even have pizza. And ice cream!"

Sis turned around. "You'd better be right," the girl snapped.

"I am. You'll see. Come on." Rae turned around and headed back to the airlock. Knowing Tabby couldn't see her face, she let her jowls droop. *Great Mother, please let them have pizza and ice cream!*

GSCS *Nightingale:* Airlock

Dale Masterson checked his timepiece again. “Eight minutes have passed, Mr. Gilbin.”

“Annnd…” Daniel burned the last few inches, then snapped off his torch. “Done!”

“Get those extractors in the door!” Masterson ordered. Dale looked on as Antonio Bruno and Jan Ebersbacher, the two largest members of the team, wedged crowbar-like devices into the seam of the door and began to tug in opposite directions. Neither Gilbin nor Masterson helped them like they had on the outer door. They were not being lazy; Bruno and the Bavarian Bluffer had made a bet with Daniel and Dale that they could do this one by themselves. Even though a six-pack of microbrew was on the line, Gilbin still cheered them on. “Come on! Av-a-go-ya-mug!”

In a few seconds, the door broke free. The air that had come with the team into the airlock rushed past them into the *Emerald Pearl*. Rose stumbled into Hamidi Abiodun.

“Woah,” Abiodun muttered, “did that wind just about knock anyone else down?”

“Don’t worry,” said Ebersbacher. “We expected ze pressure to be low in da transport ship.”

“Seems awful low to me. Low like *zero*.” Masterson checked his suit’s wrist screen once again. All the readings remained the same. Zero pressure, well below zero Celsius. But this time the observation matched the readings. He gave the German a sideways glance. “Want to take your helmet off and test the Captain’s theory, Mr. Ebersbacher?”

"No one is taking their helmets off!" Rose exclaimed. Masterson noted that her Canadian accent often got stronger when her emotions were in an elevated state, but now it sounded slightly... Australian? "Even if the readings are incorrect, there could still be a bio-hazard threat. Until I determine there's not, there will be no breaking of protocol, you...you drongos."

And Aussie slang to boot? Had Miss Vereau just chided her team chief—*him*—in front of the entire crew? It sure sounded that way. Masterson let it go because she was right, of course. Dale had only been joking; no one would be breaking Standard Operating Procedure on *his* watch. He found her choice of words amusing, though. She had been spending more off-duty time with Gilbin than he had realized if she was starting to sound Australian. Long as it didn't impact their duties, he didn't have a problem with it. *Good for Gilly,* he decided. *We should all be so lucky to land a dish like Rose.*

Ebersbacher and Bruno heaved and hoed on the inner door. As soon as a crack appeared, the opposite to what should have happened occurred. The air around them in the airlock rushed past them.

"Oh, that's not good," Masterson muttered.

"Did anyone else feel that?" asked Bruno.

Elwick's voice crackled in Dale's ear. "What just happened?"

Dale sighed. "It seems air just rushed *into* the *Pearl.*"

Several people looked at one another. Rose spoke. "Then the readings we've been picking up..."

"Are accurate," Dale conceded. "Our equipment seems to be working just fine," He closed his eyes. "Captain, I'm now not sure what—"

"The girls must be in a part of the ship that's sealed off," Elwick replied. "Right now, all we know is that the section the ship you're entering is in vacuum. The computer could have closed airtight doors nearby early on if it had detected damage to the airlock."

Dale nodded. "Possible. We'll know soon." He peered through the ever-widening crack, shining his light on an unglamorous gray passageway that ran perpendicular to the airlock. It appeared completely dark, save for several small rectangular yellow lights about a meter up from the deck panels. But were the lights powered by the *Pearl*, or from the power the *Nightingale* now supplied thanks to the Boatswain's Mate?

Once the door had been opened sufficiently for the largest team member to pass through—again, Bruno—Masterson told everyone to stand fast, and ventured a few steps inside. First, he turned to the right and shone his helmet light into the darkness. It illuminated the first few meters of a long, tunnel-like hallway with those little, rectangular lights running the length. He then turned to the left and did the same, seeing a similar but even longer hallway. Finally, he performed an about-face back to the group and raised his arms to his sides. "No one's here. And no doors are closed that I can see."

"By Jingoes," Gilbin exclaimed.

Rose asked out loud what everyone was thinking: "Where *are* they?"

GSCS *Nightingale*

"What do you mean they're not there?" Elwick asked from his command pillar on the bridge, vexed.

"Just what I said, Captain," replied Masterson. "We've called their names several times using our external suit speakers, but we get no answer. I'm now splitting my teams up as planned to take care of Phase Two."

"Understood." Elwick touched a graphic on his comm screen and spoke. "Rae? Tabitha? Where are you girls?"

"We're right here, Captain Moses. Can you maybe hurry? It's freezing in here!"

Elwick took a deep breath before responding, let it out slow. "You said you're at the airlock door, right?"

"Yes."

"The *port side* airlock door."

"Yes, Captain," Rae answered.

Moses caressed his bearded chin. "And you don't see the rescue party?"

"No, the door is still shut tight! There's no one here but us."

"Which door? Is it a small door or a really large door?"

"Um, I don't know. It's pretty big."

He sighed. "Does it say 'airlock' anywhere?"

"Right there," Tabitha said. "Airlock Two." Her voice turned monotone, like she had begun reading. "Airlock Outer Door. Caution. Stand clear when yellow light is—"

"Alright, alright, I believe you. Girls, stay right there. Don't get out of sight of the door again, okay?"

"We haven't!" Rae exclaimed. "At least, not in the last ten minutes!"

"Okay, just don't move for the next ten." Moses muted that channel so the girls could not hear his next words. "Dale, Elwick. The girls say they're at Airlock Two. I'm pretty certain it's the one on the starboard side, even though they believe it's on the port. I've instructed them to stay put. Head that way."

Moses heard no vocal reply from his friend over the comm system, only one long, deep, exasperated breath.

Emerald Pearl

Masterson took off on a slow run. A second powerful beam of brilliant white light extending from his right forearm illuminated his path better than his helmet light. He tried to be delicate over the comm with his Captain, especially when the rest of the team could hear. "You really expected two children to know the difference between port and starboard?"

"Actually, I really did think these two knew the difference," said Elwick in his ear. "Especially Rae, in this case, but both have proven themselves quite above-standard, and more than once on this little adventure."

"Well sorry to say, but your little geniuses got this one wrong." Dale hopped over debris in his path. Might have been a body. Probably just some boxes or something. "But it's okay, we'll find them."

"Let me know when you have them in front of you and I'll head down to the bay. I want to meet them when you bring 'em onboard."

"Aye aye, Captain." Masterson replied, still at a jog. He plowed through an intersection of four passageways that all looked exactly alike. He turned and found another, and then another. He thought he had memorized the old transport better than this. *This thing is a maze!* He came to a halt and called the XO over his comm.

"Ozzie here."

"Sir, if you would feed a map of this old frigate to my suit, it would make my trip to the starboard airlock a lot faster."

"No problem, Master Chief."

Dale had reached an intersection and looked each direction in turn. He paused on one hallway. "Got a body over here, I'll drop a pin as soon as we all receive the map." He squinted his eyes and shined his light that direction. A beeping from the screen strapped to his wrist alerted him he had a file waiting. He refocused his eyes and gazed upon it, and in seconds, a schematic of *Kristin's Vision* lit up on the inside of his helmet. He reminded himself the XO had found little to no data on the *Pearl* itself, so this would have to do. He studied it briefly, dropped a locator graphic where he decided the dead body to be, and moved on with a renewed confidence. Without slowing his pace and using only his eyes, Masterson shrank the map to the lower right corner of his helmet's Head's Up Display so it wouldn't impede his vision.

The gruff man had little patience for children on a normal day. Under trying circumstances, and when they out-right had refused an explanation of directions when he personally heard the Captain offer them, Dale had even less.

GSCS *Nightingale*

"Captain Moses?"

Elwick maneuvered back to his command pillar just to the right of center on the bridge. "Right here, Rae. Are you still by the airlock?"

"Yes. But the computer just announced the environmental controls have finally failed and that we need to evacuate immediately. It's super-freezing over here now! Where's the search party?"

"My good friend Chief Masterson is heading your way. It won't be much longer. Ladies, I'm afraid you may have gone to the wrong airlock," Elwick explained.

"But that's impossible," Rae told him. "You said to go to the one on the port side."

"Yes, I did. But when our party forced open the door to the port airlock, they didn't find you waiting for them."

"But how could that be?"

"We're at the wrong airlock?" Tabby's quiet voice sounded vexed, and Moses could imagine her furrowing her little brow.

"Did we get turned around somehow?" Rae asked of her sister.

"Nope," Tabby stated, as if there could be nothing more true in the world.

"It's okay, girls, no harm done, it's easy to get turned around, especially in stressful situations like you're in now. Like I said, Chief Masterson—Dale, our Search and Rescue Team leader—is on his way to meet you. It'll be just another minute or two."

"Aye, Captain," Rae replied sheepishly.

Everything will be okay, Moses told himself. *Long as there are no further mix-ups...*

41
Emerald Pearl

"Team Leader, this is Bruno."

"Masterson here."

"The bridge is just like the girls reported. Five dead, no survivors."

"Aye," Dale replied.

"But—"

"Yes?"

"These bodies…"

Dale slowed his pace. *Oh no, what now?* "What about them?"

"You might wanna take a look at 'em when you get here."

"Aye. After Abiodun accesses the main computer and starts the local data download, have him network the *Pearl's* computer directly with the *Nightingale.* He needs to coordinate with Petty Officer Connelly so Connelly can initiate a scan. I'm in no way trusting it to be accurate inside this nebula, so you and Gilbin need to conduct a *fast but thorough* physical reconnoiter of the ship to find anyone those scans miss." He added, "I know that was a mouthful. How copy?"

"Good copy, Master Chief! Hamidi's on the computer, Connelly's doing a scan, me and Daniel's on recon for survivors!"

Masterson smiled. “Roger dodger, big guy.” Of course he got it, he was speaking with an heartily seasoned sailor, after all.

“Just so you know, Chief,” Bruno continued, “Hamidi’s already on top of the download, but he’s having a bit of trouble.”

“What kind of trouble?”

Hamidi Abioudun broke in. “It’s hard to explain, Chief, but in a nutshell, I can’t for the life of me understand why the system’s so slow. Yes, I know it could be a hundred years old, but surely it’s been replaced or at least upgraded in all that time! Right?”

Dale didn’t know how to respond.

“Don’t worry, I’ll get this download started some way or another!”

“Aye, Hamidi. Keep on it. I’ll be up there as soon as I can to help out.”

“You’re going to help me network two computers that could be a hundred years apart in advancement?”

“Scratch that. I’ll cheer you on.”

Abioudun chuckled in Dale’s ear. “Aye, Master Chief!”

Around the next corner, Dale found the starboard side airlock. It looked exactly like the one on the port side of the ship. But this passageway turned out to be just as lonely as that one had been. He shone both his lights left, then right, into nothing but empty passageways. “You’ve *got* to be kidding me.”

Emerald Pearl: Airlock

"What!?" Elwick exclaimed over the comm.

"Maybe I should head to one of the *aft* airlocks?" asked Masterson.

"No, those are both in vacuum, the girls wouldn't be there," Elwick replied. "This is getting ridiculous. They must be moving around. They said they were getting cold, they're probably jogging up and down the passageways to stay warm." A mechanical sigh filled Dale's ears. The Captain sounded as frustrated as he. "Go to the bridge, Dale, I'll direct them there. There's only one bridge, and they've been there before. They can't possibly get lost."

Masterson wanted to offer a snide comment, but bit his tongue. He knew the Captain's high opinion of these children. "I have one team member there now. He's having some sort of trouble with the computer."

"I heard the radio chatter. And I'm a little curious about the bodies, which is another reason to get up there sooner rather than later."

"Aye aye, Captain." Dale didn't need the HUD displayed across his helmet to locate the bridge, all he had to do was follow the right-most wall and it would eventually lead him there. He moved out with a purpose. On his way he stopped and examined the body he saw earlier. He knelt beside it, somewhat vexed. There were blood streaks leading away from it, too faint to be the result of someone dragging the body *to* this location. More like someone (the girls?) dragged something *off* the body after it had been covered with something. A blanket or some such? But that wasn't what vexed him. The man who lay before him in no way looked like someone who had died within the past four hours. This body was actually hard as a rock. Frozen as solid as a fly trapped in a freezer.

Emerald Pearl: Airlock

"Girls, can you hear me?"

Rae busily rubbed her arms, but not too busy to answer Captain Moses! "We're still here! And still cold!"

"Girls, Chief Masterson was at the starboard airlock and he reported that he still couldn't find you. I've directed him to the bridge."

Rae sighed and rolled her eyes. That's because we're at the *port* airlock. I told you that, Captain Moses!"

"This has become too confusing, Rae. Please go to the bridge and meet Dale there. There's no way any of us can mistake the bridge for somewhere else, correct?"

Rae and Tabby eyed each other and shrugged. "Aye aye, Captain," Tabitha said, and they took off at a run.

GSCS *Nightingale*: Bridge

"Captain?"

"What is it Connelly?" Elwick rubbed the bridge of his nose in an attempt to ward off a headache.

"I have some bad news. Possibly some really bad news."

"Of course you do." He turned to face the communications station. "Okay. Let's have it."

"First, I figured out the comms delay."

"What comms delay?"

"The seven-microsecond comms delay we've been experiencing."

Elwick shook his head. "What are you talking about, Guy? I've not noticed any delay at all."

"Well, it's too short to be noticed in normal two-way communications."

"Then why does it matter?"

"Um, did I not mention this earlier?"

Osterland spun 'round in his chair to also face the comms station. "You absolutely did not, Connelly."

"Oh. Sorry, gentlemen. It wasn't any big deal at first, a little odd maybe, but nothing to worry about. Then I figured out what's been causing it. And now, well, there's definitely something to worry about."

Elwick breathed deep. "Guy, cut to the chase. What are you on about?"

"I found the other wormhole. The one we talked about earlier, the one broadcasting the *Pearl's* signals that that other wormhole was and still is spitting out. The one we're still receiving signals from."

"Wait a second," said Ozzie, "are you saying we're not talking to the *Pearl* right now? I mean literal and direct radio or QE communication?"

"No, sir. We never have been talking to that ship directly. All the transmissions we've been getting, both the original radio-broadcast distress call, and all the FTL QE voice transmissions between us and the girls, have been coming from a heading in the exact direction of that first wormhole we found. Where we thought the *Pearl* was originally. It's offset by seven microseconds, exactly like it should be considering that hole is about two hundred million kilometers behind us now, or one-fifth of a light year. QE comms is mega fast—faster than light—but not immediate."

Elwick closed his eyes. "I'm not sure I understand everything, or hell, anything you just said, but I do understand you said you found a second wormhole."

"Yes."

"Where is it?"

"It's all nice and tucked away in a place that makes this entire predicament make perfect sense."

Elwick opened his eyes, and tried to give Guy the most intense death-stare he could muster. "Petty Officer Connelly, if you don't quit beating around the bush—"

"It's right in the center of the *Pearl's* communications array, sir."

Elwick stared. "It's what?"

"Right here, look." Guy expanded a graphic display at his station, zooming in on the *Emerald Pearl's* antenna array.

"You're kidding."

"Not kidding."

"Is it stable?"

"Seems so."

"Is it moving?"

"Doesn't seem to be, sir. I don't think it poses any risk at all."

"But that sounds like a good thing."

"Oh, that part *is* a good thing."

"Then what's the bad thing? The bad news you mentioned at the start of this crazy conversation?"

"Well, sir, once I figured this out, I pieced together the rest of the puzzle. And I'm afraid it might be pretty damn terrible."

Elwick waited. He wasn't all that worried. *Honestly, how much worse could things get?*

"Sir, you know all that 'errant' data we've been receiving from our sensors and equipment? And ignoring? I now don't believe it too be errant data at all. I believe it is exactly one hundred percent accurate."

Okay, I was wrong. The situation probably just got much worse.

42

Emerald Pearl: Cryo Chamber

Rose Vereau activated the radio in her suit. "Team Leader, this is Squad Two."

"Masterson here."

"We've located the cryo chamber on Deck Three. But um—" She looked at the others, seeking help to explain the impossibility that she, Herr Ebersbacher, and Dr. Laskey had just discovered.

"Yes?"

"Dale," she let out a breath as she looked around. "It's empty. There are exactly *zero* pods in this chamber."

Emerald Pearl: Bridge

Masterson slowed to a walk and stared hard at a lump in the hallway not far past the gangway to the bridge. Probably another body, he decided. Hard to tell in the dim, yellow glow of the running lights. He'd verify later.

He stepped to his right, and his HUD notified him he was entering the "Captain's Yacht." He stomped past several offices and onto the ancient bridge. Mr. Abiodun looked up from the console at which he worked when Dale arrived. Several bodies covered with thermal blankets lay scattered about, but the two young girls he was supposed to meet were nowhere to be found. “Have you seen Rae and Tabitha yet?”

“No, Master Chief,” Hamidi replied, “they haven’t arrived yet.”

“I took my time getting here on purpose. Captain Elwick told me they took off at a run. If they were at the port airlock, we had the same distance to travel. They should have beat me here.”

“Sorry, Master Chief, if two young girls had busted into this room, I would definitely have seen them. Or heard them. Are they in spacesuits, by the way? Because my suit is reading—”

“I know what your suit it reading. It’s reading the same thing *mine* is reading. Vacuum. Negative one hundred seventy-nine degrees Kelvin. Right?”

Hamidi looked at his wrist. “Right.”

Dale did everything he could to curtail his annoyance. *This has turned into a cat-herding venture.* He was not amused. *I’m gonna strangle me two little shits if they think this is any kind of funny!*

But what had he just heard Rose Vereau say about the cryo-chamber?

Emerald Pearl: Cryo Chamber

Rose bounced from one compartment to the next. Could there be nooks and crannies in this old boat she was overlooking? Perhaps hidden compartments in the walls? She looked at her companions. The German shrugged his shoulders. The psychologist shook her head.

The radio chirped. “Miss Vereau? Say again your last.”

“Master Chief, I don’t know how it’s possible,” Rose replied, “but there are no, I say again, *no* cryo pods in the room we’re in. Is there another cryo chamber? An area we missed?” She scanned the map in her HUD as she waited for a response from her team leader. After a few more silent seconds, she broadcast again. “Master Chief, did you copy?”

“You have the *Vision’s* schematics, correct?”

“I do.” Rose poured over the thin yellow lines that filled the inside of her helmet. Her gaze zipped from side to side, north to south. She zoomed in, back out, flipped from one deck to the next in rapid but efficient succession. She let out a resigned breath. She looked over at her gray-haired friend and confidant, who waited patiently next to her. “If there indeed is a second cryogenics chamber, I can’t find it.”

Dr. Laskey shook her head. “That’s because there isn’t one.” She started toward the door.

“Doctor? Where are you going?”

Laskey paused and looked back at Rose. “I have a hunch. I just hope I’m wrong.”

Emerald Pearl: Bridge

Dale keyed his mike as he minimized his HUD, both with eye focus/gestures. “Rose.”

“I’m here, Chief.”

Masterson walked over to the nearest body. "You're one hundred percent certain there are no stasis pods in that chamber? They're not tucked away in the walls or—"

"Roger, Dale. There are mounts for pods," Rose explained, "right over what looks like doors in the deck plating."

"I can verify that, Master Chief," Laskey interjected. She sounded like she was on the move. "It looked to me like the pods have been jettisoned."

He lifted the blanket to expose the mummified face of a bridge crewmember, a young woman. "Alright, what, officially, are you telling me, Squad Two?"

"Chief," said Rose Vereau, "I'm reporting that there is no one in the cryo chamber—alive or dead—for Team Two to rescue. Awaiting further guidance."

Emerald Pearl: Bridge

Tabitha bumped into her big sister when Rae stopped running, causing Rae to stumble head-first onto the bridge. "Hey! Why'd you do that?"

Tabitha giggled. "Sorry."

Rae wanted to scold her, but couldn't bring herself to, not when they were getting along, finally. So instead, she giggled, too. She didn't even complain when Sis wanted to take "the scenic route" to the bridge instead of simply following the left wall. Yes, it took a little longer, but the more they ran, the more they warmed up! It felt so good to be laughing with her sister. She only wished it could be under better circumstances.

Now on the bridge, Rae looked around for Dale. Just like with the airlock fiasco, no one stood there to greet them. There were people there, of course, but only the *Pearl's* crew, covered with the blankets she and Tabby had laid upon them a few hours earlier. The cold air combined with the slight stench of decaying flesh filled her nose, throat, and what seemed like the whole of her insides. She shut her mouth, covered her nose with her sleeve, and took the deepest breath she could manage through the fabric. Then she ran to the communications console where she and Tabby had first spoken with crew of the *Nightingale.* She shouted into the red circle. "Captain Moses!"

"Rae?" Elwick's voice came across loud over the speakers. "Where are you girls right now?"

"We're on the bridge, but your friend isn't here yet. How long do we have to wait here? It stinks!" She took another filtered breath. Inadvertently her gaze fell upon the covered crewmembers still strewn about, the pants of their blue and black uniforms sticking out from under the small blankets. She expected Moses to reply with further instructions, but he did not. "Captain?"

"Hold on for just a minute, girls," Elwick replied. "I've got to check into something. Um, just please stay where you are, would you?"

"Ugh, do we have to? It really stinks in here!" Tabitha yelled.

"I'm sorry, girls, just a minute or two, please!"

Rae looked at her sister. "Did the Captain sound strange to you?"

Tabby breathed through her flannel bear which she held tightly to her face, all the while glancing around the quiet bridge. “Rae, I’m getting scared again.”

“Captain, please hurry!” Rae pleaded.

Emerald Pearl: Bridge

Dale Masterson took note that an unusual thing was occurring, but couldn’t for the life of him piece it together.

The Captain fumbled for words. “Master Chief, I think Petty Officer Connelly has discovered something incredibly significant. He might have noticed it before, had I not told him to ignore everything we thought were anomalous readings.”

Masterson waited impatiently.

“For starters, we’ve got another one of Bruno’s ‘little gremlin devils’ lurking between the antennae spires of the *Pearl’s* communications tower. We assume this to be the second wormhole we’ve been looking for. This would then explain the location anomaly from earlier.”

Dale shook his head, understanding none of this. *Doesn’t matter if I understand it or not.* “Roger. Is there a problem, sir?”

“Well Master Chief, the problem isn’t the wormhole per se, it’s the fact the transmissions are entering it, and then exiting the other one some two hundred million clicks behind us. And those are the transmissions we’re picking up.”

"Okay, so what does that have to do with the price of Dr. Pepper in Kansas City?"

"Connelly believes the transmissions could be time-shifted. We're trying to verify."

Dale had no idea where Elwick could be going with this techno-babbly explanation. He looked to Hamidi, who only shrugged, then continued with his work. "Captain, this is a very *old* boat. The comms are probably based on any number of old standards, any previous iterations of QE that's been invented over the decades. I'd expect the *Pearl's* systems to differ from ours. But the fact is, we still have comms with the girls, right? So I don't see how—"

"Bear with me, Dale. It'll be clear in a few minutes," Elwick said. "Please standby."

Masterson tried to calm himself. He assumed the position of "at-ease," as he often did while waiting, and stared at the overhead. He tried to make sense of the chatter over the radio—something about Barbara needing to get somewhere on the ship for some reason—before they could continue to discuss… whatever this was. Unconsciously, his stomach began to knot. In his experience, nothing good ever came from a stress knot; where his farm-raised brain failed, his gut took up the slack. And it already had everything figured out.

Dale wished it would share its knowledge with *him*.

43

Emerald Pearl: Observation Dome

Dr. Laskey basked in the red light pouring down from above. She stared intently at the couch before her and keyed her helmet microphone. “Captain, this is Barbara. I’m on the Observation Deck, under a very impressive and crazy-large transparent dome. Everything is red up here. And there are a couple of other people in here with me. People who can explain all this confusion we’ve been having.”

“People? They’re alive?” Elwick asked over the comm. “Who—”

“Mr. Connelly, would you please connect my comm ID to the *Emerald Pearl*’s comm system so that our two young friends can hear me?”

Guy piped up. “Standby.”

While she waited, Barbara’s skin tingled with gooseflesh due to a mixture of empathy, sorrow, and heartfelt appreciation for the sight before her.

The radio made a series of short beeps, then Connelly’s voice came on the line again. “Rae? Tabby? Can you hear me?”

“Hi, Guy!” Barbara heard Rae exclaim. “Just so you know, we left the bridge and shut the doors behind us. We’re sorry, but we couldn’t take the smell in there anymore! Tabby almost barfed!”

Barbara smiled, and she heard Guy chuckle. "It's okay, girls," Connelly said, "don't worry about it. I don't think you will need to go back in there."

"Good!" yelled Tabitha.

"There's a dead man out in the hallway, too," Rae added, "so we walked back to the spiral staircase by Captain Timmin's room. Quarters. Whatever they're called."

"That's fine, Rae. I have someone on the comm link who wants to talk to you both."

"Okay," the girls said in unison.

"Go ahead, counselor."

Barbara cleared her throat. "Ladies? Rae, Tabitha?"

"Hello?" one of the girls responded.

"Hello, darlings. My name is Dr. Barbara Laskey. I'm the *Nightingale's* counselor."

"Hello, Dr. Laskey, I'm Rae."

"Wow," exclaimed the younger child. "I didn't know there was a lady on board the *Nightingale!* I thought it was just packed full of a bunch of sweaty old sailor men!"

Barbara let loose a grandmotherly laugh. "You must be Tabitha! Just as precocious as I imagined. Please, call me Barbara."

"Okay. Call me Tabby."

"Yes, of course. Tabby. Such an adorable name."

The voice Laskey recognized as belonging to Rae broke into the conversation. "Miss Laskey—sorry, Barbara—are you looking for us? We're in the passageway just behind the bridge."

"No, darlings, I'm not looking for you. I've already found you."

Silence fell upon the line for a moment before Tabitha muttered, "Um… what?"

Emerald Pearl: Gangway

Now that all the comms channels had been tied together, Dale Masterson could hear the young girls' voices once again. While he had never spoken to them directly, he could tell them apart as easily as could the other members of his team. Each member of the SAR team had listened in from time to time over the past few hours as the bridge crew had attempted to coordinate the rescue with them. "I'm sorry, where did that little girl just say they were?"

SCUBA Master Hamidi Abiodun looked up from his chore of networking the two ships. "Sounded like she said they were in the passageway just of the bridge?"

After giving Hamidi a trepidatious stare, Dale jogged out the door he had entered, still open as Abiodun had left it, and into the connecting passageway beyond. He ran past several small offices and berthing compartments—only now realizing the entire front nosecone of the *Pearl* doubled as the Captain's Yacht—and finally jumped through another dogged-open door. Bursting into the large, bulky part of the ship, he tossed his beam left and right in quick succession, but saw no sign of the girls. He picked a direction—port—and darted down the passage running athwartships, shining his bright, arm-mounted beam down every dimly lit passageway he came across. He hit the far, port wall. No Rae, no Tabby. He retraced his steps, now running toward starboard. He reached the far starboard wall. Still no youngsters. "This is impossible."

Dale had seen enough science fiction holofilms to get the gist of the crazy, "Twilight Zone-y shit" that might be going on right now—he could think of no better term to call it—but he simply couldn't bring himself to believe it was actually happening in real life.

Emerald Pearl: Observation Dome

"I don't understand." Rae's voice sounded tinny over Barbara's suit communicator. "If you're not looking for us right now, well, can we just talk in person once we're on board your ship?"

"Oh, Rae, I would so love to do that. But it's just not in the cards."

"Again, I don't—"

"What do playing cards have to do with anything?" Tabby blurted. "Why are we stalling here? We just want off this cold, creepy old ship! Captain Moses! Where are *you?*"

"That was a figure of speech, Tabby," Barbara said. "Listen, girls, Captain Moses, as you call him, would agree that I'm the best person on board to tell you what I have to tell you. But before I do, I want you to know I'm here for you young ladies, in spirit and in any other way I can be. I think we're going to become wonderful friends."

"Okaaay," Rae replied, now sounding a little annoyed. "How about we become friends *after* the rescue team brings us over to the *Nightingale*?"

Barbara closed her eyes and exhaled. She tried to choose her words carefully. "Children," she began slowly. "I'm afraid I have some… some terrible news."

Emerald Pearl: Gangway

Rae's eyes had narrowed. *What was this lady on about?* "Barbara, if this is about our father, we already know. Both of us know. We haven't really had time to think about it or talk much about it, but— Wait. This isn't about Mother, is it? Or Jamie?"

Tabitha gasped. "What about Mother!? What about Jamie!?"

"Shh, Tabby!" Rae began to shake. She didn't want to hear the answer, but she was dying to know the secret this woman held.

"No, children, this has nothing to do with your mother. Is Jamie your sibling?"

"He's our brother."

"I see, well, this isn't about him either. This is about you and little Tabby." A pause. "Actually, everyone needs to hear this… Master Chief, would be so kind as to grant an old woman an audience?"

A deep voice broke the air. "Approved." A few beeps followed after him.

"Thank you, Master Chief."

"*He* sounds scary," Tabitha whispered.

"Captain, Crew, Team, Rae, and Tabitha," began the counselor, "I'm in the Observation Lounge, kneeling before two young ladies huddled on a couch together. A thermal blanket covers their laps. They are dressed in clothing I've only seen my grandmother wear in pictures when she was little. The smaller girl is wearing what looks like a short, burgundy dress and a pink sweater, buttoned up to the top. Very pretty. The older girl is wearing a pink cardigan over a cute, frilly black blouse."

Rae's breath caught in her throat. She looked at her little sister's clothes, then at her own. Twice. Most of the description sounded dead on, but the colors weren't right. "She can't be talking about us, Rae," Tabitha remarked. "My dress is blue and my sweater is white. And everything you have on is purple."

Barbara corrected herself. "Oh, girls, my colors are surely off. It's so hard to tell in this infernal red light."

Rae's hands began to shake more violently. She couldn't speak.

Tabitha never had such a problem. "Captain Moses, this counselor lady is scaring me."

"Don't be scared, Tabby," Moses' familiar voice assured her. "Everything will be okay. Just please listen to what Doctor Laskey has to say."

He sounds so sad. Rae thought. *Why does he sound sad?* Rae fought off tears. Tears due to something she couldn't understand, but which stole her voice away completely.

Emerald Pearl: Observation Dome

Barbara studied the two figures before her more closely. "The older girl is wearing a silver amulet around her neck," she said, ever-so-gently lifting the small piece of jewelry with the tips of her fingers. "It looks like a flower with five petals, but I would bet it's actually a Wiccan pentacle disguised as a flower—a talisman of protection, representing the four basic elements, and Mother Earth."

Emerald Pearl: Bridge

Rae's cold fingers fumbled about, and she soon pulled from her blouse a pendant with a five-pointed, rounded star inside a larger circle. She could see her fingers through it due to its open-air-style. "My mother gave me this. But I'm wearing it. So how could you be looking at it right now?"

"Oh sweetheart," Rae heard Barbara say, the old woman's voice trembling, "this particular amulet… it is around the neck of a very beautiful young lady. But a young lady who died a *very* long time ago."

44

Emerald Pearl

Whimpering reached Rae's ears. Tabitha. She knelt down and grabbed her sister and held her close. The little girl shook now, too.

Why would this strange woman be saying all these impossible things? Why was she deliberately trying to scare us?

Captain Moses' voice finally broke the silence. "Rae?" His voice came across like a velvety-soft blanket. "Before we jump to conclusions, I need to ask you a couple of questions."

Rae opened her mouth, but nothing came out.

"Could you please tell me what year it is?" he asked.

She tried again, but only managed a squeak. *I am not dead. We are not dead!* They couldn't be. They were standing right there in that gangway, alive as could be. A white light from the overhead shone on her hand. It shone on her sleeve. She could feel her little sister's warmth against her body, she could hear Tabitha's breathing between whimpers. Rae had just heard the Captain's voice and Barbara's voice and the scary man's voice as plain as day. Can zombies do that!?

Actually, she wasn't sure. Maybe they could?

"Rae? Are you there?" Elwick pleaded. "Can you still hear me?"

Rae managed to choke out a barely audible, "yes."

"You said it's only been a little over a month since you left Earth. Is that right? That's what the computer said, remember?"

She sniffled. "Yes."

"Rae, tell me, what month and year would that make it right now?"

Rae forced her mind to think. *Well, the computer said it's been thirty-one days since we left, so that makes it...* Math. Math seemed impossible right now.

"August fourteenth," answered a tiny voice beneath her. "I think that makes it... a Wednesday." Math proved extraordinarily easy for Tabby, no matter the situation.

"What year, sweetie?" Barbara asked.

Even I know this one. Rae yelled the answer to get it out before her sister did. "2467! We are supposed to start school this month, but Daddy," she cleared her throat, "Daddy said we would be late this semester because the trip would last too long." She then heard several exasperated voices over the comms, voices she didn't recognize. Gasps. Sighs. Words of condolence. Prayers to an "almighty god." God, *singular,* not plural. Daddy's deity. She heard what sounded like the faint sounds of a woman crying? But why? Surely not because of them. She and her sister were just fine. "Captain Moses," Rae pleaded, "I don't like this. Tabby is shaking. I'm not crying yet but I'm about to. Can we just leave already?"

"Rae," Moses said, "it's not August, my dear. And—"

"Sure it is," said Rae. "The computer said we only launched thirty-one days ago. And that was in July. So how can it be any later than August?"

"Captain Moses?" Tabitha called. "Captain Moses, we just want to go home."

"Rae, Tabby," Elwick continued, "I don't know exactly how to make you understand this without coming right out and saying it, but I'm going to try to ease you into it…"

Rae heard him take a deep breath. She dreaded to hear what he might say next.

"My darlings, from my perspective, today is Tuesday, February Eighteenth, 2541." His voice cracked a time or two as he spoke. "I'm sorry, girls. I… I know I made a promise to you, but..." He choked up, but eventually found a way to continue. "We're not going to be able to rescue you. We're seventy-four years in your future, and you're seventy-four years in our past. This is why none of us can find you. This is why you can't find us."

"But… what?"

"In your time, Rae, I haven't even been born yet. None of us have. And you and Tabby…" His voice caught, and he never finished *that* sentence.

Rae sat back on her haunches in silence. Not breathing, not blinking. Her head spun, and she was glad she hadn't been standing just now. The small, overhead lights seemed less bright than they had been just moments before. The walls that surrounded her faded. She wavered. Her resolve buckled.

Rae heard her sister scream her name before everything went black.

45

Emerald Pearl: Bridge

Dale Masterson's bright arm beam danced on the floor as he trudged back onto the bridge of the *Pearl,* arms dangling limply by his sides. If he could have seen his own face, he wouldn't have known what to make of it. He simply stared at Hamidi. He could think of only one thing to say. "What the f—"

GSCS *Nightingale*: Bridge

Moses shook his head as he looked at the forlorn faces around him. No one spoke. The XO stared at his console. *No. This isn't how it's supposed to go! This isn't how it is supposed to end. This can't be happening! Is it really happening?* His eyes filled with water, and he turned to face the conference room so his subordinates couldn't see.

Come on, Moe! Of course this is not happening. It's impossible! God wouldn't let something impossible happen. It's not his forte. Not His M.O. His Grand Design doesn't allow for "glitches" in reality. Everything fits all nice like a puzzle. A well-oiled machine. And this simply doesn't fit.

He's not the vengeful god of the Old Testament, Elwick reasoned. *He's different now. He wouldn't take vengeance out on two innocent girls, just because one of them is Wiccan. Would He? No, of course He wouldn't!*

But he took vengeance out on an innocent girl before, didn't he? A Christian girl, at that.

Alena.

Moses shook his head again and put his hands on his hips.

Even if God may allow it, I refuse to. Do you hear that, God? I have a say here! I do! And I'm saying this isn't going down like this! There's a way out. There's a way out for Rae and Tabby and I'm going to find it, so-help-me, I'm going to find it!

So... help me... please.

Silence. Silence all around him. He heard nothing, he felt nothing. Except for feeling utterly on his own.

Or... you know what? So help me not! God damn it all! I'm not giving up!

Emerald Pearl: Bridge Gangway

Rae floated.

Where am I?

She heard something that sounded like a voice. A familiar voice. But where was it coming from? She couldn't locate its source. She couldn't find anything, not in this inky darkness.

"Rae! Rae, please wake up! I don't know what to do! I don't understand! Please wake up!"

Is that Tabby?

"Rae!"

Where are we?

"Rae! Wake up!"

Senses fought to return. She grasped sound, but no sight, no smell, no taste. *Are we still on the Pearl? Are we still in trouble? Are we still alive?*

"Rae! Please don't be dead!"

The numbness drudged away. Rae felt a slight touch. The sensation strengthened. She ached for it. *Tabby...*

"Please don't leave me, too!"

Rae could feel her sister's warmth now, encompassing her body. Her little sister was hugging her, and tightly.

"What!" exploded from Rae's mouth. "What's going on? Where are we?" Her eyelids shot open, but her brain couldn't register the information that came from them.

"Rae! Thank God!"

Am I on the floor? Did I black out? What day is it? She took in the scene as her gaze darted about the room. An empty hallway. Passageway. Gangway. Empty, save for her sister, now hovering above her. Something struck Rae's mind. *Rescue!* Her head became clearer as the seconds passed. Things began to make sense again. She lifted herself up onto her elbows.

"Oh Rae, I thought you were a goner!"

"Where is Captain Moses' friend? Where's the rescue party?"

"I don't know," Tabitha replied in a sorrowful tone. "But I don't think they're coming."

Details returned all at once. Rae's heart sank through her chest and down through the decks and into the icy depths of space only a few meters beneath her. She let out a heavy breath in exasperation, and allowed her head and torso to plop back down on the hard, cold surface on which she lay. She shivered, closed her eyes, and sucked in the now downright icy air. The putrid stench of decay had followed them into the gangway, even with the door to the bridge closed. It crept deeper inside her head than ever before. She crinkled her nose, shifted to all fours, and began to dry wretch.

"Ewww!" screamed Tabby. "Stop! You're gonna make me sick too!" Sis released her grip and flew to her feet in a flash.

Rae took short, quick breaths to calm her stomach. It worked. When it felt safe to do so, she raised her head and opened her eyes again. She spotted her sister's flashlight in the now extremely dim light not far away. "It's okay. I'm not going to throw up."

"Are you sure?" The little girl's tone sounded mistrustful. "'Cause I don't wanna see it!"

"I'm fine," Rae assured her. "I just needed a minute."

Tabby stepped closer. She had both hands on her mouth, but dropped them and looked relieved upon verifying the floor was free of vomit.

"I don't know about you, Tabby, but I don't want to stay here."

"I don't either! Let's get out of this stinky hallway!"

Tabitha helped Rae to her feet, and they ran down the dark corridors, shoving death as far from them as possible. They stopped at one of the spiral staircases, near at the "housing" area where the crew lived. What did their father call them? Birthing quarters? *Wait, birthing?* Rae made a face. That couldn't be right. But it sounded a lot like that.

"Now where do we go?" Sis asked.

Good question. They couldn't go to the Observation Dome! For one thing, that's where Barbara said she had found them. For another, Captain Moses said it may be dangerous there. Her eyes lit up, and he gasped. "He was right!"

"Who was right? About what?"

"The dome!" Rae yelled, grabbed the flashlight from Tabitha's hand, and went in search of a communications panel.

"Hey! I'm using that!" the little one protested. "What about the dome?"

A short distance down the hallway/passage, Rae found a panel. She pounded her fist on the little screen above the red circle until the little blue light illuminated like she had expected. "Captain Moses! You were right!"

"What, Rae? What was I right about?" came the excited reply.

"That the dome could be dangerous, like with radiation finding its way in. Don't you see? That's probably why we died! Or, will die, I mean! So, I'm thinking, if we just stay away from the Observation Deck, we'll be okay! We'll live!"

Silence.

"Right?"

Tabitha looked up. "Rae? I don't get it."

"Tabby, listen. You and I aren't dead yet. Right now, we're still alive, right?"

Tabby pinched Rae.

"Ow!"

"You sound alive to me."

Rae groaned, but didn't retaliate. "Right! So, just because that lady said she found us dead, doesn't mean we're for sure going to die!"

"It doesn't?"

"No! Not if we don't do whatever it was that made us die in the first place! Right?"

"Oh," the little girl replied, nodding her head. "I don't get it."

"That's a very interesting viewpoint, Rae," Elwick said, breaking the silence on his end. "I don't know much about this time-shifting business, so you could very well be onto something. However—"

Rae ignored his "however" and clapped and beamed.

"—Let's not get too excited just yet," Elwick continued. "I want to check something… Barbara? You're still under the dome, correct?"

"Yes."

"The multi-function device on the arm of your suit. It's got a built-in 'Micro-R meter.' Do you know how to operate that feature?"

"Not exactly, but I think I can figure it out, Captain."

"Okay," Elwick continued, "I need to know the millisieverts. It will read 'mSv' once you're on the correct screen. Let me know when you see this."

"Got it," Barbara announced.

"Good. It's pretty straight forward once the program opens."

"I think I have it, Captain. Initiating test."

"Aye. Let me know the result."

"Aye aye."

Rae paced.

"How many women are on board the *Nightingale*?" Tabby asked, directing her voice toward the panel above her head.

"What?" asked Rae, "you're worried about that? Now?"

Tabitha shrugged. "Sounds like we have a minute."

"Four," replied Moses.

"Huh," said Tabitha. "Never would-a guessed."

Rae whispered to her sister. "What do you think the Captain and Barbara are checking?"

"I'm pretty sure he's checking for radiation," Tabitha whispered back.

"You're absolutely correct," said Elwick. "Tabitha—Tabby—remember when I told you I wasn't sure whether the glass in the Observation Dome was sufficient to protect you from the dangerous light coming from the nebula? Light that can hurt you?"

"Yes," Tabitha replied. "I know about radiation."

"Right, of course you do." His voice smiled. "Barbara is checking on just how much radiation is pouring in through the graphene dome."

"But what will that prove, Captain?" Rae asked.

"Well, it may prove your little hypothesis. On whether you might stay alive if you just stay out of the Observation Lounge, which I'm kinda hoping is what killed those two people in there right now. If so, well, maybe we have more time than we think. And maybe we can come up with other ideas on how to save you."

"Ohhh." Rae drew out the syllable, suddenly enlightened. "Tabby! The Captain thinks—"

"I heard him. I get it. I'm not stupid, I just didn't understand before. I do now."

"Oh. Okay."

"I think," she added. Then louder, "It's 'Dome' not 'Lounge'. Observation *Dome.*"

"Yes," said Moses, "I keep messing that up."

"Captain Elwick," interrupted Dr. Laskey. "I think I have what you're looking for. The number before the letters 'mSv' is 3.34. I'm not familiar with radiation measuring, except I know that five or six Sieverts will kill a person. I don't know how many millisieverts a person can safely take."

"Excellent, Barbara," Captain Moses replied. "Thank you."

Rae was impatient to learn what they had just discovered. "Okay so is that good? Or bad?"

"Actually, Rae, it's both. And neither. A reading of 3.34 on a Micro-R meter isn't enough to be harmful to human beings. So, it's good in the sense that it means the dome has been protecting you from the nebula's radiation this whole time."

"That's good!" Rae smiled at her sister. "What could be bad about that?"

"Well, it's bad in that now we haven't proven what we wanted to prove. It's still possible that the girls Dr. Laskey discovered in the Observation *Dome* died of something else, like hypothermia for instance, and not from cell damage from radiation."

Rae didn't know what to make of this new information. "Okay. What does this mean?" she asked of anyone listening. "Does this mean we still die? Or what?"

"I don't know, Rae," Elwick replied. "I just don't know. But don't worry." A long pause followed. "We're discussing other solutions, girls. I'll get back with you soon, okay?"

Rae's shoulders slumped. Her mind swirled into an ugly mess. She felt so confused. *What do we do now?* Was Captain Moses giving up? She definitely didn't want to give up, but what else could they try? What else was there to do?

She thought her little theory might still be right. Stay away from the dome. If they never go to the dome, their bodies can't be found there. "Fate and Time are just going to have to find another way to kill us," she said out loud.

Tabitha looked up at her. "What?"

"Come on. Let's go be with Mom and Daddy and Jamie."

Tabitha's mouth turned down at the corners. "Okay."

Rae led her sister down the spiral staircase to Deck Three. She teared up as they plodded along to where a room labeled "Cryogenics" patiently awaited them.

In their time, their family awaited them, too.

46

Emerald Pearl

Hamidi Abiodun checked a readout on the console he had been working at for the last half-hour. "We're at forty percent on the ship's log and data download, Master Chief."

"Aye. Captain Elwick, did you copy that?"

"Yes I did, Dale. Hamidi, do you have any ideas as to why that download is giving you fits?"

Abiodun sighed. "I had trouble linking the systems, and the download keeps pausing, don't know why. Maybe just these ancient circuits. Maybe something else."

"Understood. Dale, status of the rest of your team?"

"I've now got them scattered about below decks conducting a physical check for survivors. Or more bodies."

"Roger," Elwick replied. "We'll be over here quietly racking our brains for ideas. Please report in every fifteen minutes."

"Aye aye." Dale stared off into the red sky beyond the graphene windows of the bridge. His mind was as blank as he figured his eyes must look. *I must make myself useful.* He looked around at the multitude of consoles. "Would you look at these things? Straight out of Jules Verne."

"What's Jules Verne? Is that that new show Gilly was talking about at breakfast?"

Dale chuckled. "Nevermind. I mean it just seems so… antiquated. And they waste a lot of space here. I mean take a look at this navigation station. They've spread out across two meters what the *Nightingale* has packed into maybe twenty-five square centimeters. They use actual screens for most of this instead of holo displays that can take any shape. Why would anyone continue to use—? Nevermind."

Hamadi whispered, "The ship was probably modern when it actually *was* in use, Master Chief."

"I know, I know, I remembered before I even finished. I just can't wrap my head around this! It seems so impossible!"

"Agreed. I'm trying not to think about it and focus on this old operating system."

With the *Nightingale* trickling power to the *Pearl*, more and more consoles across the ship powered up at random. The nav station came alive beneath Masterson's fingers. "Whoa. Did you do that?"

"Don't look at me, Master Chief!"

Dale "turned some dials and flipped some switches" as the heroes in a Jules Verne story might do. "Huh. I was right."

"What's that?" asked Hamidi, without looking up.

"The *Pearl*'s destination: Preia Byoea," he read off, "QY-A C16-6. Formorian Frontier. There's only one thing out that way that I know about, and I bet there was only one thing out that way back in their day, too."

Hamidi seemed to wait patiently for Dale to continue. Either that or he didn't care.

Dale didn't need him to listen. "Preia Byoea harbors a Chinese mining colony. Sixth planet. Didn't have a name when I was—" He thought better of finishing that sentence, and instead modified it. "When last I checked. What would a transport ship full of American and European and other allied passengers be doing heading to a Chinese mining facility?"

"To work there?" Hamidi suggested. "Maybe the Chinese didn't always have it?"

"Hmm," Dale wondered. "Perhaps. Maybe it was once a free colony? Back when America and rogue Chinese factions were merely in a cold war and not at each other's throats?"

"Between the fall of the United States and before the founding of the Republic," inquired Hamidi, "weren't there independent rogue American factions in cold wars and at each other's throats? No foreign enemy needed?"

"There were, in fact! It was chaos! The wild, wild west!" Dale looked out into the red cloud all around him. "It was a simpler time. Few rules, if any at all. Must have been glorious."

47

Emerald Pearl

The girls stepped lightly into the cryogenics chamber. An odd quiet filled it now; there was no sign of the chaos that had marked their earlier experience. No alarms sounding, no lights flashing. Just the soft hum of machinery keeping their loved ones and four other passengers alive. It was also much colder here, even more so than the chilly upper decks! Rae shivered. Steam drifted from her mouth.

She stole over to their mother's and brother's pods. Rae now saw the devices only as coffins with built-in windows to view the soon-to-be-deceased. She stood directly before her mother, reclined slightly due to the incline of her pod. "She looks so peaceful," Rae said. She put a hand on the cold glass. "I'm sorry we couldn't get you out of there, Mom."

"You mean we're just gonna leave them in there?" asked Tabitha.

"What else can we do?"

"We gotta get them out!"

"And what's the point of that, Tabby?"

"I'm *not* leaving Mommy and Jamie in those things! Come on, help me break them open!"

"You can't break that glass, Tabby! It's probably made of that graphite stuff!"

"Grapheeene."

"And even if you could, would you rather them have heart attacks and die in pain and terror in broken pods, or die peacefully in their sleep? Or freeze to death like we still might?"

"I don't want them to die at all," the little girl whimpered.

Rae sighed, and saw her breath again. "Me neither, Sis." She shivered, and figured she should probably hurry if she wanted to incant a prayer for Mother and Jamie. Soon it might be too cold for her fingers to even turn the pages of a book.

My book!

Where is it!? Rae spun 'round frantically, trying to remember.

"What's wrong?" asked her sister.

"My book of Earth prayers! I must have left it somewhere!"

"Calm down," Tabitha said, unzipping her beloved teddy bear that she had been dragging everywhere. She pulled out a small, pocket-sized book from amongst the fluff. "Here."

Rae's eyes bulged. "Oh my Goddess, Tabby! You kept it safe for me?"

"You left it on the table in the kitchen. I didn't want you to lose it."

Water instantly filled Rae's eyes, and she grabbed Tabby and hugged her tighter than she ever hugged anyone.

"Okay, okay! It was just a favor! Let go, you're gonna break me!"

Rae obliged, but not before kissing Tabby on the cheek.

"Oh, yuck!" Sis screamed. "Don't ever do that again!"

Rae laughed, twirled, and opened the book. She could almost ignore the frigid air as she turned page after page scanning for a prayer that would perfectly fit the situation.

"Are we gonna stay here long? Are you gonna read one of your dumb *Earth prayers* or something?"

"Yes!"

"Well can you hurry it up? I'm freezing!"

"Okay, okay!" Rae said, "I think this one will do." She composed herself before beginning by closing her eyes, lifting her chin, taking a deep breath of cold air, holding it to the count of three, and letting it out as slow as she could. "*Mother of my birth,*" she began, "*for how long were we together in your love and my adoration of yourself?*" A larger puff of steam distracted her as she read that last word. It seemed to be getting colder by the second! But she had to finish. "*For the shadow of a moment, as I breathed your pain and you breathed my suffering. As we knew of shadows in lit rooms that would swallow the light.*"

She looked up at her mother's face. Rae wished she knew the next lines of the prayer by heart, so her gaze could remain on her mother. She raised the book high, so she wouldn't have to keep looking down and back up again and again. "*Your face beneath the oxygen tent was alive but your eyes closed, your breathing hoarse. Your sleep was with death. I was alone with you as when I was young but now only alone, not with you, to become alone forever, as I was learning, watching you become alone.*"

Rae took a deep breath, let it out slow and watched her breath evaporate into nothingness. "*Earth now is your mother, as you were mine, my earth, my sustenance and my strength. And now without you I turn to your mother and seek from her that I may meet you again in rock and stone. I love you. Whisper to the rock, I found you. Whisper to the earth, Mother, I have found her, and I am safe and always have been.*"

Rae closed the book and looked down at Tabby. She put one hand on the girl's head, careful to stay between her pigtails. Sis' pretty eyes were closed, and tears ran down both cheeks. *She might prefer to follow Daddy's Christian upbringing,* Rae thought, smiling, *but the prayers Mom taught us still touch her heart.*

48

GSCS *Nightingale*

Elwick had just absent-mindedly finished counting all the rivets in his command pillar when Connelly nearly gave him a heart attack. "Captain!"

"What? What happened?"

"Nothing's happened sir, but I may have just figured out how to save everyone! Before I spoke up, I had to check a couple of things, and now I have."

Moses smiled. *Good ol' Guy.* "Whatcha got?"

"Okay, first thing's first. Rose said the cryo chamber is empty, right?"

"Yes, but—"

"Rae, Tabby! It's Guy Connelly, please respond, it's very important." While he waited for them to answer, he looked back at Elwick. "Those pods should still be there. In our time, not just theirs. Someone dumped them."

Elwick's brow furrowed as Rae's voice finally came through the speaker. "Hi, Guy."

"Rae, listen. Did you say you were heading down to the cryo chamber?"

"Yeah, we're here now, but we're getting ready to head back upstairs. It's super freezing in here! I only came down so I could incant an Earth prayer for my mom and my brother."

"Okay great. I need you to look around. Are all the pods still there?"

"Of course. Why wouldn't they be?"

"Because they're not there in our time. The chamber is empty. Which means at some point they get jettisoned."

"Um, okay."

Elwick stepped up to Petty Officer Connelly's station. "I think I see where you're going with this," he said to Guy. Then into the comm channel, "Girls, I know it's cold, but could you please wait there just another minute?"

"Okay, Captain Moses."

Elwick made a cutting motion across his throat, and Connelly muted their microphones. "You want them to crawl back into their pods, don't you?"

Guy nodded. "Yes. That's how we're going to save them."

"You think the pods will last seventy-four years?"

"Well, if the girls stay on that ship, they die. Barbara already saw their bodies. Frozen under that dome. If they're going to die anyway, at least this way they won't freeze. They'll just go into hibernation and not wake up. And who knows? Maybe we can find those pods drifting in this nebula somewhere, and maybe they'll still be operating?"

"Connelly—"

"Look, Captain, I know it's a long shot, but—"

"Guy, those pods are surely a hundred years old!"

"Sir, you said to come up with anything and everything."

Elwick stared at his Communications Officer. "I did say that, didn't I?"

Guy nodded.

"So, Rae and Tabby somehow push all the right buttons to get the pods to re-start. Then they hop back into those coffins—"

"Please, sir, pods."

"Fine, pods, get themselves all hooked back up—sensor wires and intravenous tubes and all, in prep for hibernation—somehow eject themselves while *inside* those very same pods, hope the computer allows such a thing in the first place, especially from two young girls who are, as we already know, not on the command access roster and might need to bring Captain Timmins head with them—"

"Oh, please, sir—"

"Program the pods to initiate hibernation—again from inside the damn things—and then hope we come along in another seventy-five years and scoop them up! Two tiny needles in a haystack the size of several solar systems! And assume the pods are still going to be working and will have kept them alive after all that time. Is that about right, Mr. Connelly?"

"No sir," said Osterland. "Seventy-four years."

"Thank you, Mr. Math," Elwick snapped, giving his XO a look that clearly said, *now is not the time to be funny.*

"Sorry," Ozzie whispered.

"But is the rest of what I said just about right, Connelly?"

"Yes. Yes, sir, that's about right."

"I thought so." Elwick took a deep breath and let it out to calm himself. "Even if all went perfectly, I don't see how in all the universe those pods could keep them alive for upwards of a century."

"Some people have been known to survive after twenty, thirty years in cryo-stasis. I mean, I know it's a long time, but—"

"Upwards of a century, Connelly! Not thirty years!"

The comms officer nodded. "Yes, okay, I admit it's a little out of the specifications of any cryo pod, even in our century."

"Just a bit!"

"Well sir, even if the girls don't get inside the pods, I think it would be best to eject all of them from the *Pearl.* At least the ones with survivors."

"Oh, you do? How would that help?"

"Each one has its own distress beacon. It's possible they'll alert a passing ship in their time that could pick them up long before we arrive. Unfortunately, the beacons operate on radio, not QE—I already checked—and it's unlikely anyone would be out this way between then and now, but it's worth a shot. I mean, the *Pearl's* not providing them any additional power at this point anyway; when we had Rae and Tabitha shut the ship down, the pods were stuck with what reserves they had at the time. At least this way, the people inside might have a chance to be picked up sooner than in seventy-four years."

"But at least if they stay inside the hull of the *Pearl,*" Elwick pointed out, "the radiation won't get to them."

"I checked the specs of the pods on *Kristin's Vision.* These are surely the same. As long as they don't get hit by a gamma ray burst or float into a system with a neutron star or a black hole, nothing's getting inside. A tungsten-chromium shell auto-wraps around them upon jettisoning, covering any weak points like transparent metal and whatnot."

Elwick considered this a moment. *Connelly is probably right,* he decided. It would give every survivor that much more of a chance. And the pods are gone already, in his time!

Perhaps they're gone because the girls jettisoned them, on Moses' order? That brought up another question. What if Moses didn't tell the girls to eject them, would they magically reappear in front of the SAR team? An interesting conundrum/debate, but he had little time for academic arguments when he had two little girls freezing to death, waiting for him to come back on the line. "Okay," said Moses, nodding, "open 'er back up."

Guy touched the un-mute button.

"Girls?"

"We're here!"

"Rae, I have a question. Are your and Tabitha's cryo pods still operating? Still lit up?"

"Yes."

"See if you can start the hibernation process back up." He reached across Connelly and muted the channel on his own. "We're going to try this, Guy, because at the moment I'm out of ideas, but for the record, I'm officially against it."

The man nodded. "Aye, sir."

49

Emerald Pearl

Tabby climbed up onto her pod, threw her bear in first, then hopped in after it, smiling the whole way.

Elwick's voice came over a comm panel on the large wall that was full of information when the girls had first awoken. It was now as black as the darkest recesses of the cryo chamber. "Read me what it says on your pod's screen, Rae."

She did so, in as much detail as she could.

"Alright. Touch that re-initialize square."

Rae obliged. "I got a red warning."

"What does the warning say?"

"It says, 'Access denied. Enter command code or Cryogenics Operator code to access this operation'. And a bunch of buttons with numbers on them popped up on the right side of the screen. Are we going to need Captain Timmins again? Because I'm *not* dragging a dead body all the way down here!"

Moses sighed. "No, I wouldn't make you do that. Well, last resort."

Tabby glared at Rae, and silently shook her head violently from side to side.

Rae threw her head back and looked at the ceiling. Exhaustion crept in, deeper than the icy fingers of death. Her earlier tears had now turned to ice on her face.

GSCS *Nightingale*

"Captain?" Rose Vereau's voice came across on a line the girls couldn't hear.

Now back at his command pillar, Moses touched a virtual button that opened the channel. "Elwick here."

"I've been listening, and we might want to think about whether we want to pursue this course of action."

He looked at Guy and wanted to blurt, *You don't say?* but kept his thoughts to himself. "Go on, Rose."

"Sir, even if these girls could hook themselves up with all the necessary sensors and needles—which is ridiculously difficult even for a medical professional to do to on herself—someone *with authorization* needs to remain outside the pods to finalize the hibernation process. These aren't emergency escape pods, they are cryogenic life-process inhibitors. The process can't be completed from the inside. Even if the girls dragged Captain Timmins body down to the chamber, propped him up and figured out a way to keep his eye open so the scanner could see it, and then climbed into their pods, Captain Timmins would still need to interact with the computer, either by voice command or physically touching the controls. Otherwise, the girls will go to sleep alright, when the pods start doing their thing, but the temperature won't drop like it needs to, and their bodies will simply atrophies and wither away in seventy-degree air. But not before they die of dehydration before starving to death! The pods pump specialized fluid into veins meant to be frozen, not saline to keep someone alive at room temperature!"

It hit Moses that instant. "So you're saying—"

"I'm saying," continued Rose, "This plan might be doable, but one of the girls will have to manually initiate the sequence for the other, and then there will be no one left to initiate hibernation for the last girl."

Moses closed his eyes. *One of the girls will have to die.*

His mind reeled. Moses paced the bridge, the only sounds being the ever-present blip of the radar and the hum of the *Nightingale's* life support systems. He grabbed his command pillar with both hands and lowered his head to it.

How could he tell them? What would they say? Would one of them willingly volunteer to sacrifice herself to save the other? Yes. Each would probably volunteer. But Rae was the oldest, she should be the one to save her little sister. But could she operate the controls? Would she buckle when trying to shove needles into her little sister's veins?

Tabby would be the best candidate to figure things out. She's the one most likely to see success. *But dear God, she's only ten years old.*

How could he make this kind of choice? How could he ask them to do so? Knowing what was in store for them, would they even be able to concentrate long enough to save the other? Many adults would not be able to function under such circumstances, and he was considering asking a child to do such a thing? A tear dropped onto his console. *This is impossible. I can't get back on that radio.* "Oh Lord. Please help me. Please tell me what to do."

"Backup power level critical," Elwick heard the *Pearl's* computer announce over the comm, as if on cue. *"Environmental system now offline. Atmospheric system now offline. Cryogenic System now offline. Proceed*

immediately to lifeboats. Backup power level critical. Environmental system now offline—"

"Um, Captain Moses?" Rae's voice changed pitch. "I think something's happening…"

I think fate may have just made the decision for me.

Emerald Pearl

A red light in the corner of Rae's vision drew her attention. The screens on the eight pods still functioning flashed in concert with one another. The flashes grew faster as she watched.

"Backup power level critical," the computer repeated. *"Environmental system now offline. Atmospheric system now offline. Cryogenic System now offline. Proceed immediately to—"*

Rae interrupted the computer. "Tabby? What's happening?"

"How should I know?"

"Because you always know!"

The pods screamed with beeps and whistles. To Rae's surprise, they gained little voices of their own. Male voices. All the men seemed to sing in a chorus together.

"Attention! Cryogenic System failing. Initiation of re-animation sequence strongly suggested."

"Rae?"

The girls took one another's hand and they backed up against the wall of screens.

"Attention! Cryogenic System failing. Initiation of—" A pause, then, "*Warning! On-board Cryogenic System has failed. Initiate re-animation sequence immediately. Pod cannot sustain hibernation. Occupant in danger! Initiate re-animation sequence immediately. Warning!"*

The voices stopped. Rae and Tabby stopped moving.

"What did he say?" asked Tabby. "Are Mom and Jamie in danger?"

"Attention!" The male voices continued in unison. *"Re-animation not possible. Host vessel computer system damaged. Initiating emergency evacuation as per previous guidance protocols received from on-board brain."*

Rae couldn't move. *Evacuation? Does that mean—?*

The klaxons sounded again. Rae's mind screamed with them. *No... No, no, no, no!*

"Initiating emergency launch," came the familiar female voice of the *Emerald Pearl. "Cryo pod beacons activated. Please stand clear of pods. Repeat, please stand clear of pods. Stand clear. Stand clear. Stand—"*

"Tabby!"

The glass lids began to lower on Rae and Tabby's open pods.

"No!" Rae screamed.

All of the pods, to include those that had malfunctioned, simultaneously rose up into the walls on which each had been installed.

Rae clutched her sister as if something were about to rip the girl from her grasp. When each cryo pod was completely vertical, it locked into overhead mounts with loud *clangs,* and seemingly from out of nowhere, a shiny, gray case enveloped each pod. Yellow lights spun and flashed, and within seconds, a chilling breeze tossed Rae's and Tabby's hair about. It wasn't extraordinarily loud, nor strong enough to pull them forward, but definitely enough to activate Rae's flight mechanism once again. "Come on, Tabby! Let's get out of here!"

"No, I won't leave Mommy!"

"We have to!" Rae picked Sis up in her arms and rushed toward the open door leading to the cryo chamber.

"No!" Tabby cried. "Mommy!"

"*She's* leaving *us!*" Rae screamed. Did her sister not understand that? Behind her, Rae heard a whooshing sound. She glanced back for only a moment, and saw cryo pods drop one at a time out of sight, starting with the one she had been in, then Tabby's, then their mother's, and so on. Rae was certain they were in the process of "falling" through deep holes that had temporarily opened up in the deck. Holes that led directly into the nebula.

"Mr. Fluffles!" Tabitha screamed.

Rae turned to see her sister's bear lying face down. It, being significantly lighter than the humans, slid across the deck toward the dropping pods.

"Don't leave my bear!" Tabby wailed. "Please, Rae!"

Her father's pod dropped as she watched, followed by the others in his row.

Tabitha squirmed and tumbled free of Rae's grasp.

"Tabby!"

Sis ran to the still-sliding bear and scooped up the stuffed animal with one hand. She darted back to Rae's side in a flash, grabbed her hand, and pulled Rae toward the exit.

On the way out of the room, Rae looked over her shoulder one last time. All the pods had slipped away. She shut her eyes, releasing gushes of water that streamed down her cheeks. Tabby was already pushing the large, round hatch-like door to the cryo chamber closed, one of Mr. Fluffles' paws betwixt her teeth when Rae crossed the threshold.

"Rae! Help me!"

She began to push, but there was no longer any need. The breeze had stopped now that all the pods had been jettisoned. Both girls relaxed, and Tabby dropped to the floor. She hugged Mr. Fluffles' neck so tightly it bent backwards. The girl's lower lip quivered, and when she caught her breath, she burst into a long wail. She all but collapsed into Rae, and the two slumped to the floor.

As her sister cried, images of her parents flooded Rae's mind. She would never see them again. Not only never again in this life, but as per her and her mother's belief system, not in the existence to come.

For the first time in her life, she hoped her father had been right about the afterlife. The idea of ending up in paradise with all your family around you sounded like heaven. Also for the first time, she realized where that word had come from. She wondered if Daddy's "Heaven" included animals? She missed Lucky, the family dog. The others weren't too upset when he ran away, he had been such an ornery thing, always chewing everything up and making a mess of the house again and again. Plus, he had bitten everyone except Rae. She liked him. *Maybe he wouldn't be so ornery in Heaven?* She occasionally wondered if he really did run away, and had not been taken somewhere by their father, who then told the kids he had ran off, but she didn't want to even consider it.

Rae finally joined her sister in letting the tears flow. "Bye, Mom. Bye, Jamie. Bye, Daddy. I love you."

* * *

Rae awoke after what seemed like a brief nap, still cradling her sister on the cold, hard deck. The temperature had definitely dropped below freezing now. Her breath came out thick in the calm passageway. One thought resonated in Rae's mind. *Captain Moses!* Rae clambered mostly upright and found a nearby console. "*Nightingale?* Captain Moses, are you there?"

"Oh, thank God," came the voice from the wall. "We thought you'd been…" He took a deep breath. "I'm just glad you're okay."

"Yeah, we're okay. For now," Rae added. "Captain Moses? Is there really no way to get to the lifeboats at the back of the ship? The computer said for us to get to the lifeboats. We'd take a rickety old maintenance boat if we could find one!"

"Well, Rae, I think that was just a generic, pre-programmed warning message. We already know the lifeboats are gone, I have a someone outside your ship right now and she already verified that. It would be moot anyway; even if the boats were still there, that location is on the other side of engineering, and we've now verified that section is in vacuum. There's just no way to—" A pause. "Wait a second girls. Connelly just told me you gave him an idea. Please stand by."

The line muted, like it so often did. Rae hated that. She wanted to know what everyone was saying!

50

GSCS *Nightingale*

"Widowmakers?" Elwick exclaimed. "On the *Pearl?*"

"Yes! I can't believe I didn't think about it before! Rae's quip about maintenance craft got me thinking, and well, there they are! Look!" He enlarged a grainy image from Kelly Crawford's craft, zooming in on four bulbous objects protruding from a central, upper aft section.

"You're kidding! What luck! So, there are four of them?"

Kelly Crawford's mechanical voice broke the air. "All sittin' pretty and asleep, two by two! I can head over that way iffn ya want, get a closer look?"

"When you're finished up with the power, please do."

"Aye aye!"

"They're not like ours," Guy said, "they're a terribly antiquated design, but that actually works in our advantage. They've got a ton more shielding than ours! At least according to these schematics of the *Kristin's Vision.* They should work beautifully."

"Hold on," Osterland said, speaking for the first time in what seemed like ages, "I see several problems here. One, those things could also be in an area of ship in complete vacuum. Two, even if the radiation doesn't get them, the whole dehydration/starving thing will. It's not like these things are hibernation pods and will keep them asleep for seventy-plus years. Hell, we don't even know if those pods could do that, honestly."

"It doesn't matter," Connelly said, "even these old widowmakers have QE comms!"

"What good will that do? QE won't provide food and water! And QE didn't do shit for them before; the signal was grabbed by the closest wormhole and re-routed to us! What makes you think the same thing won't happen again?"

"Because unlike mere cryo pods, the widowmakers have ion drives! They can get away from the *Pearl.* Away from the nebula and into safe space!" Guy crossed his arms, and stood back, obviously proud of himself.

Osterland looked at Moses, seemingly for help. "So? Fine, you get the girls out into *normal* space, away from all the craziness of this red cloud, and then what? They send a signal that that deep space relay will pick up…What was the number again?"

"Sentinel 3-2-8-7," Connelly said.

"Thirty-two eighty-seven. It will relay the signal to some vessel in their day, or even Earth, and someone will send out a rescue. Do you know how far vessels could jump seventy-four years ago, Petty Officer Connelly?"

"Ummm…"

"You can look it up, but I don't think even the military got even their biggest capital ships up past three thousand light years. Five if we're lucky and they've been keeping the max distance top secret."

"They most likely were," Moses whispered.

"Most ships couldn't do more than a thousand," Ozzie continued. "This here nebula is over thirty-three thousand light years from Earth. It took us three hours just to get to the front door, and that was with a ship—this ship—that jumped twenty-eight thousand of those light years in less than an hour and a half!"

"And burned out the core in the process," Kelly muttered over the comm.

"How long do you think it will take to jump from Earth to here, or anywhere humans might be in their day to here, at three thousand light years a pop?"

Guy didn't answer.

"Well, come on, Mr. Math, how long? We need to know if we're thinking of sending the girls on an adventure."

"Eleven jumps, at three thousand a jump. So, maybe what, six hours?"

"Not so fast. You're assuming thirty minutes between jumps. We can all do *that* math. We need to add in the time it takes for one of their cores to cool down and be ready to go again after what would have been a max jump for them. And God only knows how long that would be."

"Probably eight, nine hours," Kelly said. "That's assumin' a solid forty-five minutes 'tween jumps. It can't be much more."

"Is that a guess, Kelly?" Elwick asked. "Or do you remember that from training somewhere along the line?"

"It's neither. It can't be much more'n eight or nine hours, because the girls wouldn't last longer than that. I just ran some calculations after checkin' out them schematics. Don't have a lot ta do but float around out here, you know. Anyhoo, first, those old maintenance boats don't carry enough oxygen fer an eight hour spree. Plus, they'll pro'lly run out o' power, then it'll be a race 'tween lack o' oxygen and temperature ta determine which one kills 'em first."

"So," said Elwick, who had gone back to pacing. "It boils down to the same situation they've been in all day: whether a ship could reach them in time before they freeze. Or this time, asphyxiate. Or both. Not to mention they'd each be alone this time. Fully awake, in craft built for one."

"Well, they are small," Connelly muttered.

Everyone on the bridge stared at him.

"I'm just saying they might fit in one. And not be alone. Or, even better, they'd extend their time if they each took their own craft… Might give them nine, ten hours." He shrugged. "There's a chance."

No one spoke for a moment.

"Nine hours," Moses continued. "Maybe ten. That's a long time to wait in a coffin." He gave Connelly a death stare. *Don't even try to be funny and correct me this time.*

Guy did not.

Elwick put his hands on his hips. "Okay. We'll leave it up to the girls. But even if they agree, we still have the problem of getting them there." He turned to the XO. "You were right about one thing, Ozzie. These old buckets are located in a part of the ship that's probably in vacuum. Unless the girls can find spacesuits that actually fit them, I think this is a moot argument, anyway."

"Well, gentlemen," interjected Connelly, "I hate to disagree with you, but I'm thinking that location still has air back in their time." He pulled up schematics of *Kristin's Vision* and pointed to a specific spot. "If this one door right here sealed itself like all the other doors to engineering did when the incident occurred, and we have no reason to believe it didn't, well, we may be in business!"

51

Emerald Pearl

"P-E-V-A?" Rae asked. She glanced at her sister, who only shrugged.

"Yes," Captain Moses replied over the speaker. "It stands for Personal Extra-Vehicular Activity craft."

"That's a long name," Tabby said. "How about a nickname?"

"Well, they do have nicknames, but I don't really want to say it."

"Is it a bad word?"

"No, but it doesn't imply good things."

"Oh."

"We'll just call them PEVAs for short, how about that?"

"Okay," both girls replied together, then shared an annoyed look.

"Alright, I think I've found a path for them," Rae heard Guy say, "one that avoids the areas in vacuum."

"Excellent, Connelly," said Captain Moses.

Guy continued. "There are several maintenance tubes running parallel to the ship's long axis, which lead toward aft, past Engineering, and on to where the widowmakers are."

"Widowmakers?" exclaimed Tabitha.

"What are those?" Rae asked.

"Thanks, Connelly," Captain Moses muttered over the channel.

"Is that the word you didn't want to say?"

"Sorry, sir," Guy continued, ignoring the question. "Now, of course, I'm making assumptions; I can't tell if these tubes are indeed viable, all I know is that most of them on the starboard side avoid the ruptured areas that we can see are exposed to space. In our time, the entire ship is in vacuum, but in their time, there still seems to be air in all sections other than engineering. So, I'm thinking there is still air in those tubes and the maintenance alcove where the wid—er, I mean PEVAs are."

"So…" Tabitha ventured, "now we have to crawl through some tunnels?"

"Yes, Tabby," Guy replied. "And um, I have to be honest with you, there are access doors all along the path. Vacuum could be waiting behind any of them."

"Are you nuts?" Rae heard Moses whisper. "You're gonna scare them to death!"

"Sir we shouldn't sugar coat this. This is dangerous, but at least it's a chance."

"It's okay, we're already scared, Captain Moses," said Rae, trying to laugh it off.

"I've been scared all day!" Tabby admitted.

"It's been one scary thing after another!" Rae added. "So, I guess, on to the next one! And we'd better hurry, because I could curl up on that comfy couch upstairs and go to sleep right now if I could!"

Tabitha huddled close. "Meee toooo. I'm *exhausted!*" she said, yawning, mimicking their father.

"Yes, well, please don't fall asleep, girls," the Captain said. "I just need you to be strong just a little while longer. Can you do that for me?"

Rae sighed. "I guess so." She looked at Tabby, currently curled up next to her with her eyes closed. Rae couldn't help but rue this terrible day. She had lost her mother, her father, her brother, and she may still lose her sister, not to mention her very life. She had grown sick and tired of this emotional rollercoaster a long time ago. She had reached the point where she no longer cared what happened. She just wanted the adventure to be over. Her fear and her hope—hope that had been thwarted over and over again—had given way to depression and weariness. She was almost ready to give Fate and Time what they most desired: what was left of her family.

"Are you girls ready?" Moses asked.

Rae sighed before answering. "Aye, aye," she replied, begrudgingly. "Come on, Tabby Cat, get up!"

"I don't wanna."

"Where do we go, Captain?"

Guy directed Rae and Tabitha to an access tunnel on a now even more dimly lit Deck Two, on the same wall as the forbidden doors to Engineering. The tunnel was covered by a large panel, like a miniature door. It required turning two large handles in opposite directions to open it.

"Now be careful," said Guy. "Just in case the compartment is in vacuum on the other side, I want you to turn the handle slowly and see if you hear any hissing. That will indicate air leaking from your side into it."

"Aye aye…" Rae turned the right-most handle as slow as she could.

"Anything?"

"Nothing yet…" She turned it farther, and still she neither heard nor felt any breeze. Finally, the handle creaked and hung loose. "I think it's out all the way, it is turning really easy."

"That means it's as far as it will go," Connelly agreed. "Now turn the other handle."

Tabitha turned the other one, slowly like Rae had. She experienced the same lack of hissing. It didn't take much more turning; soon and the heavy metal mini-door fell out of its mooring and banged to the deck. Tabby and Rae both yelped and jumped out of the way.

"Are you girls okay?" asked Moses.

"Yes, Captain," replied Tabby. "Just scared us when it dropped!"

"Girls," Connelly broke in, "you will likely be out of contact with us while you're in there, unless you can find a comm panel."

This made Rae hesitate. As bad as this day had been, she had found tremendous comfort in being able to talk to Captain Moses and his crew throughout the ordeal. Entering what could be a claustrophobic maze, worse than the huge one behind her on Deck Two, without the ability to call for assistance, filled her with anxiety. She looked at Tabby, who seemed ready to get on with it.

"What's wrong?" Sis asked.

Rae smiled and shook her head. "Nothing," she lied. She had to be strong for Tabby just a little while longer. *Just a little while longer.* Crouching, Rae stared into the dark. "I wish we still had that flashlight."

There came a soft zipping sound, and Tabby said, "You mean *this* flashlight?" Incredulously, Tabitha had retained not only Rae's book, but their light as well!

"How much stuff you got in that bear?"

"Just the important stuff," the little girl beamed, handing Rae the device.

Rae laughed. "You're pretty great, Tabby."

"I know. Now let's go before we freeze to death!"

Rae flicked the "ON" switch. *Whoa!* It was super bright to her eyes, which were now used to the darker hallways. She shined the light into the dark tunnel ahead. Her foggy breath now glowed in the beam. She shivered, and not entirely because of the increasing cold. "I'll go first."

Tabby nodded. "Good idea."

Rae gave her sister a sideways glance, then plunged forward. As she made her way on all fours, she imagined how difficult it must be for a full-sized adult to move through these tubes. No one could do it very quickly, that's for sure! She stopped and looked back.

"What?" Tabby inquired.

"Nothing, just making sure you were behind me."

"Where else would I be?"

Rae smiled at her sister's response. Instead of taking it as sarcasm, she chose to believe Tabby meant, "where else would I be besides by your side?"

52

GSCS *Nightingale*

Elwick listened on the SAR team channel as Dale contacted his team.

"According to my HUD," Masterson said, "it looks like Vereau and Ebersbacher are close to engineering right now."

"Aye, we are," came Rose's reply. "The Bluffer and I are on survivor detail."

"Roger. Break… Bruno, I see you and Gilbin are down on Deck Four? Is that the cargo bay?"

"Aye," replied Antonio Bruno. His reply came back staticky, like something was interfering with his signal.

"Anyone found any more bodies? I know you haven't found survivors, I would have heard about that. Right?"

"Haven't found much of anything 'cept a few pusher bots," Bruno replied. "They're just goin' 'bout their business like nuthin's even happened."

"Ah, to not have a brain…" Masterson said. "Anyway, I need you to meet Rose's team on Deck Two with your torches. See if you can get through that central door that leads to Engineering. Once through, give the girls a visual recon of what you see, paying close attention to any exposed maintenance tubes you see that they might be crawling through—or rather the one they *crawled* through, past tense.

Dear Lord, this whole thing is making my head hurt," Dale added quietly.

"Aye aye! On the way!" replied Bruno.

Elwick smiled. Dale was on top of things, as always.

Rose's voice burst across the airwaves a short time later. "Master Chief? Captain? We're at the door to Engineering. Norstrom, the engineer tech the girls mentioned, is nearby. Her body is quite well preserved. I was surprised! Seems they were all frozen good and solid before the ship lost all its pressure. I've begun our burn-through. One Antonio-sized hole coming up!"

"Aye, Rose." Elwick unmuted the channel to reach Rae and Tabitha. "Girls, we're going to get some eyes-on in the Engineering section. We hope to direct you through the tubes more safely if we can."

Silence.

"Girls? Can you hear me?"

"They're probably between comms panels," Connelly explained.

"Um," Dale said in a delicate tone, "I hate to ask, but would we even know it if they opened a door and got blown into space?"

No one spoke for a moment. Elwick looked into the eyes of those around him. Some shrugged, some did nothing.

Connelly broke the silence. "Yeah, I think we definitely would! We would have heard the channel go all whooshy, for one thing, and for another—"

"Whooshy?" asked Moses.

"Yeah, you know," and he made a sound with puckered lips that may have been humorous had the subject matter not been so morbid.

"I get it." Elwick raised a hand.

"Plus," Connelly continued, "their bodies wouldn't be on those couches in the Observation Lounge."

"Dome," Elwick said. "Why not?"

"Because history would have already changed. They wouldn't be there at all."

"But what if we changed the course of history by telling them about finding their bodies? And changes in time are slow and just haven't caught up yet?"

"I don't think it works that way."

Masterson cleared his throat. "My head is hurting again."

Elwick shook his head. "Mine too. Let's... Let's just be patient."

Only a few more moments passed before Rae's voice exploded on the line once again. "Captain Moses? Are you there?"

Elwick let loose a bit of a whoosh himself. "We're here Rae!"

"We opened a few more doors, much smaller than that first one. They swung open instead of falling. Anyway, now there's a breeze in here."

Uh oh. "Sounds like we have a leak somewhere," Elwick said. Then to Guy Connelly, "Can they bypass?"

"I'm not sure. Where are they?"

"How could we—Oh! I have an idea... Rae, how many doors have you passed through? Only the small ones."

"Um, five, I think?"

"Five," he heard Tabby agree.

"Okay," said Guy, pointing to a new place on the holographic schematic. "I think they're here." He shook his head. "They can't take a different route, not yet. The tunnel doesn't branch for another one, two, three… five more doors. They should close all the doors behind them from here on out."

"Aye. Girls, did you hear what Guy said?"

"We heard. Close that door, Tabby!"

After a brief pause, Elwick heard a thud.

Connelly nodded. "You ladies are doing great! Let us know when you get to an intersection, okay?"

"Okay!" Rae yelled.

The XO rose. "Sir, may I speak with you?"

Elwick looked up to see Osterland striding to the rear of the bridge. "Sure."

The two leaders moved into the briefing room, where Ozzie spoke in low tones. "Sir… This is going to get worse the more doors they open; there could be tiny holes in several of the tubes leading aft. I have to ask, what do you hope to accomplish with this?"

Elwick's brows came together. "What do you mean?"

"Laskey already found them. In the dome. Moe, these girls are already gone. They died a long time ago. Do you seriously think we can trick Time itself? The Universe? Mother Nature? God? Whoever or whatever you want to believe allowed this to happen? Allowed this crazy phenomenon to permit us and them to cross paths in the first place?"

"And what's the alternative, Ozzie? They go back to the dome and freeze to death? We just let them die?"

"Yes, Captain. That's exactly what we do." Osterland's look was stern. "We let them die. And they die with dignity. It's already been decided—"

"NO!" Elwick shouted. "It has absolutely *not* been decided! Not by me, not by you, and not even by God Himself! Those little girls are still alive as much as you or I am! We're talking to them!"

"They're not!"

"They're out there! How can you deny that? You just heard them!"

"I heard an echo. An echo of the past. That's what you're hearing, Moe. That's what you're talking to! They died before you any of us were ever born!"

"They're not dead!"

"But they are!"

Moses shook his head violently. "No. I will not give up on them! I will not let you, any of *you,* give up on them!" he shouted, pointing at others on the bridge. "And I will not let *them* give up on them!"

"Captain, please, this defies reason—"

"I don't care about reason!" Moses screamed. "None of this even makes sense! Reason flew out the window hours ago! What, are you going to do, apply logic next? We found them dead so *logically* they're already dead? It's fate? I don't believe in fate! I don't care about what Fate wants! I don't care what your precious Mother Nature or Time or anyone or anything else wants! Right now, I don't even care what God wants! I refuse to let any of them have their way! I can't! I won't!" Elwick's shoulders heaved as he panted and his nostrils flared. His eyes shone wild, and he stared deep into his XO's soul.

No one spoke for a good long moment while he panted, catching his breath. Then he blinked. His gaze shifted to his bridge crew. Everyone stared at him. Kitner. Burgess. Connelly.

Ozzie's eyebrows had knitted, his jaw had clamped tight. The XO leaned in close and whispered. "You want to bring God into this, Moses? Fine. My mother was a hard-nosed Roman Catholic all her life—God rest her soul—so I know a little something about the Big Guy. And guess what? He gets what He wants before any of us do. He's already mapped all this out. Time isn't the same for Him. Whatever happens has already happened. Moses, I don't care what you do. You're gonna find He's already won. He and His precious *'plan'* always wins." Osterland didn't look at him again. Ozzie calmly walked back to the navigation station and sat down. He did violently kick his console's support strut, but otherwise he remained silent.

Moses looked around the room. You could hear the proverbial pin drop. Everyone had heard their argument.

Was Ozzie right? Had fate already been decided? Should he just go ahead and call it? Should he bring all his people home, bite the bullet, and turn himself into the RNA Navy?

Doing so would leave these two precious, precocious little angels to die alone. Dear God, he couldn't live with such a thing. How could he? What, was he supposed to ignore their cries as he ordered his pilot to turn tail and head home? Have Connelly cut the comms so he could no longer hear them? How could anyone do such a thing? Orders or no? Elwick took a deep breath and walked back to stand next to Connelly.

"I, um, asked them to give us a minute," Guy said.

Moses nodded. "Thanks." He looked down and saw that the channel to the *Pearl* had been muted, but the channel to the SAR team was still wide open. Dale's team had heard everything. Likely Kelly, too. Possibly the engine rates below decks as well, if Pruitt had tuned in. *Dammit*, Moses cursed to himself. The XO had tried to have a quiet, one-on-one discussion, but Moses' emotions weren't having any of that, were they? *Way to go, Moe. You're a rotten husband, a rotten father, and a rotten CO. Not to mention a rotten, blasphemous Christian to boot, now. Had he just condemned his soul to eternal fire?* He closed his eyes, and just breathed. Could he recover from this?

Did he even care?

There was nothing to do now but own it all, even if it damned every part of him. Which it surely had, in the eyes of his wife, his crew, the Sentinel Corps, the Republic Navy, and in the very eyes of God. But like a certain obsessed sea dog chasing Moby Dick, he had committed himself the moment he chose to ignore the order to turn around. If this was to be the last thing he did in his entire career, he would give it his all. It was the *right* thing to do. Especially now that he was far past the point of no return.

He turned and addressed his bridge crew, and indirectly, the SAR team. "I'm not going to apologize for any of that. We are far too deep into this. Maybe I've turned into Captain Ahab here, and the XO's right. Maybe we are doomed to fail. But maybe not. Either way, I've got to see this through. Even if we do lose these two little angels tonight, I will not allow them to die alone, abandoned by someone—me—who promised them I would do whatever is in my power to rescue them. I will be right there with them to the bitter end. Now, if anyone had any doubt as to my intent to continue this rescue, I take it that has been cleared up."

No one moved.

"Also," Elwick continued, "I would like to take this opportunity to officially announce that, if any of you, military or civilian, think I'm mad for continuing this rescue, and want to officially excuse yourself from the rest of this mission, you may do so. No disciplinary action will come your way. You have my word. Go ahead and make way to your quarters now. If you're part of the away team, disengage and head back to the *Nightingale.* I will not judge you, nor will anyone else on this crew or in the SENTCORPS. For I probably *am* completely mad at this point, and no one would blame you. Move out now."

Moses waited. No one moved on the bridge, and no one spoke over the comms channel. "XO?"

Osterland turned his head. "Captain?"

"That includes yourself, you know."

"Understood," he replied, but didn't get up.

"SAR Team?"

Dale replied after a brief pause. "We're already over here, Captain, and we have a job to finish."

"Aye," Elwick acknowledged.

After a beat, Osterland made a motion with his hands. "Are we going to continue with this rescue or not?"

Moses tossed him a tight-lipped smile. "Indeed we are."

The others on the bridge turned back to their stations with nigh a word.

Elwick nodded to everyone, though they couldn't see him do it. "Aye."

53

Emerald Pearl

Captain Moses' faint voice had cut off mid-sentence, but Rae had heard something about God. She decided his words hadn't been meant for her and Tabitha; he had been talking to his crew.

Or rather, yelling at them.

She guessed Captain Moses' god was the same as that of her father's. Thanks to her mother's teaching and reassurances, she never feared this deity. Mother said that *if* this being exists, he could do so peacefully along with Nature. As with Allah and the Norse gods and the Roman and Greek gods and all the other wild and fantastic things people had dreamed up. They and the Great Mother could coexist as one. Together in the Great Expanse that is the Cosmos.

Now, the God of the Hebrews and His possible *will* did in fact terrify her. The cold metal around her wasn't the only thing chilling Rae to her core. For His will and that of all the gods seemed identical to the Great Mother's at the moment.

She kept moving, and her sister followed, but the look on Tabby's face made Rae question whether the girl's heart was still in this fight for survival.

At this point, Rae wasn't sure hers was.

54
GSCS *Nightingale*

Daniel Gilbin's voice broke over the comm system. "Cap'n? Gilbin here."

Elwick composed himself before answering. "Go ahead, Daniel."

"Now that we've accessed the Engineering section, we're picking up a lot o' Sieverts. And not the milli kind, either."

Crap, Moses thought.

"Also, I don't know who you had in mind to get eyes on Engineering," he said, "but as soon as the door was far enough ajar—and I mean just a crack—Rose snuck underneath me before any of us knew what was happening! Scrawny little bugger. I'll yank a knot in 'er tail for this!"

Oh, Rose! "Roger. You guys stay put, and away from that opening. No sense exposing more than one of you to the radiation that must be flooding those compartments."

"What about the little lasses?" Antonio Bruno asked. "Will the graphene structure and steel piping that're lining those tubes protect them?"

"Well, Barbara said she didn't pick up any additional radiation from the corpses, so I'm guessing they'll be okay?"

"Sir," Connelly interrupted, "any radiation their little bodies picked up has had seventy-four years to dissipate, plus, like you alluded to before, we may have changed the timeline once we notified them we found them dead. We could be—we actually hope to be—creating a new one where they don't end up on that couch all mummified."

"A new… timeline? I thought you just said time didn't work that way?"

"Well, now that I've thought about it a little more, I hope I'm wrong."

Moses drew a deep breath. The "normal" temporal effects that high gravity sources and relativistic speeds created still warped his mind; he didn't even want to *think* about causality. After all the classes and required reading the Navy and SENTCORPS had put him through, he couldn't remember anything that indicated causality could be violated. But could it?

Ironically, he was *counting* on it!

He found himself in a staring contest—to the death—with the standard model, quantum, and temporal physics all at once. But even more ironic was the fact that, even if he "won," he could still lose in a different way. "Even if you're wrong, Mr. Connelly, and we can indeed change history, Rae and Tabitha could avoid freezing to death on that ship, only to die of cancer in the days or weeks after they're rescued. And I led them right to it."

Guy didn't respond to that.

Moses looked at his XO. By the look on Quinton Osterland's face, he knew what Ozzie was thinking: *Does it really matter one way or the other? And you've sacrificed your career and the safety of your crew for this?* Maybe it didn't. Maybe none of this mattered. But to Elwick, it still did. He just couldn't give up.

He found himself beginning to understand Captain Ahab's motivation with his infamous white whale. *Only this isn't revenge. This is mercy. Surely the Good Lord will see that and reward us all for our valiant efforts!* And in turn, reward two innocent little girls with a long life!

Wouldn't He?

Perhaps He would also reward one Captain Moses Elwick with a merciful court martial sentence for saving them and, by yet another miracle, sixteen others, who were at this moment still floating about somewhere in the depths of the nebula. They, and all the souls still on board the *Pearl,* all deserved a proper burial as per their beliefs and traditions. And whose families, mainly progeny at this point, should be notified of their fate.

Moses held his breath a moment. Something nagged at him. "Guy, while we're sitting here doing nothing, would you please do whatever you can to find me sixteen cryogenic pods that have been waiting for us to find them since we entered this infernal cloud?"

Guy shook his head. "I can try, sir. But I'm thinking their power sources are long since depleted. Otherwise, I'd have picked up their beacons by now."

"Have you taken into account the jamming properties of this nebula? Just a few minutes ago, Bruno's transmission was staticky, and he wasn't even a kilometer away."

"He was inside the *Pearl's* cargo bay. Who knows what those walls are lined with?"

Elwick nodded. "You're probably right. But I'm wondering what else in this emissions nebula might be keeping us from picking up other radio signals that could possibly still be broadcasting, but so faintly, they could easily be overlooked?"

"Just about anything!" Guy paused, and put a finger to his lips. "Hmm. You know, I had thought about narrowing the search beams, similar to how we found the *Emerald Pearl* earlier, but dismissed it. However, the pods should be exponentially closer to us right now than the *Nightingale* was to the *Pearl,* which would make them larger, relatively speaking, and thus easier to locate, even if they weren't broadcasting…"

"Well, while we're still attached to the old girl, there will be no talk of another Laskey Maneuver, I'm afraid."

Connelly chuckled. "Understood, sir. But we wouldn't necessarily have to use the *Nightingale* to conduct the same trick…"

Elwick smiled and considered this. "Unfortunately, the only people qualified to fly our missile boat is over on the *Pearl.*"

The XO swiveled around to face the comms station. "Who needs Masterson and Bruno when you have a fully qualified *remote ops* pilot sitting right here? I wouldn't even have to leave this chair. I mean, it's not like I'd be taking her into combat. If I can't do a simple sit-n-spin on a little bird with a giant shark's mouth painted on it, I need to turn in my bars!"

55

Emerald Pearl: Engineering

Rose Vereau found herself awash in red light. She keyed her comm. "Captain, I'm in the Engine Room. There's a *lot* of damage, to include a massive hole in one wall that extends all the way to the outer hull. And there's a body here. He's been impaled—oh, God." She turned away and tried desperately not to throw up inside her helmet. The last time that happened she had been a mere Corpsman in the Canadian Royal Navy, but she remembered the reek of vomit as if it had happened yesterday. Inside a space suit, she understood her gag reflex was purely psychosomatic because she couldn't actually smell it, but that didn't change the fact she might still throw up. And tossing your cookies inside a space suit, well, there was no getting away from *that* smell! Not for God knows how many more hours.

"Rose?"

"Sorry, sir, just had to catch my breath," she replied. "Okay. I'm okay now." She turned back to examine the body. "The man—possibly a woman—is wearing blue coveralls. He or she has been impaled on some protruding equipment, probably from the initial blast. It looks like they died from both the impact and explosive decompression at the same time. Good thing the girls won't be coming through *this* room!"

"Now remember, Rose," Elwick said, "you can't stay in there too long. Keep an eye on your Micro-R meter. When the gauge hits the 'amber' range, you're going to want to start heading back the way you came."

Rose checked the multifunction device on her wrist and selected "Micro-R." The mSv number displayed read two Sieverts. *Wait, what? That can't be right.* She checked again. It read the same. Not two millisieverts, two *full* Sieverts.

Oh my God. The small digital line was already well into the amber and approaching the red. She sighed, then clicked unmute. "Understood, sir."

"Do you see any other personnel?" the Captain asked.

"Not yet. There's a lot of mangled equipment all around me. I'll have to look around a bit."

"How does the Zee Dee drive look?"

"Well, there's a big hole in the housing. But the magnets must be in place and the plasma tanks intact if it's been sitting here for seven decades and hasn't incinerated the ship yet."

"Agreed."

"Do you have the schematic of the Engineering section on your HUD?"

"Pulling it up now, sir." Using only her eyes, Rose maneuvered through the orange graphic displayed on the inside of the transparent graphene face of her helmet. "Okay, I've got it."

Guy Connelly's voice broke the air. "The girls are in what's labeled 'MAINT TUBE 7'. Do you see that?"

"I do," replied Rose. "It looks like it leads around here, somewhere…"

Emerald Pearl: Maintenance Tubes

Rae hated the fact she had to duck walk to get through these cursed tunnels with any speed. *Tubes? Is that what Captain Moses called them?* Tabby seemed to get getting along fine in them due to her short stature. She could simply bend at the waist and walk normally.

They reached an intersection where the tubes stretched away in both directions to their right and left. "Captain Moses?" Rae called. No answer. "Captain, can you hear me? Still no reply.

"I don't think he can," said Tabby.

Rae shone the flashlight around. "Do you see a comm panel?"

"Nope. I sure wish we had brought two flashlights."

"Me too."

"Which way do we go?" Tabitha asked.

"I guess we keep going straight. They didn't tell us to turn. They would've told us to turn if we needed to."

"Would they? Maybe they thought they'd be able to talk to us the whole way?"

Uh oh. Maybe Tabby was right. No. Surely Captain Moses would have known. Wouldn't he?

"Are you gonna make a decision or do I have to?" the bold little lady in pigtails asked.

Rae didn't know what to do. Well, she did; she needed to call the Captain and ask him what to do. But that wasn't an option. She searched down both directions for a communications panel. But her light fell on nothing but gray walls and pipes stretching off into the distance. Otherwise, everything was enveloped in darkness. It gave her more chills than the frigid air. For an instant her mind went to dark places. She imagined zombies or monsters suddenly being illuminated as the light danced around, and she shivered and looked away. Even some silly little maintenance robot would have given her a heart attack at this point.

"That's it," said Tabby, "I'll lead the way." She grabbed the flashlight as she zoomed by Rae, and continued on in the direction they had been headed.

"Wait!" Rae yelled, scrambling to catch up to the little girl, who could maneuver much faster in the claustrophobia-inducing environment.

Emerald Pearl: Engineering

Rose climbed over several pieces of blacked machinery. Wires draped from overhead in places. It looked like a fire had ripped through the entire cavernous room. *It surely had,* she thought, *and then was instantly snuffed out when all the air blew out into space.* She paused to line herself up with what she saw inside her helmet. She switched from a two-dimensional "bird's eye" view to a three-dimensional view, and then configured it to overlay with her current position in the ship. It took only a moment for the *Nightingale*'s computer to calculate the relative position with the *Pearl* and use its scanners to find her. *Ah, much better.* It wasn't a perfect correlation, but it was close.

"I see what you did there, Rose," said Elwick in her ear, "very clever."

"Thank you, Captain. Now, maybe I can figure this out a little faster! Of note, the gravity is patchy here; seems some of the grav plates got damaged in the blast. Switching on magnets."

"Aye, Rose. Please don't float off through a hole and into space. I don't want to have to send Kelly after you in the widowmaker."

"Why not? She'd love to rope my butt and haul me in!"

Emerald Pearl: Maintenance Tubes

"Whoa," said Tabby, that's a big door."

Rae agreed. "Yeah. It's different, too." She studied it. "I wish there were a comm panel around here somewhere!"

"What's this?" Tabitha asked, shining the flashlight onto a black panel on the wall.

"Hmm. Doesn't look like a comm panel. Maybe it opens the door? Touch it, see what happens."

The little girl did so. "Nada."

"Shine the light on the door again." When Tabby did so, Rae pointed to two levers. "Are those the handles?"

"Maybe."

Rae duck walked to one. "I'll take this one, you take that one. Okay, on three…"

Emerald Pearl: Engineering

Rose Vereau moved her head from side to side and turned herself where she stood. The digital lines displayed in her helmet rotated with her, thanks to active RADAR. The orange lines extended into the bulkheads nearby, and she found she could probably see the entire ship if she wanted to. But the default setting of the graphics was such that the lines dimmed with perceived distance, probably to avoid the visuals turning into a confusing mess. She silently thanked computer software coders smarter than her.

She walked along the deck tracing the path of Maintenance Tube Seven, where she understood the girls to be crawling through. At one point, the lines in her HUD stopped when they should have continued. Rose leaned forward for a better "look," even backed up a few steps, and walked forward again. Same thing. Then it dawned on her what she was seeing. "Oh my God." Rose fumbled unmuting her microphone. "Captain! The girls are for sure in Maintenance Tube Seven?"

"Yes. But we haven't heard back from them once they passed section, oh, what was it…? Okay. Connelly says section fourteen. They could be anywhere from there to section… twenty perhaps."

Rose switched some settings in her HUD until section labels appeared. "Oh my God. Tell them to hold their position! Tell them not to open any doors past section nineteen!"

"There's no way to get ahold of them. Guy," she heard Elwick exclaim, "what can we do?"

Rose heard nothing, but she imagined Guy shaking his head.

Emerald Pearl: Maintenance Tubes

"One…"

"Two…" chanted Tabby.

"Three!" the girls said together, and pulled their levers at the same time. The first "pump" of the levers opened the door a few inches, and a mini hurricane of wind blasted by them.

Tabby screamed over the roar.

Rae tumbled, and her face stuck in the opening. She could barely breathe. With one eye could see the tunnel extending before her, a red glow filling the far end.

The nebula!

Rae tried to pull herself away, but she couldn't. Blinking, she saw another tunnel straight ahead a ways further down, but between her tunnel and that one, a devilish, glowing red mist blocked her way.

"Rae!" she heard Tabby yell over the chaos.

She did the equivalent of a push-up, and only then noticed in horror that the neck of her blouse was already through the six-inch-wide gap and beckoning her to follow. "Help," she tried to scream, unsure if anything came out. Her eyes bulged as she realized her head was literally being pulled into space.

At that moment, something struck Rae in the back, and her eyes shut out the red.

"Rae!!"

It had hit right below her left shoulder blade. A piercing, like she had just been stabbed. Or what she imagined being stabbed would feel like. The pain froze her. She groaned and whimpered. Then something else hit her. Something heavy. "Ohh!" was all that came out of her. *What's on me? Get it off! Please, get it off!*

Wait a minute. Is it moving? Is it climbing on me? Not another bot!

Her head was being pulled to one side. Darkness replaced the fiery image at the end of the tunnel. As soon as it had begun, the freight train in her ears ceased. The hurricane-force winds turned into only a light breeze.

"Hold on, Big Sis! I've gotta go to the other side!"

A few clicks resounded in her ears, and the air became still again. She chanced opening her eyes. Tabby's face filled her vision. The girl's eyes were wild.

"You're okay, Rae!" she yelled. "You're okay! You'll be okay!"

"My back," she whimpered. "Something's in my back!" It seemed like dozens of tiny fingers poking her all at once.

"There's nothing in your back, Rae! You're okay, really!"

I am? She felt around, inspecting her body for anything that shouldn't be there. *Then why does it hurt so bad?*

"I think you got hit with this!" Tabby said, holding up length of metal for Rae to see. "I think it came off the wall." It looked like a connector for wires or something. Sis tossed it back down the way they'd come, then hugged her.

The girls lay there for a short time, catching their breaths. Rae squeezed her savior, her sister, her friend.

How much air do we have now after that crazy incident? Rae wondered. *Captain Moses. We've got to get back in contact with Captain Moses.*

56

GSCS *Nightingale*

"Captain?" Rose called. "Captain!"

"We're here, Rose. We're trying to get a hold of them now, please give us a minute. We have no way of knowing—"

"Would we have any way of knowing if they've already been blown out into space?"

"Connelly thinks we do. He thinks… I don't want to go into it, it's all just double-talk for the moment anyway. Just give us a minute. Please!" Then to Guy Connelly, "Ideas."

"Well, boosting the signal won't work. It wouldn't make our voices louder, just distort the speaker material and make us harder to understand."

Elwick nodded.

"I wonder…? Sir, I might be able to send over a repeating signal that will make the comm system interpret it as a warning klaxon. The sound of an alarm might get the girls attention and make them actively seek a comms panel to let us know about it."

"Do it."

Rose's voice came across the air again, more calm now. "Wait a minute. Captain, I think these tubes link up laterally."

"I saw that, Rose," said Guy almost absent-mindedly, furiously pounding away at his station. "I noticed there are two junctures."

"Right. The second one looks to be past the break, but they could reach the first intersection safely."

"Guy, you keep working, I'll handle this." Elwick studied the blue map hovering over the comms station. "Rose, it looks like they could move over to the tube along the far starboard wall of the ship. The one labeled 'TUBE 8'."

"Well," replied Rose Vereau, "they sure as hell can't head toward port. Tubes Five and Six empty out right into the giant hole that's blown into Engineering."

Moses nodded. "Let's hope they have enough wits about them to test those doors before they open any of them all the way."

Elwick heard Starman Burgess and Osterland in the middle of a quiet conversation. "—like we're only postponing the inevitable. Providing hope where there probably isn't any."

Ozzie, who had probably just become aware of the temporary silence, glanced up at Elwick. "Mind your station, Starman," he muttered.

"Aye aye, sir." Burgess said, and refocused on the pilot console.

The XO gave Elwick a look that could only mean, "You know he's right."

Moses couldn't have held Ozzie's stare if he had tried. "Did you implement your klaxon idea yet?" he asked Connelly.

"Yes, sir. No way of knowing if it is having any affect, however."

"Rae? Tabby?" Moses called. "Can either of you hear me? Please respond." He looked back to Guy, who only shook his head.

57

Emerald Pearl

"So now which way?" Rae asked once they had returned to the intersection.

Tabby shone the light down the tunnels they had found before, the ones that extended to their right and left. "Hmm," she said, a small finger to her lips. "I pick starboard."

"Okay. Why?"

"Well, when we were on the bridge, I saw a bunch of red on a little picture of the ship on this one screen. The red was in the back left corner. That's port, right?"

"That's right," Rae answered. "You've finally learned your directions onboard a ship!"

"Yes, I have," said Tabby proudly. "I figured if you can do it, I can do it. Anyway, I also learned that red usually means 'bad', and if there's red on a map of the ship, I think we should go the other way. And that way is this way!"

Rae smiled. "You know what I think? I think you're right."

Armed with the flashlight, Tabby started off down the tube leading to the starboard side of the ship.

Rae followed close. She replayed in her mind what her sister had just said. "If you can do it, I can do it." *She's only ten years old, and I'm looking up to her. But I guess that's okay. Mom and Daddy would be proud of both of us, I think!*

The sound of a far-off klaxon reached her ears. "Oh, no!" Rae exclaimed. "What now?"

Tabby stopped. "What is that?"

"Who knows! More of the ship falling apart, I'm sure! Keep your eyes peeled for a comm panel."

"Already doing *that!*" Sis announced, then took off at a trot. "Tabby! Wait up!"

"Hurry up!"

"I can't go as fast as you!"

"Rae! I see another door!"

"Don't open it!"

"Duh! What, do you think I'm stupid?"

Rae saw Tabitha's light bouncing off the walls of the tunnel as she moved down its length. *Tube,* Rae reminded herself. *Tube, Overhead, Deck, Bulkhead. If Tabby's getting this stuff down correctly now, I'd better do the same.* Rae looked behind her, into the pitch blackness. But she didn't allow the hair to stand up on the back of her neck. She knew behind her lay nothing but the empty tubes from whence they had just come. Just like there was nothing in the dark that lay between her and Tabby right now. *Funny,* she thought as she hobbled toward her sister. *Tabby's been right this whole time. It's not the dark itself. It's what might be* in *it. But there's nothing in it. Nothing but air.*

Thankfully there was still air!

But how much? And was she getting dizzy, or was it her imagination? Soon she reached Sis at the next door.

"I've got an idea," said Sis. "You stand over there. Don't do anything! I'll just *baaaarely* pull this lever. If we hear any hissing or anything at all, I'll stop. Okay?"

"Okay," Rae agreed. She prayed to the spirits they didn't have a repeat of last time. And if so, that this wasn't the only way to reach the PEVAs. Or rather, the widowmakers. *I wonder why they call them widow—* An answer invaded her mind before she even finished the question. *Oh!*

"Ready?" asked Tabby.

Rae climbed into the corner between the tube wall and the new door, then pulled her knees to her chest. "Ready."

Tabitha began pulling the lever toward her, but it didn't move. "This thing is heavy!" She set the flashlight on the deck and used both hands.

"Try harder."

"I am!"

Nothing.

"Here, let me try mine." Rae sat up and squatted before the lever on her side. She tried the gentle approach, but got no further than sister had.

"Oh! Just hold onto something!" Before Rae could, however, Tabby pulled down her lever.

Rae held her breath. The door popped open three inches on one side. No hurricane returning, not even a hiss.

Rae grabbed the flashlight and shone the beam into the crack. "Looks normal. No red!"

"Thank God!" Tabitha pumped the lever as before. After several clicks, her side had opened fully, and she jumped past the threshold. "Don't open your side, just climb through here, you'll fit. We have to close it behind us anyway."

"Good idea," Rae said, and somewhat painfully crawled through. The walls of the tube brushed her back and reminded her of the blunt injury. *I'll probably have a giant bruise there!*

"Let's go!" said Sis, snatching the light back and taking charge.

Soon they reached yet another door. "Rae, look!" exclaimed Tabby, pointing down the tube. "I think that's a comm panel!"

Rae's heart leapt. By the time she reached Sis, the little girl had already activated the red circle.

"Captain Moses? It's Tabby. Can you hear me?"

Elwick's voice exploded in the small space, and echoed all around. "Oh, thank God!" He liked to say that a lot, Rae observed. Not unlike their Father. Both men's habits were probably why the phrase was beginning to fall from Tabby more often. But Rae didn't mind. It's what they all believed, and she didn't want someone telling *her* what to believe. "Are you girls okay?" he asked.

"Well, said Tabby, "Rae almost got sucked out into space, but she's okay now."

"Oh, Dear Lord! Are you sure you are alright, Rae?"

"I'm fine," Rae replied. "It was terrifying there for a minute, but Tabby came to my rescue." She patted her sister on the back, which made her sister smile.

"Well, we were pretty terrified here on this end, too," Moses said. "We found some areas of the tubes that are open to vacuum. All we could do was sit tight and hope you didn't get, well, exactly what you described almost happened."

"Yeah, we learned to be careful and not open doors all willy-nilly-like," said Rae. She hoped that phrase was correct, and still used in the future. She had heard her mother use it a time or two.

"It's okay, Rose," Moses said, obviously to another member of his team. "They're okay." Then, "So girls, where exactly are you right now?"

"Um," said Rae, "oh! There's some lettering on this door. It says 'SECTION 30'."

"Section thirty!" Elwick repeated.

"Here it is sir!" shouted Connelly. His voice echoed even louder than Moses'. "They made it! They made it to stern!"

"Hi, Guy!"

"Hi again, Tabby!"

Rae interjected. "There's another alarm going off now, by the way!"

"Oh!" Connelly exclaimed, "that's me. Just a second."

A moment later, the klaxon ceased.

"You?"

"We were hoping you would hear it and stop opening doors and search for a panel to let us know about the alarm! Mission accomplished!"

"Well, I just thought it was the computer telling us something else on the ship had broken! We would have called you anyway, soon as we found a panel. Which we finally did!"

Moses broke back in. "Girls, it looks like the PEVAs are just down the hallway past that door you're at. But be careful!"

"We will, Captain Moses!" exclaimed Sis, already grabbing the lever on her side.

"Just like last time," said Rae.

Tabby nodded. "One… two… three!" She pumped her lever once. As before, the door slid three inches toward her side. Also as before, no hiss or hurricane came. "Whew!"

But there was a red glow.

Oh no.

"Wait," Tabitha said. "I'm confused. How can we see a red glow, but still have air?"

Rae found herself vexed, too. She peered through the small crack and saw a full-size passageway, dimly lit like in other parts of the ship. "Open it more." Tabby did, and Rae poked her whole head and flashlight through, shining the light around. To her left was a dead-end with a ladder heading downward. To her right, the hallway extended toward port. Halfway to that side of the ship, the passage turned bright red.

Rae's heart stopped for a second, but then she realized they were in no immediate danger; the red light was filtering through skylights in the overhead, rather than a gaping hole in the hull. She sighed. "Tabby, it's okay, open it up all the way. *Nightingale*," she hollered, "we're okay! We found a passageway! We'll call you again when we find the PEVAs!"

"Aye, Rae," Moses replied.

"Again, very official, Big Sis."

"Thank you, Tabby."

The girls climbed through, then joined together to seal the door shut behind them. Soon they noticed a foul smell alighted the air here. Rae crinkled her nose.

"Eww, what's that?" Tabby asked. "It smells like poopy."

Rae didn't answer, instead holding her breath. After a few steps down the passageway, she spotted what looked like two piles of clothes up ahead. She froze. She knew what those were.

58

Emerald Pearl

The piles of clothes resolved themselves as the girls drew closer. Two bodies, spaced fairly far apart. Up ahead lay an intersection. Rae tiled her head as she approached. On the left appeared to be an alcove, and across from that, on their right, a set of double-wide doors. Large letters read "Engineering." "Not opening that!" she said.

"Is that more blood?" Tabby asked. She pointed at something dark on the face of one man, lying on his back.

Like the bodies on the bridge, these were completely red due to the light from the nebula pouring down from the windows above. "I don't know. I don't really wanna—" She paused. He looked fine other than his nose. His guts weren't splattered on the walls like so many others, but his head was definitely twisted too far to one side. But like the others, his eyes stared into infinity, unblinking, soulless. His eyes… "Hey. That kinda looks like the guy who was arguing with Captain Timmins." Rae ventured closer. "I think it *is* him!"

"Huh?"

"It was when me and Daddy were on the tour. The guy was being super disrespectful and rude, and Captain Timmins put him in his place! It was really funny! What was his name…? Naff, Naffur? Oh, I can't remember. But what is he doing here? He's a passenger. He should still be in one of the pods."

"Napharr?" Tabby asked.

"Maybe."

"I tried to tell everyone this morning that someone else was in his pod, and it looked like one of the crewmembers. But *nooobody* would listen to me." She turned and walked away.

"Why would a crewmember be in a cryo pod?"

Tabby shrugged. "Oh wow, look at the hole in *this* guy! It looks… funny."

This piqued Rae's curiosity. She turned the flashlight on the body her sister now bent over. The second man lay on his stomach, and had a glistening hole bigger than Rae's fist in his back. Near the hole his tunic was flowered outward, like something had exploded. Rae realized she was gawking at the man's insides, and tried to look away. *Oh my Goddess, is that bright pink stuff bone? Maybe cartilage?* She finally closed her eyes and covered her mouth.

"Why does it look like that? Like something punched through him?"

"Oh, sweet Goddess! Tabby, get away!"

"He's not gonna hurt me!" she spat back, her face hovering right over the bloody hole.

Why is this not affecting her? How is she so brave? How does she do it? "Fine, you stay and play with the dead guys," said Rae. "I'm checking out the PEVAs!" She spun 'round and peeked ever-so-carefully into the alcove, scared she might find more bodies. Sure enough, a third dead crewmember lay in the center of the room. This one was not quite as red as the others; one of the white spot lights shone down upon it. The light didn't seem as bright as it should be.

Rae wondered if the power failure the computer announced earlier had anything to do with how dim the overhead lights were getting. Probably.

She shined her flashlight about the dead man, and soon found another red and yellowish "flower"-type wound. It lower, near his stomach. Liquid of various colors had poured out and made a fairly large puddle beneath the man. This is where the rotten stench seemed to be coming from, directly from this man's gut! Rae started to wretch. She had held her stomach in check before, but this was just too much to handle. She spewed a fine mist into the air trying to hold it in.

"Oh, groooohhhhhss!" yelled Tabby, now fanning the air and remaining at the intersection.

Rae turned and shoulder-checked her little sister as she flew back into the passageway and threw up some more, not far from the two dead men.

"Hey!"

There wasn't much left in her stomach anymore. The bile burned her throat. Rae coughed a few times, and looked for something to wipe her face. She found nothing but her sleeve, which would have to do. And there was nothing to drink, to get the terrible taste out of her mouth. Her eyes welled with tears. Not from sadness, just from the act of puking. A warm hand fell gently upon her shoulder, and a small pair of shoes appeared next to her. Rae relaxed and grabbed her sister's hand.

Tabby knelt down. "It'll be okay, Rae."

Rae wiped her eyes with the sleeve she hadn't soiled with bile. "Thanks, Sis," she choked. *But will it?* She wanted to believe it, but doubt had crept back into her mind. She had been so sure of rescue all day. Especially after Captain

Moses and his ship arrived. But now, bent over dizzy in that red hall, surrounded by death, her tummy aching, her body exhausted, her mind still in shock over the day's events, she had less and less faith everything actually would be okay. *Goddess,* she said to herself, *let us be rescued. Help us, Great Mother, please. If not me, then at least save my sister? She's the strong one. She has what it takes. She doesn't deserve any of this. She's so young. So innocent. Please... Please.*

Tabitha patted Rae on the back. "You okay now?"

Rae looked up at her and sniffled.

"Let's check out these widowmakers. Just don't breathe on me, alright? Or I'll throw up next."

Rae chuckled, then nodded.

They re-entered the alcove. Four doors stood, two by two, on a semi-circular wall. Each door had a number on it, from "01" on the far left to "04" on the far right, plus a round, black window inset in the upper portion. Tabby skirted the dead man, ran to the first door, and jumped. She tried again. Three times. "I can't see!"

Rae picked door number two and jumped once. She saw only black. *That's good, isn't it?* She tried the other windows. They were all the same. "I think the PEVAs are still here!" The overhead light illuminated her breath and reminded her how cold it had become. She glanced down and noticed the small smears of bile and tears on her sleeves had turned to ice.

Tabby busily waved her hand before her face. "Yuck! When you talk it smells like throw-up!"

"Sorry," Rae said.

Tabby held her nose, and sounded funny when she spoke. "Okay, well, now what? How do we get these doors open? There aren't any handles!"

Rae looked around and found this room's comm panel. She stomped over to it and punched the red circle. "*Emerald Pearl,* can you open the doors to the PEVAs?"

"Request not understood. Please restate the inquiry."

"Can you open the doors to the widowmakers?" asked Tabby.

"Request not understood. Please restate the inquiry."

"Hold on, Tabby, I think I'm getting the hang of this. *Emerald Pearl,* what room is the panel in that I'm talking to you on right now?"

"You are currently making an inquiry from the panel in the Maintenance Extra-Vehicular Activity vehicle disembarkation alcove."

"They're called MEVAs!" Tabby exclaimed. "That's why she didn't know what you were talking about!"

Rae stifled a laugh. Such a small difference. "*Emerald Pearl,* please open all four doors to the M-E-V-As at this location."

The four doors in the vestibule made a popping sound, slid a few inches either left or right, then slowed to a crawl. Rae could swear the overhead light dimmed while the doors were moving. They would take a while to move to the point the girls could enter the vehicles. *The power.* The *Pearl* was running out of it.

Tabitha cocked her head. "Do you hear that?"

"What?"

"That whistling noise?"

A slight chilly breeze arose from behind the girls, and realization hit Rae in an instant. "Oh, Goddess! Where is it coming from?"

"Tabitha ventured to the door labeled "03." "I think this one!"

"Get back, Tabby! *Emerald Pearl,* close the door to MEVA number three!" The door stopped, and after a moment, started moving in the opposite direction. When it closed, a whistling noise rose.

Tabby looked back at Rae. "I think we have a prawww-blemmm…"

Rae slammed her palm on the blue screen above the red circle. "Captain Moses! Captain Moses, are you there?"

"Yes, Rae, I'm here."

"We found the PEVAs—they're called MEVAs here—but anyway one of them is leaking air for some reason! The door to it is shut but it's whistling. That means air is still leaking out, right? We have a super chilly breeze in here!"

"Yes, it sounds like you're losing air, but that's okay, you're leaving. Go ahead and hop into the MEVAs."

"Do you want us to each get in one, or both of us get in one together?"

"Will you both fit in one vehicle?"

"I'm not sure. Maybe?"

"Either way, long as you can still work the controls. We're going to have to figure out how to work them together; these things are much older than ours. But the first thing you need to do after powering them up, is to close the door behind you!"

"Okay!" Rae turned to her sister. "Which one do you want?"

"Umm, give me the flashlight," Sis said, "I want to figure out which one is nicer!"

Rae rolled her eyes but gave the girl the light. "I'm sure they're all the same, Tabby."

The little girl shined the beam on each one in turn, first starting at the closest one, labeled "04." "Hmm," she said. She kicked the door of number three on the way past it, then moved onto "02," and finally "01." "Hmm," she said again. "They all look yucky!"

"Well, they're maintenance craft, right? They probably get dirty and greasy a lot."

"Yeah, but these are *really* gross! Like… burnt yucky."

"Burnt yucky? What does that mean?"

"It means what I said. They look burnt!"

Rae snatched the light from her sister and took a look for herself. "Eww! You're right! They do look burnt! They also look broken."

"Do you mean, 'don't look like they will fly' broken?" Sis asked gingerly.

"Yes. I wonder if number three is the same?"

"Um, I'm thinking number three has a hole in it."

"Girls?" Moses again.

Tabby answered with a yell. "Yeah?"

"Which of the PEVAs is leaking?"

"Number three. And they're MEVAs!"

It took a few seconds before he spoke again. "I'm having our chief engineer swing over take a look at it, just out of curiosity."

"Okay."

"Are you in the MEVAs yet? Do you think you can power them up on your own?"

"Um, we're not inside them yet."

"Why not?"

"Well, the insides of all of them look like they were set on fire."

No reply.

"Captain Moses?"

59

GSCS *Nightingale*

"I got eyes on widowmaker three, Cap'n,"

"Aye, Kelly," Elwick acknowledged, pinching the bridge of his nose again, not even wanting to ponder the latest problem the girls had just discovered. "What do you see?"

"Captain Moses?" Rae again.

"Give us just a minute, Rae."

"It's not good," Kelly replied. "And it's confusin'. I couldn't tell much 'till I shined a white light on it, but that number three's got tiny perforations all over its hull. And one of its arms is clean blown off!"

"I see. These perforations, do they look like shrapnel damage, maybe from the accident that stranded the ship here? Or micrometeor punctures, or what?"

"Looks like micrometeors, but meteors that punctured the darn thing from the inside out!"

From the inside out? That didn't make sense. "Dale, could you get Rose to continue on to the rear of the Engine room on Deck Two? I think we need eyes on these things."

"Aye aye, sir."

Rae's voice came across the airwaves once more, "Captain Moses!" She sounded as annoyed as he had become.

"Yes, Rae?"

"Tabby and I think we have a really big problem. All of these PEVAs or MEVAs or whatever they're called are broken. And we're talking so broken they won't even turn on. We tried! I don't think we're going to be able to fly them. And not only that, I think all our air is still being sucked out this door! Or blown out, I mean."

Moses threw his head back and gazed toward where he believed Heaven might be. He did his best to stare down the Almighty. *Really, God? Why!?*

60

Emerald Pearl: Engineering

"Rose, Master Chief."

Rose Vereau looked to the spot on her HUD that would unmute her microphone. "Rose here."

"How's it coming?"

"I'm about three quarters of the way through. Give me… about two minutes."

"Understood. Masterson out."

Rose muted the circuit and continued cutting, only pausing long enough to check her R-meter. It was high. Extremely so. She decided not to look at it again.

She focused on completing burning a round hole in the ridiculously thick door before her. The hole's circumference would only be large enough to fit Bruno's head and shoulders, but Rose would soon be able to zip her slender frame through it like a gymnast. Which she still considered herself, dammit! And she wasn't going to let a somewhat bulky spacesuit, nor middle age, slow her down.

She didn't let a little—or in this case, a lot of—radiation poisoning concern her, either. Doc Galloway could put her in stasis for the trip back to Earth, halting cell destruction until they could get her into the Susan Aline Ives Cancer Center in Omaha, Druthers Province. Shouldn't be in statis more than four months or so. Maybe six. There were just so many people to heal nowadays.

And if she got stuck over the derelict ship *too long*, eh, so be it. The exposure was for a good cause. And who wants to live forever anyway?

Plus, she couldn't have let any of those other apes do it, they all have children and grandchildren to watch grow up. *Me, who do I have?*

Well, I guess I might have one *crazy soul who loves me.* She sighed. *Fine, I'll hurry.*

Emerald Pearl: Outer hull, MEVA Docking Point

"BM1?"

Kelly paused. *That's kinda odd,* she thought, now having to click two buttons before answering. "Crawford here, Cap'n. Wonderin' what the reason is fer you to be on a private channel during a rescue op—"

"Rose just reported she's cut through the door to the, I guess it's called the 'MEVA disembarkation alcove', and will be checking out the vehicles. You did say you were able to see into the vestibule, through the cockpits of the craft and that the doors to each one was still open?"

"Aye. All doors 'ceptin' fer widowmaker number three, o' course. Why d'ya ask?"

"I want you to position yourself so you can get a good look at her. I need you to use your helmet's optics and zoom in on her face, and send the video feed directly to Doc Galloway."

"Well, if that ain't the oddest request I ever heard!"

"Doc's been watching her vitals from Sick Bay. Namely her radiation exposure. If things are as bad as I fear, I want you to rip one of those MEVAs out of its housing, have Rose grab onto a claw, and ferry her back to the *Nightingale*. Pronto."

Shit. "Aye, aye, Cap'n!"

Emerald Pearl: MEVA Disembarkation Alcove

Rose Vereau shook her head at the scene around her. "Captain Elwick? Vereau here."

"Go ahead, Rose."

"I can tell you what the girls meant by burnt. The cockpits are charred black. Looks like someone took some kind of shotgun-torch-lightning gun to their dashboards. I mean, these things are destroyed. There's no way these things are going to fly ever again."

"Understood," Moses replied. "That's all we needed. Thanks for getting eyes-on."

"Roger. By the way, there's a dead guy in here. Couple more in the passageway. Two are dressed like crewmembers, one is in civilian clothes. They all have broken limbs, but their wounds look different from the others. If I didn't know better, I'd guess these guys were killed before the incident happened."

What? "What makes you say that?"

"Because this looks more like a crime scene than an accident scene. I've seen enough of each in my life."

Elwick tucked that last bit of info away for later. Rose was definitely one interesting lady. "Curiouser and curiouser, as Alice would say. The Navy's going to have a blast trying to piece this one together."

"So, you want me to stay here, go back through Engineering, or—?"

"Stay where you are for just a minute. Oh, and Rose, can you see Kelly? She should be right outside. Could you wave to her from one of the cockpits?"

"I suppose. She feeling lonely out there, or something?"

"Something like that. Switch to channel eight to speak to her."

"Okaaay." Rose climbed into MEVA "02" and put her helmet to the glass to get a good look at the widow maker parked right outside the alcove. Everything was so red out there! She would never have known the vehicle Petty Officer Crawford piloted was construction-yellow had she not known better; it looked an odd shade of orangey-pink. Using her HUD, she switched to the comm channel labeled "8." "Hi, Kelly," she said, waving.

Crawford waved back. "Hiya, Rose! How are ya?"

"I'm fine. A little bird told me you got a promotion. Congratulations. It's very well-deserved. You're the best bosun around!"

"Aww, thank ya, Rose! That was mighty nice of ya to say! I'm really excited about it, I— Hold up a sec…"

Rose waited. Kelly looked as though she was talking to someone on another channel. Soon the Chief nodded, and the circuit opened up again.

"Rose, I'm gonna need you to stand back. I'm about to rip one of these critters out of its hole."

"Oh, oh dear! Okay," she said, stepping back. "Why?"

"After I do, I'm gonna need ya to crawl through the empty hole 'n hop on board. I'm yer taxi back to the *'Gale!*"

Rose only now pieced together *why* this was all happening. She somehow forgot the *Nightingale's* Sick Bay can keep an eye on all their vitals in real-time. Someone must have spotted her mSv numbers. "Hey, Kelly? Can we not let Daniel know about this? Not just yet, I mean?"

Crawford chuckled. "I don't even know what yer talkin' 'bout! All I'm doin' is givin' ya a ride!"

Emerald Pearl: MEVA Disembarkation Alcove

"Rae," she heard Captain Moses say, "I'm sorry the PEVAs or MEVAs didn't work out. My crew is trying to figure out what other options—"

"*Emerald Pearl,*" Rae called loudly, "are there any other MEVAs on this stupid ship? Any escape pods left? Any lifeboats? Anything?"

"MEVAs one through four are not responding. Escape pods one through forty were jettisoned between 13:24 and 13:26 this afternoon. Lifeboats removed at previous refit and not replaced. Captain's yacht is reading inoperable and unable to detach from host vessel. Damage to guidance system, quantum entangled communications pod, propulsion—"

"It's okay, you can stop, we get it!" Rae's heart sank, and with it, she sank to the floor. The air hurt her lungs now. If she had the energy to cry, she was certain her tears would freeze before they ever dripped from her chin, especially in the chilling breeze passing over them now. She shivered.

"Captain's yacht!?" exclaimed Tabby. "I never saw anything like that! Where is it?"

"Who knows?" Rae muttered. "Doesn't matter."

Tabitha looked upward. "You could have told us all that first off, you mean old lady!" the little girl spat. "Before we came all this way and nearly got sucked out into space!"

Blown out, Rae thought, but she didn't correct her.

"Why were even trying this?" yelled Tabby. "Any of it? Why? This was so stupid!"

"Tabby." Captain Moses spoke in a soothing tone. "We just had to try every option we had available to us."

Tabby crossed her arms and plopped down next to Rae. "So stupid!" she screamed.

"Wait a minute," Rae heard someone on the line say quietly, almost but not quite out of earshot, "what time did the explosion occur again?"

"I think it was around fourteen hundred?" Rae recognized this voice as Guy Connelly's. "We'll check the logs when Hamidi finishes the download. Looks like we're at eighty-seven percent."

"Why were the escape pods jettisoned *before* the explosion?" Moses asked, in low tones but still loud enough for Rae to hear. "That doesn't make sense."

"Unless Mr. Osterland's theory is correct."

This last voice was a new one that Rae didn't recognize. But she no longer cared what the *Nightingale's* crew were on about. She had reached at her wit's end. *Everything we did today... Running all over this ship looking for a way off... Running around trying to find Captain Moses' people...*

Crawling through all those long, ice cold tunnels... Me almost getting squished through a four-inch slit and blown out into that nasty red nebula, and now our air about to leak out into space... It was all for absolutely nothing. There was never any way off this stupid old boat to begin with!

Her mind raced as she heard Captain Moses and his crew continue to debate their latest mystery. Rae didn't care. She closed her eyes tight.

What did any of it even matter anymore? Her father was dead. Her mother and brother might still be alive, but had just been shot out into a cloud of red-hot plasma, so they were probably going to die soon, too, if they weren't dead already. What chance did they have of surviving the seventy-four year gulf between now and when the *Nightingale* shows up to "rescue" all of them? Their home back on Earth had surely been torn down by now; there would be no calling Aunt Beccah and trying to get it back. In fact, Aunt Beccah was probably dead, as was everyone else they knew. Many of their schoolmates might still be alive, but now as old as dirt. Her best friend Sallie would be... Rae did the math in her head... eighty-seven. Eighty-seven years old! Rae despaired. She almost wanted to go back to that one panel, the one that opened to the nebula, and just get this whole mess over with.

One thing stopped her. Okay, two things. One: that horrific informational holo she saw in school regarding what happens to a human body when exposed to vacuum. She didn't want to put herself through the trauma that one unlucky little boy went through. She didn't want her last moments in this universe to be filled with excruciating, unbearable, self-inflicted pain. Even if it was for only a few seconds before everything went dark. That would be worse than simply freezing to death!

But wait, wouldn't that happen soon anyway? Once all the air flitted out through the crack in the MEVA door? She and Sis were going to die in a freezing vacuum no matter what!

Tabby, as if reading her every thought, curled up in her arms. The little thing was shivering all over, and her lower lip trembled.

Rae's heart went out to her, and she hugged her tight. She was reason number two. "Captain Moses? I have a question."

Moses' voice came back, loud enough for her to hear easily. "Sure, Rae, what is it?"

"What's going to happen to our mother and our brother? And our father's body? Do you think anyone will ever find them?"

"I'm glad you asked," he said. "Guy has located all sixteen cryo pods! We're in the middle of scanning each one, and sending out a remote drone to retrieve them and bring them on board. It will take a while, they're all pretty far away after drifting for seventy-four years, but a few of the ones we've scanned show valid life signs! Weak, but there. That means the occupants are still alive in those!"

"You mean Mom and Jamie are alive?"

"Well, we can't tell which pod is which at this distance, but considering we've already found some survivors, chances are good that most or all of them made it through the decades. We'll recover them, and ever-so-carefully bring them back. They'll be out of time, fish out of water, but alive."

Rae began to cry. "At least Mom and Jamie will make it. I'm glad about that."

"But we won't," Tabitha whispered.

"Tabby," Moses said in a soft voice, "we're not giving up. There may be another way. We haven't explored the entire ship yet. We haven't gone through the logs yet. When the data is downloaded from the *Pearl*'s computer to the *Nightingale*'s, we can go through the schematics and see what we may have missed. Maybe power can be routed to the Captain's yacht?"

"And how much time will that take?" Tabby yelled.

"Well…"

"More time than we've got, right Captain Moses?"

"We're losing our air!" screamed Rae.

"We definitely need to get a seal on one of the tunnel doors you girls came through. The area you're in right now will lose its air, but we will stop the air from leaving the rest of the ship. After that, we might be able to find a way to generate more power, maybe using one or more of those pusher robots in the cargo bay that my people found. Surely they're operating in your day if they're still lumbering around in ours."

"They are. One scared the life out of me!"

"Sorry to hear that. But you might be able to use them in *your* time to do things we can't in *our* time. If you can make your way down to the cargo bay—"

"I don't want to go down there again!" Tabby yelled.

"But the robots have power cells. With enough of them, we might be able to—"

"Stop! I don't want to hear any more of this!" screamed Tabitha. "Might, could, maybe, your day, my day, your time, my time! I don't understand it! Any of it! I'm getting dizzy!

I'm really tired and I'm freezing and I just want to go to sleep! I want all this all to be over with! No more! I'm not going back down into that dark, scary place! Not again!"

"Tabby, please—"

"I said no more!" Tears streamed down Sis' cheeks. She began to whimper. "No more."

Rae hugged her, felt her shiver. Tabby's tears were crystalizing before they could drop onto her clothing. Rae had heard somewhere that it took salt water a lot longer than fresh water to freeze, so it must be far below freezing at this point. It's probably why her fingers and toes had hurt earlier. They were now numb.

"I just want to be with Daddy!" Tabby whined. "I just want to be with Mommy and Daddy! Oh, Daddy! Why did you have to die? Why? Rae, why!?"

Rae held the little girl tight. It all had finally crashed down upon her. Tabby had weathered the crazy events of the day much better than Rae had. All of them. At times, Rae wanted to crumble, to give up, but Tabitha remained strong. Her strength had pushed Rae along. She admired her little sister for that, and wished she could be more like her. But had it all been a façade? This whole day, had she just been acting strong in an attempt to outlast and outshine her big sister? Just another game at which to beat her? If so, Tabby now appeared to be giving up just before the finish line. It now seemed the strain, the worry, the heartache, the gravity of their impossible situation had all finally caught up to her. She had finally broken.

Be strong, Rae told herself. *Be strong for Tabby. Be* like *Tabby. She comforted you not half an hour ago when you needed it. Now it's time to comfort her.* "It'll be okay, Tabby. It'll be okay."

"No! It won't!" the girl shouted, then buried her face in Rae's shoulder. When Sis spoke again, her voice came muffled. "It will never be okay again! We're orphans! We're all alone! And we're gonna die alone!"

Rae allowed small fingers to dig into her clothing. It hurt, but only a little. Rae ignored it. Sis then let loose an ear-splitting scream. Rae pushed her little face into the fabric of her blouse to muffle it as best she could so as not to hurt her ears, and let Tabby wail to her heart's content. She held the girl close, tighter than she ever had before.

Exhaustion overpowered Rae. She was tired of getting their hopes up time and time again, only to be let down. Tired of fighting. Tired all over. And it was oh, so cold. Getting colder by the second now, surely, what with all the power depleted. Not to mention what with the *Pearl's* air zipping by them in a breeze colder than she'd ever experienced, even in the coldest Winter in what was once called Wisconsin. She remembered that from Educata. Why could she remember facts that didn't matter, but not the really important things?

The flashlight. It seemed to be giving up, too. Or was it just hard to see the beam through all her tears? She should shut it off to conserve power.

Hold on, what did she just say? *Who cares about flashlight batteries! None of it matters anymore!* Once again, Rae found herself on a cold, hard floor, rocking back and forth with her sister. *What else can we do? Go to the dome? Where the Fates have seemingly already decided we would end up?*

After a few minutes, Tabby calmed down. She shook from time to time as people do right after they cease a violent cry. "Rae?" The girl sniffled.

Rae relaxed her hold and pulled away so she could see her sister's face. "Yeah, Tabby?"

As if she could read Rae's thoughts she whimpered, "Let's go to the dome. It will be warmer up there."

Rae opened her mouth to object, but nothing came out.

"It's the only place to see outside," Tabby went on between post-sobbing heaves. "Well, besides the bridge, which is stinky. And the hallway over there, which is also filled with dead bodies. I don't want to be around all these smelly dead people! And I don't want to freeze by this stupid, leaky door!"

Rae nodded, wiping tears from her eyes. "Okay. Okay." She helped Sis to her feet.

"Plus the couch is comfy."

"It *is* comfy, isn't it, Tabby?"

Tabitha nodded.

"Maybe we can grab some thermal blankets on the way? And shut all the doors behind us?" She turned and looked at the comm panel in the wall. "We won't be completely alone, either, Tabby, no matter where we are on this ship. So, I guess the Dome is as good a place as any." She raised her voice. "Captain?"

"I'm here."

"We've decided—"

"We heard," Moses replied.

61

GSCS *Nightingale*

"I'm heading over," said Elwick.

"Sir?" Osterland inquired.

"I just want to spend some time with a couple of special little ladies, that's all."

Ozzie nodded.

Moses committed the deck plan of the *Emerald Pearl* to memory before departing the ship, and knew exactly where to go. He had not donned a spacesuit in a long time. It felt awkward. How much time did he have before the RNA Navy arrived and took him away in handcuffs? *Who cares? They'll have to come get me.*

Kelly had returned with Rose Vereau, and Doc Galloway had started radiation treatment on her. The old, gruff Australian had given her a fifty-fifty chance, but Moses would be damned if he would be going to the Canadian beauty's funeral any time soon. There had been enough death today to go around, he didn't need to be burying a member of his own crew! He told himself Rose would be fine; she was now in good hands, and Moses had a mission to complete.

A failed mission. Okay, maybe only partially failed. They still had survivors, just not the survivors he so longed to have.

How much time did the girls have left? That was the foremost question on his mind. Temperatures in his time had reached nearly a hundred and seventeen degrees below zero Centigrade, and he had no way of knowing exactly how cold it had gotten in Rae and Tabitha's time without asking them. And he didn't want to bother them with trivialities anymore. It would only make them focus on the details of what's to come, and he didn't want to put them through that.

He pushed his bulky suit faster. He had to make it to the Dome before they drew their final breaths. It was something he absolutely had to do.

Emerald Pearl: Observation Dome

Moses entered the Observation Lounge for the first time, via the aft-most spiral stair. He looked up at the elaborate, seemingly delicate latticework above his head, the skeleton of the graphene dome keeping the glowing monster outside at bay. Barbara had been right, it was a remarkable sight, a beautiful feat of engineering.

The overwhelming nature of the color *red* in this room took him aback. The nebula enveloped everything; the walls, the floor, the long dead plants and trees, the lush couches, soft chairs and tables that scattered around the room. Barbara Laskey and Jan Ebersbacher sat on one couch. Antonio Bruno stood nearby, as did Dale Masterson, Hamidi Abiodun, and Daniel Gilbin. Moses only just now thought about how unusually quiet Gilbin had been from the moment he had stepped on board the *Pearl.* Perhaps this place freaked him out. It rose Moses' hackles, that's for sure.

And then he saw them.

On the opposite sofa, across a glass "coffee table," sat the bodies of two other people slumped together, as if they were sleeping. They looked so small. And young.

Rae and Tabitha.

Moses could not take his eyes off the two girls as he moved toward them. Their fragile bodies, laps covered by a silvery blanket, looked completely intact, like they had just died a few days ago. It looked as if the tissue had frozen long before the air finally leaked out of this deck, meaning the girls had—hopefully—still been in full atmosphere when they died, and hadn't been subject to the horrid effects of vacuum while still alive. He saw no after-effects of outgassing, swelling, leaking of blood. Their faces looked perfect; their skin was simply devoid of color. Gray. But even in this macabre state, they were still beautiful to him.

"Captain Moses?"

Elwick jumped. *Oh my God!* To hear Rae's voice in his headset while staring at her corpse scared the bejesus out of him.

"You said you were heading to the Observation Dome, right?"

It was uncanny. He had been talking to that little girl for hours, but to actually see her sitting there lifeless, an unwrapped mummy cuddled up with her sister… and then to hear her speaking! The hair rose on the back of his neck and gave him gooseflesh on his arms, and all the way down his back.

"Captain Moses? Are you there?"

"Yes. Yes, Rae. I am here. I'm in the Dome." Elwick did his best to not let his voice show the horde of emotions running through him. Well, at least not the undesirable ones, ones that may hurt little Rae and Tabby's feelings. "Barbara and I are both here, along with other members of the Search and Rescue Team."

"Okay. We're here now too." Her voice shivered. "Just walked in."

Elwick was almost afraid to turn and look, but he did so anyway. But of course, he saw no one enter from either the fore or aft stairwells, nor through any of the other ingress points. He looked around the room. The others did the same, looking for ghosts. *Dear God, this is so strange.*

"Was Doctor Laskey telling the truth? Do you see our bodies?"

"Yes, sweetheart. I do. You two are adorable. More beautiful than I imagined you to be." Elwick noticed the items in the perfect little hands of the dead girls. "Tabby, that's a very cuddly bear you've got there."

"This is… Mr. Fluffles," the little girl replied. Her voice sounded strained. It trembled a bit. The extreme temperature? Or sadness? Perhaps both.

Elwick leaned over and looked into the face of the bear. "Well, hello, Mr. Fluffles. It's nice to meet you."

No further response came from Tabby.

"Rae, I love your blouse," said Barbara, shining a white light on the girls. "Purple is my favorite color."

"Really?" the girl asked. "Mine too!" Her voice beamed.

"Rae," Moses said, "you're cradling your prayer book. It's open to a page… I'm trying to see which—"

The girl sighed over the comm. "I knew Barbara wasn't lying. But I guess I was just hoping it all wasn't true after all."

"I'm so sorry, Rae. I wish it wasn't. I so desperately wish it wasn't true."

"You can see *me*. I wish I could see *you*. I'll never know what you look like."

"It's probably for the best," Moses joked, "I'm not much to look at anyway."

"The Captain's being ridiculously humble, Rae," Barbara interjected. "You want me to describe him to you?"

"Please?"

"Well, he's got beautiful dark brown hair—clean-cut of course— with just a twinge of gray at the temples. Big blue eyes. Chiseled, scruffy jaw with a hint of a gray there, too. Broad, strong shoulders. He's brave. Bold. Stoic. Doesn't know when to stop; doesn't know the word 'quit.' Probably to the point of fault. He puts his family and crew far above himself. I know, being ship's counselor, I've spoken to everyone on the ship. Not to mention the fact I've glanced at his... sealed military files."

Elwick gave her a harsh stare.

Laskey only smiled. "Girls, this is a man other men strive to be like. His sailors will follow him into Hell and damnation and not complain. Case-in-point, if you take a look outside." She breathed deep, and in a way that made Moses wonder whether she wasn't suffering ill-effects of being in a spacesuit too long at her age. "It is a pleasure to serve under his command."

Elwick mouthed the word, "Enough."

"Thank you, Miss Laskey," Rae said. "That at least gives me a picture in my head."

Barbara stood and sat next to Tabitha. When Moses saw this didn't disturb the bodies, he walked over and sat down next to Rae.

It was just surreal. Moses had seen far too many dead bodies in his day, but these girls didn't look dead at all. If he didn't know better, he would swear they had merely been too weak and exhausted from their ordeal to keep their eyes open any longer. That they had simply fallen asleep. *That's exactly what happened,* Moses told himself.

"Will you stay with us until…?"

He waited, but she didn't finish her sentence. "Yes, Rae," he promised. "I'm sitting next to you and I'm not leaving your side."

"Whoa. You're… *right* next to me? Right now?"

Moses looked into the gray faces before him. "In my time, I am. And Barbara is sitting next to Tabitha."

"I wish you could be here. I mean in our time."

"Me too, Rae. If I only knew how, I would be there in a heartbeat."

He looked down at the book again, and gently slid it from under the gray hand of the corpse. Even without the support, the hand did not fall to Rae's chest or lap, but remained frozen in mid-air.

Frozen in time.

62

Emerald Pearl: Observation Dome

Rae and Tabitha both looked around when their new friends said they were in the room with them. Rae now wished all the ghost stories she had heard had been true, because it seemed like she had been talking to ghosts this whole time. *Or are Tabby and I the ghosts?*

It was hard to comprehend, but if she understood correctly, her new friends had not even been born yet. They existed seventy-four years into the future. Even if she and her sister had survived this accident, they would be very old women in Captain Moses' time. But they would have lived their whole lives by then, so it would have been okay.

Rae thought she had come to accept the fact she and Tabitha were probably going to simply fall asleep and not wake up. But now, so close to it becoming real, she hoped that somehow, they might still be rescued. *Why can't the captain find a way?* He still had a way to *talk* to them! Why couldn't he find a way to *get to* them? *Because it's not in his power, Rae,* she scolded herself. *It's not in anyone's power. Maybe it is in God's power? Daddy said the God of the Hebrews could do anything. ANYTHING.* But if he could, why hadn't he saved them by now? Would he not save them at all? Two little girls who had their whole lives ahead of them? *Hmm. Maybe he would save little Tabby, because she believes in him. But not me, because I don't.*

There was another possibility. *Perhaps Daddy was wrong? Perhaps not even the most powerful god of all the gods can control the strangest things in the universe?*

Or maybe he simply did not want to do so?

Rae considered this last possibility a mean thing to do. Maybe even downright evil. A being with the power to do anything it wants, and it doesn't use it for *good?* To save people? *Maybe that's why Mommy did not believe in Daddy's god?* Her mother never said so, but Rae knew she did not. *Mom supported their father because she loved him.* Now their father was dead.

And God did not save *him*.

Rae found it ironic that her mother was still alive, albeit now floating around in the nebula somewhere and some*when* in the future. *She will live longer than Daddy!* But soon she would be waking up and asking questions and asking about… about her family. What will she be told? Just that her two little angels were gone, and they died three-quarters of a century ago? It made Rae tear up all over again.

Daddy. Mom would learn about Daddy, too. Rae wondered then, if his soul was even now traveling to the safe haven of which he spoke. "Heaven" he had said it was called. Just as when her mother died, her spirit would travel back to Mother Earth to join—

Wait.

Rae experienced that gnawing feeling again. *We are a long way from Earth! A very long way.* Would her parents' immortal souls find peace at all? What did that mean for Rae and her little sister? Would their souls find their way home?

Or would they be stuck here as ghosts on this derelict ship for all eternity?

A revelation hit Rae full-force. *Maybe that's where ghosts come from!? And they are indeed real! Maybe people get trapped between life and true death, unable to find Heaven or Gaia, doomed to haunt the halls in the house—or in the ship—where they died?*

Forever!

This idea would have terrified Rae had something funny not struck her at that moment. She realized she had picked one of the empty couches at random. Had she chosen the same couch on which Moses "now" sat? The same one on which Barbara had found their bodies the first time? What if they moved to another couch right now? Would their future bodies still be in the same place as the Captain described? Or would they suddenly disappear before everyone's eyes, and pop up on another couch? *How funny would that be!?* She giggled at the idea of their dead bodies teleporting, surprising Captain Moses and everyone else on board with him, all while she could hear them! She almost wanted to try it, just to see…

"What's so funny?" Tabby whimpered.

Rae told her about the teleportation joke.

"Oh. I don't get it."

Rae smiled. "Nevermind." She found it nice to think about something humorous instead of the heavy matter concerning the dealings of their souls.

"Sis? Mr. Fluffles wants you to read… one of the poems from your book." Her breath caught in the middle of her sentence; it had begun to get hard to breathe.

"They're not poems, Tabby. They're prayers."

"Whatever. Just read one like… Mom used to."

Rae considered it. "I can't just incant prayers without—"

"Please?"

Did Tabby just say "please?" That was the second time today! Or was it the third? Rae dreamed Tabitha had said it while she had been passed out on the bridge earlier, but she couldn't be sure whether that had been real or imagined. *Wow. This really had been a tremendous day of firsts!* Of high adventure! Of sibling rivalry and of sisterhood. If only they could take this day into the future with them! Rae sadly accepted the fact they could not.

She thought of an appropriate prayer. Rae had many of them memorized, but not all. Not even half. However, today she knew exactly which one she wanted to read. "Okay," she said, then opened up her book and cleared her throat. "*Soul of Earth, sanctify me*," she began. "*Body of Earth, save me. Blood of Earth, fill me with love.*"

Tabitha snuggled closer to her sister. Rae was very thankful for Sis's warmth. She could not imagine being alone at that moment. She spread a large, thermal blanket across their laps.

"*Good Earth, hear me,*" Rae continued, pausing longer at each comma than she meant to, but the cold made it difficult to get out more than a few words at a time. "*Within your wounds, hide me. Never let me be... separated from you.*" Rae's throat had constricted without warning. She took a deep breath and held it a moment in an attempt to warm the air. The frosty air seared her lungs. She had to get through the prayer. "*From the power of evil, protect... me. At the hour of ...my death, call me. That with your... living ones I... may thank you. For all eternity... Amen.*"

Tabitha shivered, and she and her little flannel bear snuggled even closer to Rae.

If Rae had been frightened over the fate of her immortal soul before, after reading this prayer, she was terrified. "Captain Moses?"

"What is it, Rae?"

"What will… happen to us?"

"Don't worry, sweetheart, you can be sure we will treat you and your sister with the utmost respect. And we'll find your father, don't worry. You'll all receive proper burials as per Interstellar Maritime Law."

"That's… not what I meant."

Silence on the line.

"What I meant was, this… far away, will… our spirits find their way back… to Mother Earth?"

No answer came.

Perhaps the Captain does not understand? Or does not know? Maybe—

"I was just told you may be Wiccan, is that true?"

"Yes."

"I see," Elwick said. "I don't think I'm qualified to answer your question, Rae. I am a Christian. I'm afraid I'm not too familiar with your theology."

"Rae," Barbara Laskey interjected, "I think I understand your concern. I am not spiritual in the sense your mother was, but I have studied many different religions, to include Wicca. Am I right when I say you believe that when you die, your soul becomes part of the world from whence it came?"

"Yes. We become part… of the trees. The rock. The… animals, even the… clouds," Rae explained.

"And now you're worried that, because your bodies are so far from home, your souls will get lost and not find their way back. Is that right?"

"Yes."

Tabitha shivered again, and breathed heavy. Rae hoped she dreamed of pleasant things.

"Well," Dr. Laskey said, "I don't believe our souls can ever get lost, per se. They transcend space and time. Even though you and I are separated by decades rather than light years, even though—from my and Captain Elwick's perspective—your spirits have long since departed your bodies, your souls are still a part of these events, part of this very discussion. No matter how far away from its starting point, the soul can always find its way home in the blink of an eye. Rest assured, girls, both of you will find your way home. Both of you will find peace."

"And my… father?"

"Your father too."

"Do… you promise?"

"Yes, I promise," Barbara said confidently.

Rae waited a moment before uttering her blatantly petulant next words. "Captain… Moses broke his… last promise."

No response. Perhaps she had gone too far? If she had, she didn't care.

* * *

The blanket had held its warmth for only an hour, if that. Now it did little good and was downright frozen itself! The warmth from their own bodies was no longer sufficient to provide enough heat to maintain their lives for much longer, let alone allow them to be comfortable in their final moments.

"Backup power level at critical level," the computer said. Its voice seemed somewhat shaky, too. Rae guessed the speakers were frosting up, but it sounded like the woman in the computer was freezing like they were. *Good! Mean old lady.*

"Not enough power to maintain voice-activated computer communication system. Audio broadcasts from the on-board Ship's Brain will now cease. Voice recognition is now unavailable. Please use installed comm panel keyboards or biometric verification devices to make requests of Brain, and to request further announcements and updates."

"There… are keyboards?" Rae thought out loud. Her breath came out in puffs of steam now, as did Tabitha's. It took great effort to speak more than a few words.

The announcement must have awoken Tabitha. She spoke through chattering teeth. "I thought Captain… Moses said the computer would… last hundreds of years?"

Rae shrugged. "Maybe this… is how it's… going to do it?"

"Oh. Is the… lady inside… the computer dying too?"

"I don't know… One good thing… we don't have… to listen… to her rambling… on anymore."

"Oh. Good," Sis said. "I didn't like… her anyway."

Rae took a deep breath in order to let her sister know they were in 'violent agreement', as she had heard her father say once. "Me neither!" Her fingertips had gone numb, and her hands hurt as she rearranged the blanket over herself and Tabby.

It didn't help.

63

Emerald Pearl: Observation Dome

Time passed.

Elwick could still hear breathing on the other end of his suit's comm system.

"Captain… Moses?" came a much weaker voice over the channel.

"Yes, Rae?"

"Captain… You s-said you… have… my b-book?"

"Yes, sweetheart, I have it right here."

"Could you…"

Elwick waited for the girl to finish her sentence. But she did not. "Rae? Rae are you there?" He heard what sounded like someone taking a quick breath, then some fumbling about.

"Could you… read… me a… pr-prayer? Can… can't…"

"Of course, Rae," Moses interrupted. The poor girl could barely speak; she was surely much too frozen to get her fingers to turn the pages of a book. Moses felt delighted and honored to read to her, like he had read to Alena when she was little. "Which one?" he asked.

"My… fav… favorite…"

Again, he waited.

"P-p-page three… oh-two…"

Moses flipped to page 302. Turned out, turning pages while wearing spacesuit gloves was not the easiest task. "Is it about flowers?"

Another pause. Then, "Y-yesss."

"Okay." Elwick swallowed and began. "*Flowers have come!*" He swallowed before continuing, as his voice was already beginning to crack. *"To refresh and delight you, princes... Princesses,*" he corrected, veering from the printed word; Moses thought it only appropriate. "*You see them briefly as they dress themselves, spread their petals, perfect only in spring—countless golden flowers!*"

The breathing became less frequent. Moses continued. "*The flowers have come to the skirt of the mountain! Yellow flowers. Sweet flowers. Precious vanilla flowers. The crow's dark magic flowers, weave themselves together.*"

Silence on the line. Then a couple of quick breaths.

His eyes watered so much he could barely see to read. He couldn't wipe his eyes while wearing the helmet, so he squeezed his eyes tight to let the tears fall away, down his cheeks. "*They are your flowers, God. We only borrow them: your flowered drum, your bells, your song.*"

Silence hung in the room like a heavy blanket.

"*They are your flowers, God.*"

Moses stared at that last sentence for a long time. He held his breath and listened.

But he heard nothing.

"Rae?" Elwick waited. "Tabby?"

No answer. He called Rae's name once more, but this time he barely choked it out.

Moses stared into nothing across the cold red room, waiting for a reply he knew would never come.

64

Emerald Pearl: Observation Dome

A hand touched his arm.

Moses opened his eyes and looked into the blurry face of Barbara Laskey. He blinked more tears away as best he could, and now, through the glass of her helmet, he could see her glossy eyes and pursed lips. He took a deep breath. "Give me a minute."

She nodded.

Moses sat in silence next to Rae and Tabitha's small bodies, struggling to suppress his emotions. He still had a duty to perform, a mission to complete.

He closed the book and delicately placed it under the hand of the dead angel where he had found it. As gently as he could, he rested a gloved hand on the thermal blanket on Rae's lap, closed his eyes, and said a silent prayer of his own. When finished, he looked over at Dr. Laskey, who waited patiently next to Tabitha. "Time to go, doctor."

As Moses stood to leave, he heard a clinking sound which he couldn't zero-in on through his helmet. He looked at Barbara, who stared at the floor. Elwick followed suit to find Rae's pentacle amulet at his feet. He gasped, then leaned forward to examine the girl's neck. The necklace was indeed missing from where it had been only a moment before. It wasn't hard to deduce the amulet had slid down the thermal blanket, then clanged to the floor after being stationary for seventy-four years. But how had it broken free? He had tried to be overly careful not to disturb either of the little flowers on the couch. Barbara had been careful too, of that he was certain. But they had obviously failed. "The movement of the cushions must have shaken it loose."

"Perhaps it had not been not clasped completely to begin with?" Barbara asked.

Should I put it back? Elwick shuddered. He feared Rae's little body may be so fragile it might crumble at his touch. If her head toppled from her body he would be mortified! He could not bear the idea of desecrating this somehow still beautiful corpse just to return a trinket. But was it merely a trinket? Or something more? It had definitely been something more to Rae. Disturbing the dead was not something to be taken lightly in any belief system. *No. I will keep it,* Elwick decided. Rae would surely have wanted him to have it, would she not have?

Moses swore a promise to her then and there, one he could most definitely keep, unlike the last one he had made to her. "I will treasure this all the days of my life, Rae." Holding the amulet tightly to his chest, Elwick paused a moment to reverently gaze one last time upon both of the little gray girls before him. Rae's head still rested on Tabitha's. They appeared only to be resting peacefully, and not gone from this universe. "Protect their souls, o' Lord," he whispered. "Let them find the peace they so deserve."

With that, he followed Barbara and the others out from under the Observation Dome, and off the *Emerald Pearl,* for the first and last time.

65

GSCS *Nightingale*

"Captain?" PO2 Guy Connelly's voice violently tore Moses away from his tranquility.

"Captain, the *Jeffrey Buker* just jumped in."

Elwick sat at his beaten-up desk in his office on board the *Nightingale,* motionless in the hard, functional chair. He turned Rae's silver amulet over and over in his fingers, ensuring the delicate silver chain remained untangled as he twirled it. He stared at the star-shaped flower inside the circle for what seemed like an eternity.

Barbara Laskey's distant voice interrupted his non-thoughts. "Captain?" Moses barely heard it.

After a few seconds, Connelly called him again. "Captain did you copy my last?"

Elwick's eyes moved to the screen at his elbow, and he keyed the comm. "Aye."

"The RSS *Buker—*"

"I heard you."

"Right."

"XO?"

"Ozzie here, Captain."

"Did Doc come back with a completed report of the pods we collected yet?"

"Aye."

"Let's have it."

"Two were empty. I'm assuming those had been Rae and Tabitha's. Eight of them contained mummified human remains, which we expected. And of the six that were still operational, Doc reports all six patients are alive and in recovery. She's still assessing radiation exposure, but it sounds like all but one of them have been very-well protected by their ancient pods. The ones who are awake aren't on their feet yet, but they've begun asking questions."

Moses perked up. He looked at the woman sitting across from him, who smiled big and clasped her hands over her heart. "Thank you, Lord," he whispered. Then to Osterland, "Roger! I'll get Barbara down there before Doc Galloway's horrendous bedside manner gives them all heart attacks when she blurts out what the current date is."

"Ozzie, have we identified which ones are Rae and Tabby's mother and brother?"

"Unknown. I'll find out."

"Aye."

"Also, we're to turn all survivors over to the Navy once Doc signs off that they're ambulatory. Or at least able to be moved without harm."

Elwick laughed. "Galloway's gonna drag that out as long as she can, I'm sure. They'll have to send the Master at Arms over and wheel those folks outta her sick bay by force, if she has anything to say about it."

"I'm sure you're right," Osterland agreed. "One last thing, sir. Admiral Frontera suggests a Zero-Nine-Hundred start time tomorrow morning for the memorial service."

Barbara's eyes grew wide. "Frontera came all the way out here?"

"Send concur." Moses replied. "Thanks for the update, Ozzie. Elwick out."

Barbara shifted in her seat. "Has our old friend dropped you a line yet? I'm hoping he won't be expecting you to report to his office until *after* the service…?"

"He did. His communiqué consisted of exactly three short sentences. I won't bore you with the details but the word 'disappointed' was in there, along with 'out of character', and a time and date he *suggests,* read *demands,* I report to his office. And yes, he's given me a stay of execution until after the service. Preliminary discussion prior to legal counsel in prep for Captain's Mast. Can't wait." He glanced up at his dress uniform, now hanging on a hook near the door to his stateroom. "Eh, probably high time someone on this ship ended up at the receiving end of a Court Martial anyway."

Laskey shrugged. "Maybe it won't be so bad. At least something good came of today. Six somethings!"

Elwick nodded. "Six very good somethings." He sighed. "I wish there had have been a couple dozen more. Or at least two more."

"You did all anyone could have done, and you handled it brilliantly."

Moses scoffed. "Lot of good it did."

"It *did* do a lot of good! You comforted two little lost souls who would have died terrified and alone had your leadership of this crew not been there for them. You didn't have to take on this mission. Scuttlebutt says you were directed to turn the ship around. Ignore the distress call. But you didn't. Which is what I assume this Captain's Mast is all about."

"Heard that, did you?" He sighed, wondering if the XO let it slip, or if Connelly or one of the other nosy apes on board had cracked the classified code out of morbid curiosity. If so, there may be another Captain's Mast in the *Nightingale's* future. But that won't be his problem, it will be Ozzie's. Or that of some random captain who doesn't yet know he's about to receive a Triple S and all the scoundrels that come with it. But none of that was Barbara's fault or concern, and she was awaiting an answer he couldn't officially provide.

"I'll assume so, based on your silence. Without our intervention, the RNA Navy would have taken matters in their own hands in the name of national and galactic security, and that destroyer out there would have surely scuttled the *Pearl* before anyone ever discovered the fate of those two very delicate, very lovely, very precocious little souls."

"Had they boarded that ship they would have found them, just like we did."

"But they would have meant nothing to them. Rae and Tabitha actually meant something to us. And their story will mean something to their mother and brother. When I get around to telling them, that is. I plan to give them a day or two to recover first, but I doubt their mother will want to wait that long."

"You know the first thing she'll ask isn't going to be 'where am I?' or 'what happened?' or 'what day is it?', but 'where are my daughters?'!"

Barbara's volume shot up. "Oh, I know it's the first thing *I'd* ask!"

"What I want to know is something none of us will ever find out."

"Oh? What's that?"

"The cause of the accident. Which I think was anything but. There's just too much evidence of sabotage. The premature jettisoning of all the escape pods. The destruction of the MEVA craft. The almost surgical damage to the Captain's Yacht, the one thing with its own mini Zee Dee core that could have allowed any and all crew to eventually get back to occupied space."

"Really, Moses? Nothing about the murders?"

"The murders! I mean come on, that right there is enough to open an international, interplanetary, interstellar investigation! But what does the Navy do?"

"Quarantine."

"Quarantine! Which will ensure no media, no historical organizations, no nothing! That ship is a hundred years old! It's got ten times more historical significance than this stupid pen even!"

"Why do you keep that nasty thing, anyway?" Barbara asked, motioning to the pen Kelly liked to toy with on occasion.

"Dale would have to kill you if I told you," he muttered, and quickly changed the subject. "The *Pearl* disappeared without a trace seventy-four years ago," he went on raising his voice once more, "and lo and behold someone found it, but now it's going to be swept under the rug. Like none of this ever happened!"

"But the survivors will talk. They're displaced out of time, they have to be re-acclimated into society. What will be their excuse for being three-quarters of a century out of date with the zeitgeist and just general knowledge?"

Elwick shook his head. "I don't know, the military will come up with something. We'll all have to sign nondisclosure agreements, and be debriefed. You knew that, right?"

"Not until now. Ah! That explains why the comms are suddenly on the blink."

"Communications blackout. Enacted before anyone even read my report, which I'm sure will be redacted heavily. As you well know, all this is standard procedure when sailors come across something the government doesn't want getting out."

"Should have known," Barbara said, standing up and turning her back to Elwick. "Fucking Navy," she muttered.

"Barbara!" Moses exclaimed. "I didn't even know you knew such words!"

The old woman shrugged. "I looked it up," she joked. "Sometimes certain words just fit the situation."

Elwick chuckled. "Yeah. I guess so. You heading down to Sick Bay?"

"I am. Gotta head off ol' Doc Galloway at the pass, as they used to say in the old holos." Before she reached the door, however, she turned around. "Oh my God, how could I have forgotten?"

"What?"

Barbara stared at him a moment and smiled. "I found their pictures."

Moses' eyes bulged. "Rae and Tabitha's?"

"You want to see them?"

"Are you kidding!?"

Barbara walked around Moses' desk and operated the built-in controls.

"You could have led off with that, you know!"

Her smile grew large. "I was saving it for the right time."

Two 3-D, holographic images appeared above his desk. Moses stared into the faces of two vivacious young ladies he had been blessed to know for too short a time. Rae and Tabby smiled beautifully in their passport holos, staring back at Moses from three-quarters of a century ago. They were dressed in their quaint period clothing, similar to what they had been wearing when they died. Their full names displayed at the lower left of each three-dimensional image.

Rae Annabel Marshall.

Tabitha Lenore Marshall.

"They were adorable, weren't they, Moe?"

"Beyond words."

To Elwick's delight, Barbara had found holos of each passenger. Hugh Marshall, the girls' father, had been a strong-looking man. In his official passport photo, he wore the scruffy beard of a seasoned miner. Carmella, their mother, had the most mesmerizing green eyes Moses had ever seen. In her holograph, her long, golden-brown hair was braided beautifully on top of her head, with a thick, excess braid falling upon one shoulder and down past her breast. She looked to Elwick like someone who would most definitely own a book of Earth prayers. He could see from where Rae and Tabby got their amazing smiles. Their eyes, however, were all Hugh. Elwick looked closer at the young girls' photographs and discovered Rae sported two gazing gems of deep emerald, while Tabitha's irises were the refreshing azure of a cloudless day.

Their brother, James Sean Marshall, was—and likely still is—a strapping, soon-to-be adult of seventeen. He smiled mischievously in his photo, and had the same stocky build as his father, but the same light blue eyes of his littlest sister.

Probably ornery just like her, he mused. "I'll be sure to say a quick prayer for their souls tonight."

"I already did, but one more can't hurt."

Moses blinked, taken aback. "I didn't think you were religious!"

"I'm not."

He laughed. His gaze fell upon two model ships that sat on the shelf by the door. One was the model of the *Republic Star Ship Elliott* that Dale enjoyed playing with seemingly every time he came to Moses' cabin. But he knew the reason for that; Moses and Dale served together on that old boat in another life, dozens of years and thousands of light years ago. Next to it stood a majestic Tall Ship from a distant age, when men used only the power of the wind and the currents to master the mighty seas of Earth. He followed the lines of its deck, admired the full sails. He took a deep breath, and imagined the salty sea breeze filling his nostrils. He yearned for those days, for a simpler time. When the only worries were the well-known perils the Good Earth had to offer. The mysteries of outer space—if even considered at all—were far, far away. "It's not fair, what happened to these people." he said.

"Normally I would spit out some trite saying when someone uttered that phrase to me," Barbara replied, "like, 'whoever said life was fair?'. But in this case, I wholeheartedly agree with you."

Moses nodded.

"This ship would have probably become a shrine, were it not in so dangerous a region. And veiled in such secrecy." Barbara shook her head. "Thanks to the Navy keeping all this under wraps, the families of the *Pearl's* crew and passengers may never know what happened to their loved ones. Such a shame. Families are the most important thing there is, when all is said and done."

She said more, but Elwick didn't hear her. His thoughts fell upon Alena. And Zoey. How he longed for earlier days. When life had been wonderful. When he had a family, not an estranged wife and the memory of a daughter. But Zoey wasn't estranged by her own accord. No. By his hand alone. It was only after Barbara called his name a few times that Moses realized he had been staring off into nothing. Again.

"You okay, Captain?"

"Yeah. Sure. Sorry." Moses checked his timepiece. "There's time… There's still time!"

"Time for what?"

He jumped up from his desk and darted into his stateroom. Moses gently draped Rae's necklace over Alena and Zoey's photo, ensuring the circled star flower did not cover either of their beautiful faces. "I have something I need to be getting to, Doctor," he called over his shoulder. "My apologies for kicking you out!"

"No, no, I need to be getting down to Sick Bay anyway," Barbara said from his office.

"Okay. Please close the door on your way out?"

"Certainly. Everything okay?"

He poked his head back into the office and smiled at the good and wise counselor. "It will be," he said, nodding. "It will be."

Moses heard Barbara closing and latching the door behind her as he donned a fresh shirt, then bolted into the head and combed his hair. His beard too, for it was a scraggly mess. Satisfied, he returned to his beat-up old desk, and breathed deeply in an attempt to calm his nerves. He gazed at the overhead, as if toward Heaven, even though directions in space were meaningless; they only depended on the observer's point-of-view. He figured God would understand. "I have been a selfish fool, haven't I? And I needed a hard slap in the face. Thank you for that." He let the tears flow once more. For Rae. For Tabby. For Alena. And for Zoey, from whom he had distanced himself for nearly a full year. And for what? Anger. Guilt. Pain. Shame. Regret. A longing for revenge. He had punished Zoey for far too long. It was time for a long-overdue reconciliation.

Way past time.

Unfortunately, he couldn't do it in person. He was still some thirty thousand light years away from his wife, and he had no idea when SENTCORPS would allow him to return to Earth. If ever. Heck, he could be in prison before the week was out. He may never see her again.

He couldn't wait another day. Another hour. Another minute! *Sorry, Zoey, a face-to-face holo-call is the best I can do.*

66

GSCS *Nightingale*

"Oh muh God," is all she said before long-fingered hands covered her mouth and nose.

She looked affright, but to Moses' eyes, she couldn't have been more beautiful. "Hi, Zoey Joey," he said in as sweet a voice as he could.

She simply stared at him for a moment. "Is it really you? I mean, I saw the name on the incomin' message, but I figgered it *had* ta be a glitch or somethin'! Or Kelly playin' another prank on me!"

Moses laughed. "No, it's really me, babydoll. How are you?"

"Whew! Ya gotta give me a minute, Moe! My hair's a mess! I just woke up!" She pulled several strawberry-blonde strands away from her face and mouth and tucked them behind one ear. "Heck I'm still not sure if I'm not just dreamin' here!"

"You're not dreaming, darling. I've just been through something life-changing, and I think it's way past time to, well, let you know I still love you, and see if you still love me."

Her face twisted all up in that cute way it does when Zoey couldn't for the life of her figure something out. "What are you talkin' 'bout, Moe? Why wouldn't I love you!?" She scoffed. "If anythin', I'm the one over here's been wonderin' if you still loved *me*! I mean, it's been… well, it's been a whole mess o' months now, hasn't it?"

"Since we sat down for a real conversation? Not just a necessary text-only message? Yes. And that's my fault. All my fault. I admit that."

"Yer darn right it is!" she shouted. But then she immediately followed that up with, "I'm sorry, I shouldn'ta said that. It's just… whew! Seven months of not seein' your husband's face and barely hearin' from him all that time will do that to a girl! A wife can only survive for so long on the occasional un-intimate note before her head starts a-comin' up with all sorts of things!"

Had it been that long? He had thought Kelly was exaggerating earlier. "It's perfectly alright, babydoll, I deserved that. I completely understand. I've been a fool."

"Yeah ya have!" she replied. "I needed ya, Moe." Tears welled up out of nowhere. "I mean, I didn't know if ya wanted a divorce or if ya just wanted ta forget you ever met me, or what!"

A pang shot through his chest. "Oh, Zoey, of course I didn't want a divorce! And I could never forget you! I just… I just didn't know how to process what happened. I didn't know what to say to you. I felt so much pain, so much guilt, so much anger—"

"What, ya think you're the only one ta run through a whole gamut of emotions? She was my little girl, too, ya know! I've been on a rollercoaster over here! Most days are okay. Some days are bad. Really bad. Other days, I'm just numb. And I've got no one to anchor me. No one to curl up with. No one to tell me it's gonna be okay. I mean, sure, I've got Kelly, but she's out gallivantin' around with you all the time! But at least she calls me once a week," she added under her breath.

"I know, I know, you're right about all of it, baby. You are. I just didn't know… I didn't know how to handle this. I was angry with you, at Kelly, at God, at Alena's abductor, at everyone."

Zoey said nothing to this, merely stared at him across the light years, tears now streaming down her beautiful, full cheeks.

"I blamed you all, all this time. I couldn't understand why God would let something like that happen, so I blamed Him, too. What I had done to warrant his wrath? What you might have done. What Alena might had done. And I know it's nothing any of us did. I just wanted someone to blame. And I took it out on the one person I never should have."

"Moe, God had nuthin' ta do with what that terrible man did to our little girl. I guess it coulda been a woman, but that tent was filthy! No woman would let her campsite get like that! No, sir. Messy, maybe, but not outright disgustin'. No, it was definitely a man. And if I ever catch that man, Lord help me, what I'll do to him…"

Moses nodded. The idea of someone camping in the woods right behind his house was bad enough. But a sexual predator? God only knows how long he had been watching, waiting for just the right moment to strike.

That's right. God *did* know how long. Why didn't he do anything to save her? God also knew about Rae and Tabitha. Why didn't he do anything to save them? In his younger days, Moses might have thought it was because Rae and her mother practiced witchcraft. He had decided now, after years of experience and introspection, that notion was ridiculous.

No truly loving god would condemn an innocent Christian girl and her wayward sister for the sins of their mother. Or would He? Their mother had indeed survived, and would soon be told her daughters and husband were gone. If that wasn't punishment for sacrilege, what was?

"Are ya comin' home?" Zoey asked.

Moses lowered his head. "Not just yet, babydoll. I still have some things to—" He cut himself short. Why sugarcoat it? Why keep anything from her at this point? She should know her husband's fate, right? Decide for herself whether she wants to stay with him, not held hostage like he had been doing to her all these long months. "I may not get back to Earth for a while, Zoey. Possibly a long while. I got myself into some trouble. If I'm court martialed—"

"Court martialed!?" Zoey shouted. "Moses Ulysses Elwick, what have you gotten yerself into?"

He sighed. "Doing the right thing. For once! Well, in my eyes anyway. Hopefully in God's eyes. But not in the eyes of the SENTCORPS or the RNA Navy. I went on a rescue despite being ordered not to."

"Did ya save the people, at least?"

"We saved six of them. Out of..." he tried to count, "I think twenty-five, maybe thirty. Actually, we don't know the exact number yet, some people were likely blown out into space and we haven't located them yet. We may never. And we may never know just how many people were aboard the ship in the first place. We had started going through the logs, but the Navy confiscated those before we even scratched the surface. Made us purge them from our system and everything."

"Really? Wow, that's a new one. What type a' naval ship was it? Some kinda big, new, secret boat or somethin'? Somethin' you and Kelly can't tell me about? Uh-gain?"

"It wasn't a Navy ship at all. Civilian vessel."

"Civilian!" Zoey exclaimed. "What right does the Navy have to it, then? This is all completely irregular, as Dale likes to say."

Moses was treading dangerous waters, and knew darn well he should stop talking. But he wanted to tell his wife everything, like he always had, even though he knew it would complicate her life and violate several security policies to boot. Not only get him deeper into trouble, but possibly her as well. He had said too much already. He waved it all off. "Look, Zoey, it's complicated. The important thing is, irregular or not, it doesn't matter now. It's all locked away behind closed doors, and it's none of our business. What matters is that I love you. I love you and have since the day we met. And I hope you still love me, despite how dumb I've been, and will surely be in the future. There's nothing to forgive, neither with you or with Kelly. I'm sorry, *truly* sorry, that I wasn't there for you when you needed me the most. When we needed each other, to find strength in one another. To be each other's rock. It'll never happen again, Zoey. I promise that. If I can just have another chance, I promise I'll never abandon you again."

Zoey was crying a full geyser of tears now, and Moses couldn't understand what she said next due to how much sobbing was taking place. Sometimes he couldn't understand her words through her thick accent anyway, but now it proved basically impossible. "I can't understand what you're saying, baby. I'm sorry."

She waved her hands in front of the camera and shook her head. Moses took that to mean it didn't matter. She took some deep breaths and tried to compose herself, wiping tears from her cheeks and then drying her hands on a pillow she presently pulled onto her lap. "You've made my night, Moses Elwick. My week. My whole year! I love you, Moey Poey."

"I love you, too, Zoey Joey."

67

RSS *Jeffrey Buker*: Sick Bay

Ezra Mi-Ling's eyelids snapped open.

Where am I?

He did not recognize this room, but recognized it had to be a hospital.

He tried to turn his head, but it wouldn't move it. He could move his eyes, though. Next to him lay a female with a whole lot of brown hair, most of which had been tucked into a sloppy bun under her head. She lay on a thick hospital bed, her back raised slightly. Above her bed was a large, boxy machine. A blue laser shone from a small protrusion on the box and painted small but bright patterns on various points on her mostly naked body, pausing from time to time before hopping to another location. Ezra Mi-Ling soon realized he lay in a similar position, also naked, with a large, boxy device hanging precariously over him as well. Out of the corner of his eye he caught a glimpse of a similar blue light dancing around his own body. He then realized he couldn't move anything at all, with the exception of his eyes. Some kind of induced temporary paralysis, he assumed, due to the medical procedure currently underway. He wondered if he they had intended him to wake up prematurely? Probably not.

Thankfully there was little pain. He wondered if the doctors had somehow pinched his spinal cord at the neck? Possibly even severed it with nanobots that stood ready to repair the damage on command? Such things had been readily available to even urgent care clinics in his day, but did they have such things in *this* time? This unknown, future time?

He realized then that he had no idea what the date might be. He could have been in that pod a full year. Ten years, even. A century? Very probably not; those old pods couldn't have been rated for more than two decades, tops.

Around the room lay others, also in beds like his. On the other side of the middle-aged woman lay a young boy. Next to him lay a middle-aged man. Finally, the last two, an older man and an older woman, probably a couple. The first three looked American or possibly European, but the two older patients appeared to be of African descent. None were a threat. None knew anything about him or why he was there. In fact, he reasoned, the medical staff and authorities of this vessel or station knew nothing of importance either, or else he would surely be in shackles. Unless the doctors weren't planning on repairing his spine at all, if indeed that's how they had immobilized him.

He had been fortunate the transport ship hadn't been completely destroyed in the deliberate de-folding into the nebula. He yearned to learn of his level of success. If the timeline had been altered, and in what way? If Emperor Wu was finally the rightful ruler of China, and how much China had prospered due to his faithful service. But right now, he would be happy merely learning the date. The year. The century!

Above his hospital bed floated a glowing, ever-updating chart, that told the doctors and nurses details about their patient. He focused on the name, for *that* above all else would make him a target for enemies both Chinese and Republic. It was hard to read in the bright overhead lights of the surgical room, but he eventually made it out.

"Patient Name: Greg Napharr," the chart read.

Greg Napharr!? Who the hell is that?

"Gender: Male (assumption due to presence of Y chromosome)."

"Age: Unknown; 29 based on various biological samples."

"Nationality: Chinese based on DNA."

"Disposition: Passenger, Survivor #3 of 6, Civilian Transport Ship *Emerald Pearl.*"

Mi-Ling couldn't help but laugh, but it hurt, and what came out sounded more like a series of staccato breaths. He only then realized he wasn't breathing on his own, and that his attempt at laughter had interrupted an auto-breathing machine that lay out of his sight. He settled down and merely smiled at his good fortune. Ling had escaped, and more completely than even *he* had planned, for no one would be looking for him. Not as Ezra Mi-Ling, not even by his given name: *Kho Lok.* But as Greg Napharr…

He was certain Napharr was not the name of that undercover, former RNA special forces plant that had disposed of his every means off that ratty old transport, but Kho Lok had got him in the end, in the aft alcove. *And with his own weapon!* The agent had been a formidable and honorable opponent. Lok regretted his death, as he would any person of respectable profession, possessing learned and applied talent, knowledge, strategy, and skill. Wisdom, that took longer. Wisdom was something of which Lok had been planning to be a student all his life.

As Kho Lok's gaze followed the healing blue laser light, he tried to say the mysterious name out loud. "Greg Napharr." *Likely,* he mused, *Napharr was that crazy man who tried to assist the agent...* The unskilled but admittedly brave passenger who valiantly gave his life in the blink of an eye when Lok broke his neck. And who later gave up his cryo pod, so that Ezra Mi-Ling/Kho Lok could live.

And continue his work.

Fortune and Luck smiled upon him. Now he could continue to serve and bestow glory and honor to the one true Emperor of China, Wu Heng Guang, who surely had taken control of the country and islands that rightfully belonged to China by now. Possibly, he ruled the entire continent! *Not much more,* he decided, *or every label around here would be written in Cantonese or Mandarin.* Lok soured as he listened to the quiet ramblings of the nursing staff, all of whom spoke English. That meant there was still a *lot* of work to do. Now that he had escaped with his life, and more importantly, his identity intact, there was plenty of time to plan.

Kho Lok closed his eyes, and allowed himself to fall into a much-needed slumber. He would need to be fully healed for what was to come.

68

GSCS *Nightingale*

In the mirror of his small, personal head, Captain Moses Elwick squared away his tie after donning the jacket of his Service Dress Blue uniform. Due to it being winter back on Earth, the "Blue" dress uniform—actually black in color—was to be worn as opposed to the white, which is normally reserved for summertime. While the seasons mattered not one iota in the depths of space, the Navy, and therefore the Sentinel Corps, still followed tradition. Plus, Moses decided dark colors more appropriate for a funeral, anyway. The color matched his mood.

Satisfied all rank and medals were properly aligned, he made his way down to the Mess Decks on Deck Two, where the crew and company had already assembled.

Upon seeing Elwick, every voice hushed, and they all assumed a position of crisp attention. Each looked sharper and more cleaned-up than he could ever remember. The only crew not present were the still-Officer of the Day Lieutenant Kitner and Helmsman Starman Apprentice Burgess. Elwick imagined them standing dutifully at attention behind the helm one deck up, watching the service on a 3-D display above the pilot's central console.

"At ease," Elwick said softly. The crowd parted for him to meander to a window towards the port side of the wide room, where a narrow podium had been set up for the event. Moses stood beside, rather than behind the podium. and turned to face the crowd. The reddish light of the nebula washed upon everyone present.

He picked out Dale Masterson and Antonio Bruno. Moses found comfort in the faces of his two closest comrades-in-arms. They regarded him solemnly, and Bruno gave him a tight-lipped, funeral-appropriate smile. He returned the gesture.

He picked out Kelly Crawford. Her usually explosive red hair, now up in a tidy, regulation bun, combined with an unusually clean jumper, complimented her in ways he never realized were possible. The standard jumper, also black this time of year and worn by all enlisted men and women of E-6 grade and below, was often called the "Cracker Jack" uniform by landlubbers outside the Navy. Moses didn't have a clue as to why, probably some tradition from centuries ago he never bothered to look up. Come September, Kelly's uniform would not be all that different from his, Dale's and Bruno's—a crisp suit and pants. Or the conservative, regulation skirt, if she chose to expose those mile-long knacker crackers, but he would let her decide that detail. He wondered if she had spoken with her sister Zoey since he had. By the way she was smiling at him, probably. He nodded acknowledgement.

With family by his side, Moses could get through any day. With his buddies-in-arms by his side, he could get through any mission. But they also reminded him of shipmates lost in the war stories that haunted his memories as much as little Alena. It was time to put the ghosts of the past behind him. Move forward. Alena would want that. So would Rae and Tabitha.

The events of the last two days sparked a revelation in Moses he wished he could have found on his own, but could not. Moses' experience with Rae and Tabby would heal the broken connection between Husband and Wife. It would mark the beginning of a new era for a family torn apart, that would finally be put back together. Eventually, anyway. Once his judicial punishment was complete. Whatever that turned out to be. He mentally checked off his crimes, of which insubordination at the Flag level seemed the least damaging of all, and that was pretty bad in itself. He faced charges of commandeering of a SENTCORPS vessel, endangering the crew of said vessel, haphazard if not neglectful use of SENTCORPS equipment (the vessel and everything within her), breach of national security, breach of galactic security, and whatever else the RNA Navy and the Sentinel Corps wanted to pile on. He figured he might see the light of day again by his ninetieth birthday.

Elwick turned to face the as-yet officially unnamed nebula. On behalf of the *Nightingale* crew, he would suggest it be named the Marshall Nebula, after Rae and Tabitha. Even though they had left the damn thing two full light years behind, the red cloud still filled the 180-degree observation windows of the *Nightingale's* Mess Decks. Elwick had a feeling of dread when gazing upon it; this particular emission nebula, while beautiful from a distance, harbored mysteries that should remain forever hidden from the human race. Only terrible things could be found there. Pain. Heartache. Death.

He looked to his left. The RSS *Shawnee* had parked alongside the *Nightingale* specifically for the service. It had spent the last several hours towing the *Emerald Pearl* out of the nebula and had deposited it several thousand kilometers away. For what purpose it had been left there, Moses could only speculate. But that sense of dread included it as well. Mixed with a little fear and not a little anxiety.

On the other side of the *Shawnee* lay the RSS *Jeffrey Buker,* where Moses was to report immediately following the funeral. He may as well go in his Service Blues for his ass-chewing and likely arrest. It never hurt to look sharp in such situations; perhaps it would ever-so-slightly sway the Judicial Board when they reviewed the hologram.

Moses looked about, but saw no other vessels in the sky other than those two. He had hoped to see at least one media boat. He had dreamed of looking out to see a small chunk of the fleet for such an historic occasion! But alas, he figured the dead were lucky as-is. They could just as easily have been met by a lone destroyer and a lone missile, by the sound of that top secret communiqué and the obvious hush-hush nature of this incident. And Elwick himself was lucky he had been allowed to remain on the *Nightingale* with a front row seat to the memorial, rather than facing four, ten-by-ten gray walls over on the *Buker*. Possibly lucky the *Nightingale* had even been allowed to remain in the area. Not that it *could have* been sent away, what with an inoperable space-folding drive, but it could have been ordered into the *Buker's* cavernous fighter bay, and the crew locked down tight in guest quarters.

Elwick's brow furrowed. *Actually, why hadn't that happened...?*

The service began on time at 0800, or "eight o'clock sharp." Admiral Frontera, still onboard the *Buker*, thankfully, and said a few opening words. They were the usual, customary generic things Fleet Officers say when they're about to bury someone at sea or in deep space. Elwick didn't pay much attention, but rather stared at the slowly rotating *Pearl*. This sailor, while a good man with whom he had shared many a battlefield, didn't know these young girls. Hadn't spent the last umpteen hours fruitlessly trying to save them. Hadn't spent a seeming eternity listening to them die. Experiencing their deaths via a radio window to the past which shouldn't even exist.

After Frontera finished speaking, Dr. Barbara Laskey stepped up to the podium. Elwick turned his attention her direction. Her voice filled not only the room but the entirety of the *Nightingale* via the 1MC circuit, not to mention every passageway of the other two ships alongside them.

"Shane Timmins," she read from her notes, "Captain of the *Emerald Pearl,* born 2399, graduated RNA Naval Academy in 2421. Retired from the Navy after twenty-six years, and joined the Merchant Marines, in which he served until his death at age sixty-eight, in 2467, seventy-four years ago. Final assignment: Captain of the transport ship, *Emerald Pearl.*"

Barbara then told a brief history of the *Emerald Pearl,* how it had started life christened the Republic Star Ship *Holloway*. "The *Holloway* served the Republic of North America in a time of peace, between the two Asia-America wars. Upon decommissioning, after twenty-three years of worthy service, it underwent several renovations to become a civilian transport, ferrying passengers of all socio-economic classes across the vast Milky Way. The *Pearl* was mysteriously lost among the sea of stars in 2467, but found by the stalwart crew of the GSCS *Nightingale* in 2541."

Moses smiled at the blatant self-promotion for posterity.

Barbara went on to honor the *Emerald Pearl's* Executive Officer and other key members of its ill-fated crew. She was somehow able to piece together short, quick blubs of each crewmember—the ones they knew about anyway—and to honor each deceased passenger. She elaborated on the Marshalls. Elwick expected nothing less. "Hugh Marshall had been an illegal weapons smuggler," she began.

Elwick's eyes bulged.

"…who, while in prison," Laskey continued, "was extraordinarily productive, earning advanced degrees in geology, chemistry and mineralogy. There he accepted the Christian faith, and met his wife upon his release four years later. Soon afterward, Jamie, Rae and Tabitha came along, and Hugh took the more difficult but much more rewarding path of dedicated father and hard working off-world miner."

Elwick looked around to see faces showing equal surprise.

"He received accolades from his company, earning the title 'Most Innovative Engineer' in the year 2466, just one year prior to the *Emerald Pearl's* ill-fated voyage."

Moses nodded. *That explains why his daughters were so good at, well, everything they had been good at.*

Barbara continued. "Hugh was offered the position of governor of what was to be a new mining colony in the then-recently discovered Preia Byoea system. Due to the inherent dangers of daily mining, his wife had urged him to take the more comfortable, safer, and higher-paying position, even though it meant leaving Earth for an indefinite number of years. Hugh Marshall jumped at the opportunity. He did not die at the business end of a gun—as a judge once warned him he might, according to court records—or in the depths of a hostile moon deep underground, but while ushering his family to a better life."

Dr. Laskey then told those assembled of Rae and Tabitha's achievements in Educata, to include some of their extracurricular activities. "Rae was an accomplished sailor. She had won two first-place trophies racing sail boats with her father at a young age."

Ha! Moses smiled inwardly. *So, she* did *know port from starboard after all!*

"Tabby held a deep interest in science and technology," Barbara added, "likely influenced by her father. This probably explains her understanding of advanced concepts, and her ability to quickly manipulate the *Emerald Pearl's* complex systems, assisting the *Nightingale* in its rescue efforts."

As I said, Moses proudly told himself.

Barbara touched the screen before her, indicating the turn of a page. "These brave souls will not be forgotten. While they perished, six survived. Their names follow."

What? She discovered the names of the survivors in the pods? As she read, Moses listened for anything familiar. None of the names rang any bells at all. He wondered if any were familiar to Naval Intelligence, members of which were surely hanging on every word as diligently as everyone on those Mess Decks. Two names Moses did recognize: Mrs. Carmella Marshall and Mr. James Marshall, or 'Jamie,' as he had been called by his sisters.

"I am told Rae and Tabitha's mother and brother are still in medically-induced comas to assist in recovery following their extremely long hibernation, but we will soon welcome them into the Twenty-Sixth Century with open arms."

The room erupted with murmurs. All around him, Moses saw smiles.

"May your gods bless all of you on your journeys. *Deliver All...*"

"*Thwart Death!*" Elwick said reverently, his voice joining a chorus of others in the room. He nodded to Barbara. Her conclusion with the Search and Rescue motto had been the perfect touch.

Elwick took her place at the podium. It took longer than expected to collect himself, but the crew stood motionless, waiting in revered silence. He drew in a long breath and forced out the words. "I only knew Rae and Tabby for… not even twenty-four hours. But in that time, I grew to love them. They proved intelligent, clever, vivacious, precocious, and unbelievably strong to the very end. Stronger than I." He paused to take a breath, and to hold back tears. "All day yesterday, I battled with something. I asked myself, why would God allow something like this to happen? Why does He allow children to die? Why do aberrations of nature exist? Like these wormholes that thwarted our rescue efforts? Why allow us to get to know these little girls at all, if the experience was only going to end in heartache?"

He paused to let his crew and anyone else listening to think about the question for a moment.

"With the Lord's help," he continued, "I came to a conclusion. Perhaps not an absolute answer, but one I can live with, one that will allow me to sleep at night. *Is* this wormhole an aberration of nature? That anomaly came about without any human intervention. Perhaps God, or Mother Nature, or whatever deity you may believe in, made it specifically for us? Perhaps our purpose here was not to be a witness to tragedy for tragedy's sake, rather, perhaps it was to aid in finally solving the mystery of the *Emerald Pearl,* gone missing these past seventy-four years? Perhaps it was a mission of mercy? To be here, at least in some capacity, at the end of the lives of two beautiful little souls. Souls that God would not allow to die alone and afraid. To provide these little angels some comfort in knowing they wouldn't be forgotten. To know that their memory would live on in the minds of so, so many." Elwick chewed those final words, hoping it would remain accurate, even after what would surely be days of naval debriefings and the subsequent government coverup that was certainly coming.

He remained at the podium to let those in attendance know he wasn't finished, but he found it was becoming increasingly difficult to remain upright. He grabbed both edges of the wooden podium, found his military bearing, and continued. "Let us not forget the six souls who we pulled from yonder hydrogen cloud. They may have been stranded out there for all eternity if not for the efforts of the brave men and women of the GSCS *Nightingale*." Yes, he joined Barbara in tooting their own horn with that one, but his intent was to toss well-deserved accolades to his crew while he still could. "So, I offer you, that these wormholes, these 'devilish gremlins' as they are called by one particularly seasoned and lovable sailor, may not represent the evil these anomalies have been feared to be. During this mission, they became enablers of not only comfort and closure, but of continuing life."

He took one last, deep breath, pushing the tears down as best he could. "I will leave you with that thought to ponder, and to draw your own conclusions, and find peace within your own faith or spirituality." He brought himself to the position of attention and said in a resounding, confident tenor, "*Deliver All...*"

The chorus rose again: "*Thwart Death!*" A bit louder this time, but somehow more somber.

With that, Elwick stepped away from the podium and focused on the nebula. Soft music played a remorseful tune, and a few sang the words quietly. Moses did not bother to wipe the streams from his face this time.

While his crew sang, a white streak departed from the RSS *Jeffrey Buker* in the direction of the *Emerald Pearl*. Elwick's heart stopped. Just as he had feared, a lone missile had the *Pearl's* name on it. The weapon soon disappeared as the kilometers grew between it and the vessels standing vigil.

Moses closed his eyes. He lost track of the seconds. He thought of Rae and Tabby. Their tiny bodies snuggling on that ancient, icy couch, still hugging one another in a futile attempt to stay warm. Embracing as sisters. As friends. So far from home. Alone.

But also, *not* alone.

A brief flash forced his eyes open. A small ball of white light appeared in the distance where the *Pearl* lay moment before. It was as if everyone present together witnessed the birth of a new star before their eyes. A new giver of life before the blood red curtain that filled half the sky.

But it was not a star. Rather, the equivalent of a reverent burial at sea. It flared twice more as it ignited minor gasses in its vicinity, then began to sparkle and fade. Moses stared at the tiny light until it winked out completely. "Goodbye, my little flowers. You're free. Go now. Find your way home."

Appendices

Appendix A	on Space-Folding Drives
Appendix B	on Defying Gravity
Appendix C	on Ion Base Factors
Appendix D	on “QBert” QE RADAR

Appendix A

On Space Folding Drives

QE Communiqué to Mrs. Elwick, Zoey A., from Lieutenant Junior Grade Elwick, Moses U., RSS *Helling*, RNA Navy, 10 August 2521:

Dearest Zoey, my musings for the day…

I have to admit, I'm a little worried about this "jumping" business. Going from one place to another by folding space. I understand we travel within the quantum foam, the substructure of the universe. I don't even know where that is.

The worst part about it is being aware of the passage of time inside what I'm calling the purgatory of folded space, the netherworld visited between physical locations. In my experience, it only ever lasts a maximum of a few seconds, ten tops, but I've heard of people being stuck in there for not merely seconds, not even minutes, but hours! Talk about a living hell! It's not so much the sensation itself, but the terror of not knowing if you'll ever "unfold" back into the real world.

Not to worry you or anything, but I don't want to keep secrets from you, either. You should know the risks I have to take, just so you're prepared…

I have learned that, when a catastrophic Zhédié system failure occurs, it means a "Zee Dee" drive could do a number of nasty things. One of the better possibilities being to fold its ship into something that no longer exists when viewed edge-on, and then never return it to three-dimensional space! But these instances are very rare, or so I'm told.

I think it's better to be vaporized in my own universe rather than lost in another, in which I might never be found. Or are the crews of such ships killed outright?

Hopefully.

But if not, could these people even age and die in two-dimensional space? Or in a parallel, but still three-dimensional one? That might not be too bad, depending. But what if they ended up in some weird dimension where their bodies didn't even really exist? Could they die, then?

I figure some part of them must still live on in these nether worlds—the brain, or at least the consciousness—if people are aware of the passage of time while within the quantum world. I imagine it a type of purgatory, a terrifying locale from which even my soul may not know how to escape.

The idea of being stuck between "real" and "not real" for all eternity makes me shiver every time it crosses my mind! Surely the Good Lord would not allow such a travesty of nature to occur, would He? Or if so, surely He would rescue those souls from such a fate, right? Especially if it happened while said souls were in the service of the Republic, fighting a just and righteous war, right?

Right?

Miss you! Love you!
Moe

QE Communiqué to Lieutenant Junior Grade Elwick, Moses U., RSS *Helling*, RNA Navy, from Mrs. Elwick, Zoey A., 11 August 2521:

Moey Poey,

You don't have to tell me all your musings. In fact, you should keep most of them to yourself from now on.

Love, Zoey Joey

Appendix B

On Defying Gravity

QE Communiqué to Mrs. Elwick, Zoey A., from Lieutenant Junior Grade Elwick, Moses U., RSS *Helling*, RNA Navy, 14 September 2521:

Dearest Zoey, just one more. This one isn't scary like the last one, I promise!

Gravity. We still don't entirely get it, even eight hundred years after Newton. The only thing the engineers can really do is mimic it. We can't actually create *real* gravity waves.

You'd think they'd just use gravitons, right? But they don't. I've heard they exist, but who really knows? I've never seen one. I've seen a photon. I've seen an electron. I've never, ever seen a graviton. Dale says you can feel them. I don't know what he's talking about.

But the beautiful thing is, you don't have to understand it to use it to your advantage. Boosting your jump distance, for instance. And don't worry, I won't go all surreal on you again about all the terrible things that can happen to a person if the jump goes wrong. Sorry about that. I like to ramble sometimes, you know that.

Anyway, here's what I learned. The force—ironically the weakest of all the forces in the universe—when emitted from any group of molecules, large or small, permeates throughout the entire universe in varying degrees depending on distance. And we have made sensors that are fine-tuned to pick it up. To a certain level, of course, one that matters in a practical sense. So, gravity waves aren't going to sneak up on us or anything. They can't; they can only propagate at the speed of light. We can jump away.

But what if a really bad dude took a gravity plate and amplified it with a Zee Dee core and switched it on? Would it pull ships to it? If he used a racing core or a war core, could it pull larger things to it like asteroids? Or moons? Or pull entire planets out of their orbits? And what happens if you're on one of those planets? Can you imagine the earthquakes? All the death and destruction? You could destroy entire solar systems with it! It would be the ultimate weapon, and nobody would even be able to get close! If they fired a missile at you, you reverse the polarity of the plating and it shoots right back at them! Or you create a warping grav field and curve it over so it hits some other target!

Could you get into a gravity contest with a black hole?? That would be sooo coool!

QE Communiqué to Lieutenant Junior Grade Elwick, Moses U., RSS *Helling*, RNA Navy, from Mrs. Elwick, Zoey A., 15 September 2521:

Moses,

Don't write me again until you're at least a commander. And stop hanging around all those stupid lieutenants.

By the way, my little sister is talking about joining the Navy after her final semester of Educata. Speaking of gravity, she has no idea how heavy the gravity is on Earth. I tried to warn her, but she won't listen. I'm trying to talk her out of it. Wish me luck. If she actually does it, I'm keeping her far, far away from *you.*

Zoey

Appendix C

On Ion Base Factors

Excerpt, *Lessons Learned from the First China-America Conflict,* Chapter 4, para 1-2, "Introduction to Ion Drive Base Factors," dated September 2403, by Admiral (ret) Jeffrey Buker, RNA Naval Academy, San Diego, Voilition Province, Republic of North America, Earth

Ion Drive is sub-light propulsion, but drastically more powerful than maneuvering thrusters. Each Ion Base is a doubling of the preceding factor. Ion propulsion began its development in the 20th Century, but saw minimal development for the next two hundred and fifty years. In the early 2200s, ion propulsion advanced to the point it could be used for more than tiny, unmanned craft. Humans used IB 4 for manned missions to all eight primary planets and associated moons in Earth's solar system, reaching Neptune in only two months. When IB 10 was achieved in the late 2200s (1/8th lightspeed)—which appeared to be the upper limit of ion tech—humankind used it to explore several neighboring stars, reaching Proxima Centauri in only 34 years, a staggeringly impressive feat at the time.

In the 24th Century, the year 2312 in fact, Ion Base 11 was achieved, breaking the 1/4 light speed barrier, a feat deemed all but impossible only a decade prior. Speed wasn't a factor so much as structural integrity of even the heartiest racing craft and battleships. The general populace still laments that the breakthrough came one year too late. To this day, politics are blamed for the poor timing.

By the 25th Century, Ion Base 12 (1/2 of lightspeed) is the upper limit allowed by Interstellar treaty (no intergalactic "speed limit" is enforced). IB 12.01 is possible only by illegal racers using dangerous, souped-up experimental craft, so far achievable only for a few seconds before either the core shuts down or the craft is vaporized.

The "unachievable goal" is now set at IB 13, which equates to over one billion kilometers per hour, and is very near lightspeed. Even the most optimistic of scientists do not believe such speeds can be reached without a breakthrough in ship design and ion engine materials. Power is not an issue; ion propulsion only uses a fraction of the energy produced in Zhédié core powerplants. In fact, due to Zhédié Shikōng technology, there is little need for such speeds and stresses on spacecraft (except in extremely rare situations where space folding motors cannot be used).

Note to 26th Century readers: the only known spacecraft launched from Earth that achieved interstellar flight prior to the discovery of Zhédié technology were four tiny exploration probes, each launched from Earth in the late 20th Century. Two were named Pioneer, two were named Voyager. For nearly 500 years, Voyager 1 maintained the title for the fastest man-made object ever built, under no propulsion except what it obtained from its original launch vehicle and slingshot maneuvers involving Sol's gas giants (anhydrous hydrazine was used in its thrusters, but this was merely for attitude adjustments). Ancient astronomical records indicate it reached speeds of up to 61,500 kilometers per hour before exiting the Sol system and entering interstellar space. This is equivalent to approximately. Ion Base factor 0.25. While this seems a mere snail's pace compared to spacecraft of the current century, keep in mind this feat was achieved almost 600 years prior to the lifetime of Admiral (ret.) Moses Elwick (b. 2496, d. 2588).

All four spacecraft are still crawling through the interstellar medium to this day, each traveling in a different direction away from Sol, on their way toward various stars. Voyager 1 will pass within two light years of the Gliese 445 solar system in approximately forty thousand years.

Note to tourists: each of these "ancient metal birds" is protected by international agreements and interstellar law, but space history enthusiasts can book tours that visit one or all four probes. Please note that tourist vessels, personal EVA pods, and powered EVA suits are required to maintain a distance of one kilometer from all probes at all times. No person or vehicle is allowed to fly directly in front of any of these historical objects for a distance of 0.1 light year. To further avoid disruption of the probes' ongoing flight, only passive methods to visually or audibly record visits are allowed. This means multi-dimensional holographic scanning is forbidden due to electromagnetic radiation pressures that could be unintentionally exhibited on the ancient craft, which could disrupt their flights or even damage their sensitive structures. Two- and three-dimensional photography is allowed and encouraged!

Standard IB factors	**Fraction of lightspeed**
1	1/4096=73 km/sec=262,800 km/hr
2	1/2048=146 km/sec=525,600 km/hr
3	1/1024=293 km/sec=1,051,200 km/hr
4	1/512=586 km/sec=2,102,400 km/hr
5	1/256=1,171 km/sec=4,204,800 km/hr
6	1/128=2,342 km/sec=8,409,600 km/hr
7	1/64=4,684 km/sec=16,819,200 km/hr
8	1/32=9,369 km/sec=33,638,400 km/hr
9	1/16=18,737 km/sec=67,276,800 km/hr
10	1/8=37,474 km/sec=134,553,600 km/hr

Questionable factors [1]	**Fraction of lightspeed**
11	1/4=74,948 km/sec=269,107,200 km/hr
12	1/2=149,896 km/sec=538,214,400 km/hr
13	1/1.4=299,008 km/sec=1,076,428,800 km/hr
∞ [2]	1=c=299,792 km/sec=1,079,251,000 km/hr

Footnotes:

[1] All questionable Ion Base factors are considered theoretical. Speeds in excess of IB 12 are currently unachievable due to modern limits of structural designs and materials of both spacecraft and ion engines using superheated liquid propellant. Power is not an issue due to Zhédié Shikōng technology. An engineer known for his controversial and reckless experiments has proposed a typical Zhédié core motor of the mid-26th Century could hypothetically power an ion engine with a base factor of up to 358 (when not being utilized for space folding trajectories). The same engineer has also calculated that the IB factor could reach in the millions if quantum structural foam folding technology becomes viable. This would allow spacecraft to reach severe relativistic speeds. However, due to limitations in currently-known construction materials (biological limitations should also be taken into account), these calculations should be considered merely for academic debate and entertainment.

[2] Unobtainable; this factor is equivalent to lightspeed.

Appendix D

On "QBert" RADAR

Excerpt, *Lessons Learned from the First China-America Conflict,* Chapter 23, para 1-1, "Quantum Entangled RADAR: History and Observations," dated April 2399, by Admiral (ret) Jeffrey Buker, RNA Naval Academy, San Diego, California, Republic of North America, Earth

It was (again, suspiciously) the Chinese who figured out Quantum Entanglement-Boosted Radar Targeting, or "QE-BRT." Like Zhédié Shikōng technology, the RNA acquired this advanced RADAR tech toward the end of the Second Asia-America War from captured Chinese warships of rogue nations under various self-proclaimed Emperors.

Affectionately dubbed "QBert" by the developers, it could identify targets up to eleven light years distant. This distance is of course entirely ineffectual when ships could jump up to ten thousand lightyears in a single hop. [see footnote 1]

The fact that the accuracy of Radio Detection and Ranging decreased with distance was bad enough, but QBert RADAR was completely useless detecting ships jumping in from Folded Space; neither person nor device could see a ship coming before it arrived, immediately bringing guns to bear on an unsuspecting enemy. An advanced type of RADAR is needed to detect ships the moment their Zhédié core initiates a space folding event from anywhere in the galaxy, giving ships and personnel near the exit point valuable seconds to prepare. This tech, known as [REDACTED], was discovered in the year [REDACTED], near [REDACTED]. Its mere existence is considered top secret (compartmented, sensitive). It is rumored to be close-held tech utilized sparingly by various space-faring Chinese factions claiming or vying for legitimacy, unrecognized by NATO member nations, member worlds, and asteroid-based and station-based member colonies. [see footnote 2]

Footnotes:

[1] Eleven lightyears is the *unclassified* effective range of QE-BRT RADAR the RNA government allowed the manufacturer to release. Scuttlebutt boasts an effective range closer to twenty light years, but this is unverified.

[2] For a complete, unredacted version of this excerpt, forward a bio-verified, signed request through Commander, Naval Intelligence, Department of the Navy, San Diego, CA, Republic of North America, Earth, ATTN: Office of the Adjutant, J-2

Dear Reader,

Thank you for reading Distress Call! I hope you enjoyed it.

Now I have a favor to ask. *Would you please leave a quick review of Distress Call on Amazon?* Leaving reviews is the absolute best way to reward an author for his or her hard work, and to let other readers know what they're in for. Like I've often said, a review, good or bad, is better than a Reese's Peanut Butter egg washed down with a tall glass of cold milk any Spring day! And RPB eggs are *puh-rrrretty* darn good.

Also, if you find a typo, or an error with my math or science—invented or real—e-mail me about it!
rod@rodwerks.net

Rod Galindo
February, 2024

Acknowledgments

The following prayers and poems appear in Distress Call:

1. "Mother of my birth, for how long were we together," by David Ignatow.
2. Excerpt from an adaptation of *Anima Christi,* "Soul of Earth," credited to Sister Jane Pellowski.
3. "Flowers have come!" by Aztec King, Warrior, Philosopher Nezahualcoyotl ("Fasting Coyote").

First off, I want to thank my father, **Mitchell Galindo, Jr.**, for introducing me to science and science fiction and all things wondrous and speculative and amazing in this universe at an early age (like five years old). And for encouraging me every step of the way in this life to be the best I could be. Even if my early drawings and writings sucked (which they did), he still said they were "really neat." Which is all I cared about; if it made him proud of me, I was happy. Eventually my creative musings got better, which I'm sure made him happy and alleviated his certain torture. Thank you for being a good dad, Dad. I've tried to emulate your example, and as a result have some amazingly intelligent, creative little critters of my own who love to speculate as much as I do about what might be "out there."

Second, there's a ton of people I'd like to thank for all the science, math, foreign language, and writing assistance. You might recognize the names if you make it all the way through the *SENTCORPS* series!

Jeni Frontera, fellow Wordwraith, who shredded my first chapter over and over until it was fit for human consumption, and set the tone for the rest of the story. There are too many other writerly things to list, Jeni, but you already know how thankful I am to have your friendship, so I'll just leave it at that. Everyone else, just know that *this* is the lady you want in your Writer's Toolkit. Trust me.

Jeff Buker, who let me know in no uncertain terms that the real Navy is *nothing* like Starfleet, and whose time as a U.S. Navy Commander was instrumental in getting the general "tone" of the *Nightingale* up to speed.

Jim Shoemate, whose time as a U.S. Navy Petty Officer First Class helped breathe realism and life into all the *Nightingale*'s non-commissioned officers and enlisted men and women.

Shane NeeCowen, Australian Accountant Extraordinaire, who was not scared to let me know my first-round "maths" were a mess. I had no idea I needed an accountant to run through my stories, but after the uber-thorough treatment he gave to Distress Call, he's running through every technical novel I write from this point forward. He just doesn't know it yet.

Jasmine Elliott, sci-fi and gaming fangirl, who I was dating when I finished the first draft and was so happy that she wanted to read it, and actually finished it, she got the honor of having Elwick's ill-fated destroyer named after her. It was an amicable parting and life and fate took her far, far away. She is an excellent sounding board and one of the most resourceful and knowledgeable people I've ever met. Sorry I made you cry at the end, Jasmine!

Mark Manley, one of my old high school gaming buddies who is also a fellow writer, who really laid into me on Draft 1 and made me think twice and reconsider a lot of things that were just, well, a little off. I also stole *Mylar's Pub* and *Corg* from him, but I prefer to call it "paying homage." The planet Corg was actually named after a great warrior and mentor to gladiators, of whom you can learn more about in Mark's "Dark Arena" fantasy series set in the "Duel 2" (formerly Duel Masters) game universe. Book One was illustrated by yours truly.

John Holloway, beloved science teacher at Blue Valley Northwest, who built me this incredible, interactive, Microsoft Excel-based relativity chart! A chart that I ended up not using in the SENTCORPS series at all as soon as I discovered something called "Space Folding," and could then thankfully throw relativistic effects out the window as readily as Gene Roddenberry did. But it did come in super handy for another work yet to be published, so I'm still more than grateful!

Christopher Johnson, who I never would have met were it not for the urging of members of my writing group to send Distress Call off to an Ozark Romance Authors promo, where three certified ORA judges analyze your work and gives you a *quantifiable* score. From two judges, across a dozen categories, I got 9s and 10s across the board, out of a possible 10. I was feeling pretty good about myself! Then I got to the third judge. He only gave me 7s, 8s, and 9s. Maybe one 10. But he also wrote back and asked if I would allow him to read the entire manuscript! I was ecstatic. He pointed out things I hadn't thought of, and called me out on many sci-fi clichés which I never even realized, some of which I just couldn't fix without ripping entire character arcs to shreds. So, I hope he forgives me. I hope the sci-fi community forgives me!

Xinru Pan, without whose help with Mandarin I would have totally dorked up most of the "stolen Chinese technology" of the 22nd through 26th Centuries.

He Liu Dan/Dawn Ho, who did her best to straighten me out with Cantonese and Mandarin; I hope I don't embarrass her. She also proved to be a fun writing group attendee when we could temporarily escape our military duties in Jordan!

I could never acknowledge my killer writing collective to the level they deserve. The unstoppable **Wordwraiths,** based out of Kansas City, Missouri, has provided me advice, education, and unending inspiration and motivation to finish my projects Since the Fall of 2013. The group has changed radically over the years, but the spirit remains. Combined with NaNoWriMo (National Novel Writing Month) and other literary events all throughout the year, and their insightful, sometimes harsh, but very much needed critiques of my work, they have given me something lasting that *no* amount of money could ever buy. For their continued support and friendship, I am forever appreciative and grateful. Here's where I'd shout our group catchphrase or battle cry if we had one, something like, "Never Give Up, Never Surrender!" or "So Say We All" or even, "Goonies Never Say Die!" But alas, all we have is "Stay on Target," which is emblazoned on a shirt I wear to every business meeting. We have a tendency to get a little sidetracked on occasion.

About the Author

Rod A. Galindo arrived on Earth in the Spring of 1970. He's been trying to stay out of trouble ever since, but has now accepted that finding it is one of the three things he does well, right behind drawing and right ahead of spelling. He's beamed all around the world thanks to various military and government positions, but proudly calls Kansas City home. Mainly because his request for transfer to Stargate Command was denied. AGAIN.

"Major Galindo" retired with 28 years of service under his belt in the US Army, both Active Duty as an enlisted M-1A1 Abrams tank crewman in Operation Desert Storm, and in the Kansas Army National Guard as a Field Artillery cannoneer and officer. He served in Operation Noble Eagle (as a Platoon Leader on a homeland security mission), in Operation Iraqi Freedom (as a Battle Captain in Baghdad, Iraq), and in Operation Inherent Resolve (first as a Division Plans Officer and later as a Forward Logistical Base Commander/Mayor in the Hashemite Kingdom of Jordan).

"Rod Galindo" is a worn-out father of four; two cyber-smart boys, who he has to keep reminding himself are no longer teenagers, one German Army (Bundeswehr) Soldatin who is as dangerously clever as she is beautiful, and he fills in as full-time father to a special young lady who never really had a dad to call her own.

Rod is a fully assimilated and overly active member of the Wordwraiths Writing Collective and Wordwraith Books, LLC (learn more about our authors and books at Wordwraiths.com). Enjoy his shiny art or delve into his literary musings at RodWerks.net or RodGalindo.com.

www.ingramcontent.com/pod-product-compliance
Lightning Source LLC
Chambersburg PA
CBHW030542020726
47494CB00005B/1449

* 9 7 8 1 9 4 6 9 2 1 3 5 2 *